WITHDRAWN

ANIMERICA EXTRA GRAPHIC NOVEL

fushigi yûgi™

The Mysterious Play
VOL. 8: FRIEND

Fushigi Yûgi
The Mysterious Play
VOL. 8: FRIEND

This volume contains the FUSHIGI YÛGI installments from ANIMERICA EXTRA Vol. 5, No. 7 through Vol. 6, No. 1 in their entirety.

STORY & ART BY YÛ WATASE

English Adaptation/Yuji Oniki
Touch-Up Art & Lettering/Bill Spicer
Cover Design/Hidemi Sahara
Graphic Designer/Carolina Ugalde
Editor/William Flanagan

Managing Editor/Annette Roman
Sr VP of Sales & Marketing/Rick Bauer
Sr VP of Editorial/Hyoe Narita
Publisher/Seiji Horibuchi

Printed in Canada

Published by VIZ, LLC
P.O. Box 77010, San Francisco, CA 94107

10 9 8 7 6 5 4 3 2 1
First printing, April 2003

www.viz.com

store.viz.com

ANIMERICA EXTRA GRAPHIC NOVEL

fushigi yûgi™

The Mysterious Play
VOL. 8: FRIEND

Story & Art By
YÛ WATASE

CONTENTS

CHAPTER FORTY-THREE
THE SEALED CASTLE WALL................................9

CHAPTER FORTY-FOUR
THE SPARK OF COMBAT.............................38

CHAPTER FORTY-FIVE
HEARTLAND..68

CHAPTER FORTY-SIX
MAELSTROM OF FEAR.................................107

CHAPTER FORTY-SEVEN
WATCHING YOU ALWAYS.............................137

CHAPTER FORTY-EIGHT
SORROW IN THE SNOW...............................164

STORY THUS FAR

Chipper junior-high-school girl Miaka is physically drawn into the world of a strange book—*The Universe of the Four Gods*. Miaka is offered the role of the lead character, the Priestess of the god Suzaku, and is charged with a mission to save the nation of Hong-Nan, and in the process grant her three wishes.

While Miaka makes a short trip back to the real world, her best friend Yui is sucked into the book only to suffer rape and manipulation which drives her to attempt suicide. Now, Yui has become the Priestess of the god Seiryu, the bitter enemy of Suzaku and Miaka.

The only way for Miaka to gain back the trust of her former friend is to summon the god Suzaku and wish to be reconciled with Yui, so Miaka reenters the world of the book. The Seiryu warriors ruined Miaka's first attempt to summon Suzaku, but the oracle Tai Yi-Jun has a new quest for Miaka and her Celestial Warriors of Suzaku—to obtain treasures that will allow them to summon the god. On the way, a storm caused by Seiryu Warrior Soi causes Miaka's ship to be beached on a mysterious and dangerous island.

THE UNIVERSE OF THE FOUR GODS is based on ancient China, but Japanese pronunciation of Chinese names differs slightly from their Chinese equivalents. Here is a short glossary of the Japanese pronunciation of the Chinese names in this graphic novel:

CHINESE	JAPANESE	PERSON OR PLACE	MEANING
Hong-Nan	Konan	Southern Kingdom	Crimson South
Qu-Dong	Kutô	Eastern Kingdom	Gathered East
Bei-Jia	Hokkan	Northern Kingdom	Armored North
Tai Yi-Jun	Tai Itsukun	An Oracle	Preeminent Person
Shentso-Pao	Shinzahô	A Treasure	God's Seat Jewel
Nucheng-Kuo	Nyosei-koku	An Island Kingdom	Woman Fort Country
Hua-Wan	Kaen	A Woman	Flowery Grace
Dou	To	A Tribe	A Measure
Tomolu	Tomoru	An Elder	Earth Silent Duty
Teniao-Lan	Touran	A City	Unique Crow Orchid

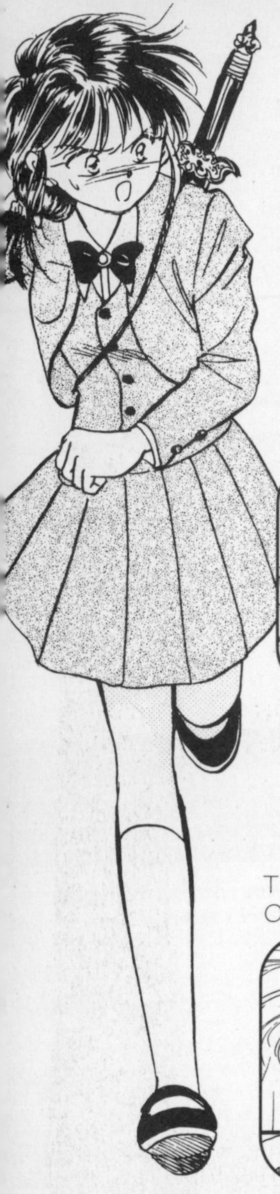

MIAKA
A chipper junior-high-school glutton who has become the Priestess of Suzaku.

THE CELESTIAL WARRIORS OF SUZAKU

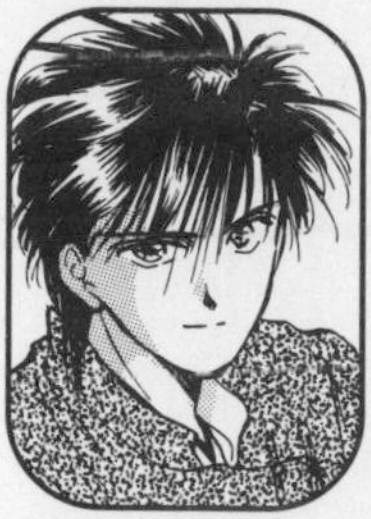

TAMAHOME
A dashing miser.

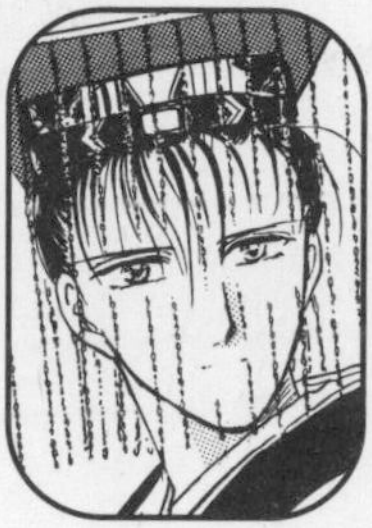

HOTOHORI
The beautiful emperor of Hong-Nan.

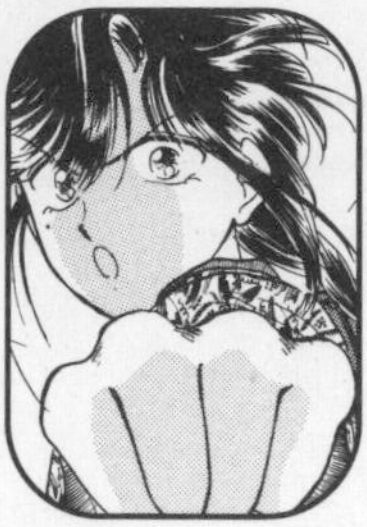

NURIKO
An amazingly strong cross-dresser.

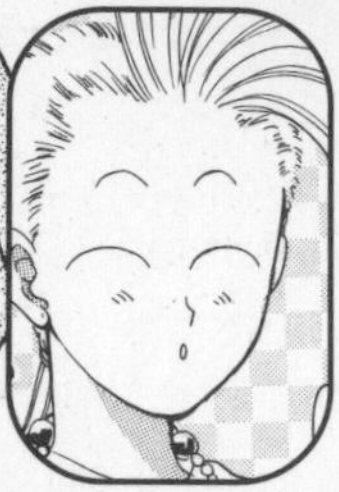

CHICHIRI
Former disciple of the oracle.

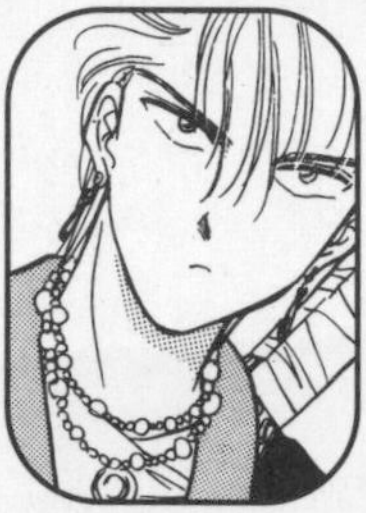

TASUKI
An ornery ex-bandit.

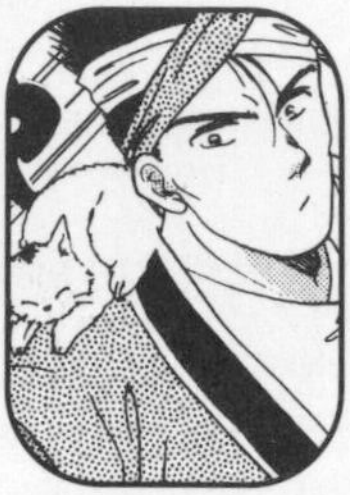

MITSUKAKE
A silent healer.

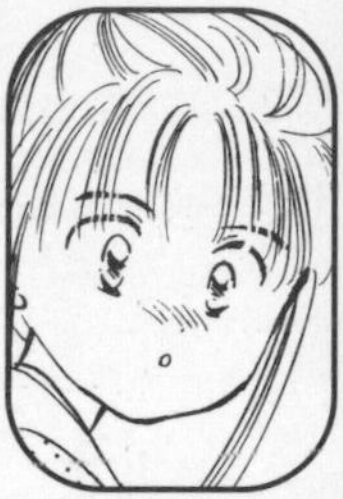

CHIRIKO
A child prodigy.

THE FOLLOWERS OF SEIRYU

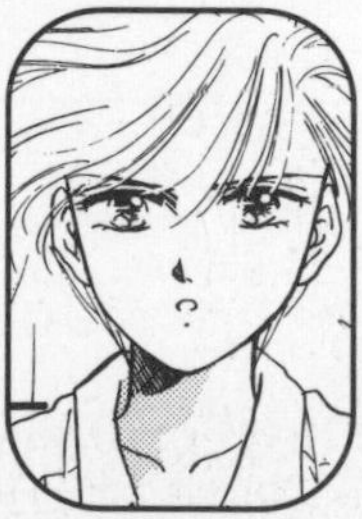

YUI
Miaka's former best friend, but now her enemy and the Priestess of Seiryu.

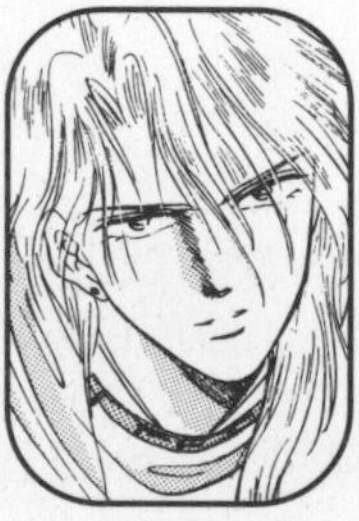

NAKAGO
A general of Qu-Dong and a Celestial Warrior of Seiryu.

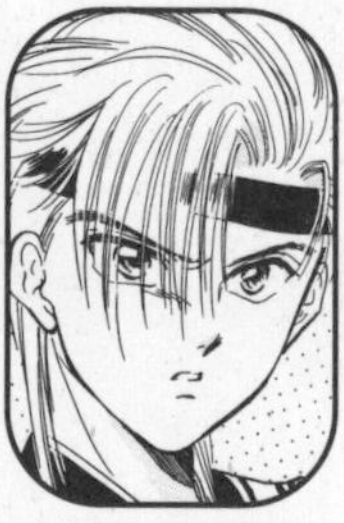

SUBOSHI
A young warrior who has vowed revenge for his twin brother.

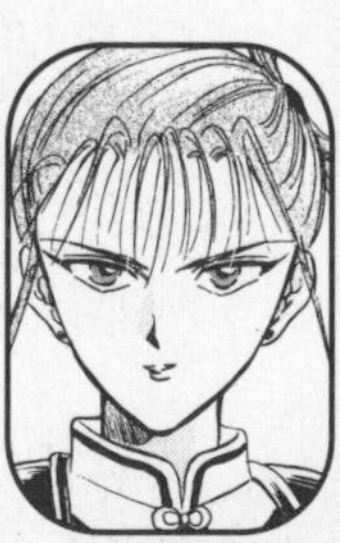

SOI
A mistress of lightning.

CHAPTER FORTY-THREE
THE SEALED CASTLE WALL

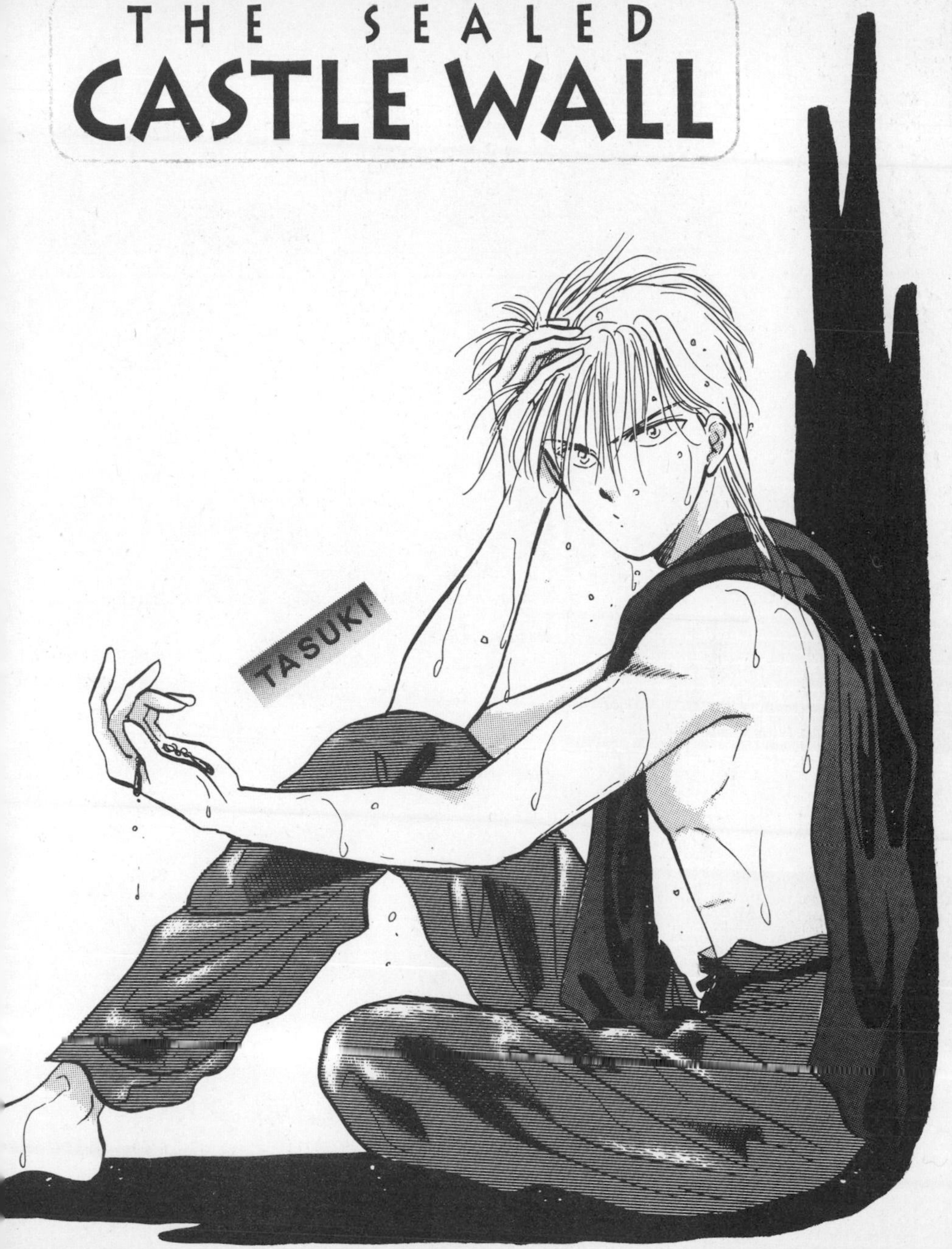
TASUKI

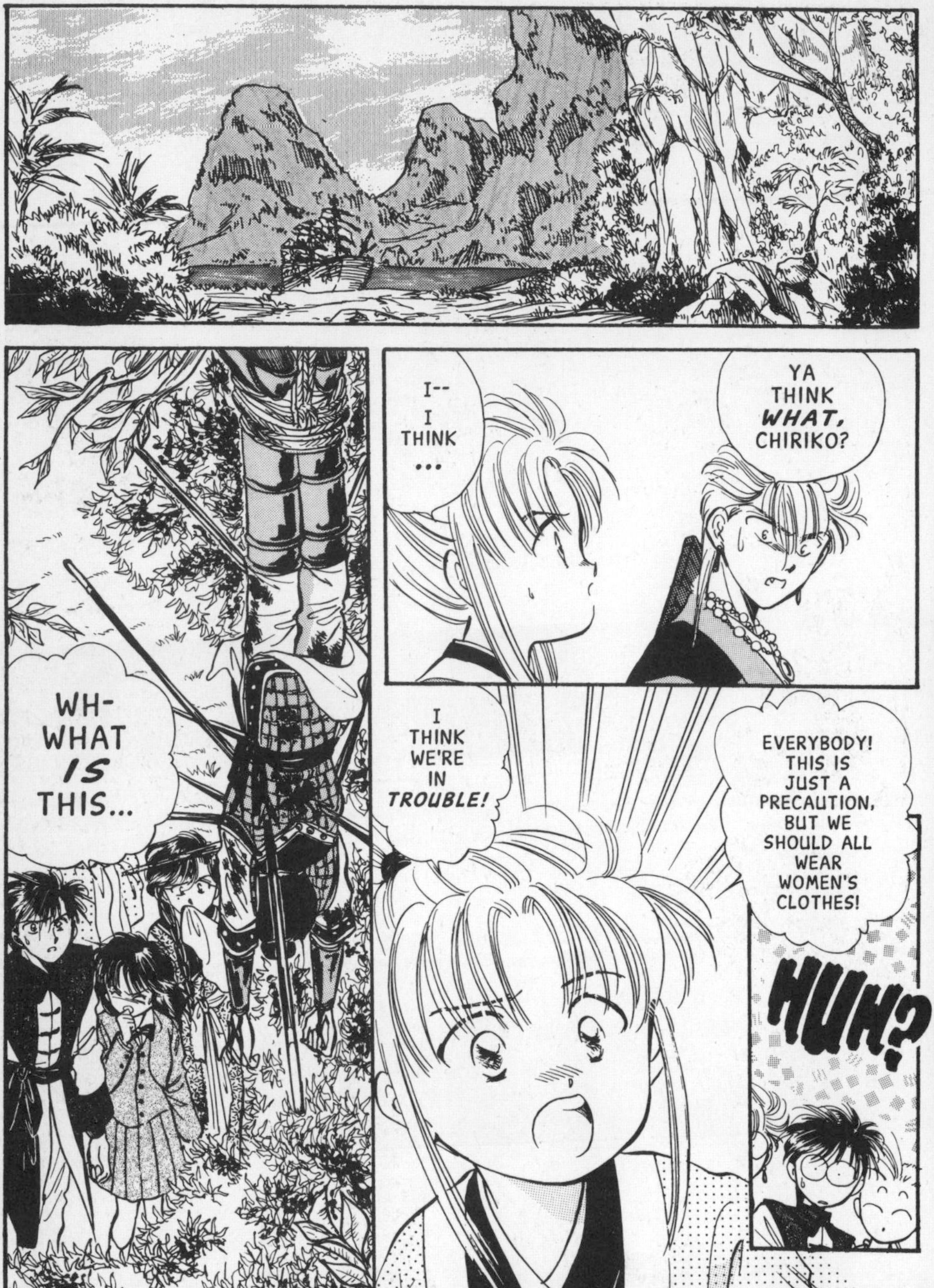
WH- WHAT *IS* THIS...
I-- I THINK ...
YA THINK *WHAT,* CHIRIKO?
I THINK WE'RE IN *TROUBLE!*
EVERYBODY! THIS IS JUST A PRECAUTION, BUT WE SHOULD ALL WEAR WOMEN'S CLOTHES!
HUH?

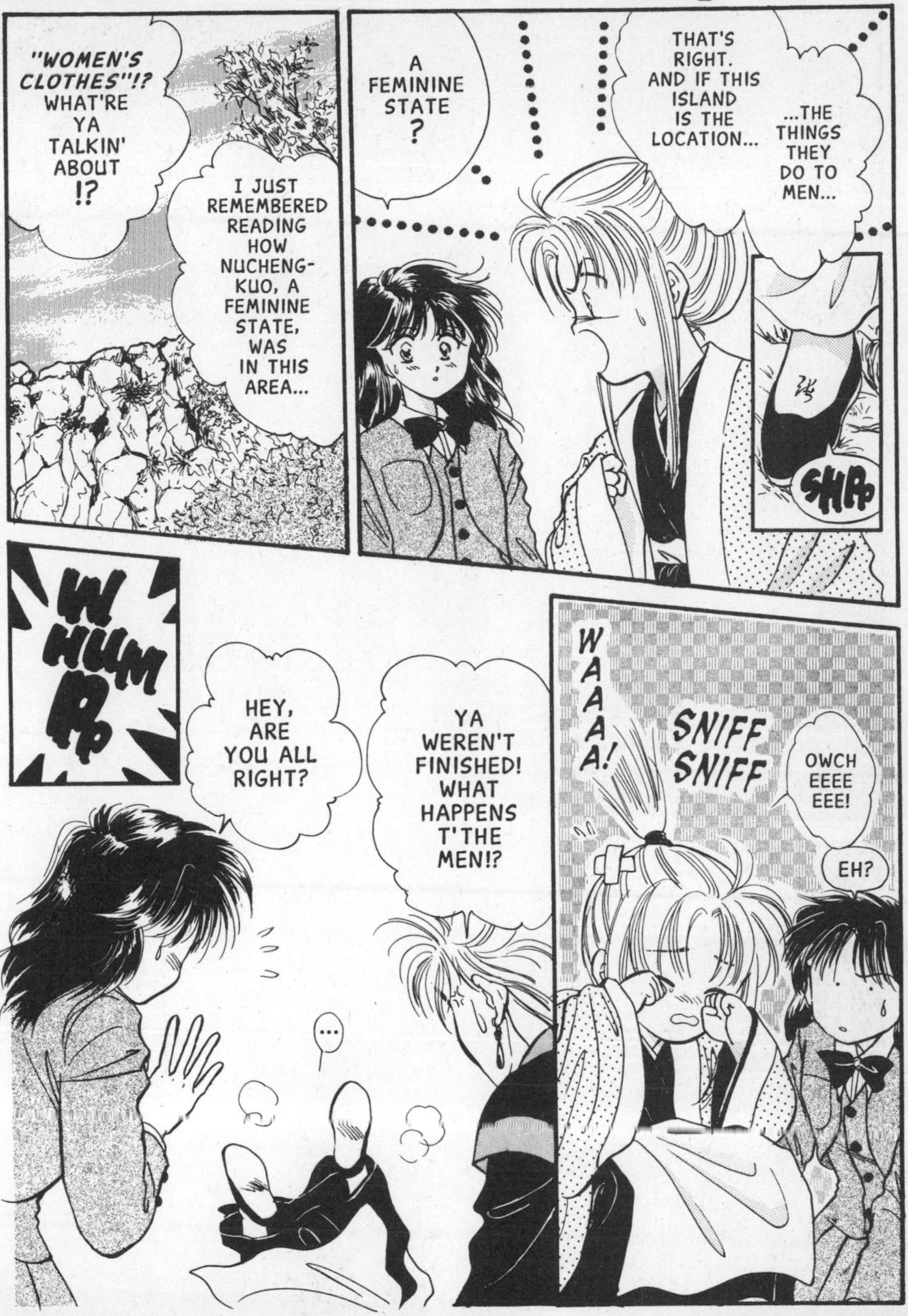
"WOMEN'S CLOTHES"!? WHAT'RE YA TALKIN' ABOUT !?
I JUST REMEMBERED READING HOW NUCHENG-KUO, A FEMININE STATE, WAS IN THIS AREA...
A FEMININE STATE ?
THAT'S RIGHT. AND IF THIS ISLAND IS THE LOCATION...
...THE THINGS THEY DO TO MEN...
SHIPP
WHUMP
HEY, ARE YOU ALL RIGHT?
YA WEREN'T FINISHED! WHAT HAPPENS T'THE MEN!?
...
WAAAA!
SNIFF SNIFF
OWCH EEEE EEE!
EH?

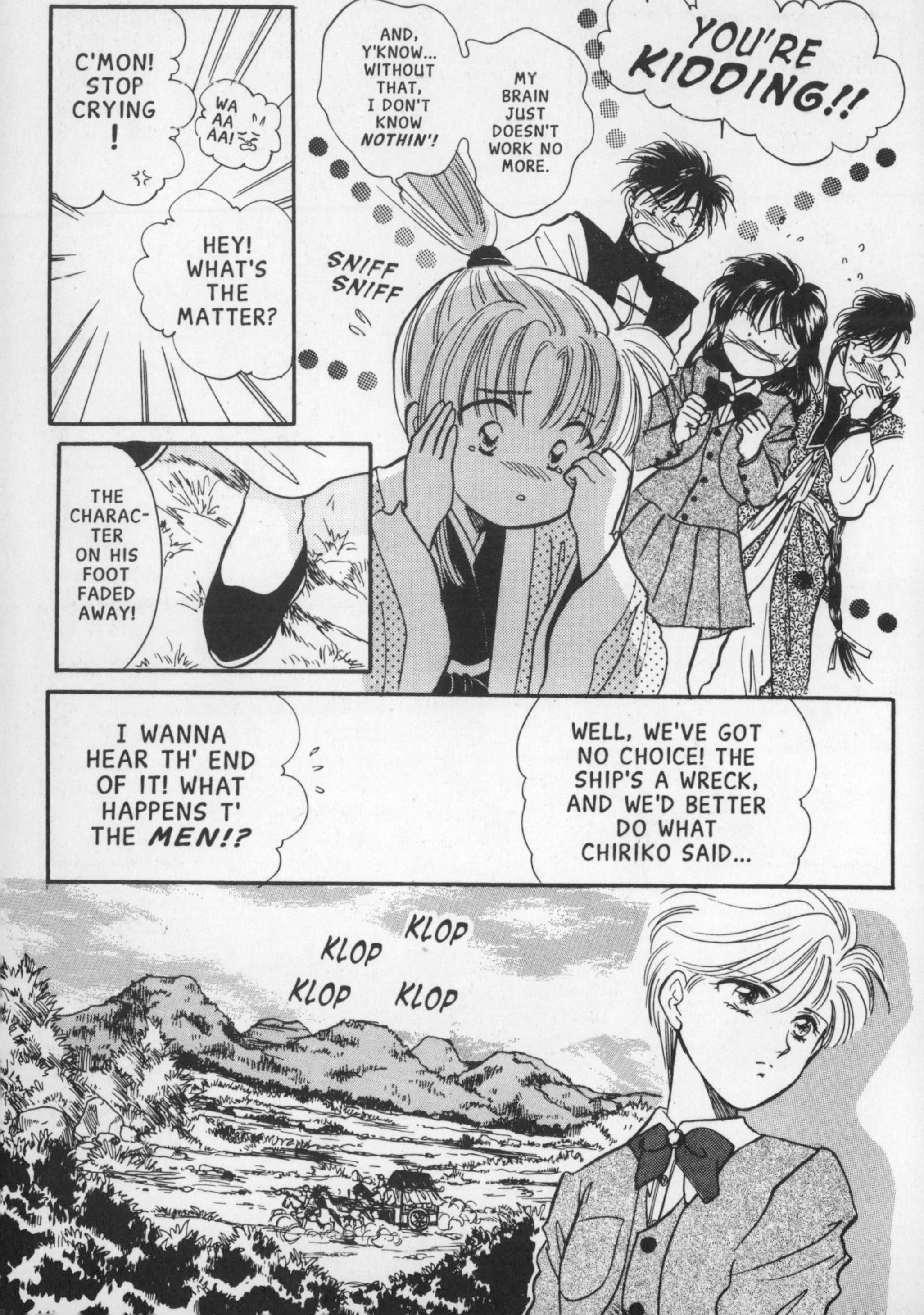
C'MON! STOP CRYING!
WA AA AA!
HEY! WHAT'S THE MATTER?
THE CHARAC-TER ON HIS FOOT FADED AWAY!
AND, Y'KNOW... WITHOUT THAT, I DON'T KNOW NOTHIN'!
MY BRAIN JUST DOESN'T WORK NO MORE.
YOU'RE KIDDING!!
SNIFF SNIFF
I WANNA HEAR TH' END OF IT! WHAT HAPPENS T' THE MEN!?
WELL, WE'VE GOT NO CHOICE! THE SHIP'S A WRECK, AND WE'D BETTER DO WHAT CHIRIKO SAID...
KLOP
KLOP
KLOP KLOP

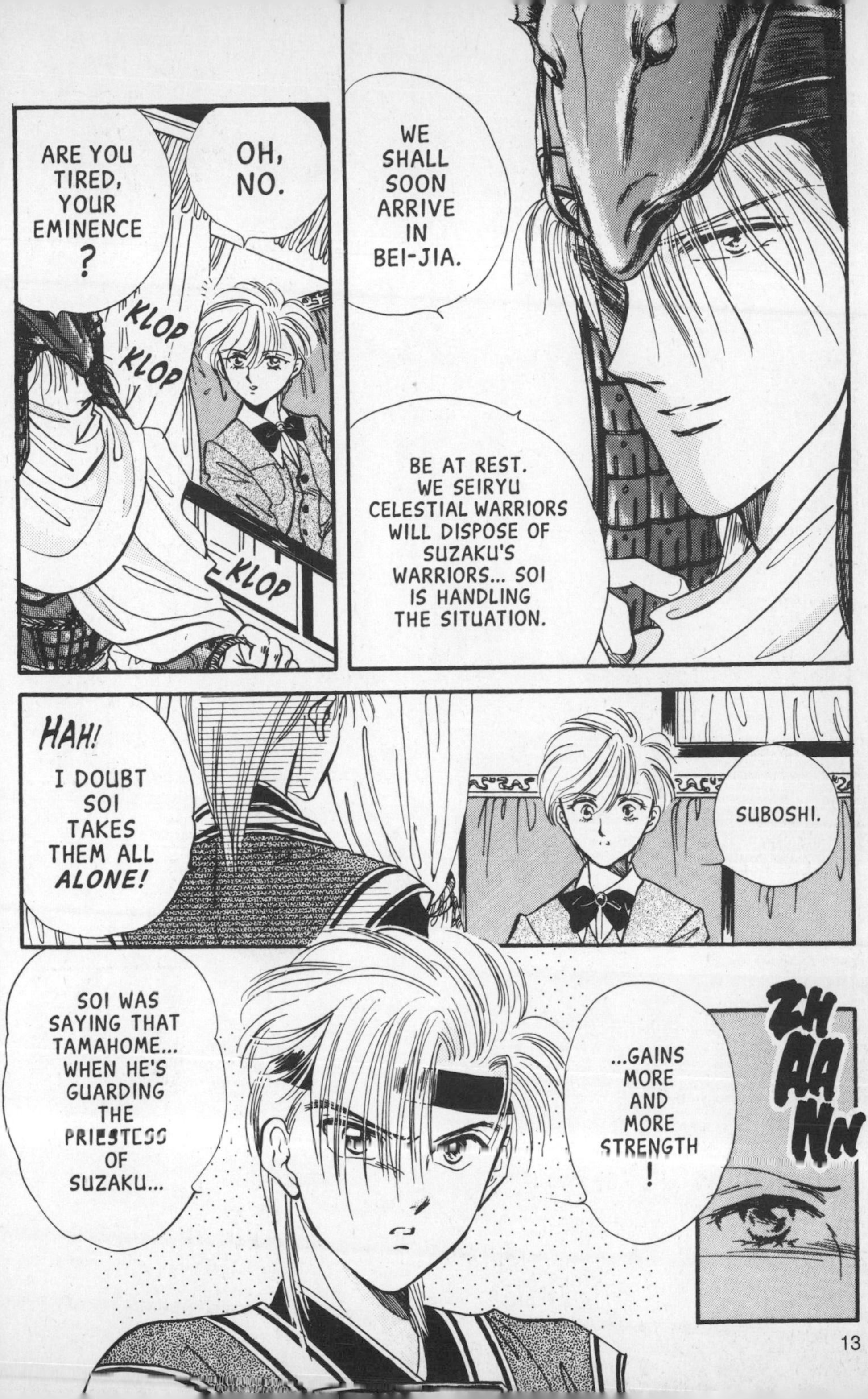

ARE YOU TIRED, YOUR EMINENCE ?
OH, NO.
KLOP KLOP
KLOP
WE SHALL SOON ARRIVE IN BEI-JIA.
BE AT REST. WE SEIRYU CELESTIAL WARRIORS WILL DISPOSE OF SUZAKU'S WARRIORS... SOI IS HANDLING THE SITUATION.
HAH! I DOUBT SOI TAKES THEM ALL *ALONE!*
SUBOSHI.
SOI WAS SAYING THAT TAMAHOME... WHEN HE'S GUARDING THE PRIESTESS OF SUZAKU...
...GAINS MORE AND MORE STRENGTH !
ZHAAANN

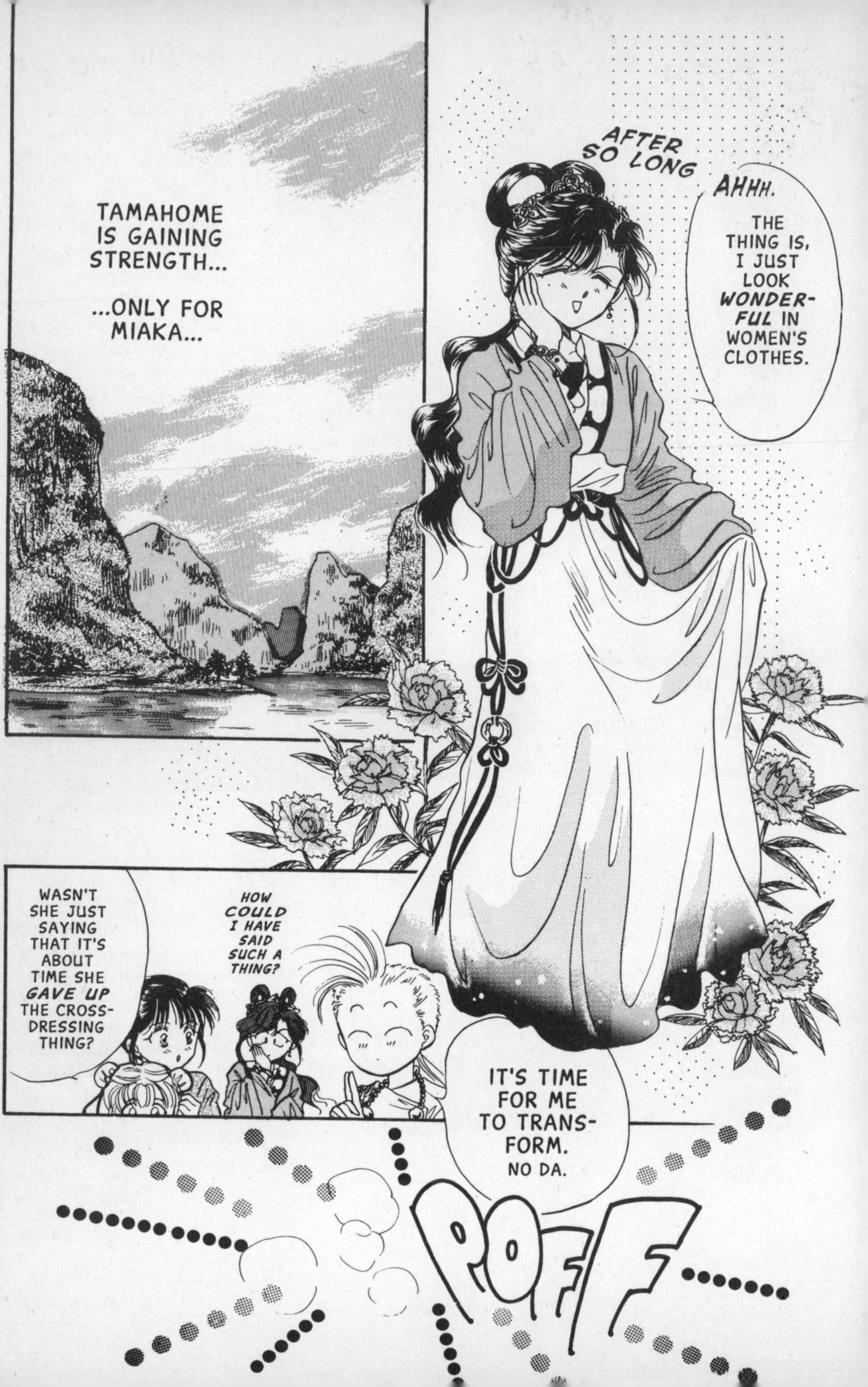
TAMAHOME IS GAINING STRENGTH...
...ONLY FOR MIAKA...
AFTER SO LONG
AHHH.
THE THING IS, I JUST LOOK WONDERFUL IN WOMEN'S CLOTHES.
WASN'T SHE JUST SAYING THAT IT'S ABOUT TIME SHE GAVE UP THE CROSS-DRESSING THING?
HOW COULD I HAVE SAID SUCH A THING?
IT'S TIME FOR ME TO TRANSFORM. NO DA.
POFF

POP

NO DA!

YOU'RE A CUTIE!

I'M CUTER!

KLAP KLAP

WOW. YOU'VE EVEN CHANGED INSIDE.

QU-QUIT IT. NO DA!

NOW FOR THE PROBLEM THREE... I HAD TO WORK ON THEIR MAKEUP.

DON'T BE SO BASHFUL. COME OUT!

TWITCH

....

❧ Friend ❧

Hello. This is Yū Watase. I want to wish you all a "Happy New Year." My new year is off to a great start.

At the end of October, my stress level began to take its toll on my body. I was in such poor shape, I couldn't even let my assistants into the office! So I went to see a doctor. *I'm all right now.* Stress can be scary! In November, while working on manga, I started wondering why I was putting myself through this... And that's when I realized I was in trouble. 🌀 The sight of my office was enough to make me feel nauseous. My right hand ached, and I kept on dropping my pen. But I worked when I could, and I managed to finish my installments on my own. So I can calm my stress all by myself. (Although when I work alone, I do end up putting a little too much detail in each frame. ♡) *My assistants did help me out on volume 8 here.*

I'm such a delicate creature. (Are you callin' me a liar?) I put up a tough front, but I really need to be bolder and more self confident. 🌀

● And so this volume was written by a woman under stress ♡ so please take that into consideration when you read it. 🌀

● Last volume, I ran on and on with talk about my dog, and in this one, I think I'll tell you about my trip to China. Well, let's see what I come up with as we move through Fushigi Yūgi.

NI

HAO

WATASE DOES NOT LOOK GOOD IN THIS STYLE.

15

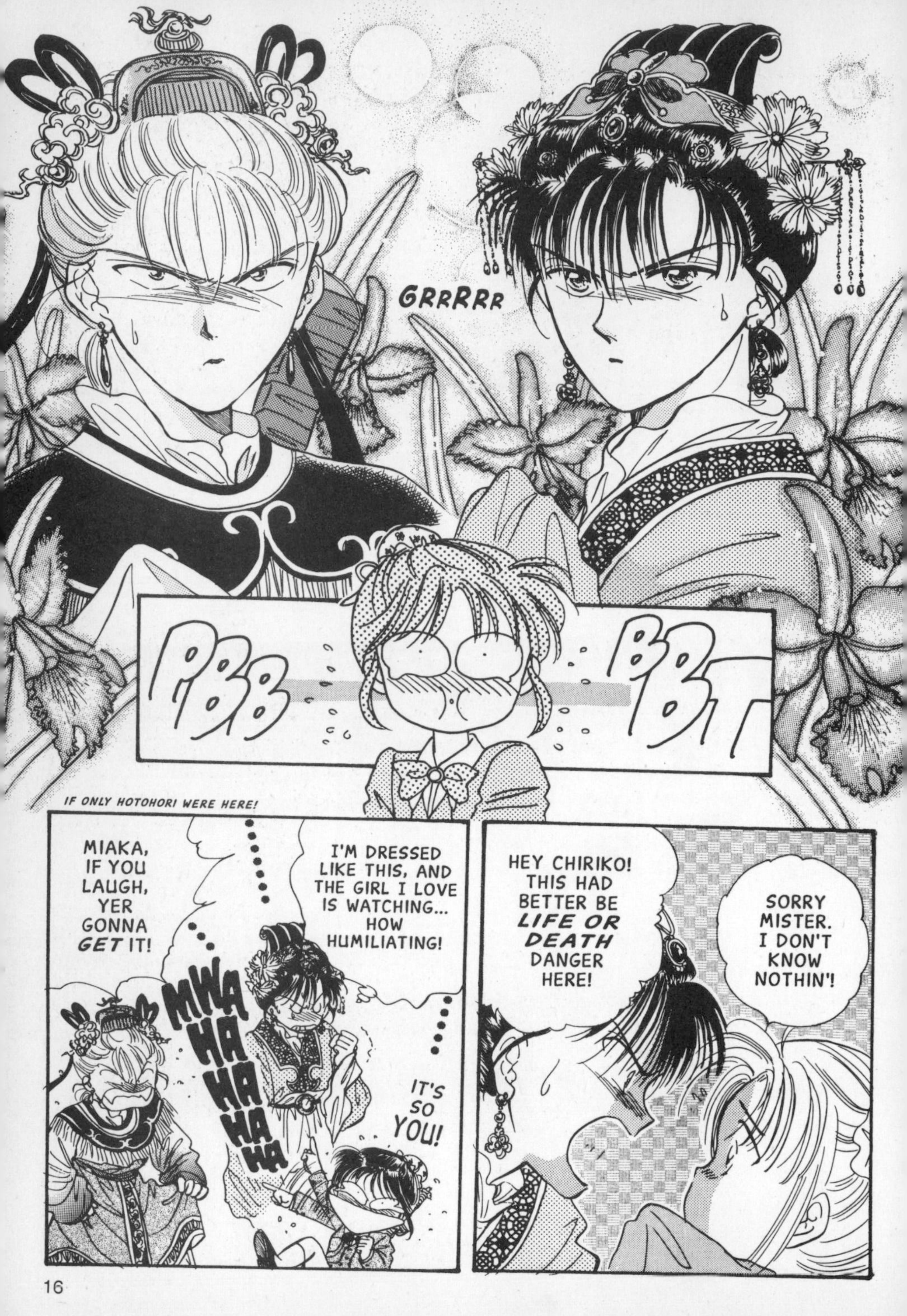
GRRRRR
PBBBBT
IF ONLY HOTOHORI WERE HERE!
MIAKA, IF YOU LAUGH, YER GONNA GET IT!
I'M DRESSED LIKE THIS, AND THE GIRL I LOVE IS WATCHING... HOW HUMILIATING!
MWA HA HA HA HA HA
IT'S SO YOU!
HEY CHIRIKO! THIS HAD BETTER BE LIFE OR DEATH DANGER HERE!
SORRY MISTER. I DON'T KNOW NOTHIN'!

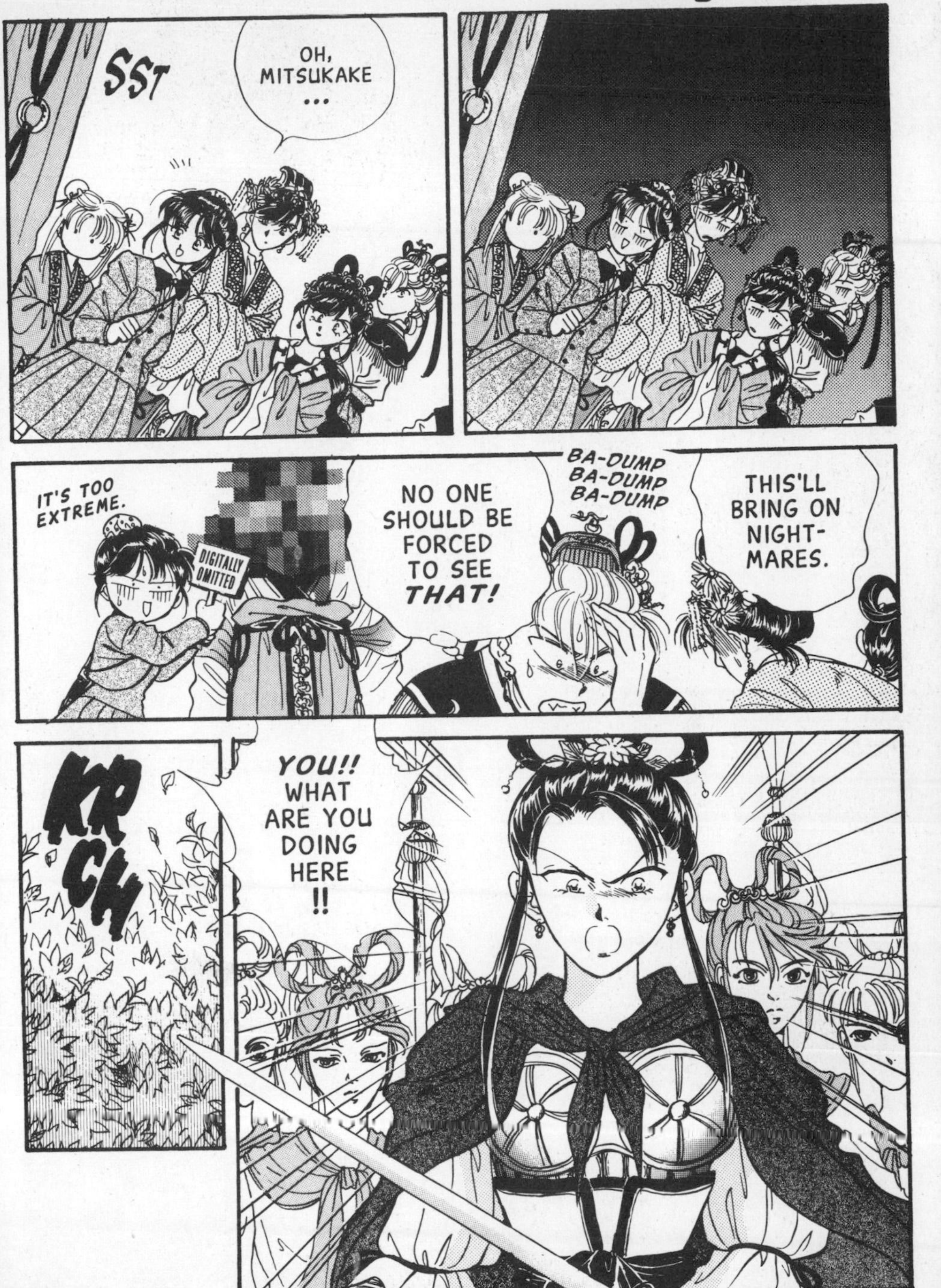
SST
OH, MITSUKAKE ...
IT'S TOO EXTREME.
DIGITALLY OMITTED
NO ONE SHOULD BE FORCED TO SEE THAT!
BA-DUMP BA-DUMP BA-DUMP
THIS'LL BRING ON NIGHT-MARES.
KRCH
YOU!! WHAT ARE YOU DOING HERE !!

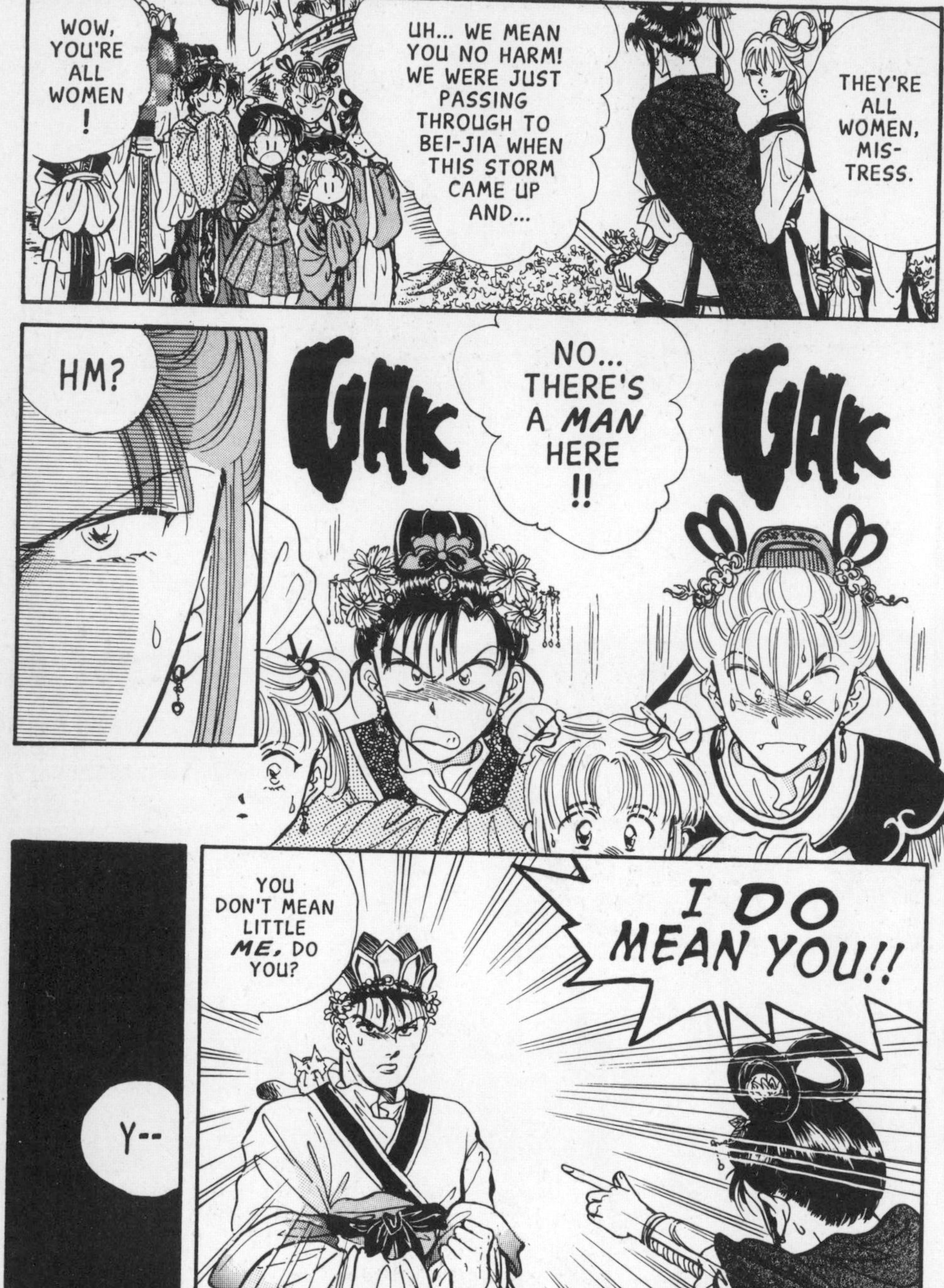
WOW, YOU'RE ALL WOMEN !
UH... WE MEAN YOU NO HARM! WE WERE JUST PASSING THROUGH TO BEI-JIA WHEN THIS STORM CAME UP AND...
THEY'RE ALL WOMEN, MIS-TRESS.
HM?
GAK
NO... THERE'S A *MAN* HERE !!
GAK
Y--
YOU DON'T MEAN LITTLE *ME,* DO YOU?
I DO MEAN YOU!!

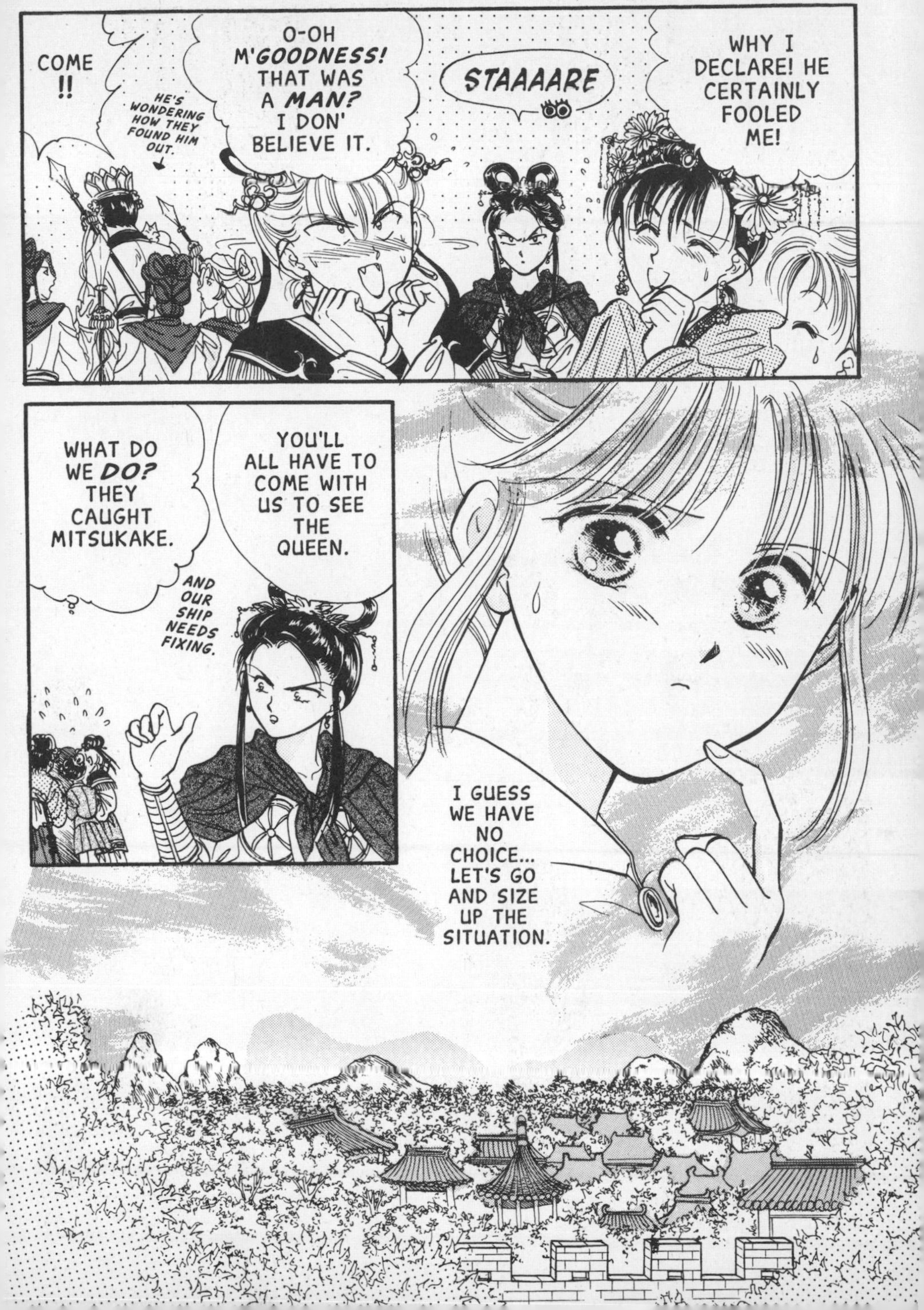
COME !!
HE'S WONDERING HOW THEY FOUND HIM OUT.
O-OH M'GOODNESS! THAT WAS A MAN? I DON' BELIEVE IT.
STAAAARE
WHY I DECLARE! HE CERTAINLY FOOLED ME!
WHAT DO WE DO? THEY CAUGHT MITSUKAKE.
AND OUR SHIP NEEDS FIXING.
YOU'LL ALL HAVE TO COME WITH US TO SEE THE QUEEN.
I GUESS WE HAVE NO CHOICE... LET'S GO AND SIZE UP THE SITUATION.

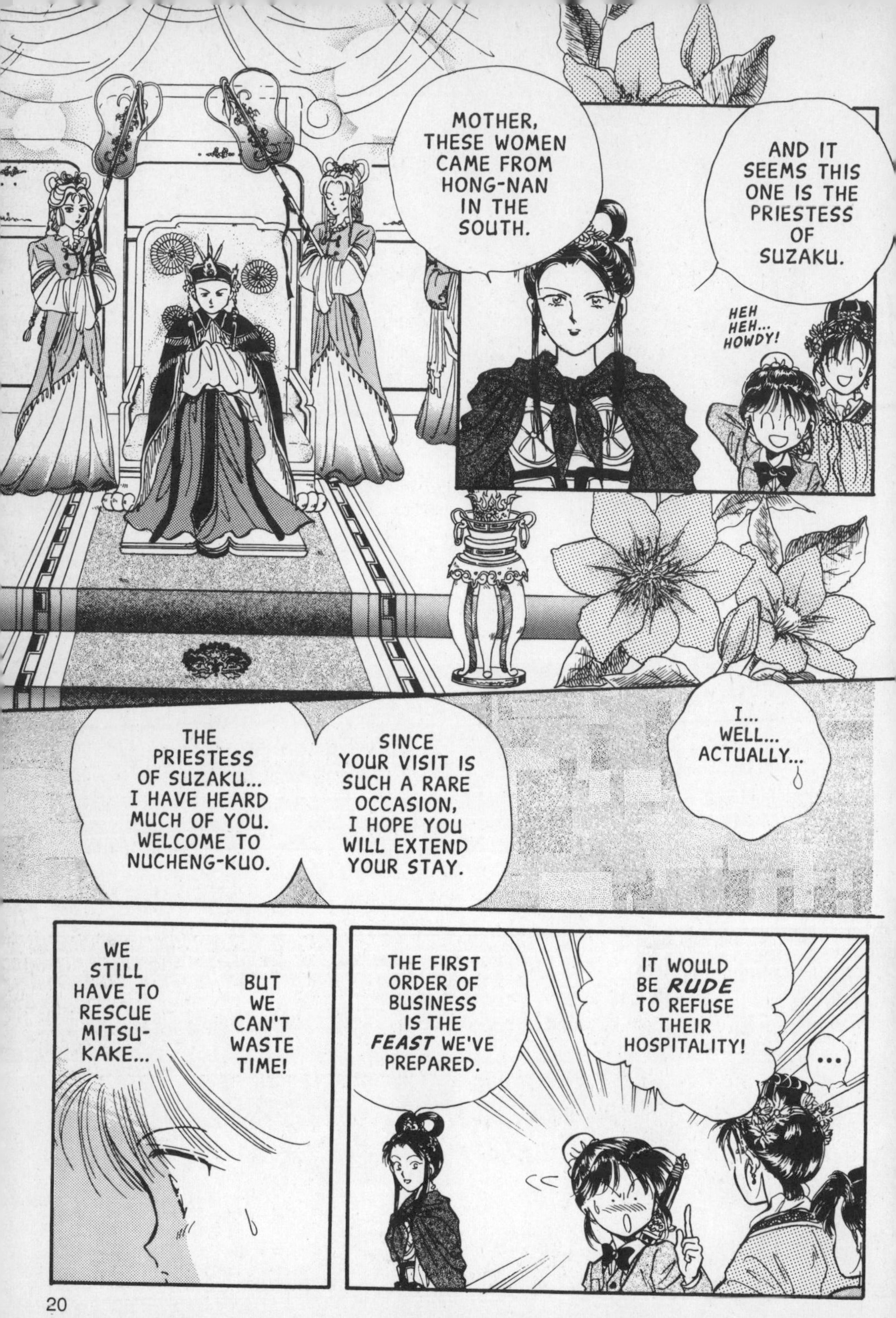
MOTHER, THESE WOMEN CAME FROM HONG-NAN IN THE SOUTH.
AND IT SEEMS THIS ONE IS THE PRIESTESS OF SUZAKU.
HEH HEH... HOWDY!
THE PRIESTESS OF SUZAKU... I HAVE HEARD MUCH OF YOU. WELCOME TO NUCHENG-KUO.
SINCE YOUR VISIT IS SUCH A RARE OCCASION, I HOPE YOU WILL EXTEND YOUR STAY.
I... WELL... ACTUALLY...
WE STILL HAVE TO RESCUE MITSU-KAKE...
BUT WE CAN'T WASTE TIME!
THE FIRST ORDER OF BUSINESS IS THE *FEAST* WE'VE PREPARED.
IT WOULD BE *RUDE* TO REFUSE THEIR HOSPITALITY!
...

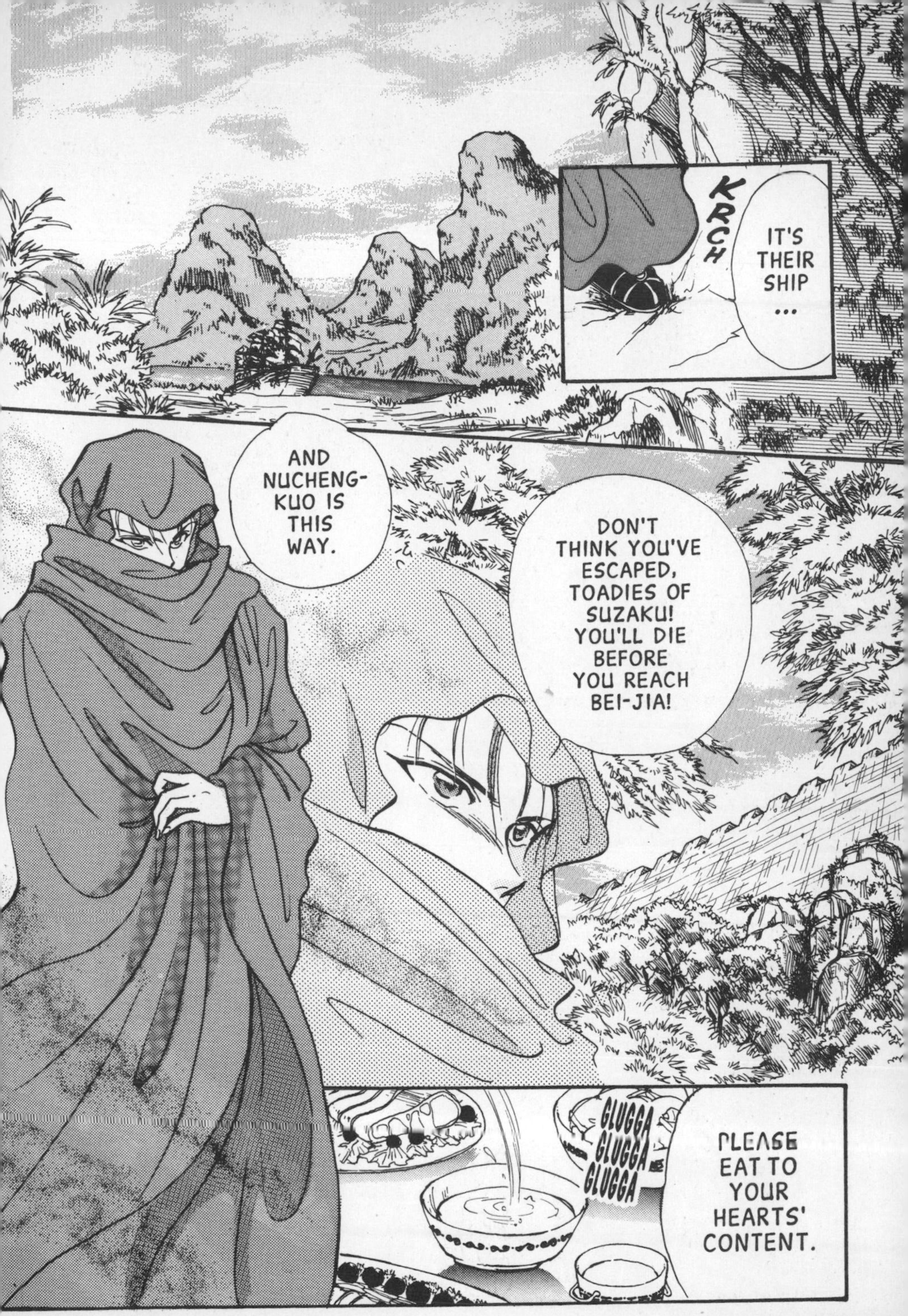
KRCH
IT'S THEIR SHIP ...
AND NUCHENG-KUO IS THIS WAY.
DON'T THINK YOU'VE ESCAPED, TOADIES OF SUZAKU! YOU'LL DIE BEFORE YOU REACH BEI-JIA!
GLUGGA GLUGGA GLUGGA
PLEASE EAT TO YOUR HEARTS' CONTENT.

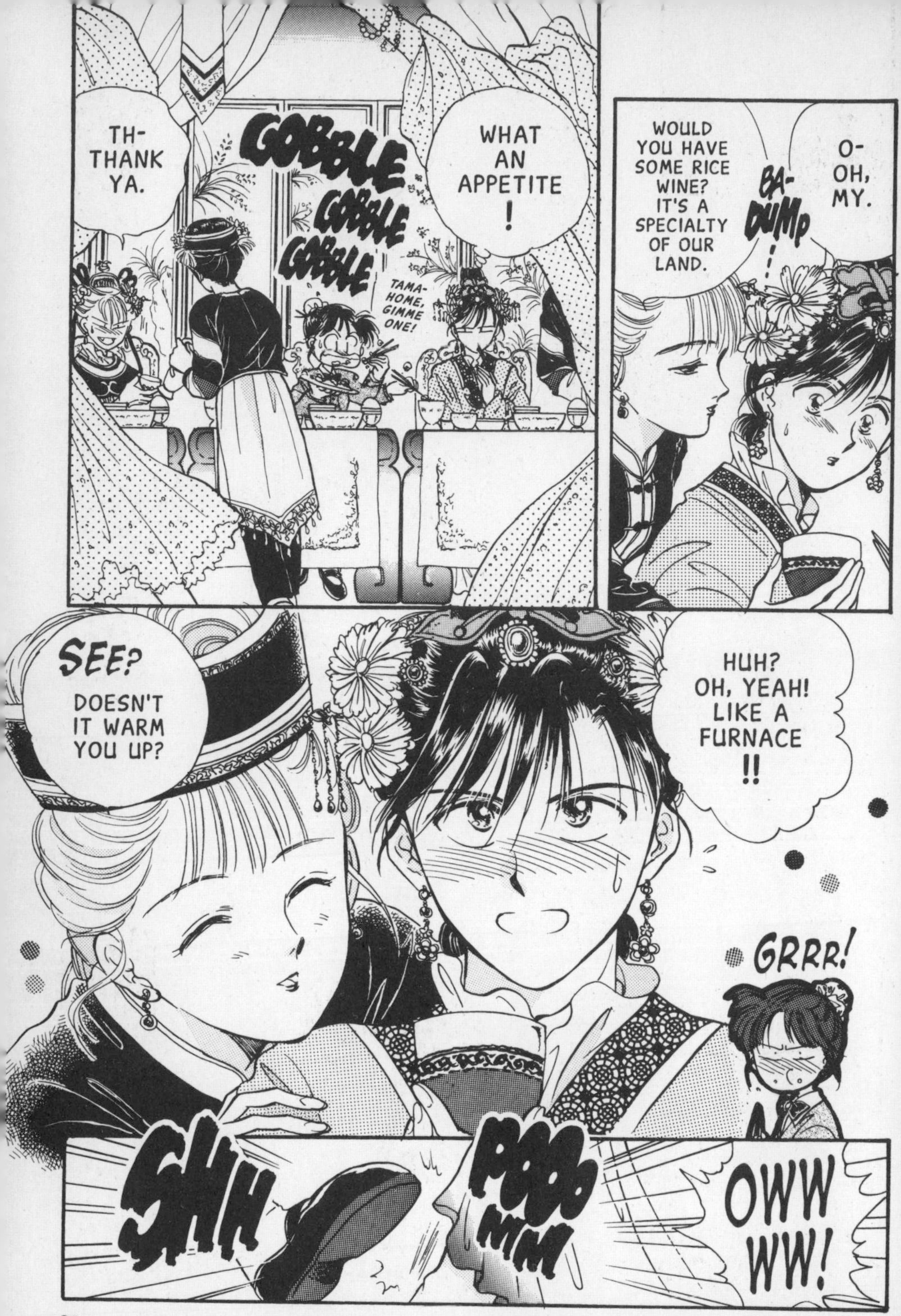

TH- THANK YA.
GOBBLE GOBBLE GOBBLE GOBBLE
WHAT AN APPETITE!
TAMA-HOME, GIMME ONE!
WOULD YOU HAVE SOME RICE WINE? IT'S A SPECIALTY OF OUR LAND.
BA-DUMP!
O- OH, MY.
SEE? DOESN'T IT WARM YOU UP?
HUH? OH, YEAH! LIKE A FURNACE!!
GRRR!
SHH
POOOMM
OWWWW!

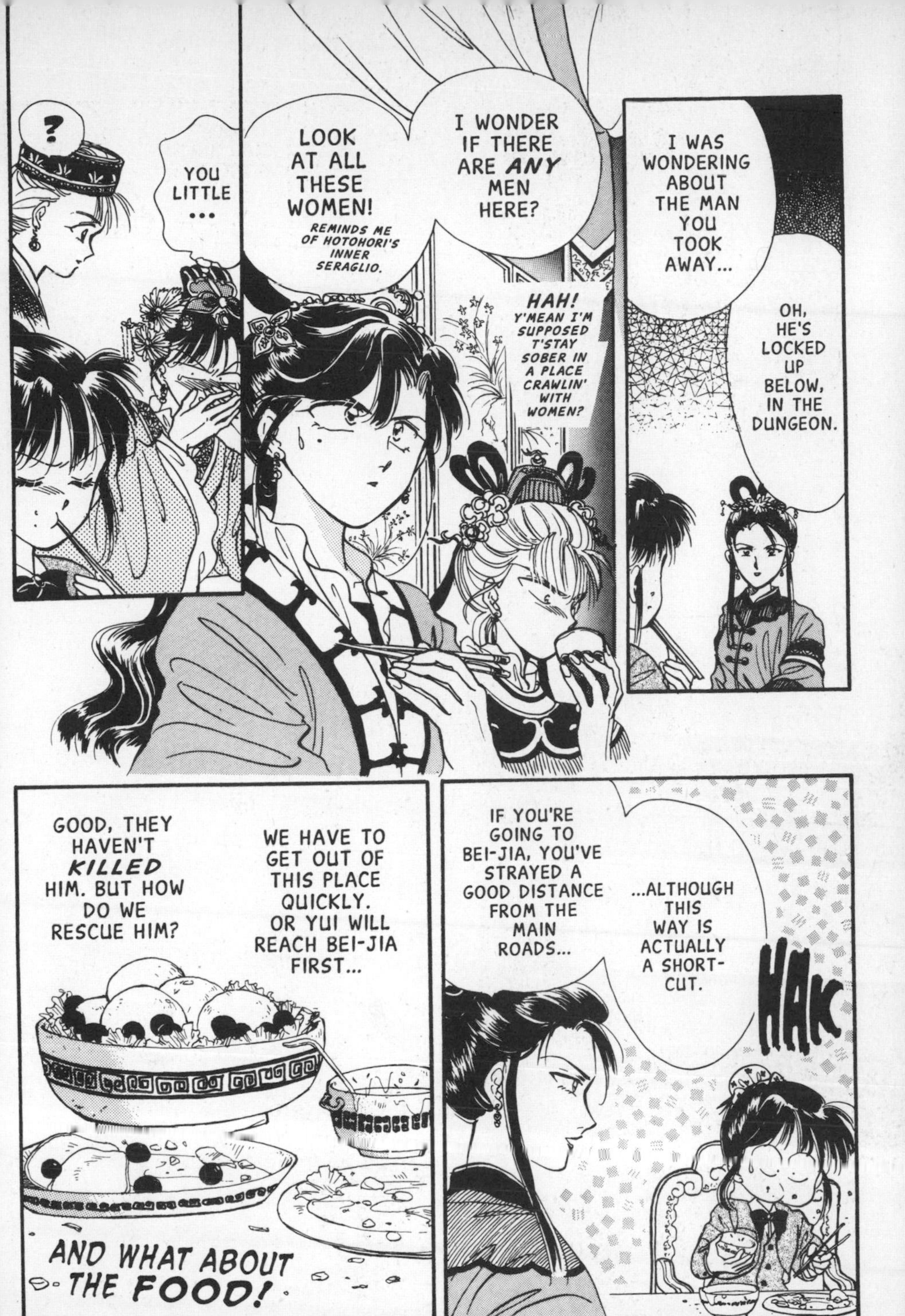
?
YOU LITTLE ...
LOOK AT ALL THESE WOMEN!
REMINDS ME OF HOTOHORI'S INNER SERAGLIO.
I WONDER IF THERE ARE *ANY* MEN HERE?
HAH! Y'MEAN I'M SUPPOSED T'STAY SOBER IN A PLACE CRAWLIN' WITH WOMEN?
I WAS WONDERING ABOUT THE MAN YOU TOOK AWAY...
OH, HE'S LOCKED UP BELOW, IN THE DUNGEON.
GOOD, THEY HAVEN'T ***KILLED*** HIM. BUT HOW DO WE RESCUE HIM?
WE HAVE TO GET OUT OF THIS PLACE QUICKLY. OR YUI WILL REACH BEI-JIA FIRST...
AND WHAT ABOUT THE **FOOD!**
IF YOU'RE GOING TO BEI-JIA, YOU'VE STRAYED A GOOD DISTANCE FROM THE MAIN ROADS...
...ALTHOUGH THIS WAY IS ACTUALLY A SHORT-CUT.
HAK

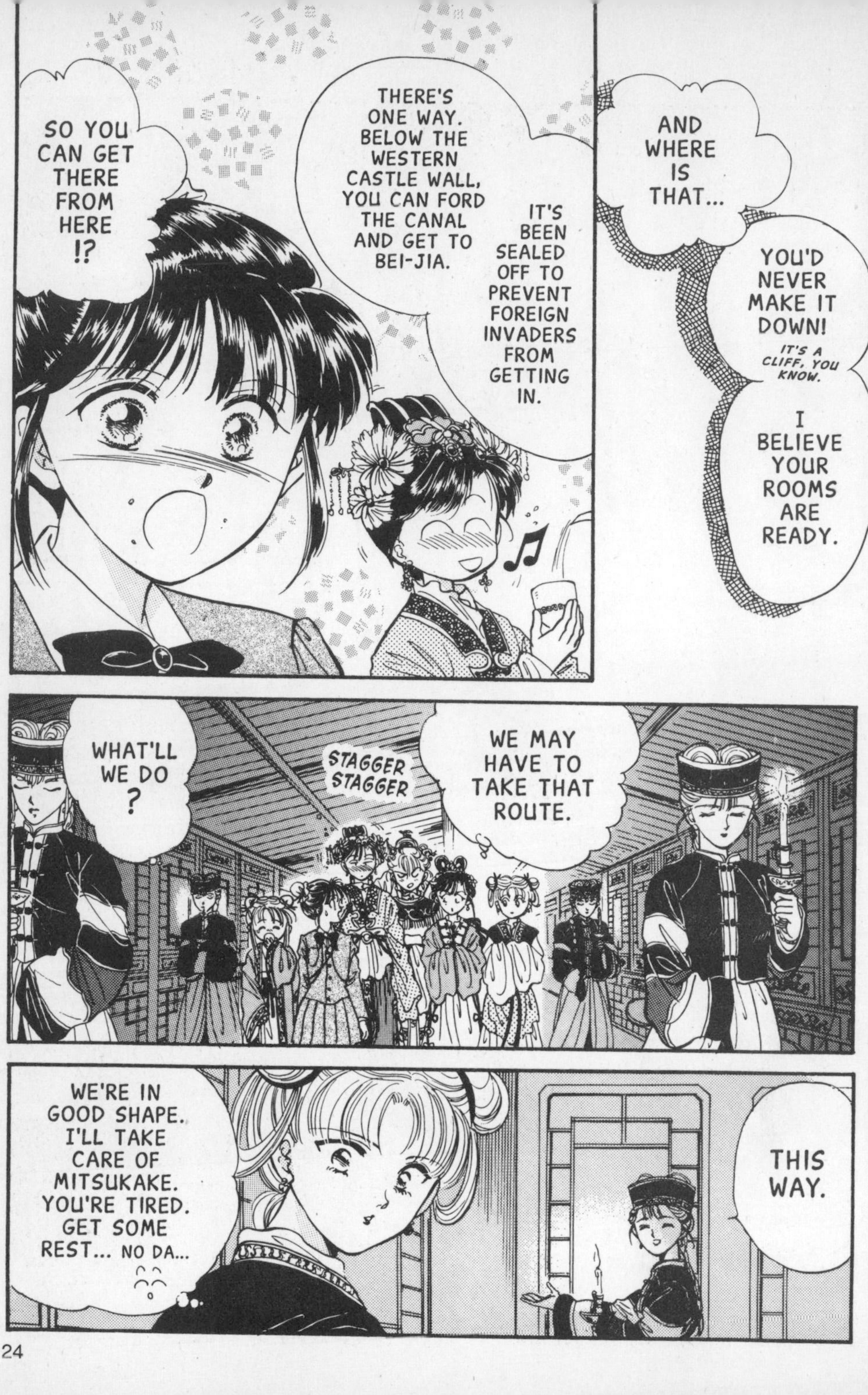
SO YOU CAN GET THERE FROM HERE !?
THERE'S ONE WAY. BELOW THE WESTERN CASTLE WALL, YOU CAN FORD THE CANAL AND GET TO BEI-JIA.
IT'S BEEN SEALED OFF TO PREVENT FOREIGN INVADERS FROM GETTING IN.
AND WHERE IS THAT...
YOU'D NEVER MAKE IT DOWN!
IT'S A CLIFF, YOU KNOW.
I BELIEVE YOUR ROOMS ARE READY.
WHAT'LL WE DO ?
STAGGER STAGGER
WE MAY HAVE TO TAKE THAT ROUTE.
WE'RE IN GOOD SHAPE. I'LL TAKE CARE OF MITSUKAKE. YOU'RE TIRED. GET SOME REST... NO DA...
THIS WAY.

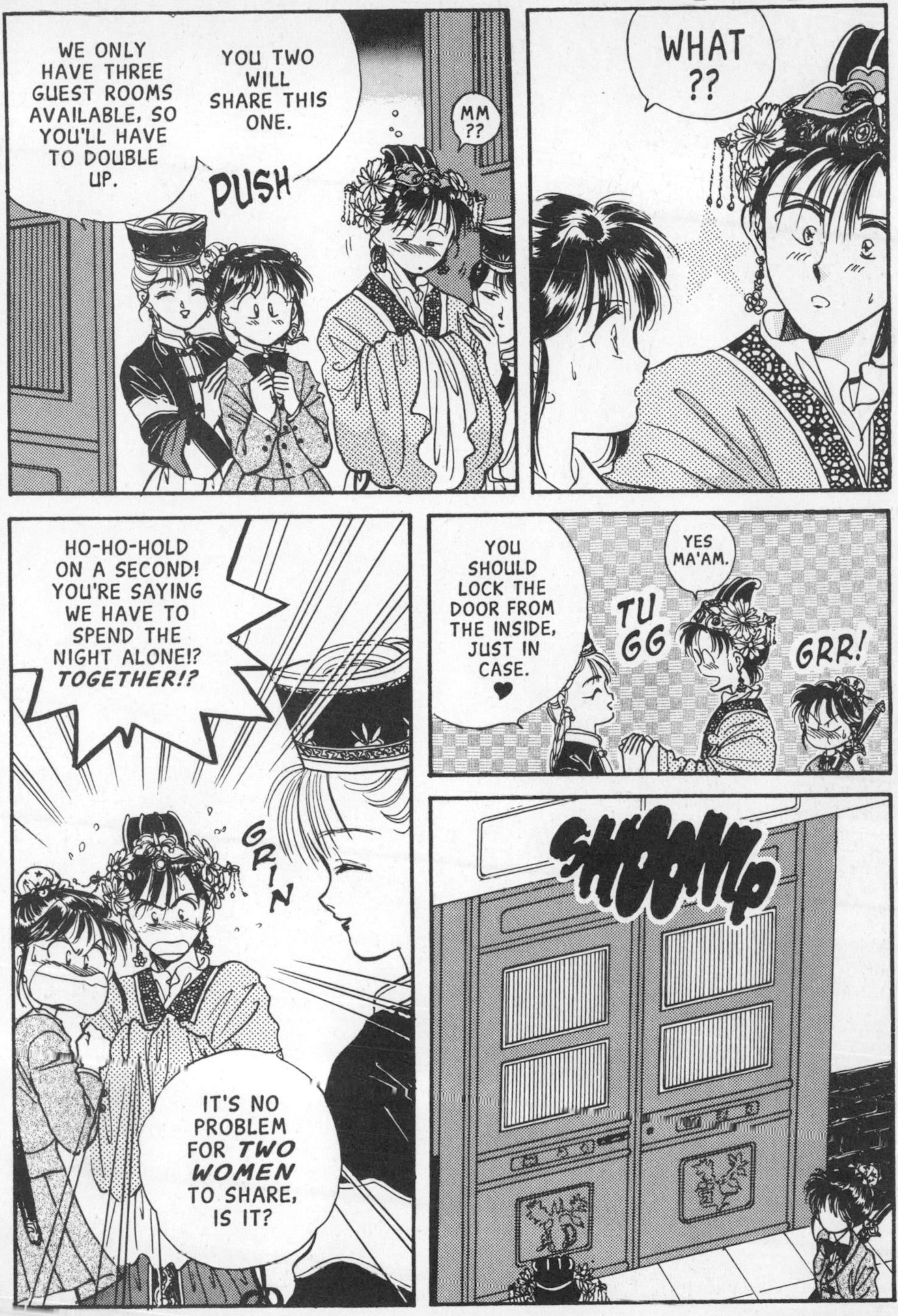
WE ONLY HAVE THREE GUEST ROOMS AVAILABLE, SO YOU'LL HAVE TO DOUBLE UP.
YOU TWO WILL SHARE THIS ONE.
MM ??
PUSH
WHAT ??
HO-HO-HOLD ON A SECOND! YOU'RE SAYING WE HAVE TO SPEND THE NIGHT ALONE!? *TOGETHER!?*
GRIN
IT'S NO PROBLEM FOR *TWO WOMEN* TO SHARE, IS IT?
YOU SHOULD LOCK THE DOOR FROM THE INSIDE, JUST IN CASE. ♥
YES MA'AM.
TUGG
GRR!
SHOOMP

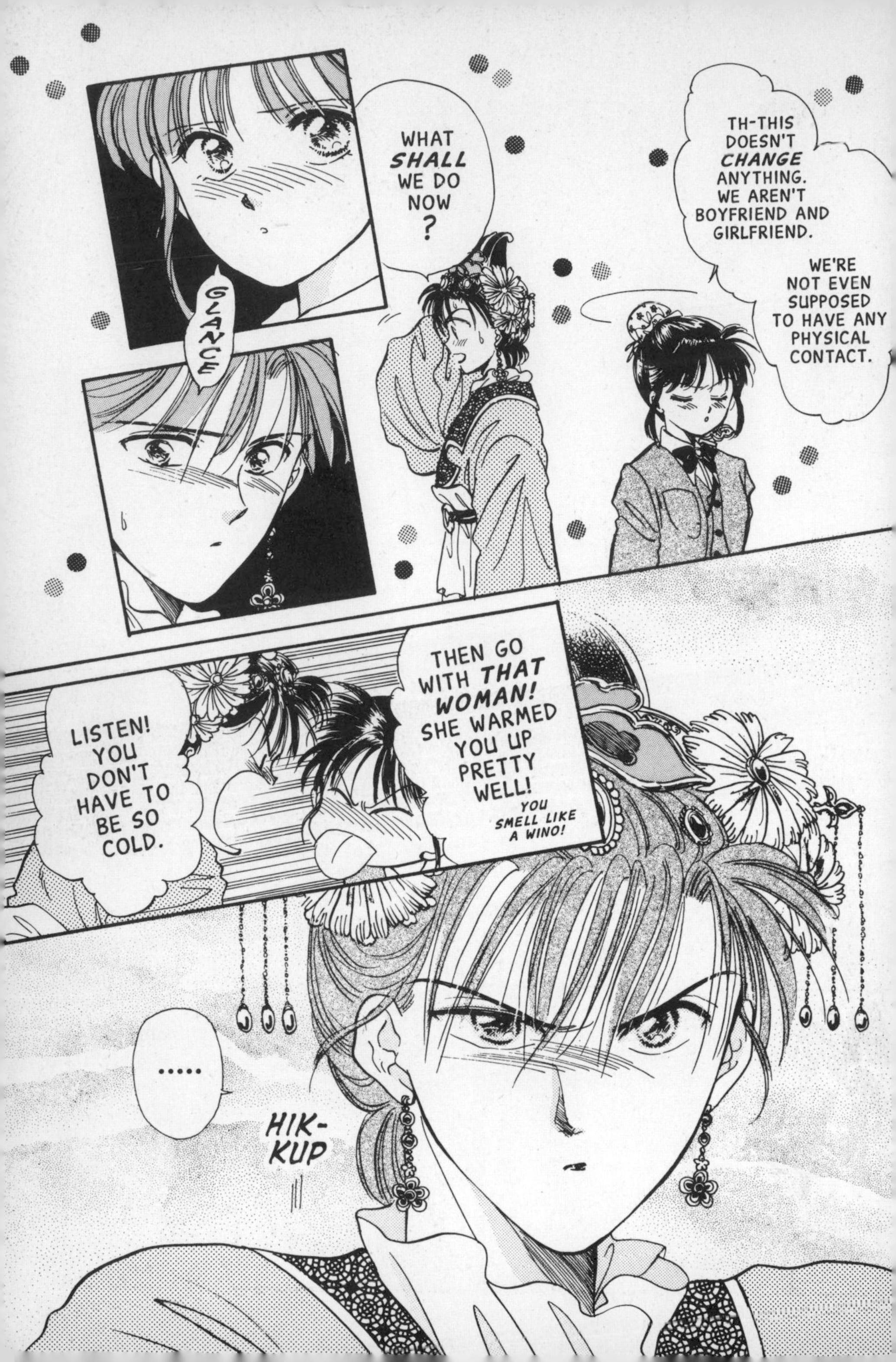
GLANCE
WHAT SHALL WE DO NOW?
TH-THIS DOESN'T CHANGE ANYTHING. WE AREN'T BOYFRIEND AND GIRLFRIEND.
WE'RE NOT EVEN SUPPOSED TO HAVE ANY PHYSICAL CONTACT.
LISTEN! YOU DON'T HAVE TO BE SO COLD.
THEN GO WITH THAT WOMAN! SHE WARMED YOU UP PRETTY WELL!
YOU SMELL LIKE A WINO!
.....
HIK-KUP

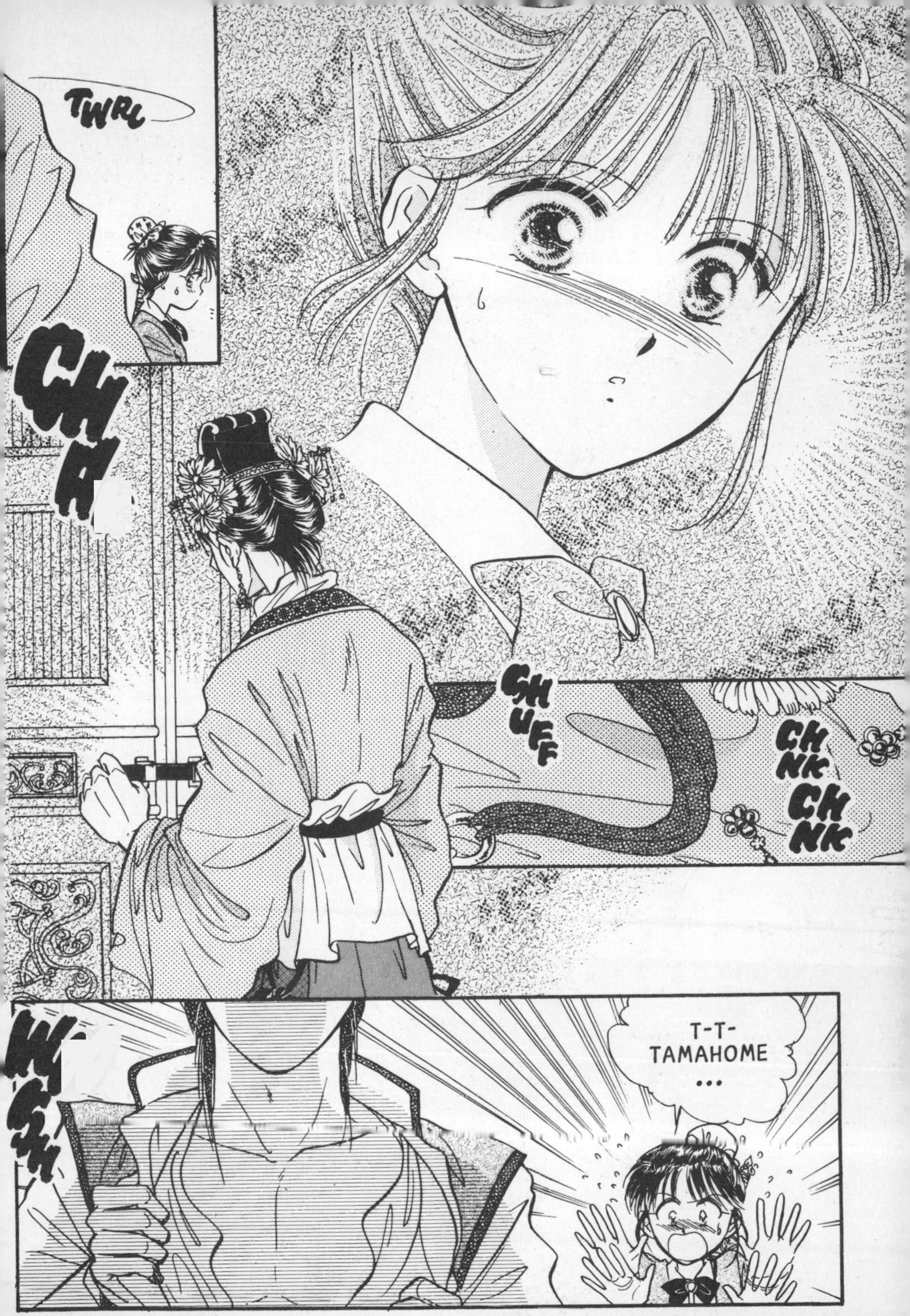
TWRL
CHA
SHUFF
CHNK CHNK
T-T-TAMAHOME...

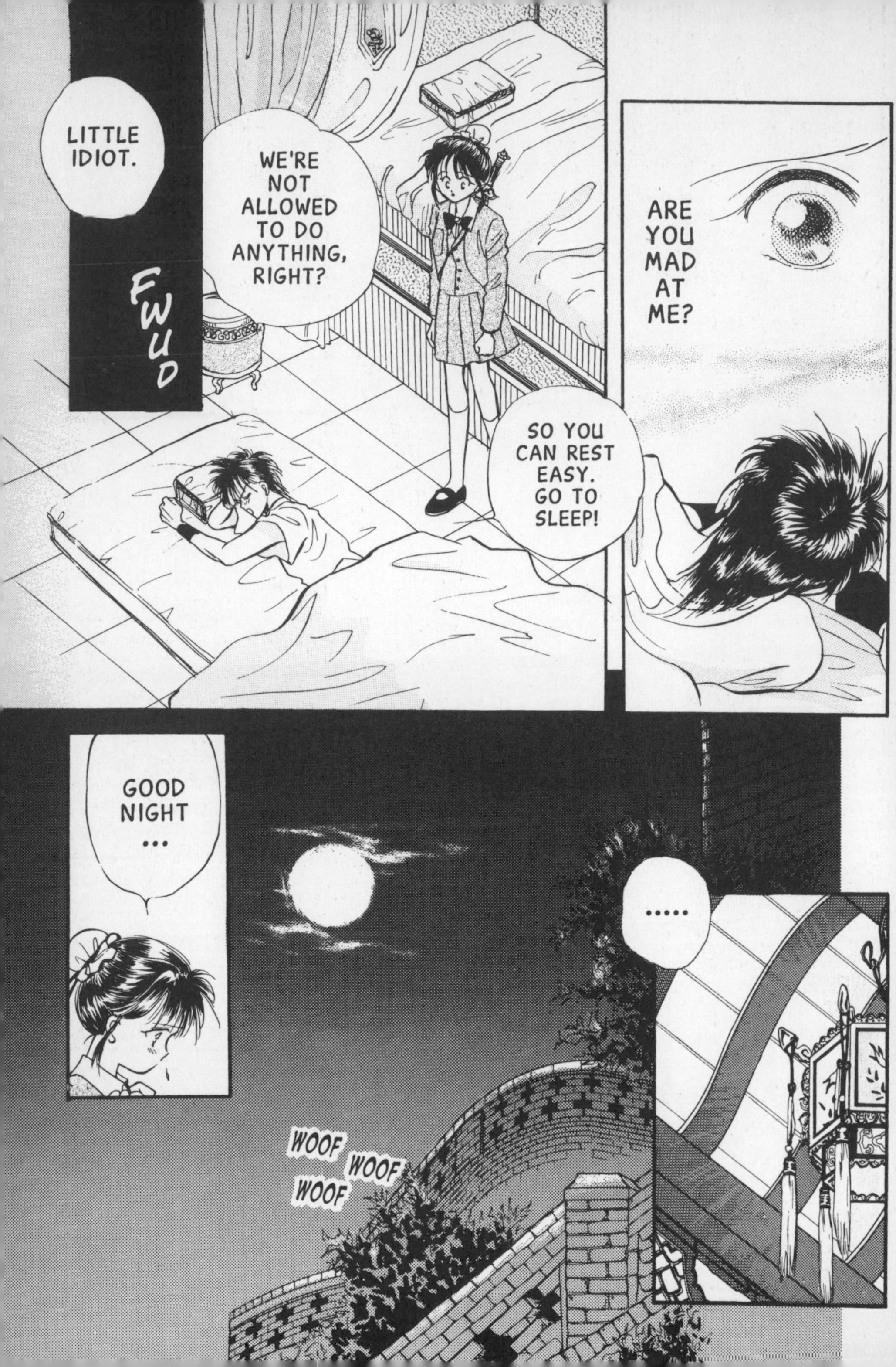
LITTLE IDIOT.
FWUD
WE'RE NOT ALLOWED TO DO ANYTHING, RIGHT?
SO YOU CAN REST EASY. GO TO SLEEP!
ARE YOU MAD AT ME?
GOOD NIGHT ...
.....
WOOF WOOF WOOF

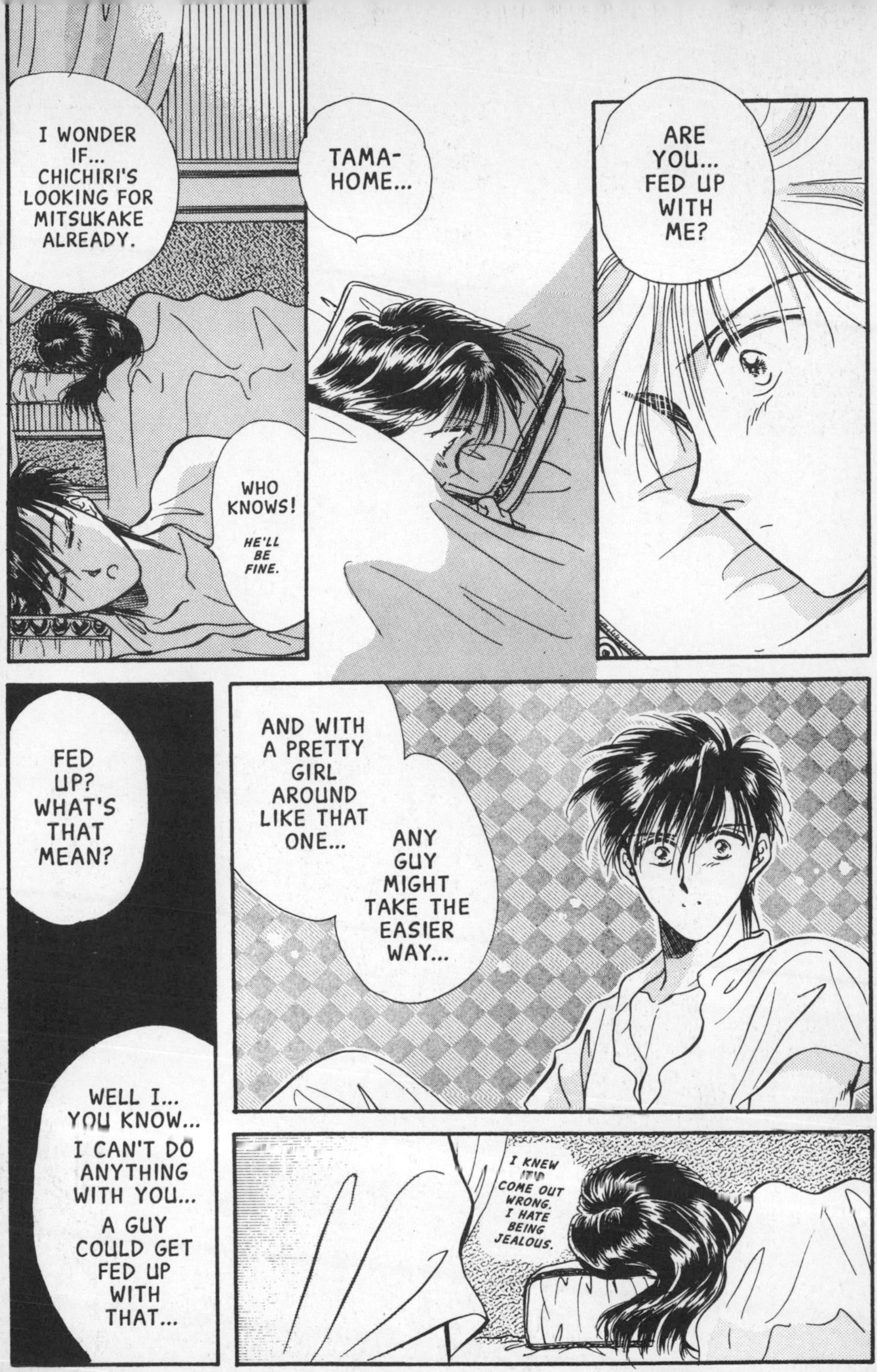
I WONDER IF... CHICHIRI'S LOOKING FOR MITSUKAKE ALREADY.
WHO KNOWS!
HE'LL BE FINE.
TAMA-HOME...
ARE YOU... FED UP WITH ME?
FED UP? WHAT'S THAT MEAN?
WELL I... YOU KNOW... I CAN'T DO ANYTHING WITH YOU... A GUY COULD GET FED UP WITH THAT...
AND WITH A PRETTY GIRL AROUND LIKE THAT ONE...
ANY GUY MIGHT TAKE THE EASIER WAY...
I KNEW IT'D COME OUT WRONG. I HATE BEING JEALOUS.

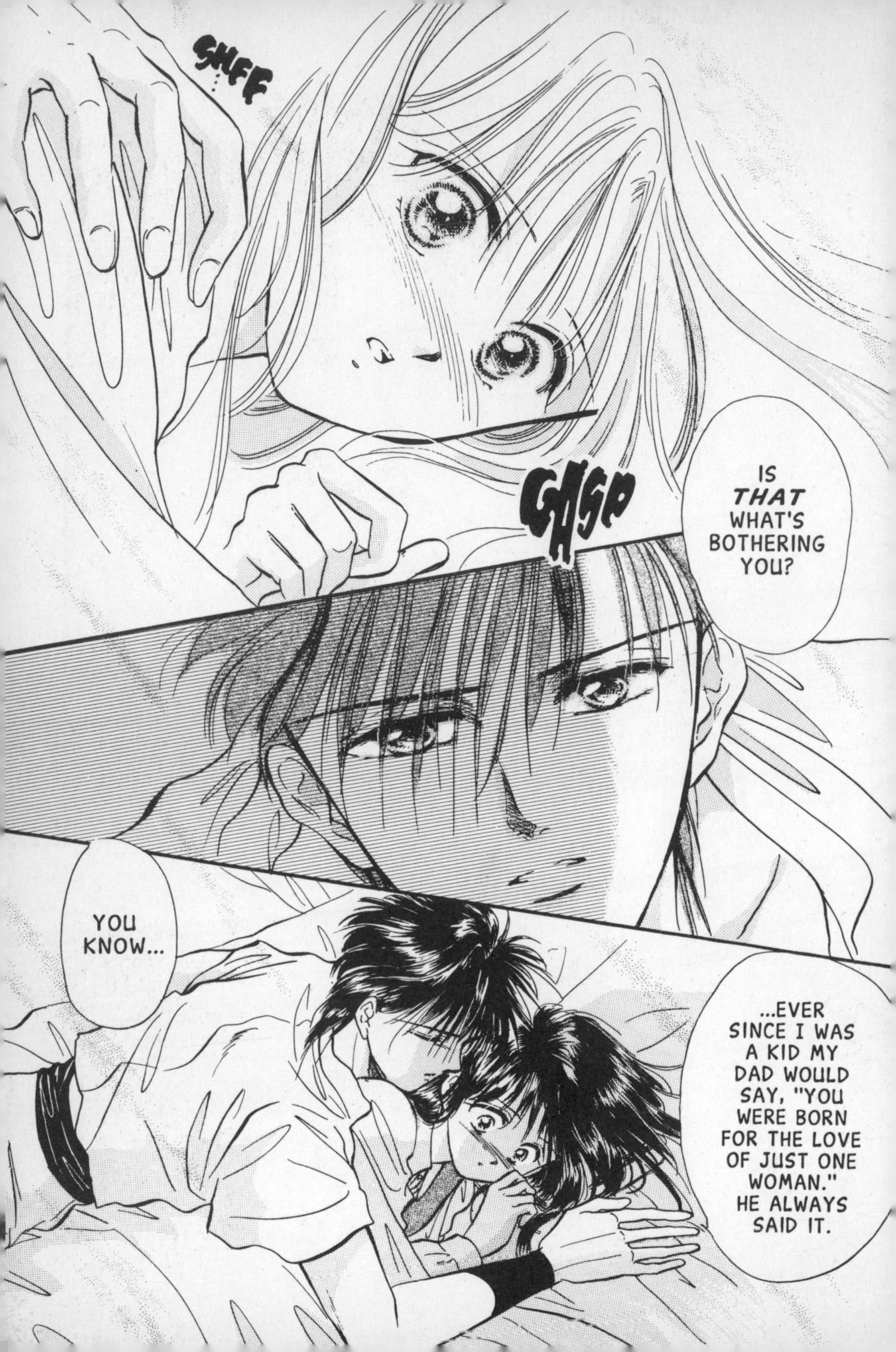
SHFF
GASP
IS *THAT* WHAT'S BOTHERING YOU?
YOU KNOW...
...EVER SINCE I WAS A KID MY DAD WOULD SAY, "YOU WERE BORN FOR THE LOVE OF JUST ONE WOMAN." HE ALWAYS SAID IT.

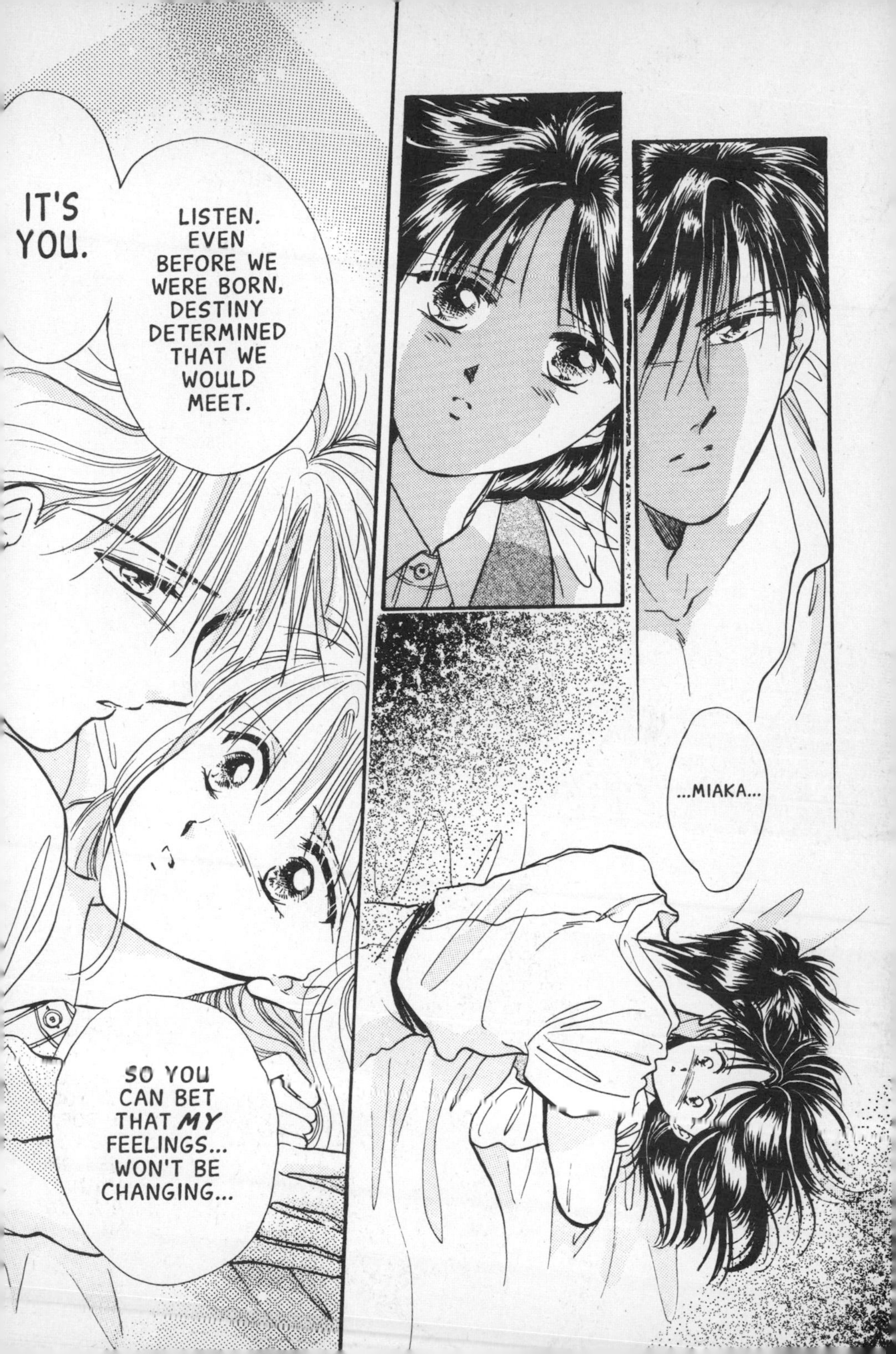
IT'S YOU.
LISTEN. EVEN BEFORE WE WERE BORN, DESTINY DETERMINED THAT WE WOULD MEET.
SO YOU CAN BET THAT *MY* FEELINGS... WON'T BE CHANGING...
...MIAKA...

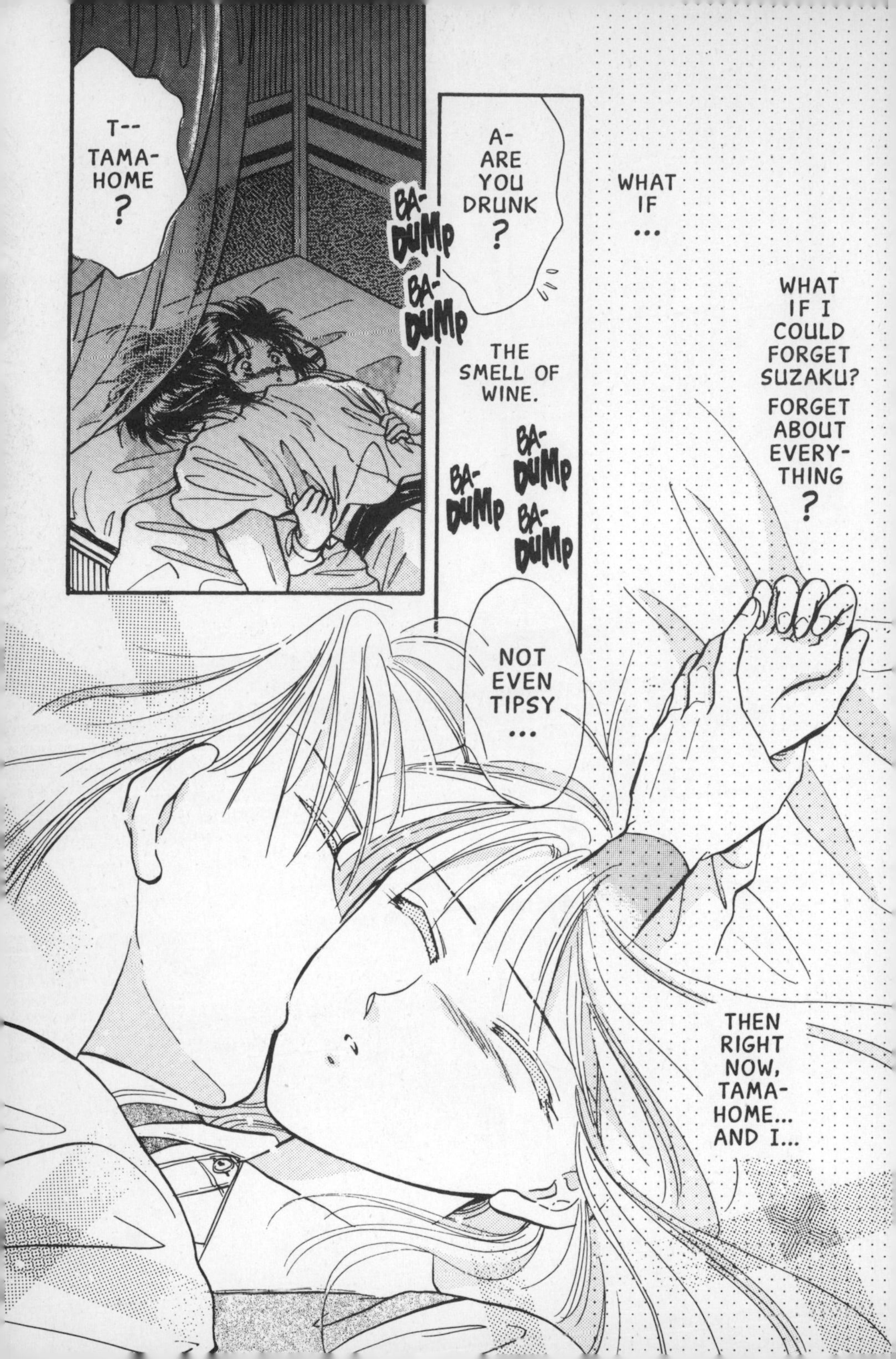
T-- TAMA-HOME?
A- ARE YOU DRUNK?
BA-DUMP
BA-DUMP
THE SMELL OF WINE.
BA-DUMP
BA-DUMP
BA-DUMP
NOT EVEN TIPSY...
WHAT IF...
WHAT IF I COULD FORGET SUZAKU?
FORGET ABOUT EVERYTHING?
THEN RIGHT NOW, TAMA-HOME... AND I...

W-WE CAN'T!!

I'M THE PRIESTESS OF SUZAKU. I CAN'T--

AH!

"YOU ARE NOT TO HAVE ANY FEELINGS FOR MEN, NOR ARE YOU TO HAVE ANY BODILY CONTACT WITH THEM."

SSSHHHH

SCHORR

WHAP

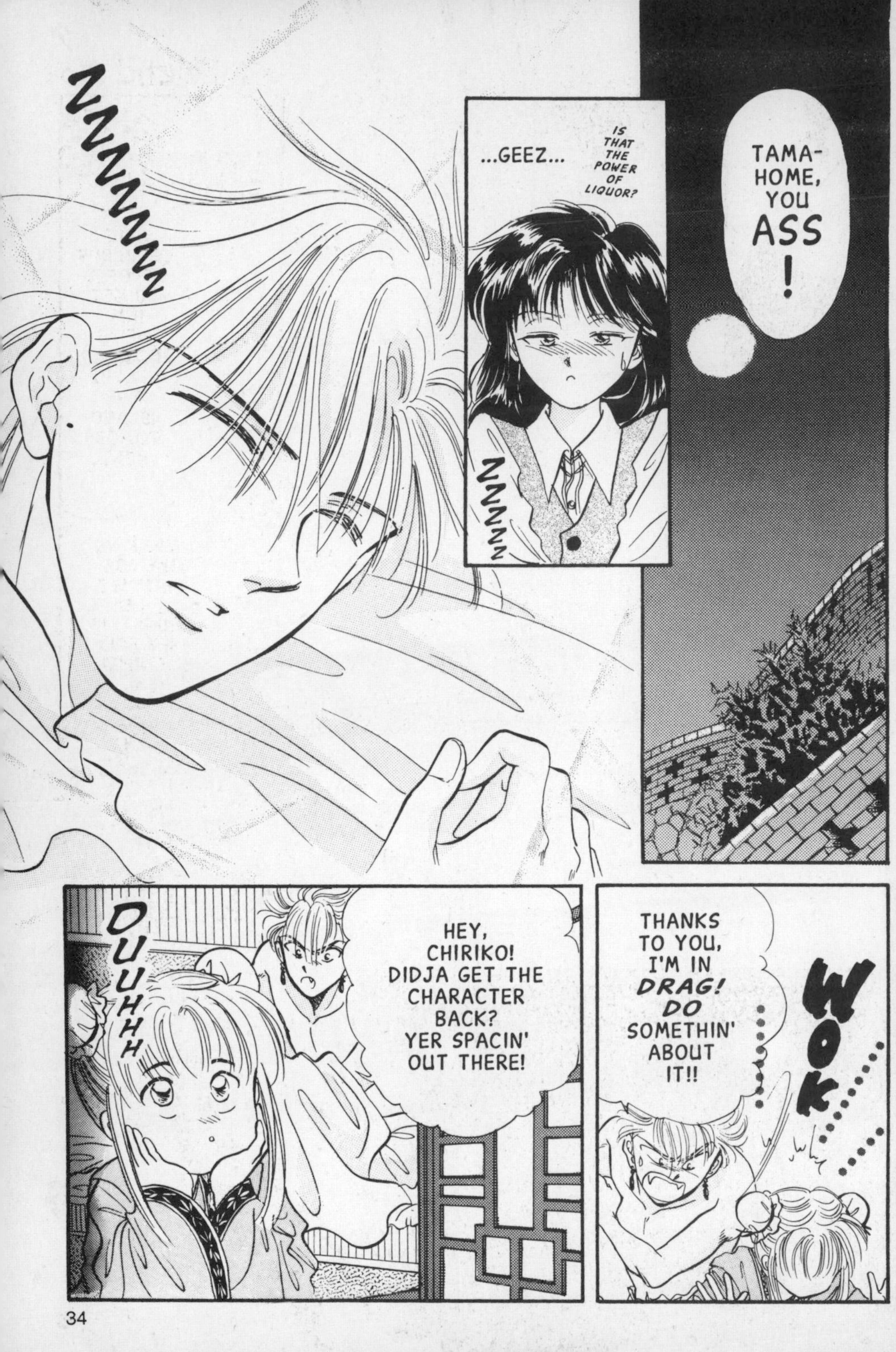
ZZZZZZZZZZZZ
...GEEZ...
IS THAT THE POWER OF LIQUOR?
ZZZZZ
TAMA-HOME, YOU ASS!
DUUHHH
HEY, CHIRIKO! DIDJA GET THE CHARACTER BACK? YER SPACIN' OUT THERE!
THANKS TO YOU, I'M IN DRAG! DO SOMETHIN' ABOUT IT!!
WOK......

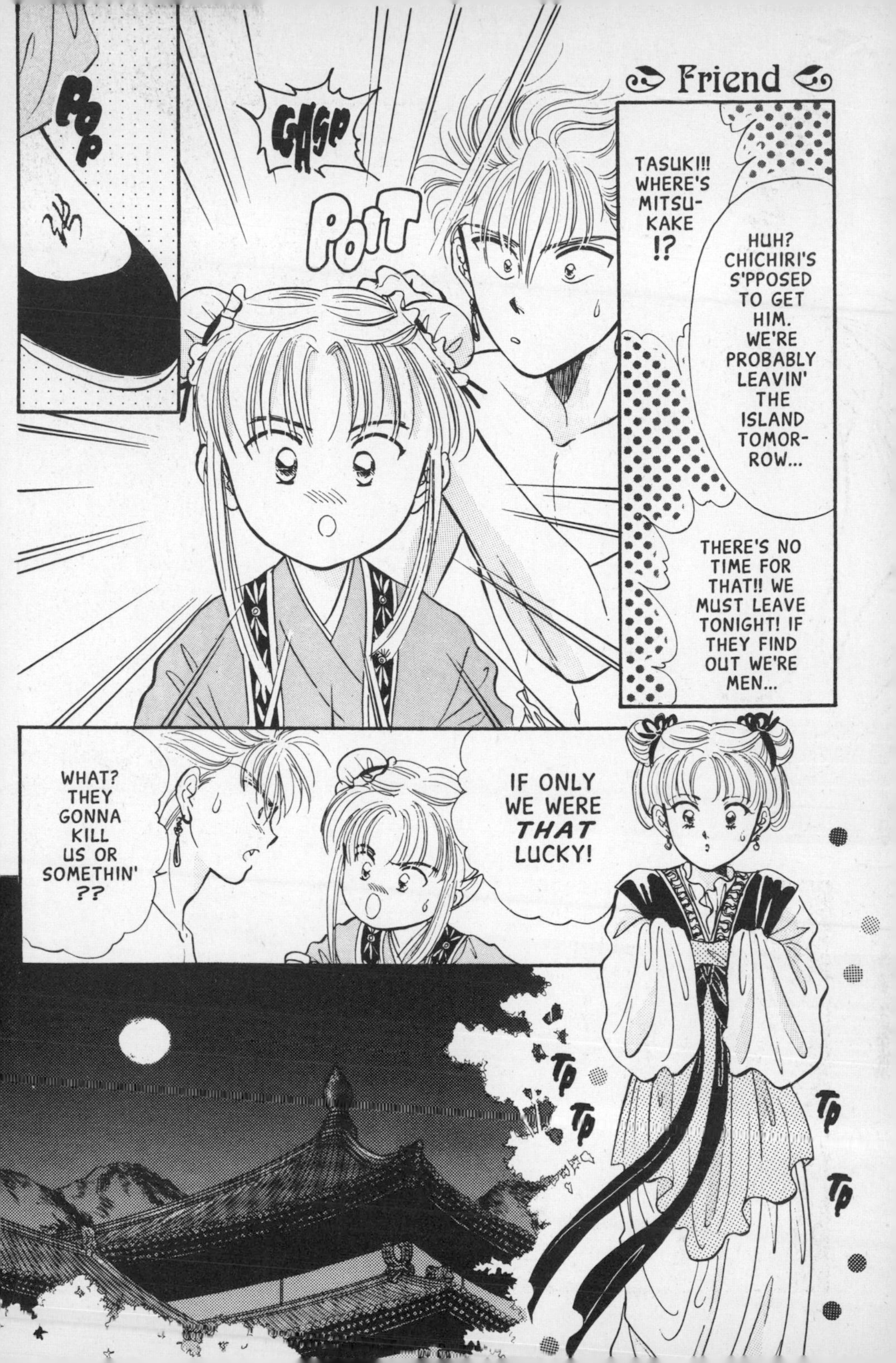
POP
GASP
POIT
TASUKI!!! WHERE'S MITSUKAKE !?
HUH? CHICHIRI'S S'PPOSED TO GET HIM. WE'RE PROBABLY LEAVIN' THE ISLAND TOMORROW...
THERE'S NO TIME FOR THAT!! WE MUST LEAVE TONIGHT! IF THEY FIND OUT WE'RE MEN...
WHAT? THEY GONNA KILL US OR SOMETHIN' ??
IF ONLY WE WERE *THAT* LUCKY!
Tp
Tp
Tp
Tp

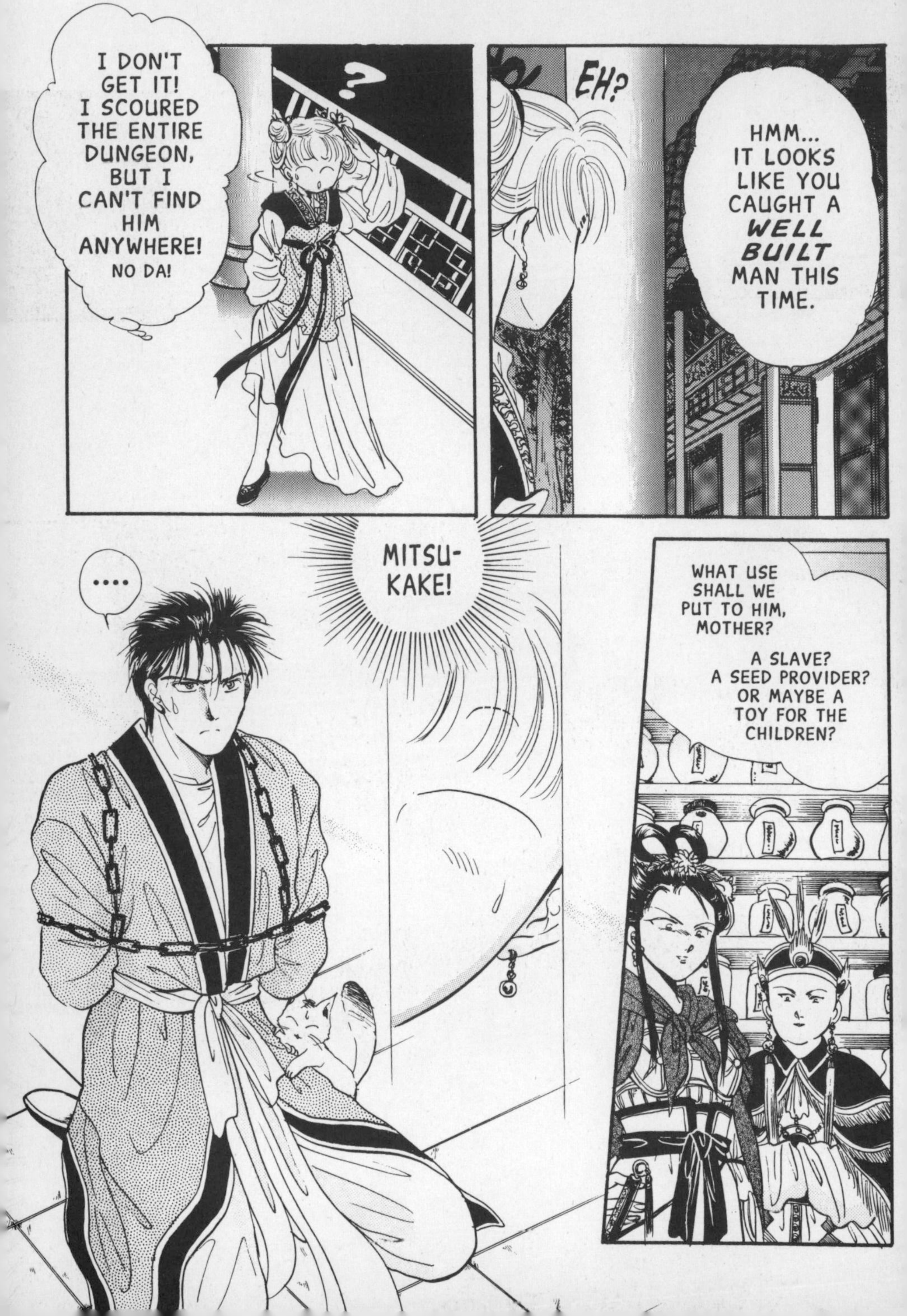
I DON'T GET IT! I SCOURED THE ENTIRE DUNGEON, BUT I CAN'T FIND HIM ANYWHERE! NO DA!
?
EH?
HMM... IT LOOKS LIKE YOU CAUGHT A WELL BUILT MAN THIS TIME.
....
MITSU-KAKE!
WHAT USE SHALL WE PUT TO HIM, MOTHER?
A SLAVE? A SEED PROVIDER? OR MAYBE A TOY FOR THE CHILDREN?

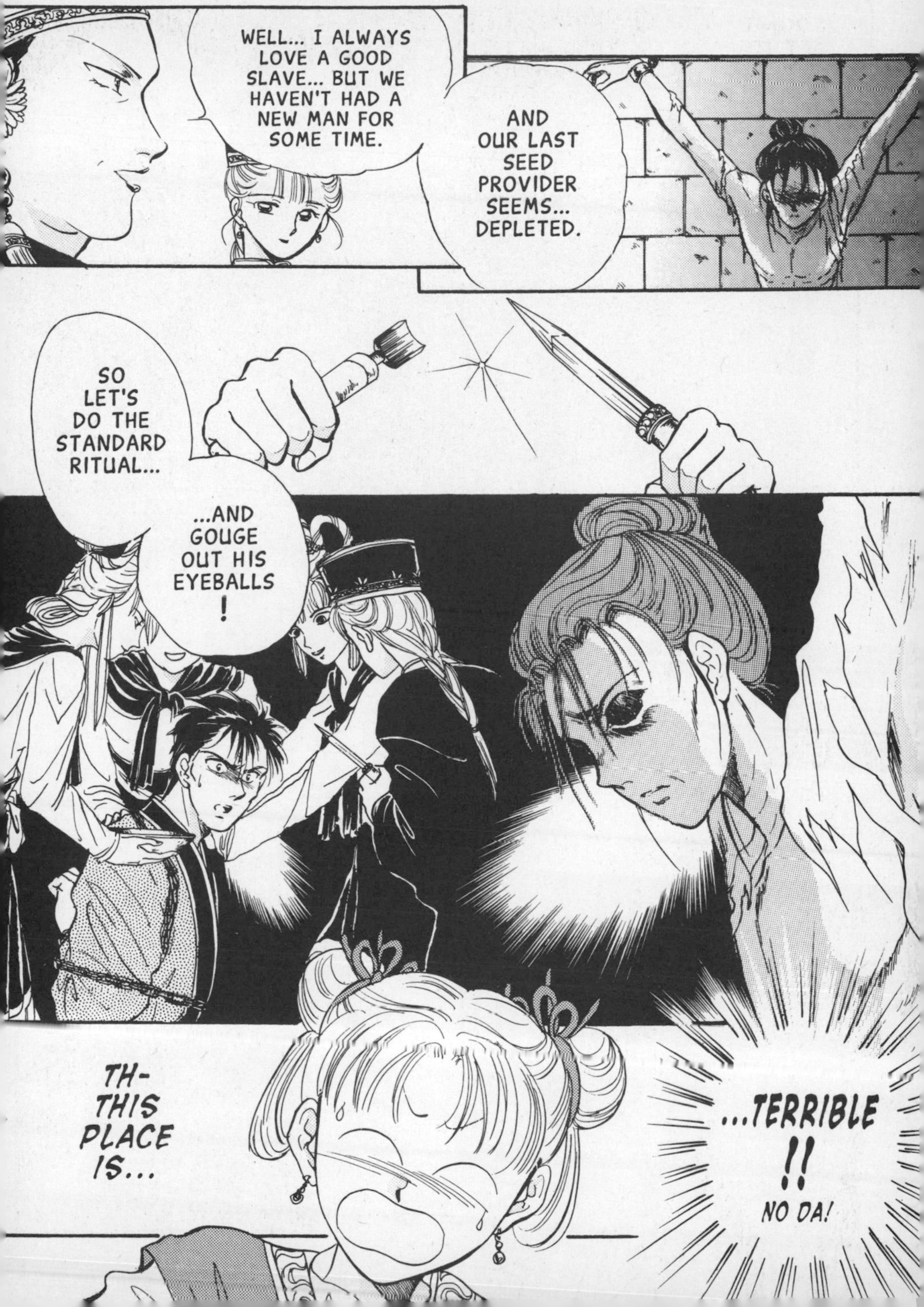
WELL... I ALWAYS LOVE A GOOD SLAVE... BUT WE HAVEN'T HAD A NEW MAN FOR SOME TIME.
AND OUR LAST SEED PROVIDER SEEMS... DEPLETED.
SO LET'S DO THE STANDARD RITUAL...
...AND GOUGE OUT HIS EYEBALLS !
TH-THIS PLACE IS...
...TERRIBLE !! NO DA!

CHAPTER FORTY-FOUR

THE SPARK OF COMBAT

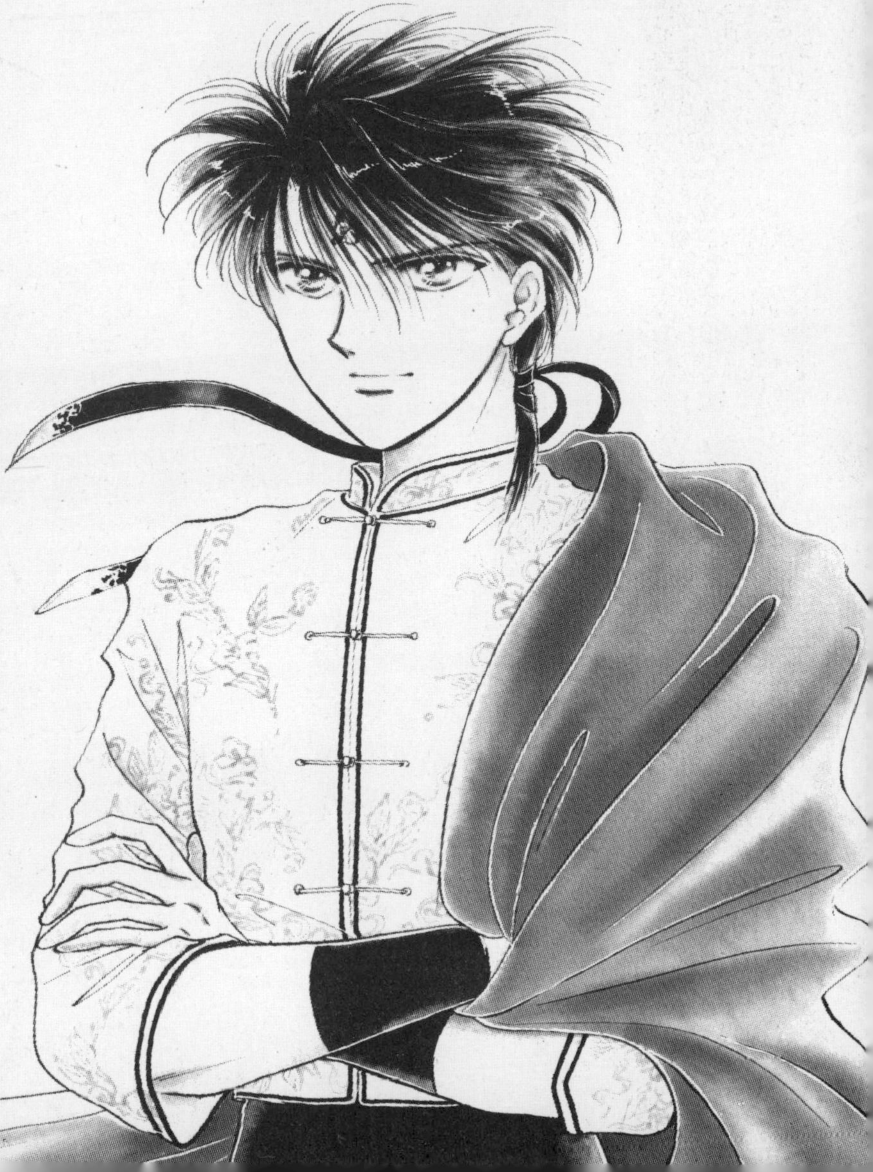

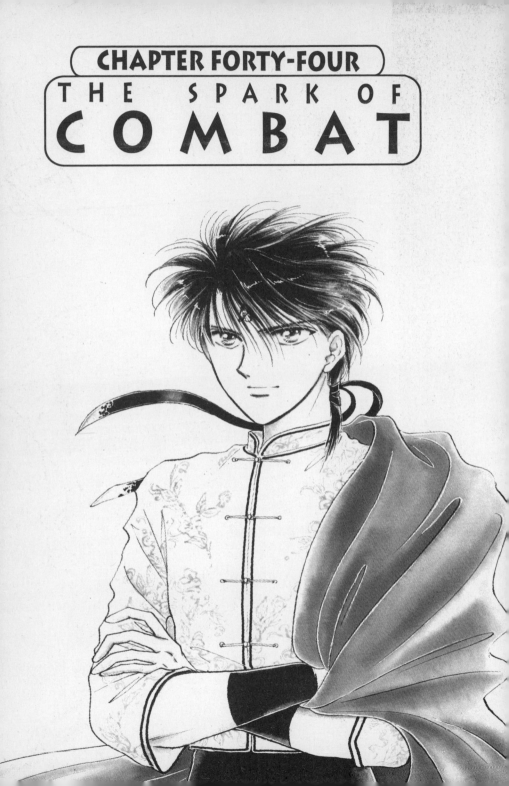

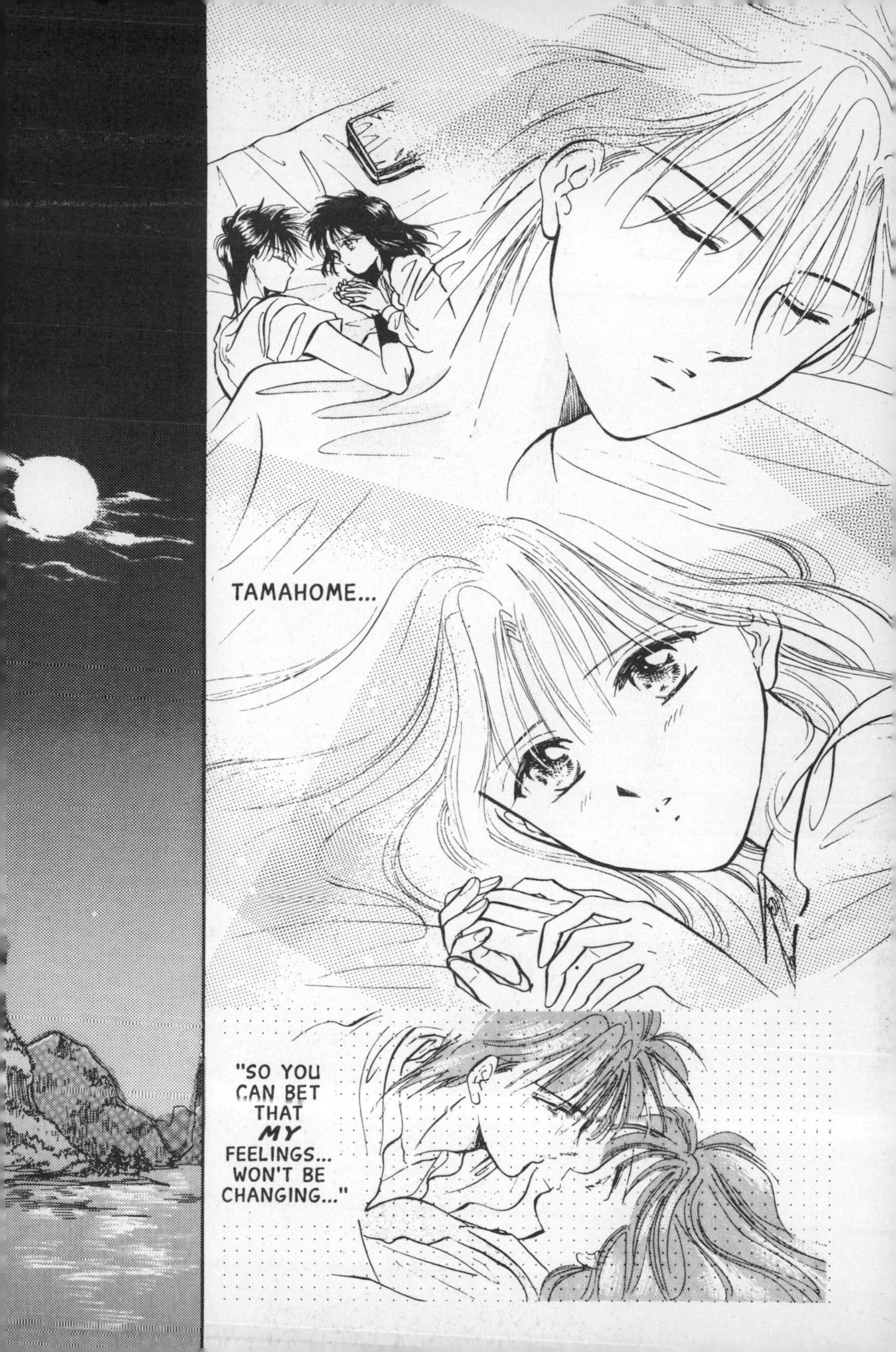
TAMAHOME...
"SO YOU CAN BET THAT *MY* FEELINGS... WON'T BE CHANGING..."

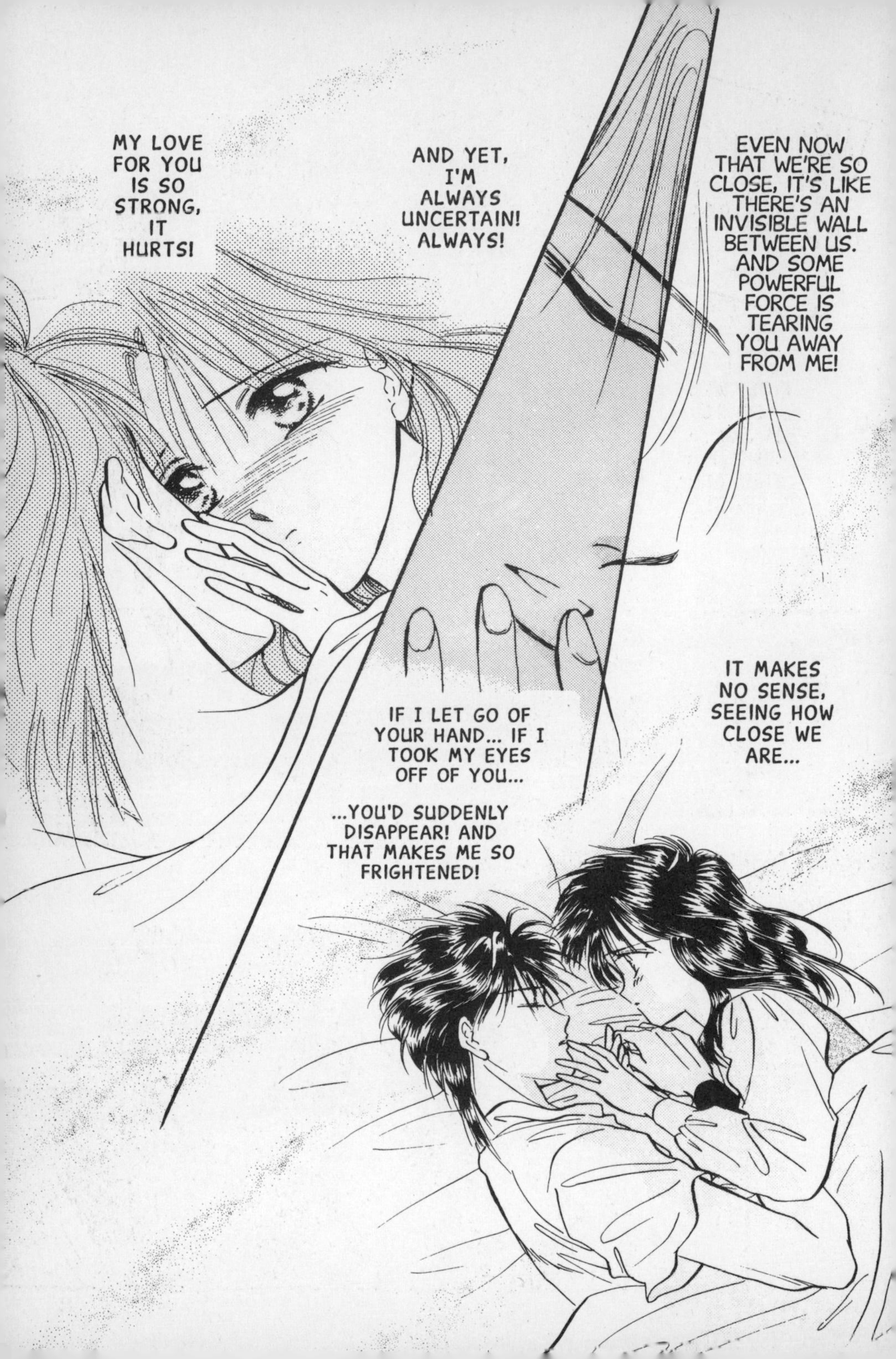
MY LOVE FOR YOU IS SO STRONG, IT HURTS!
AND YET, I'M ALWAYS UNCERTAIN! ALWAYS!
EVEN NOW THAT WE'RE SO CLOSE, IT'S LIKE THERE'S AN INVISIBLE WALL BETWEEN US. AND SOME POWERFUL FORCE IS TEARING YOU AWAY FROM ME!
IF I LET GO OF YOUR HAND... IF I TOOK MY EYES OFF OF YOU...
...YOU'D SUDDENLY DISAPPEAR! AND THAT MAKES ME SO FRIGHTENED!
IT MAKES NO SENSE, SEEING HOW CLOSE WE ARE...

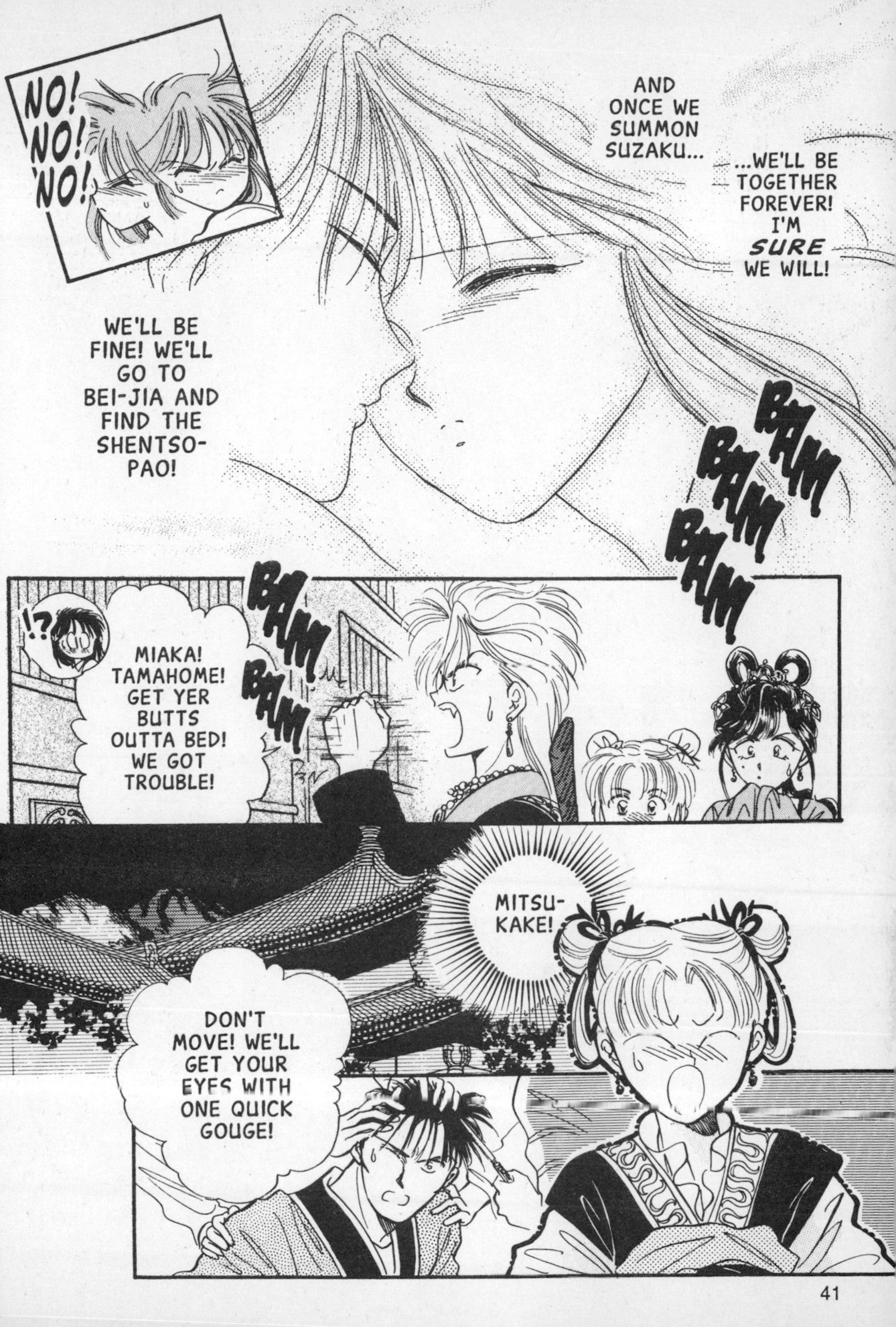
AND ONCE WE SUMMON SUZAKU...
...WE'LL BE TOGETHER FOREVER! I'M SURE WE WILL!
NO! NO! NO!
WE'LL BE FINE! WE'LL GO TO BEI-JIA AND FIND THE SHENTSO-PAO!
BAM BAM BAM
BAM BAM
!?
MIAKA! TAMAHOME! GET YER BUTTS OUTTA BED! WE GOT TROUBLE!
MITSU-KAKE!
DON'T MOVE! WE'LL GET YOUR EYES WITH ONE QUICK GOUGE!

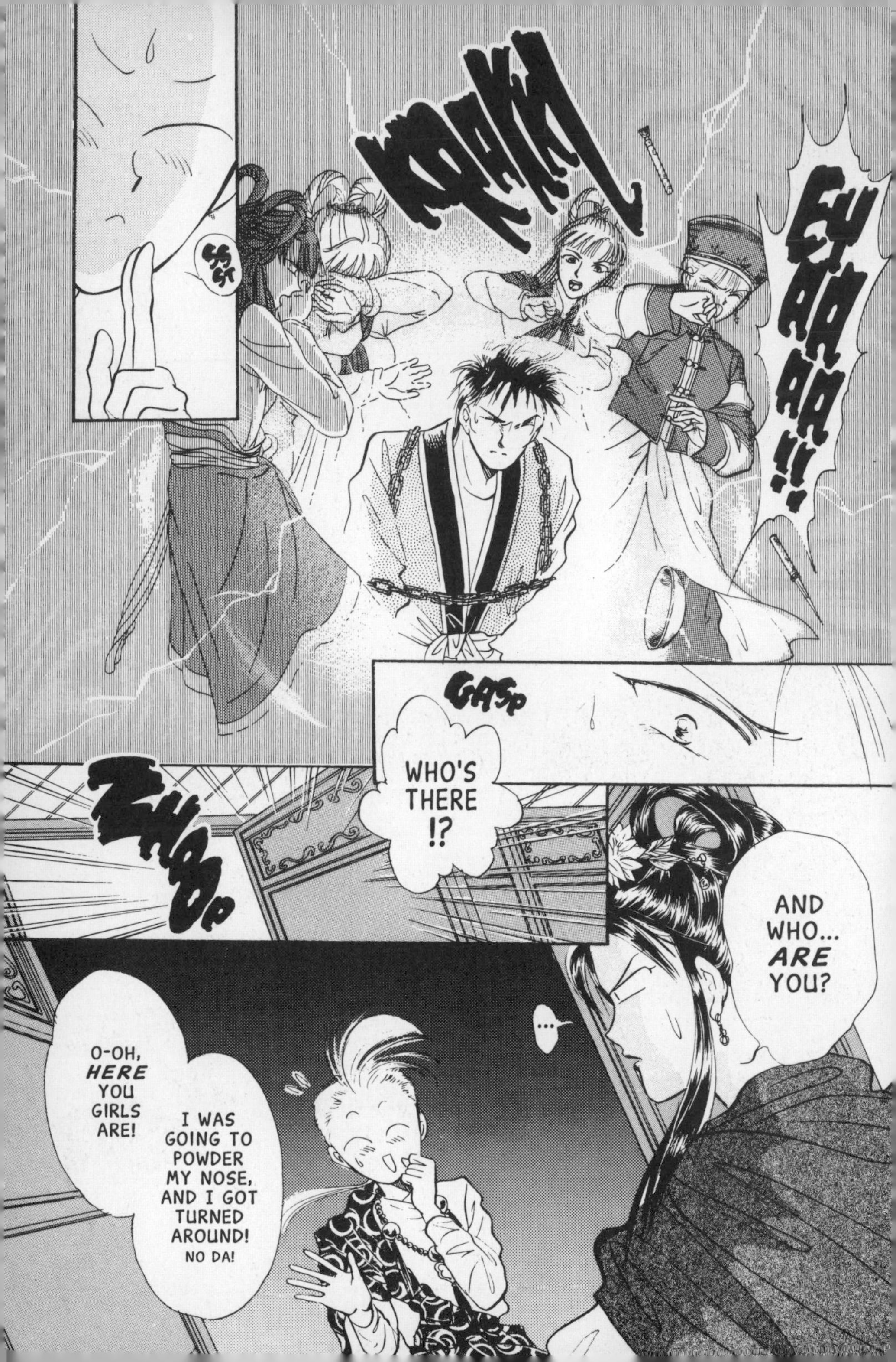
SSST
ZHOOP
GASP
WHO'S THERE !?
AND WHO... *ARE* YOU?
O-OH, *HERE* YOU GIRLS ARE!
I WAS GOING TO POWDER MY NOSE, AND I GOT TURNED AROUND! NO DA!
...

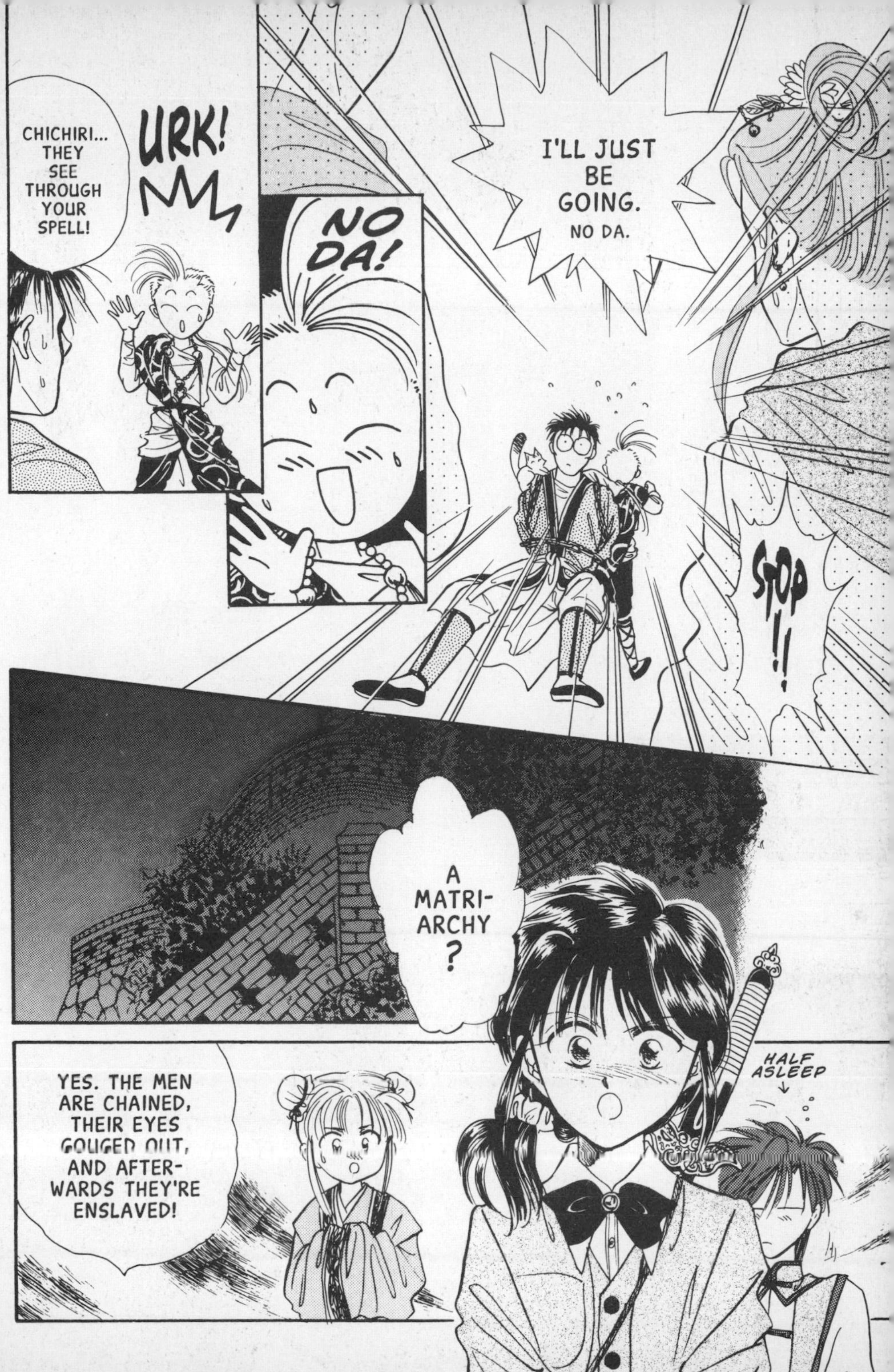

CHICHIRI... THEY SEE THROUGH YOUR SPELL!
URK!
NO DA!
I'LL JUST BE GOING. NO DA.
STOP!!
A MATRI-ARCHY?
YES. THE MEN ARE CHAINED, THEIR EYES GOUGED OUT, AND AFTER-WARDS THEY'RE ENSLAVED!
HALF ASLEEP

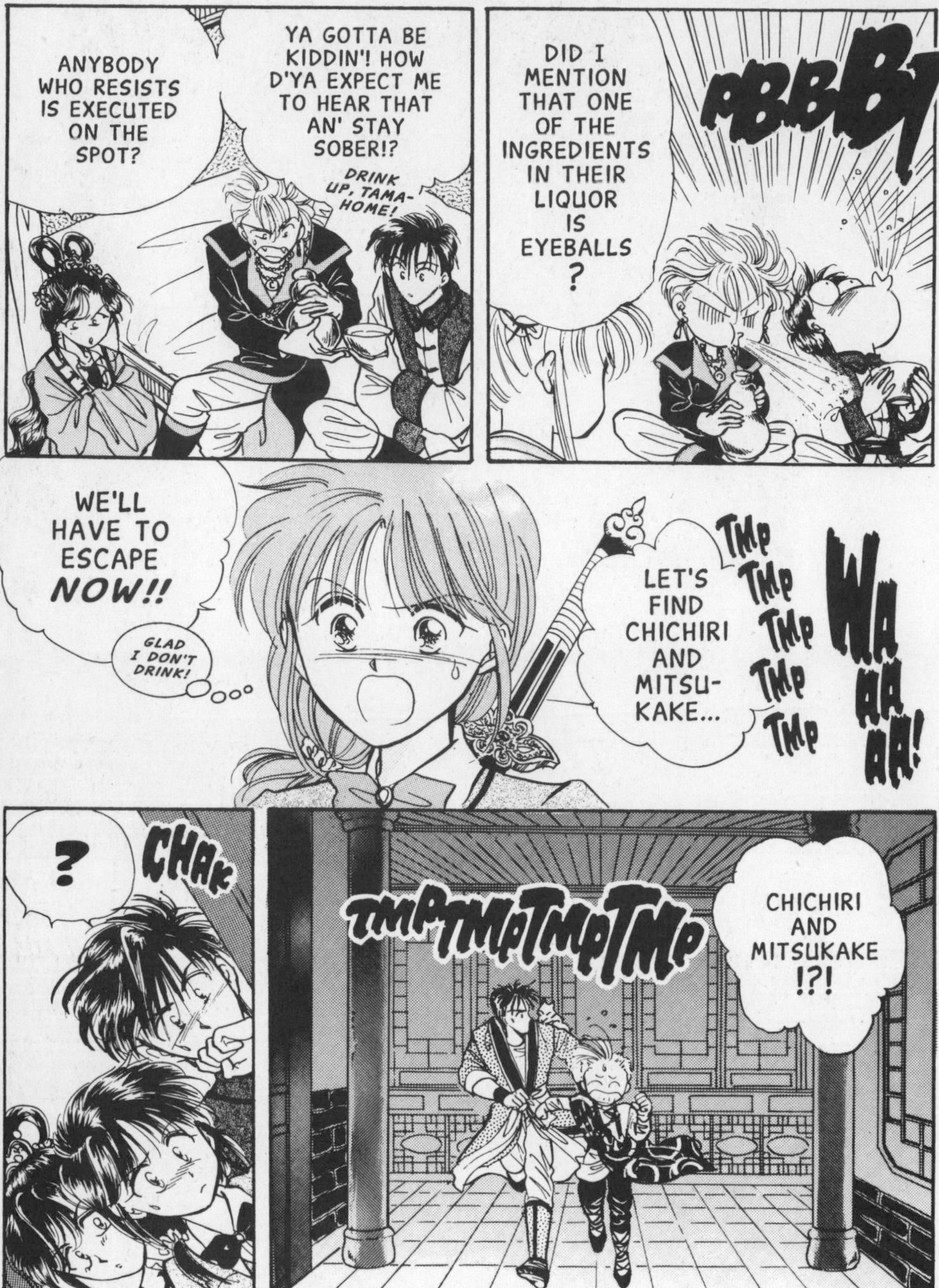
ANYBODY WHO RESISTS IS EXECUTED ON THE SPOT?
YA GOTTA BE KIDDIN'! HOW D'YA EXPECT ME TO HEAR THAT AN' STAY SOBER!?
DRINK UP, TAMAHOME!
DID I MENTION THAT ONE OF THE INGREDIENTS IN THEIR LIQUOR IS EYEBALLS ?
PBBBT
WE'LL HAVE TO ESCAPE NOW!!
GLAD I DON'T DRINK!
LET'S FIND CHICHIRI AND MITSUKAKE...
TMP TMP TMP TMP TMP TMP
WAAAAA!
?
CHAK
TMPTMPTMPTMP
CHICHIRI AND MITSUKAKE !?!

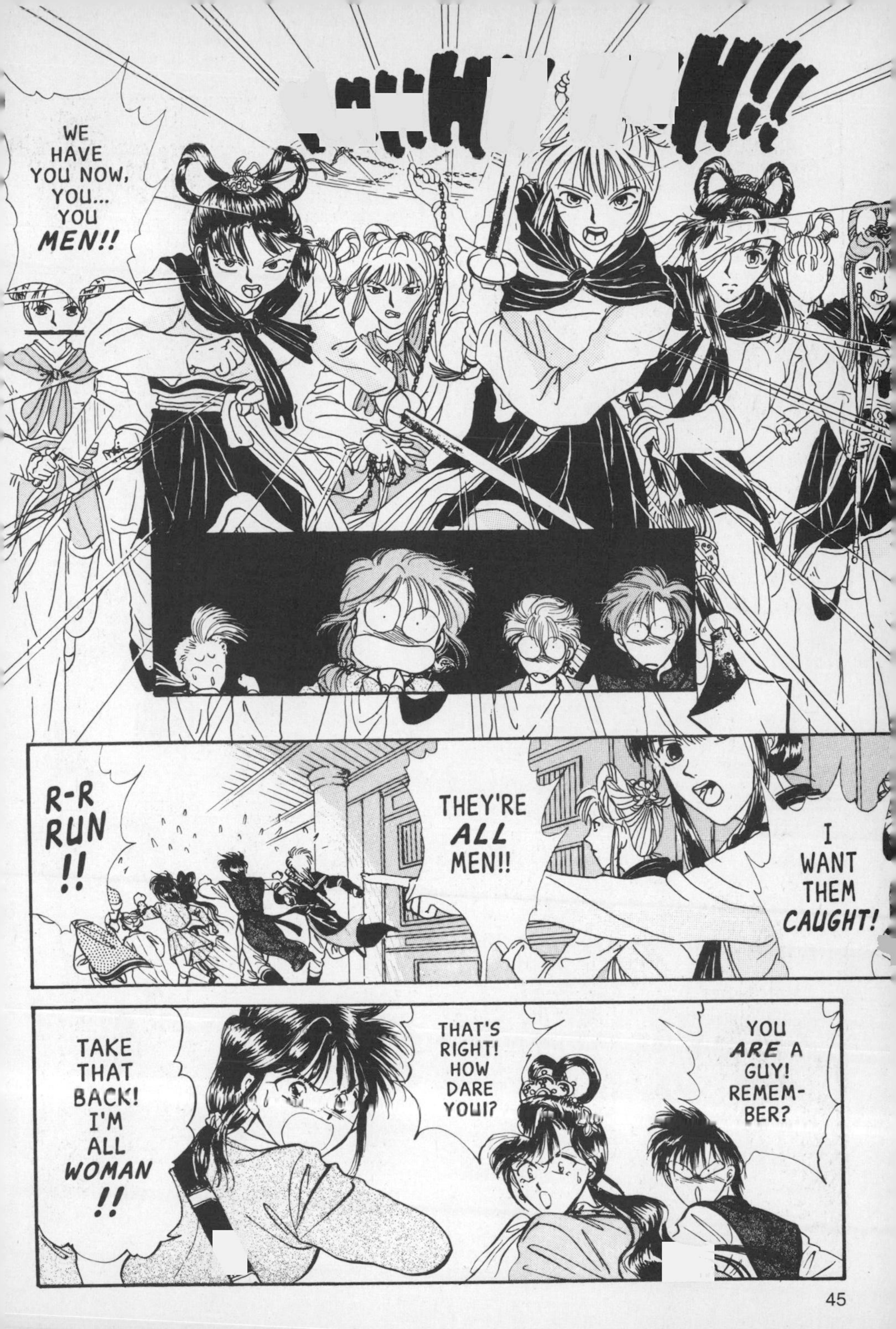
WE HAVE YOU NOW, YOU... YOU MEN!!
R-R RUN!!
THEY'RE ALL MEN!!
I WANT THEM CAUGHT!
TAKE THAT BACK! I'M ALL WOMAN!!
THAT'S RIGHT! HOW DARE YOU!?
YOU ARE A GUY! REMEMBER?

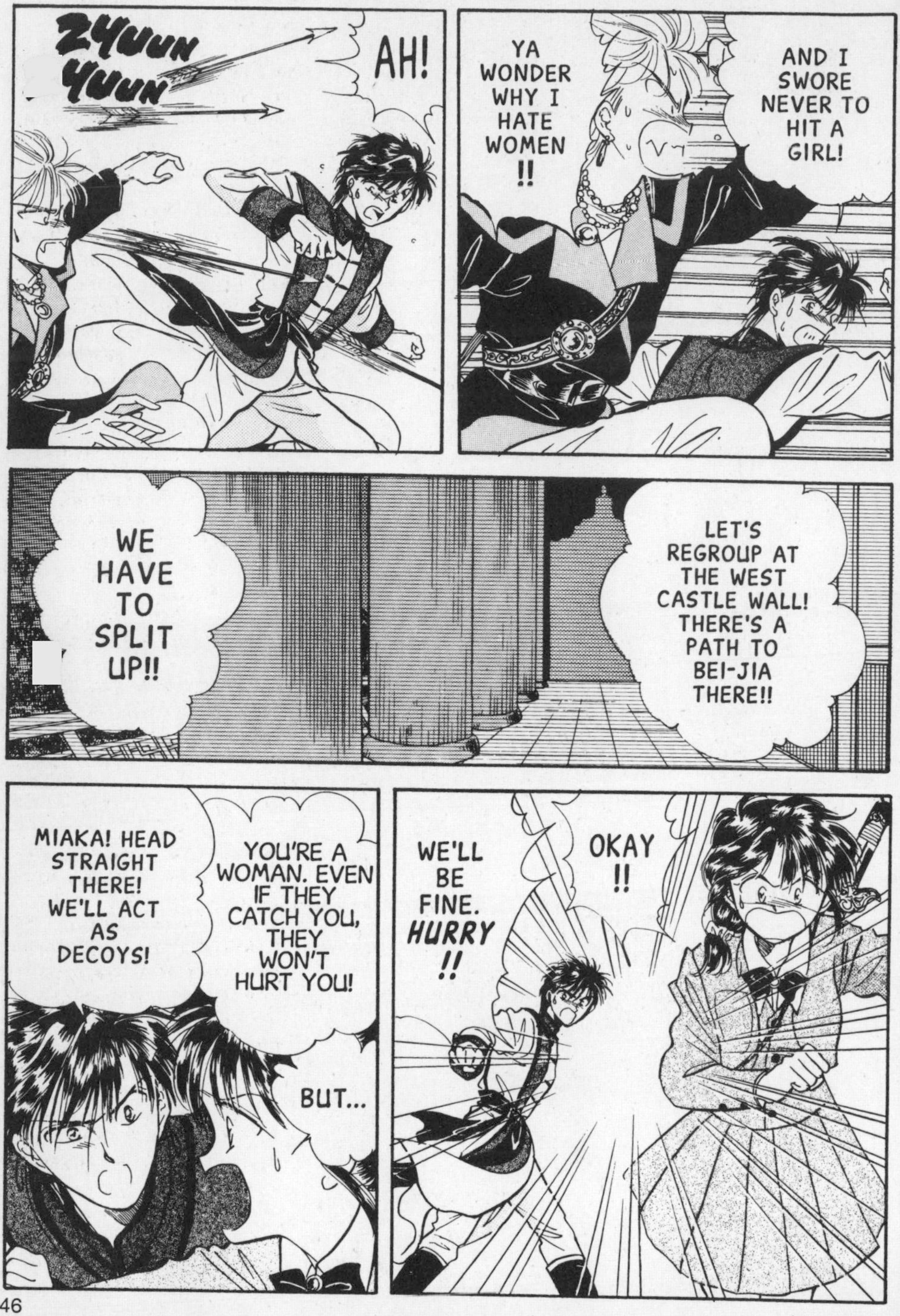
ZYUUN
YUUN
AH!
YA WONDER WHY I HATE WOMEN !!
AND I SWORE NEVER TO HIT A GIRL!
WE HAVE TO SPLIT UP!!
LET'S REGROUP AT THE WEST CASTLE WALL! THERE'S A PATH TO BEI-JIA THERE!!
MIAKA! HEAD STRAIGHT THERE! WE'LL ACT AS DECOYS!
YOU'RE A WOMAN. EVEN IF THEY CATCH YOU, THEY WON'T HURT YOU!
BUT...
WE'LL BE FINE. HURRY !!
OKAY !!

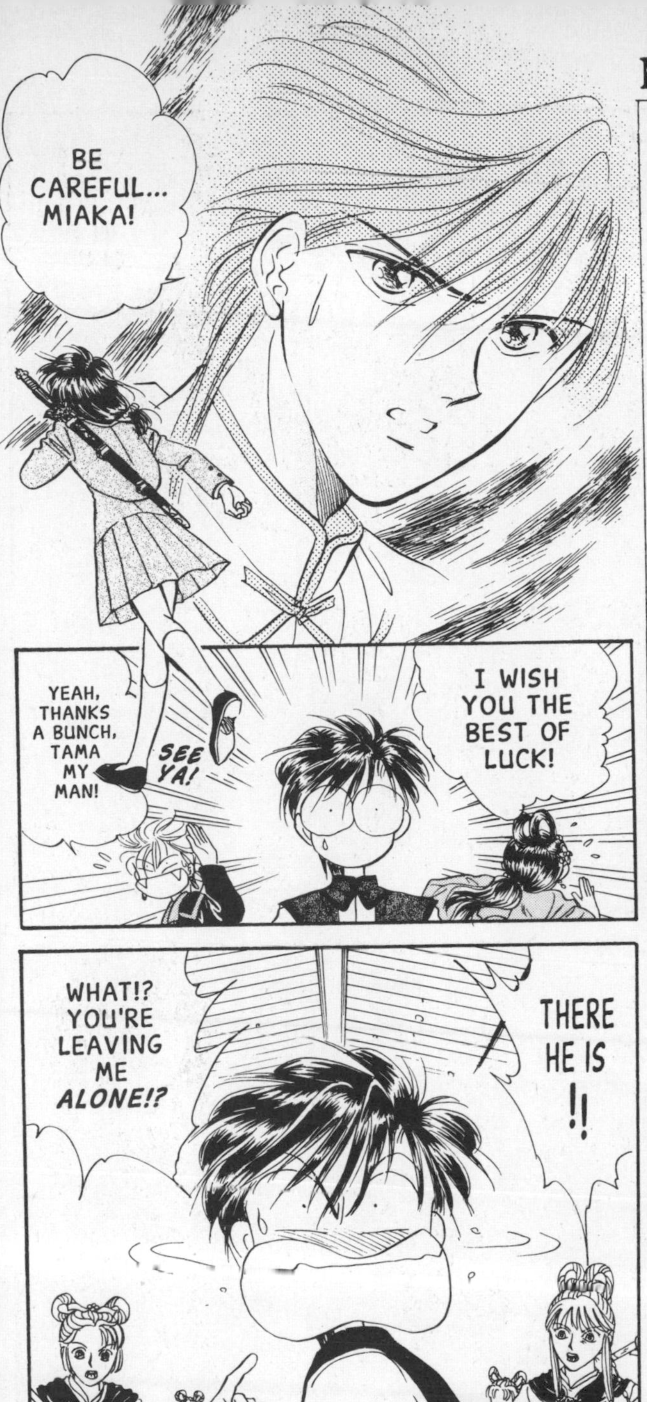
BE CAREFUL... MIAKA!
YEAH, THANKS A BUNCH, TAMA MY MAN!
SEE YA!
I WISH YOU THE BEST OF LUCK!
WHAT!? YOU'RE LEAVING ME *ALONE!?*
THERE HE IS !!

July 26 through August 3, I went to China (from Beijing to Xian to Guilin and finally to Shanghai) with my editor K for nine days. We had trouble from the very beginning -- our JAL flight was blocked at Beijing Airport by a Chinese airplane. It just wouldn't get out of our way! So we waited for a half an hour, and finally, we managed to get off the plane. We took the bus to the famous Tiananmen Square. It was so huge, with so many people that I wondered what they were all there for! There were even people flying kites.

I was in search of the palaces I've been drawing all this time, and I took loads of photos. The gates are so big. My drawings were based on travel brochures, but the real thing was awesome!!

The meals, of course, were Chinese! They were really tasty (at least for a while...)

Of course with Beijing, the ultimate place is the Forbidden City (the old Imperial Palace) where the "Last Emperor" took place. Our first day there, we had a view of the entire palace. (It was really huge!!) "Wow!" Then the next day, we visited the inside of the building! I was so excited! I mean, it's a real palace (duh).

Apparently, it takes a week to view the entire palace, so we went straight to the middle portion. The ceilings were incredibly high, the columns really wide, and the interior decoration and designs of the walls and ceilings were wonderful!! I got it all on film, but it'd be impossible to capture it in a drawing. India was the same! It was in the realm of art! The border between reality and manga became blurred.

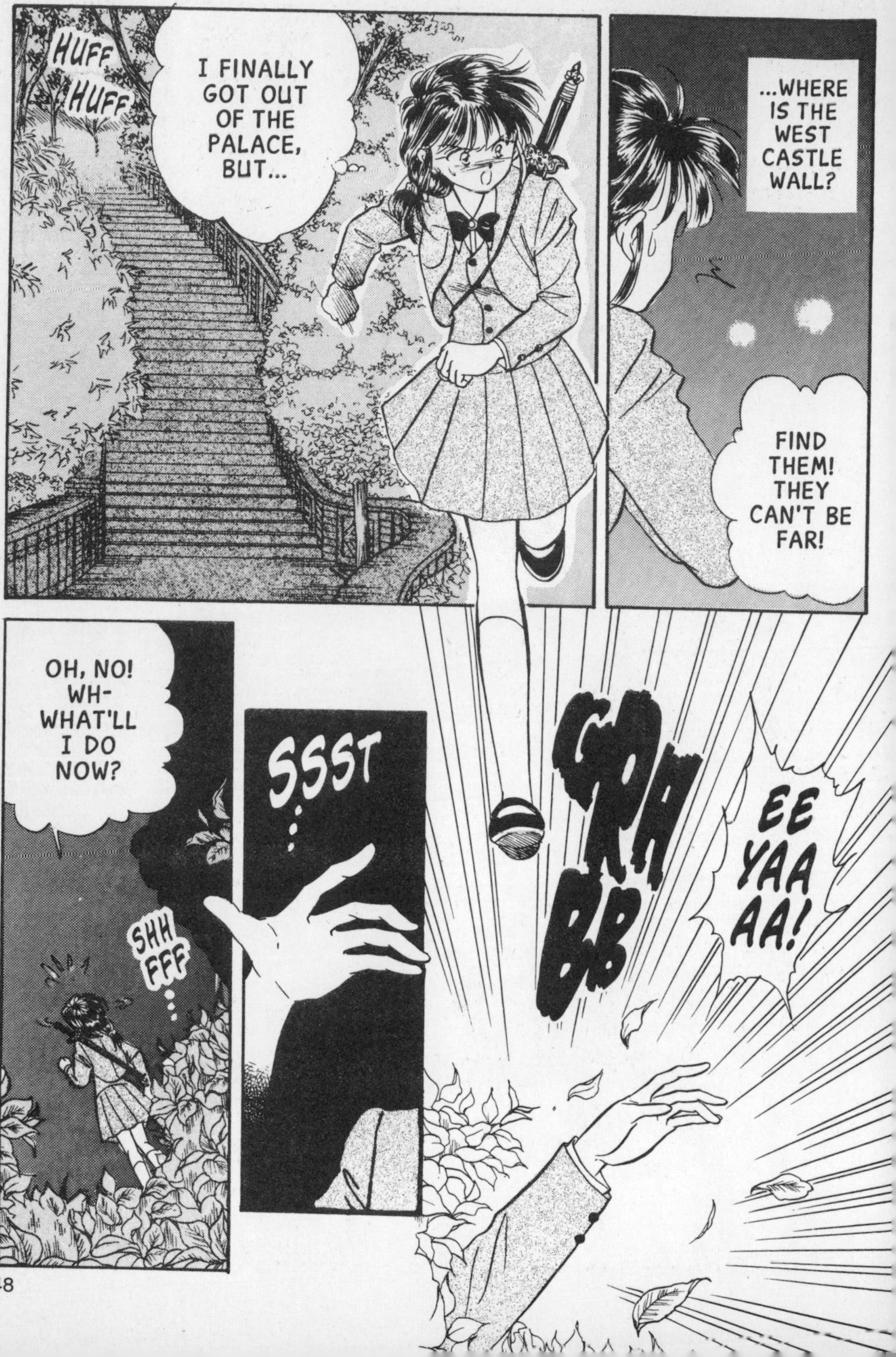

HUFF HUFF
I FINALLY GOT OUT OF THE PALACE, BUT...
...WHERE IS THE WEST CASTLE WALL?
FIND THEM! THEY CAN'T BE FAR!
OH, NO! WH-WHAT'LL I DO NOW?
SHH FFF
SSST
GRAB
EE YAAAAA!

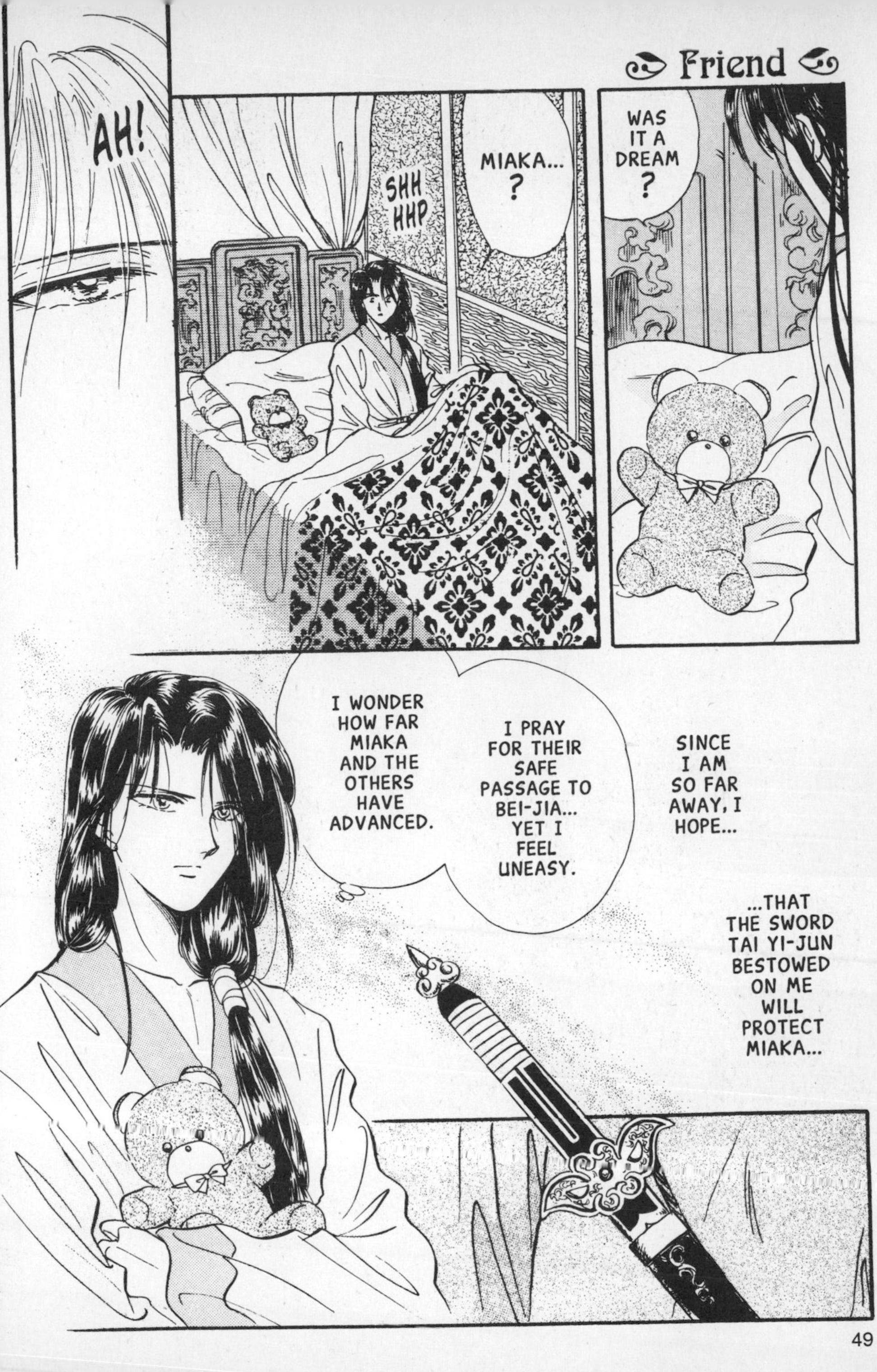
AH!
SHH HHP
MIAKA...?
WAS IT A DREAM?
I WONDER HOW FAR MIAKA AND THE OTHERS HAVE ADVANCED.
I PRAY FOR THEIR SAFE PASSAGE TO BEI-JIA... YET I FEEL UNEASY.
SINCE I AM SO FAR AWAY, I HOPE...
...THAT THE SWORD TAI YI-JUN BESTOWED ON ME WILL PROTECT MIAKA...

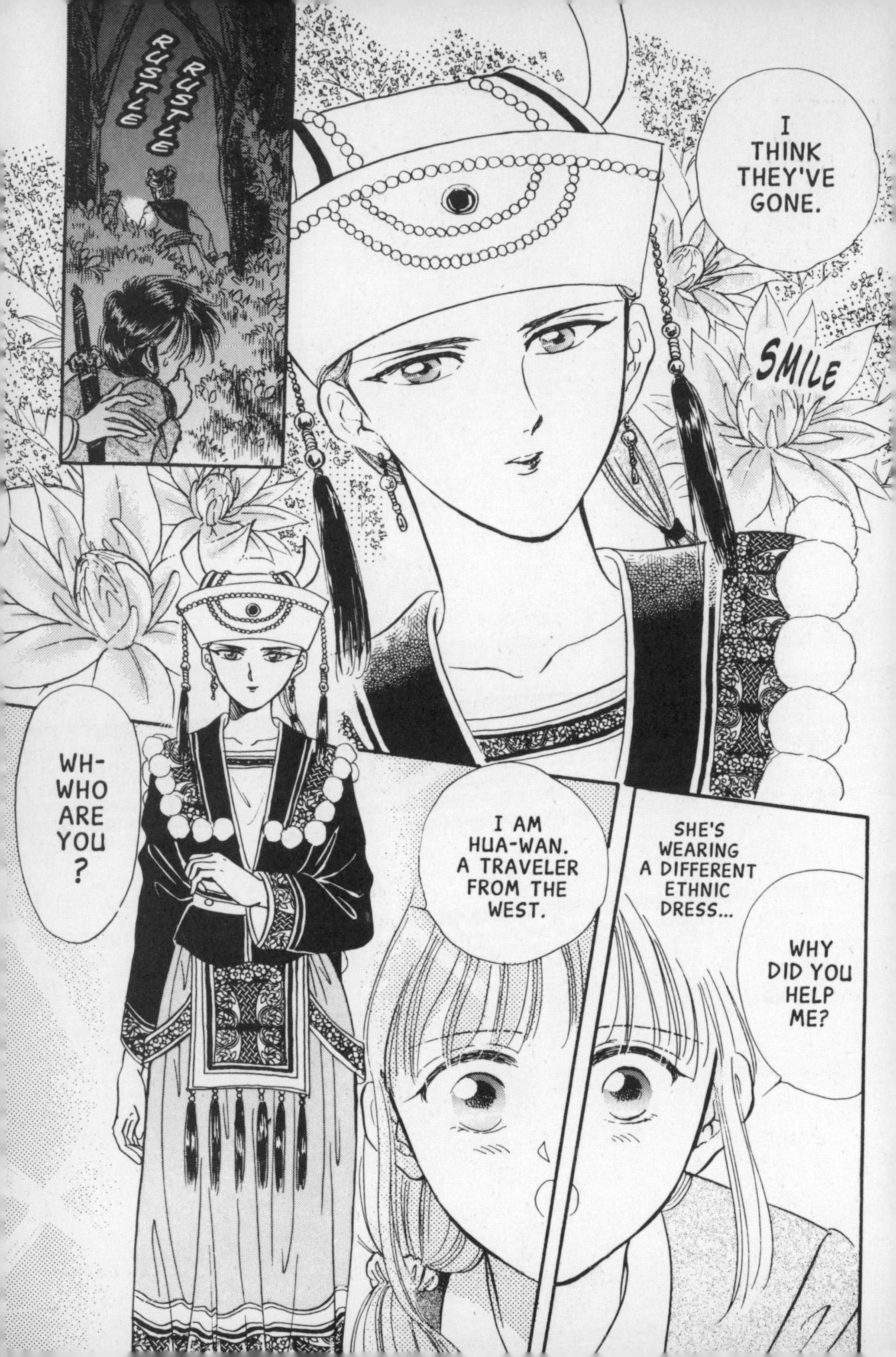
RUSTLE RUSTLE
I THINK THEY'VE GONE.
SMILE
WH-WHO ARE YOU?
I AM HUA-WAN. A TRAVELER FROM THE WEST.
SHE'S WEARING A DIFFERENT ETHNIC DRESS...
WHY DID YOU HELP ME?

ABOUT A MONTH AGO, I WAS... ON MY WAY TO BEI-JIA, AND MY SHIP DRIFTED ONTO THE SHORE OF THE ISLAND...

BECAUSE I'M A WOMAN, THEY WELCOMED ME... BUT... THEY WON'T LET ME LEAVE...

THEN I HEARD ABOUT YOUR GROUP, AND I THOUGHT YOU MIGHT TAKE ME WITH YOU.

GRABBIE

SMALL, BUT THEY'RE THERE!

OH, WHAT A RELIEF. THEY SEEMED TO THINK YOU ALL WERE MEN!

THEN COME WITH US! I'M MIAKA YŪKI!

I'M HEADED TO MEET MY FRIENDS AT THE WEST CASTLE WALL.

WONDERFUL! THANK YOU, MIAKA!

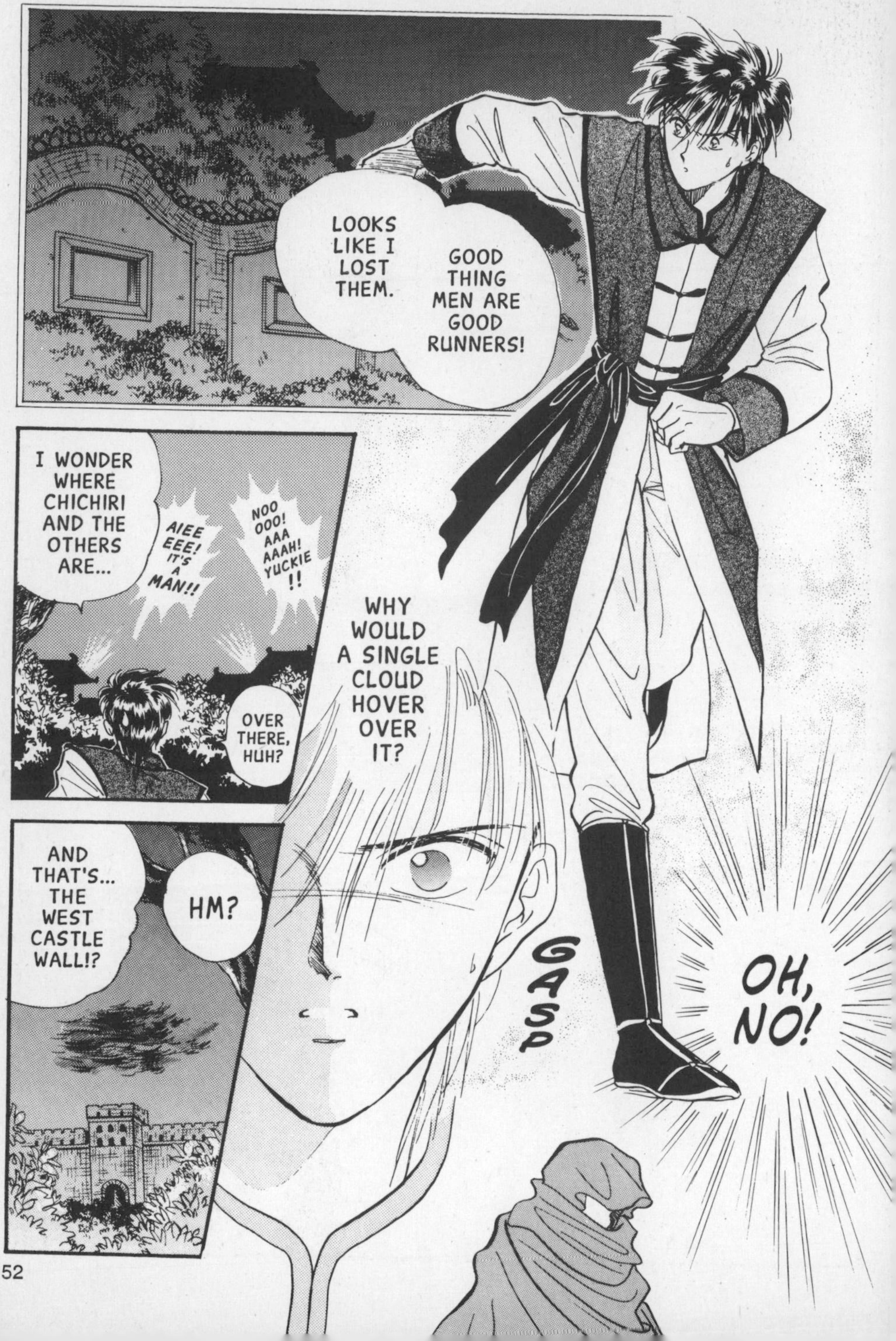
LOOKS LIKE I LOST THEM.
GOOD THING MEN ARE GOOD RUNNERS!
I WONDER WHERE CHICHIRI AND THE OTHERS ARE...
AIEE EEE! IT'S A MAN!!
NOO OOO! AAA AAAH! YUCKIE !!
OVER THERE, HUH?
WHY WOULD A SINGLE CLOUD HOVER OVER IT?
AND THAT'S... THE WEST CASTLE WALL!?
HM?
GASP
OH, NO!

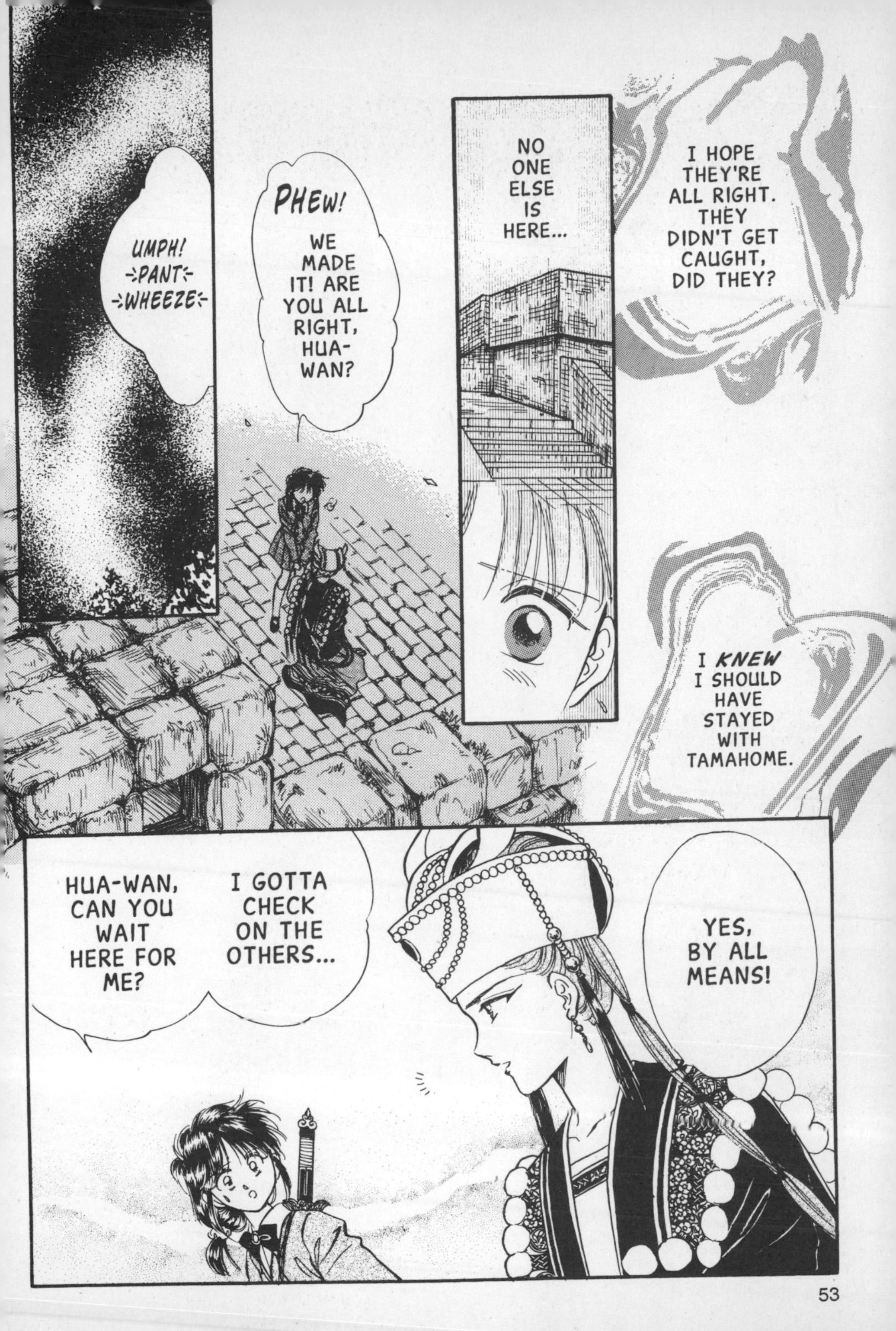
UMPH! -PANT- -WHEEZE-
PHEW! WE MADE IT! ARE YOU ALL RIGHT, HUA-WAN?
NO ONE ELSE IS HERE...
I HOPE THEY'RE ALL RIGHT. THEY DIDN'T GET CAUGHT, DID THEY?
I KNEW I SHOULD HAVE STAYED WITH TAMAHOME.
HUA-WAN, CAN YOU WAIT HERE FOR ME?
I GOTTA CHECK ON THE OTHERS...
YES, BY ALL MEANS!

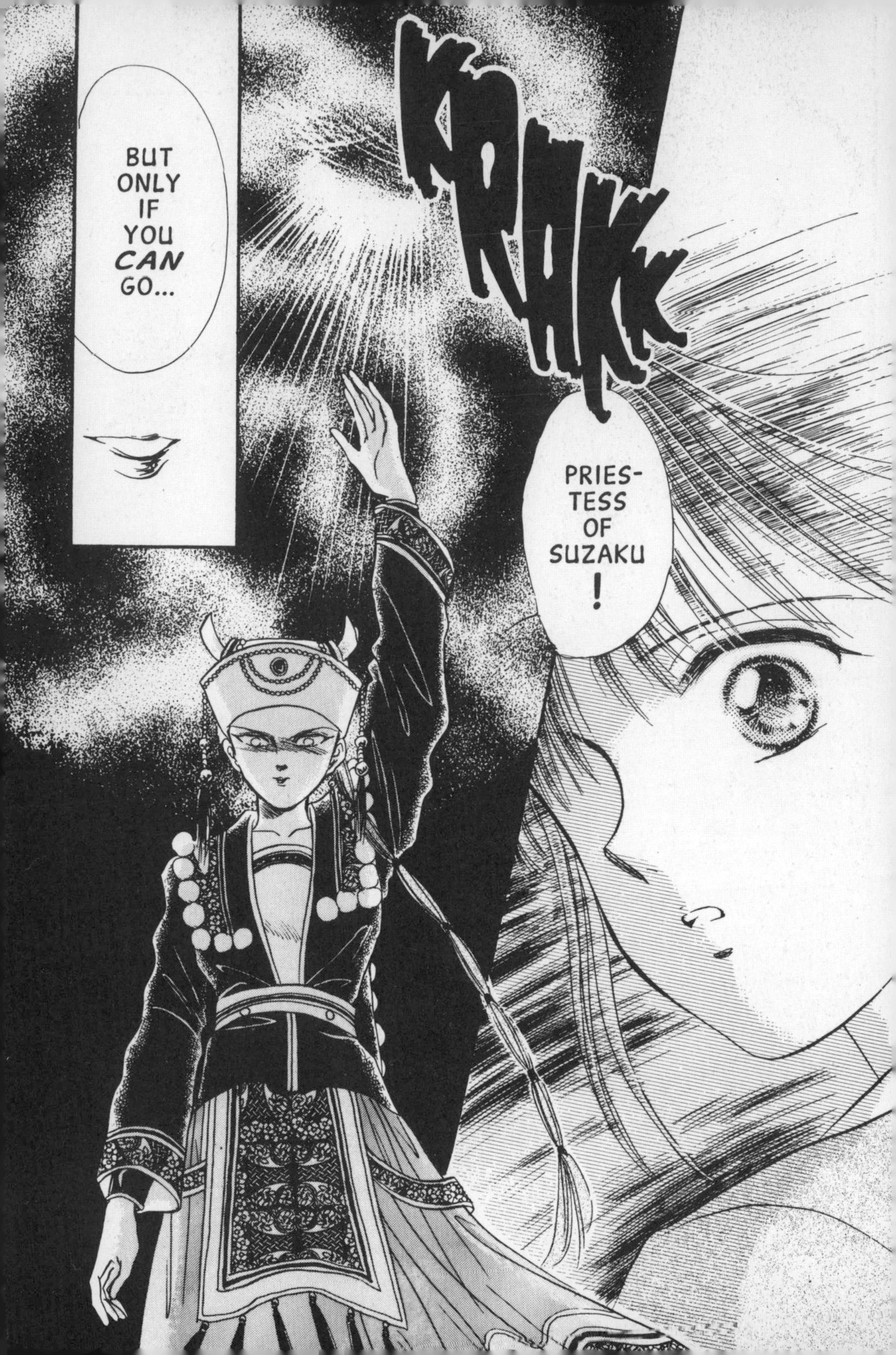
BUT ONLY IF YOU *CAN* GO...
KRAKK
PRIES-TESS OF SUZAKU !

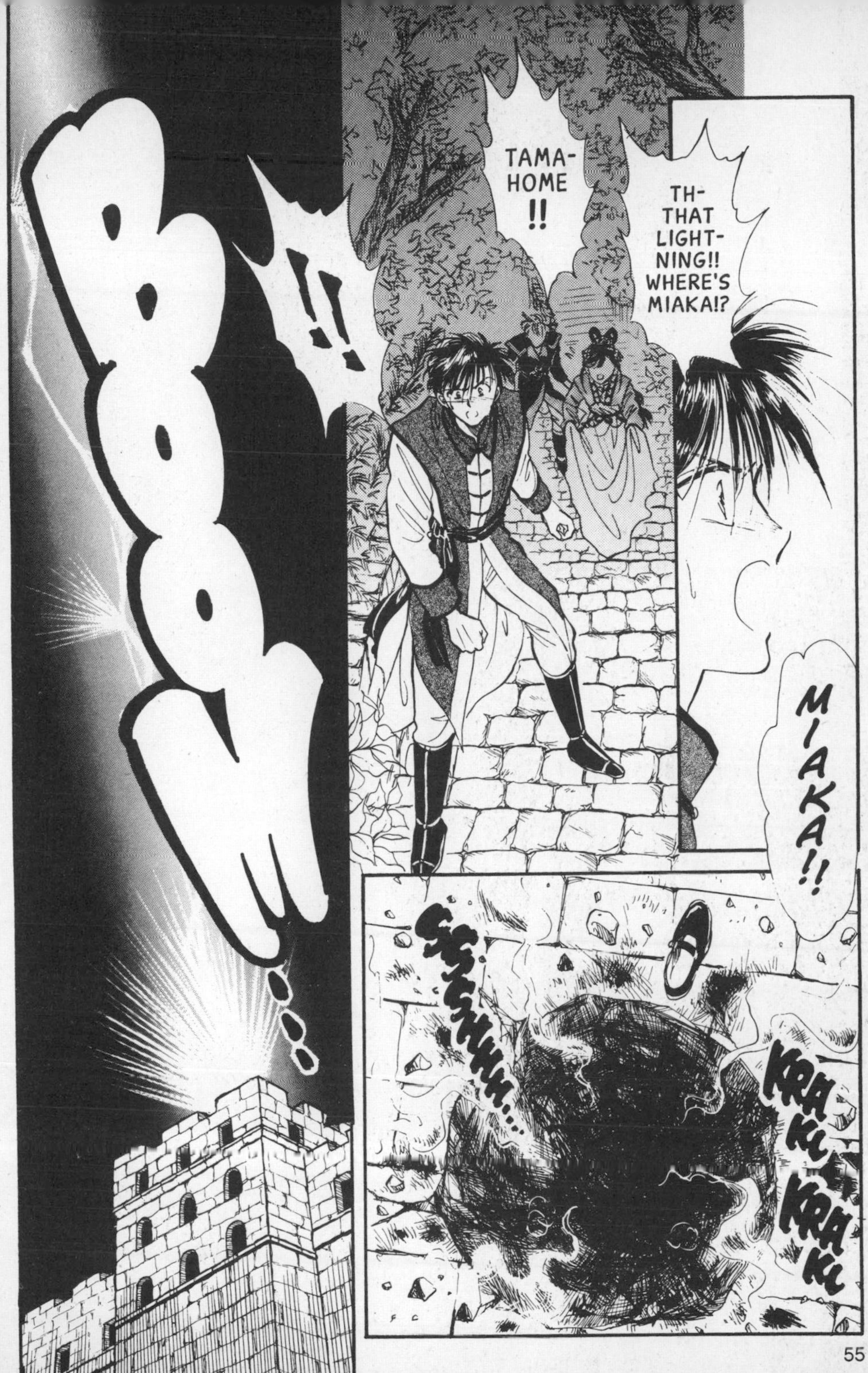
BOOOM!!...
TAMA-HOME!!
TH-THAT LIGHTNING!! WHERE'S MIAKA!?
MIAKA!!
KRAKU KRAKU

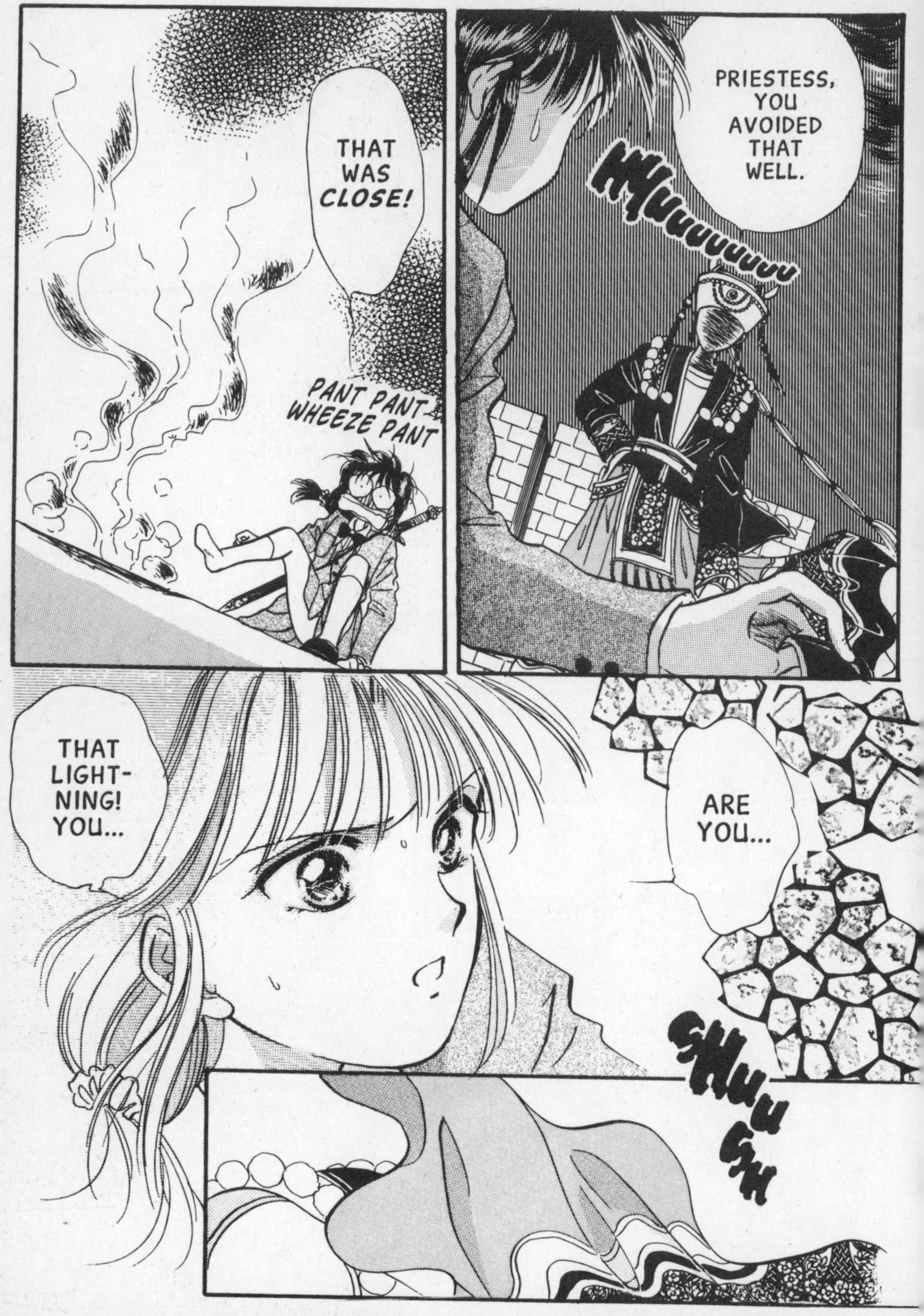
THAT WAS CLOSE!
PANT PANT WHEEZE PANT
PRIESTESS, YOU AVOIDED THAT WELL.
WHUUUUUUUU
THAT LIGHT-NING! YOU...
ARE YOU...
SHUUSH

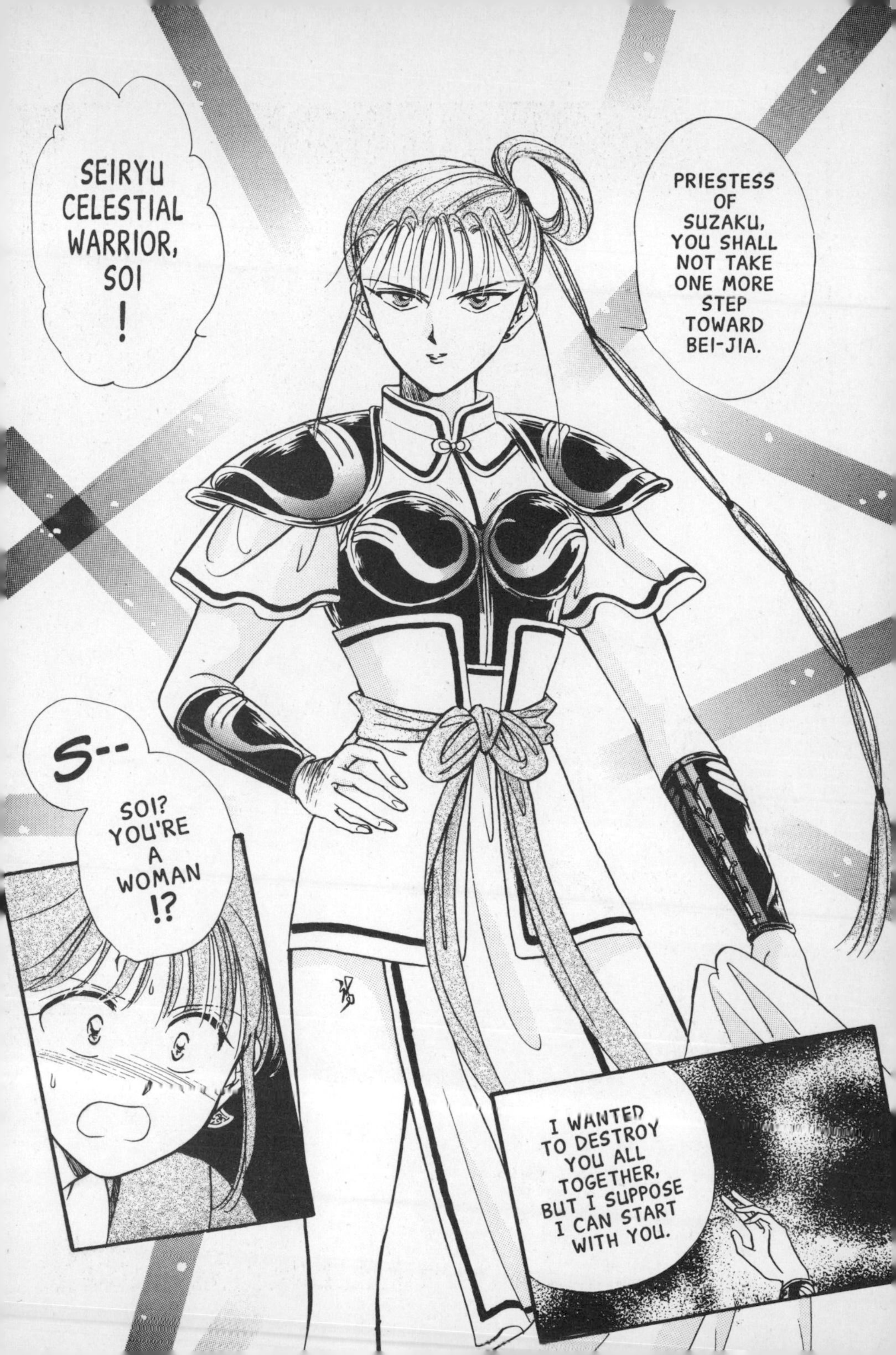
SEIRYU CELESTIAL WARRIOR, SOI !
PRIESTESS OF SUZAKU, YOU SHALL NOT TAKE ONE MORE STEP TOWARD BEI-JIA.
S--
SOI? YOU'RE A WOMAN !?
I WANTED TO DESTROY YOU ALL TOGETHER, BUT I SUPPOSE I CAN START WITH YOU.

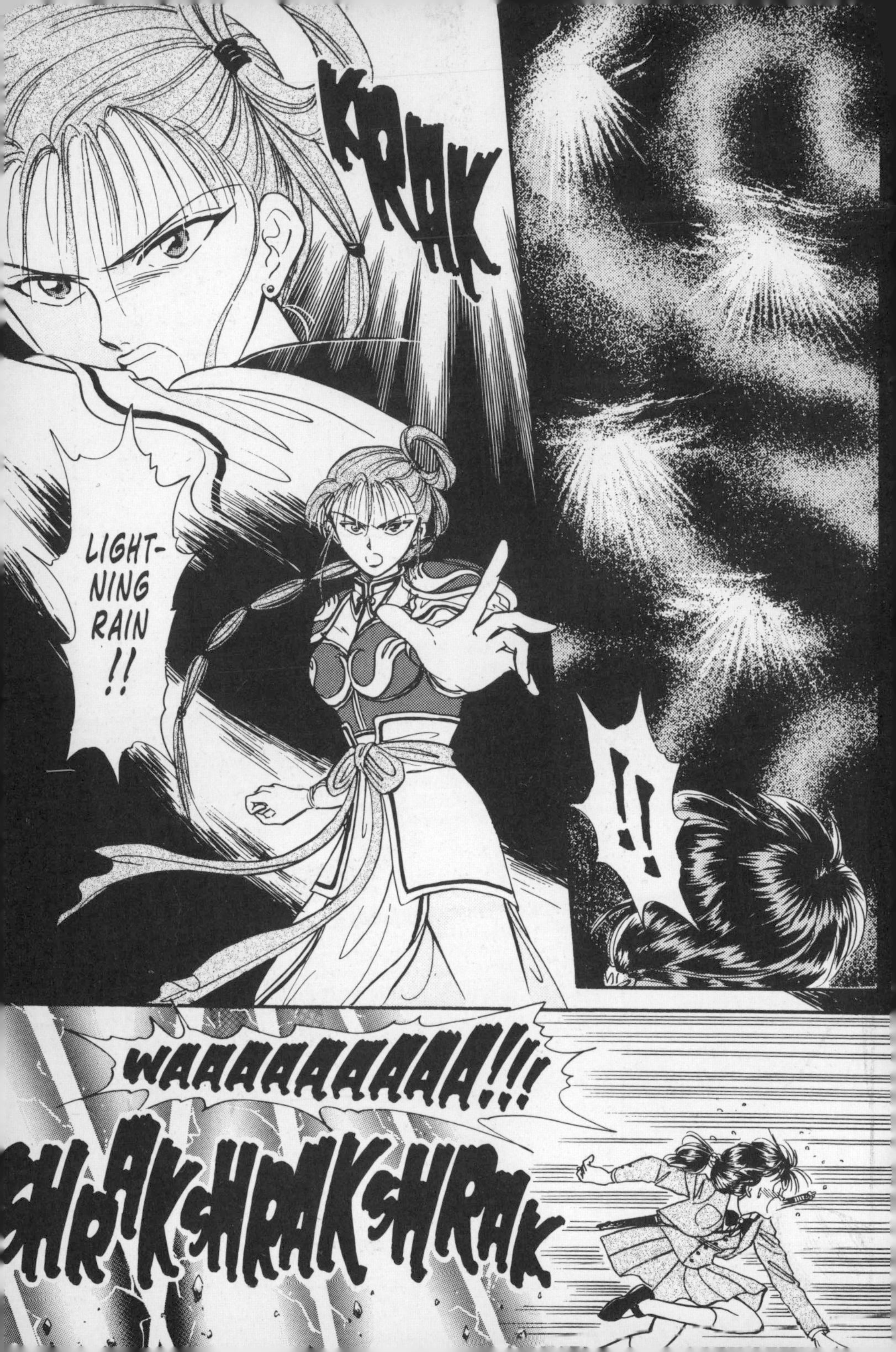
KRRAK
LIGHT-NING RAIN!!
!!
WAAAAAAAAAAA!!!
SHRAK SHRAK SHRAK SHRAK

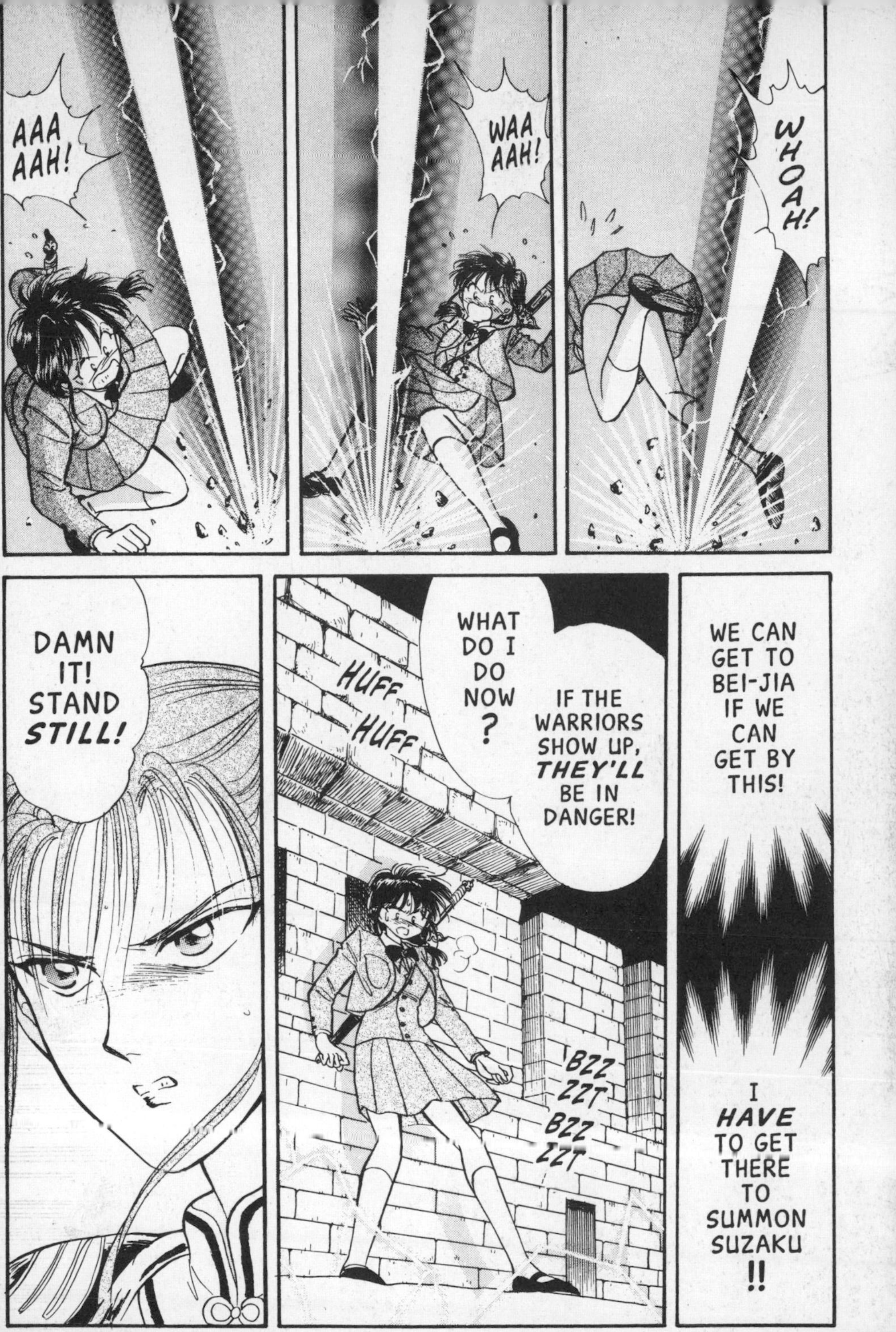
AAA AAH!
WAA AAH!
WHOAH!
DAMN IT! STAND STILL!
HUFF HUFF
WHAT DO I DO NOW?
IF THE WARRIORS SHOW UP, THEY'LL BE IN DANGER!
BZZ ZZT BZZ ZZT
WE CAN GET TO BEI-JIA IF WE CAN GET BY THIS!
I HAVE TO GET THERE TO SUMMON SUZAKU!!

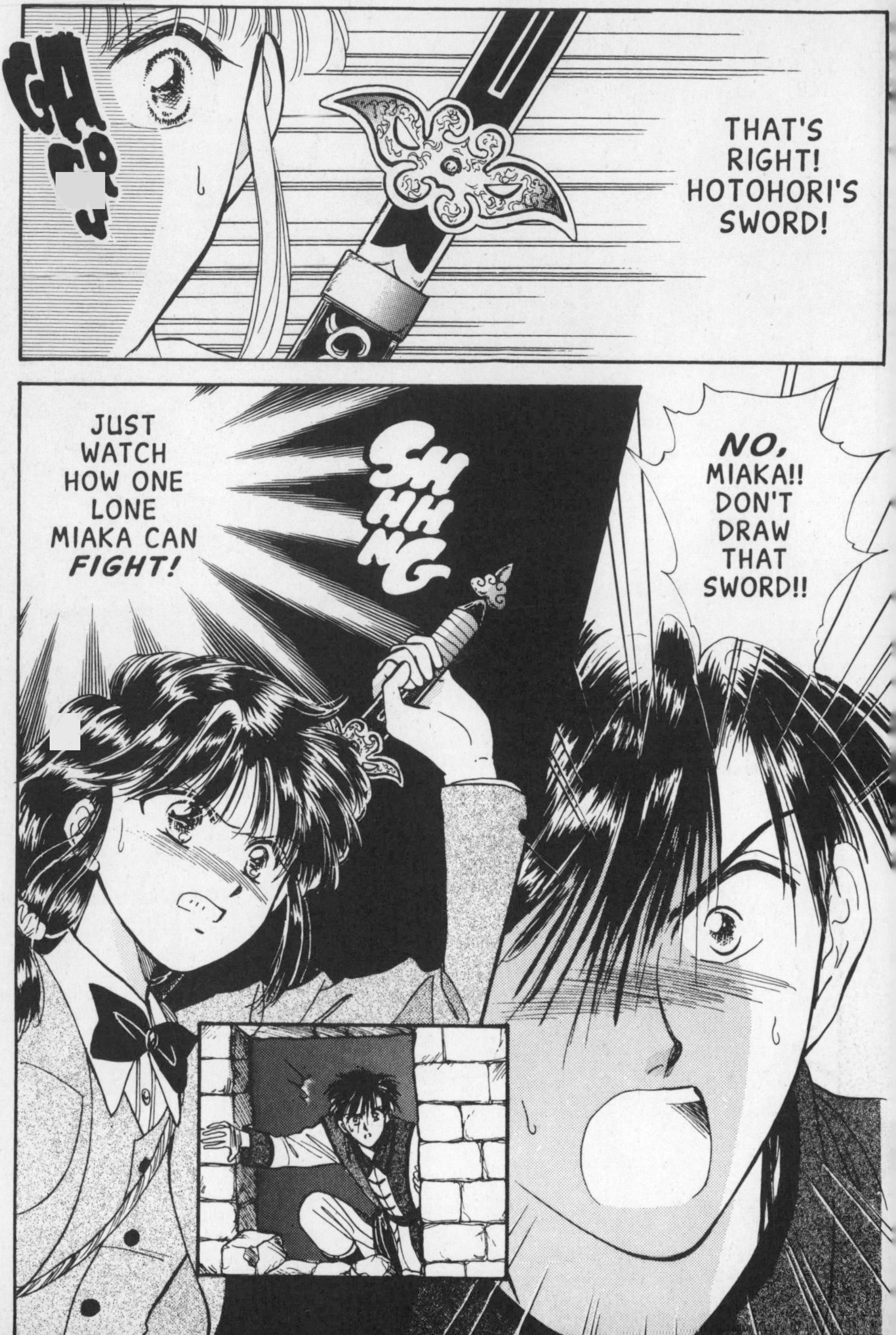
THAT'S RIGHT! HOTOHORI'S SWORD!
JUST WATCH HOW ONE LONE MIAKA CAN *FIGHT!*
SHHHNG
NO, MIAKA!! DON'T DRAW THAT SWORD!!

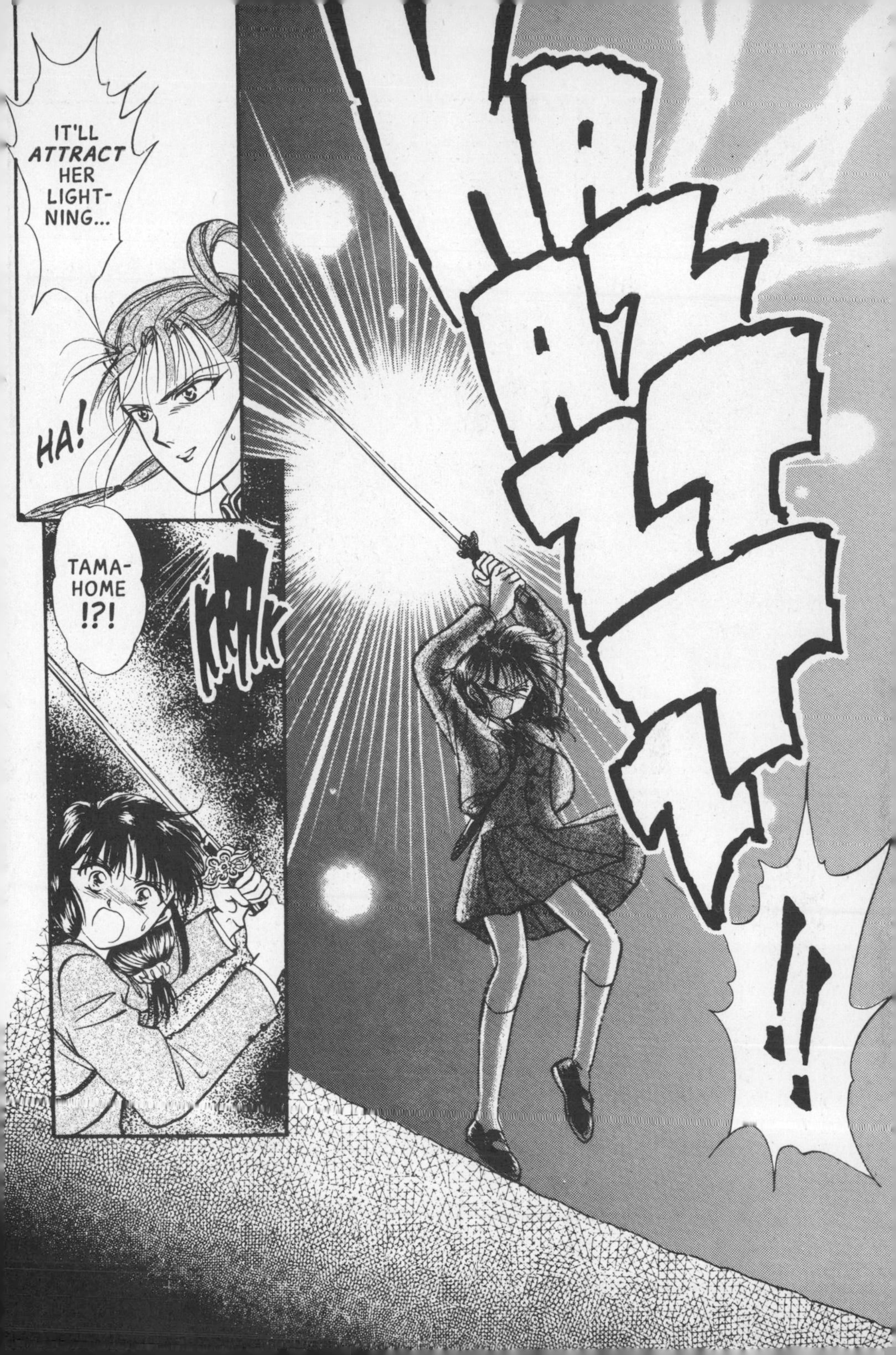
IT'LL ATTRACT HER LIGHT-NING...
HA!
TAMA-HOME !?!

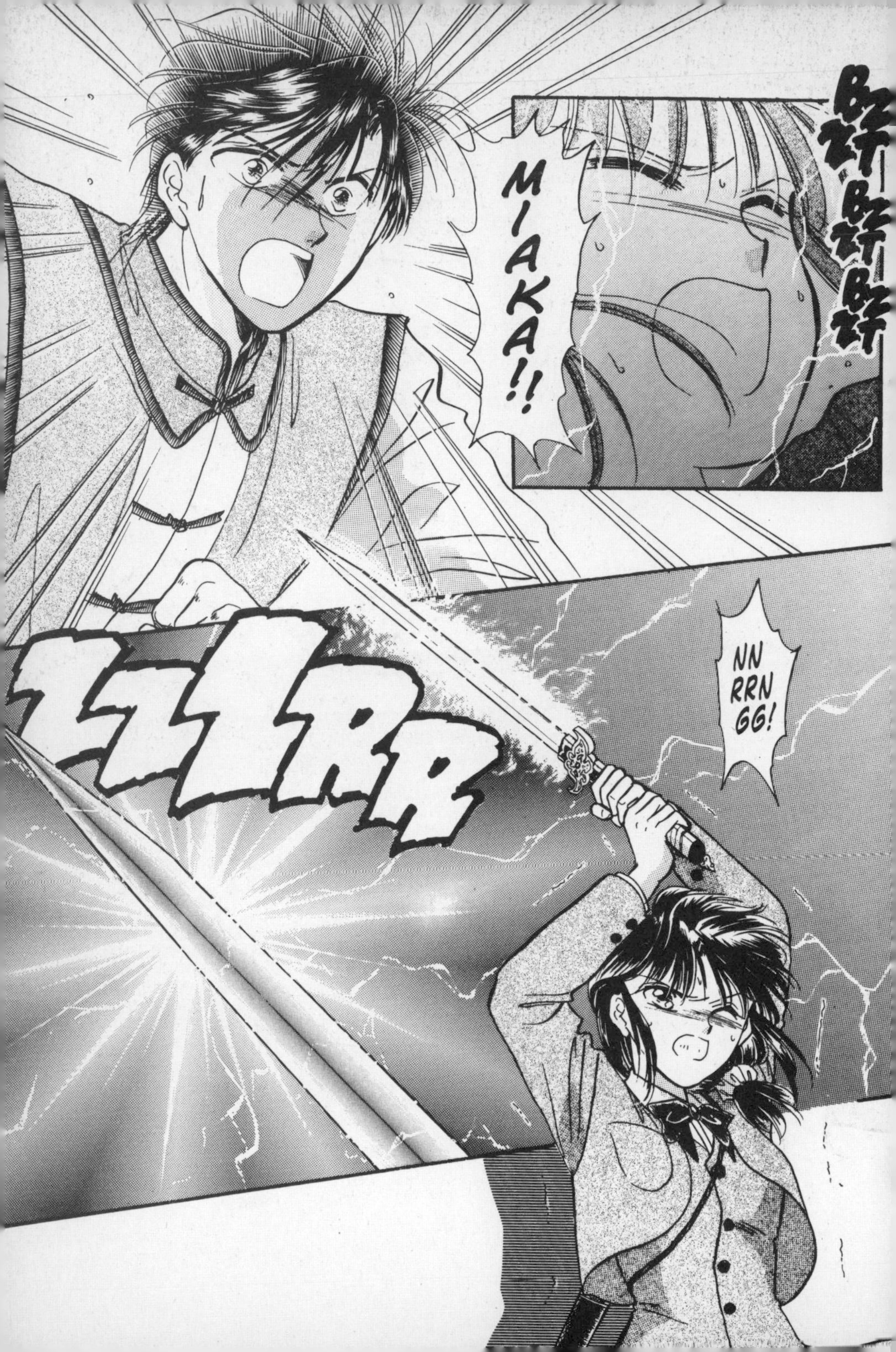
MIAKA!!
BZT BZT BZT
ZZRR
NN RRN GG!

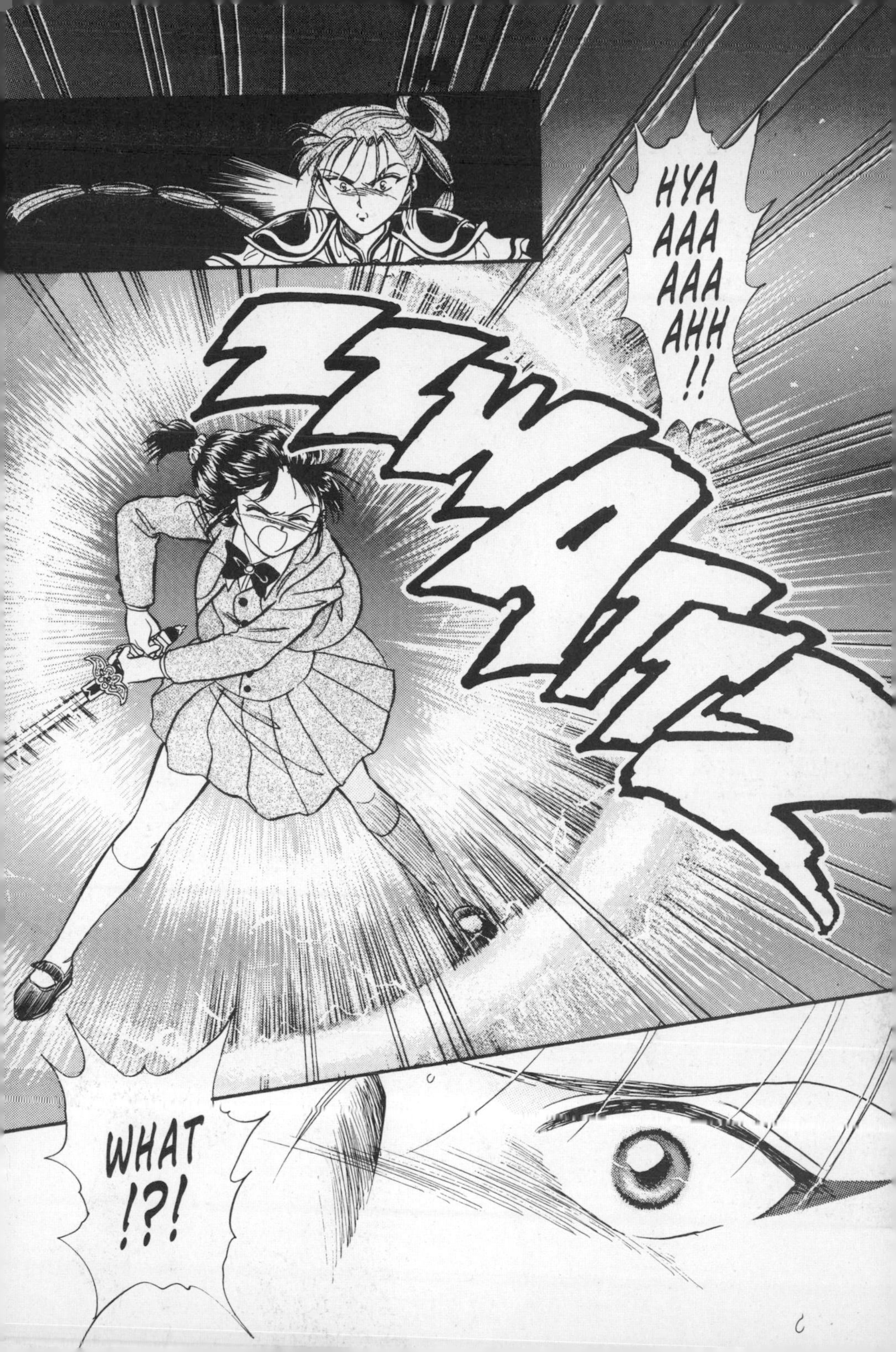
HYA AAA AAA AHH !!
WHAT !?!

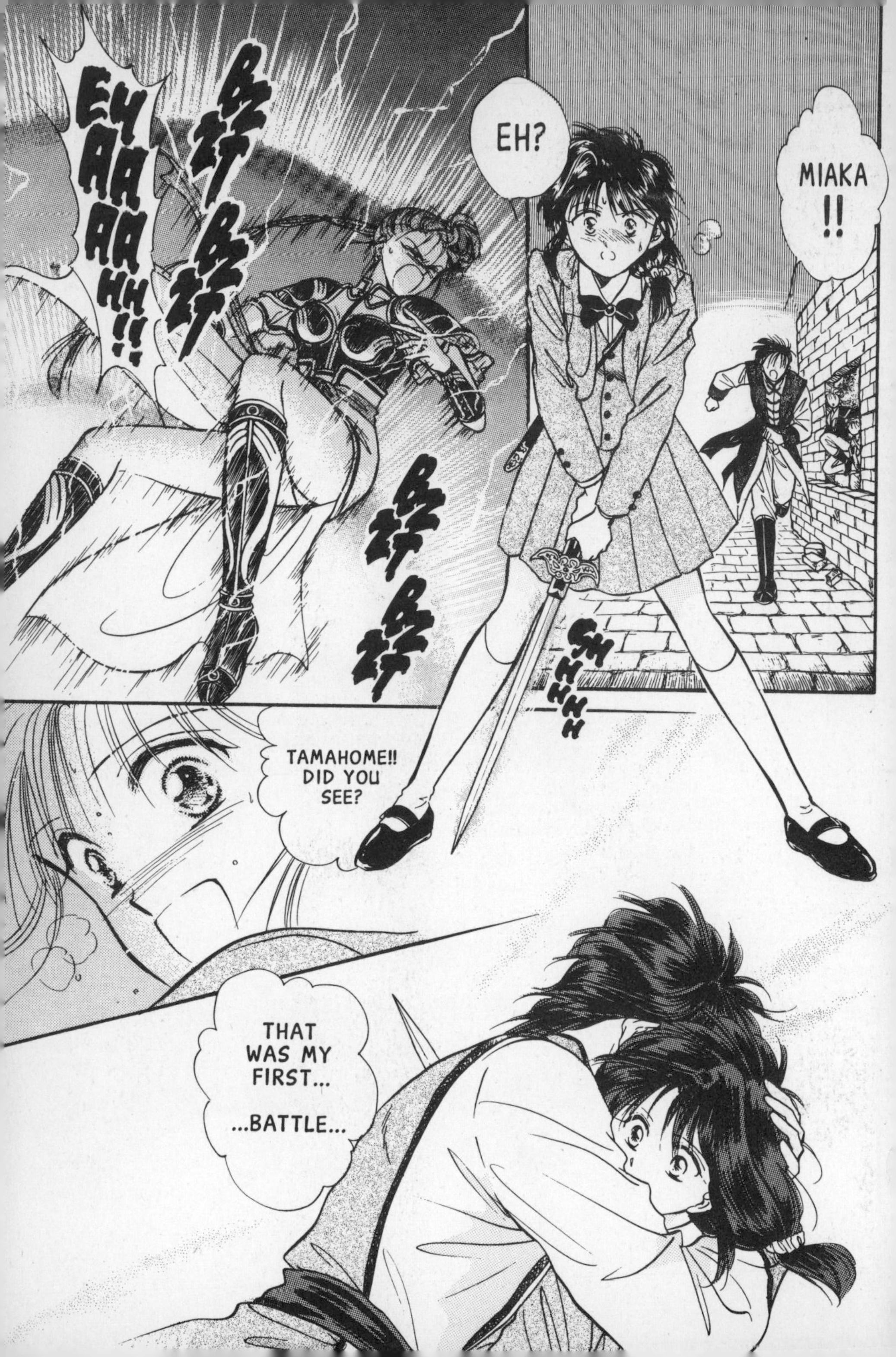
EYAAAAHH!!!
EH?
MIAKA !!
SHHHHHH
TAMAHOME!! DID YOU SEE?
THAT WAS MY FIRST...
...BATTLE...

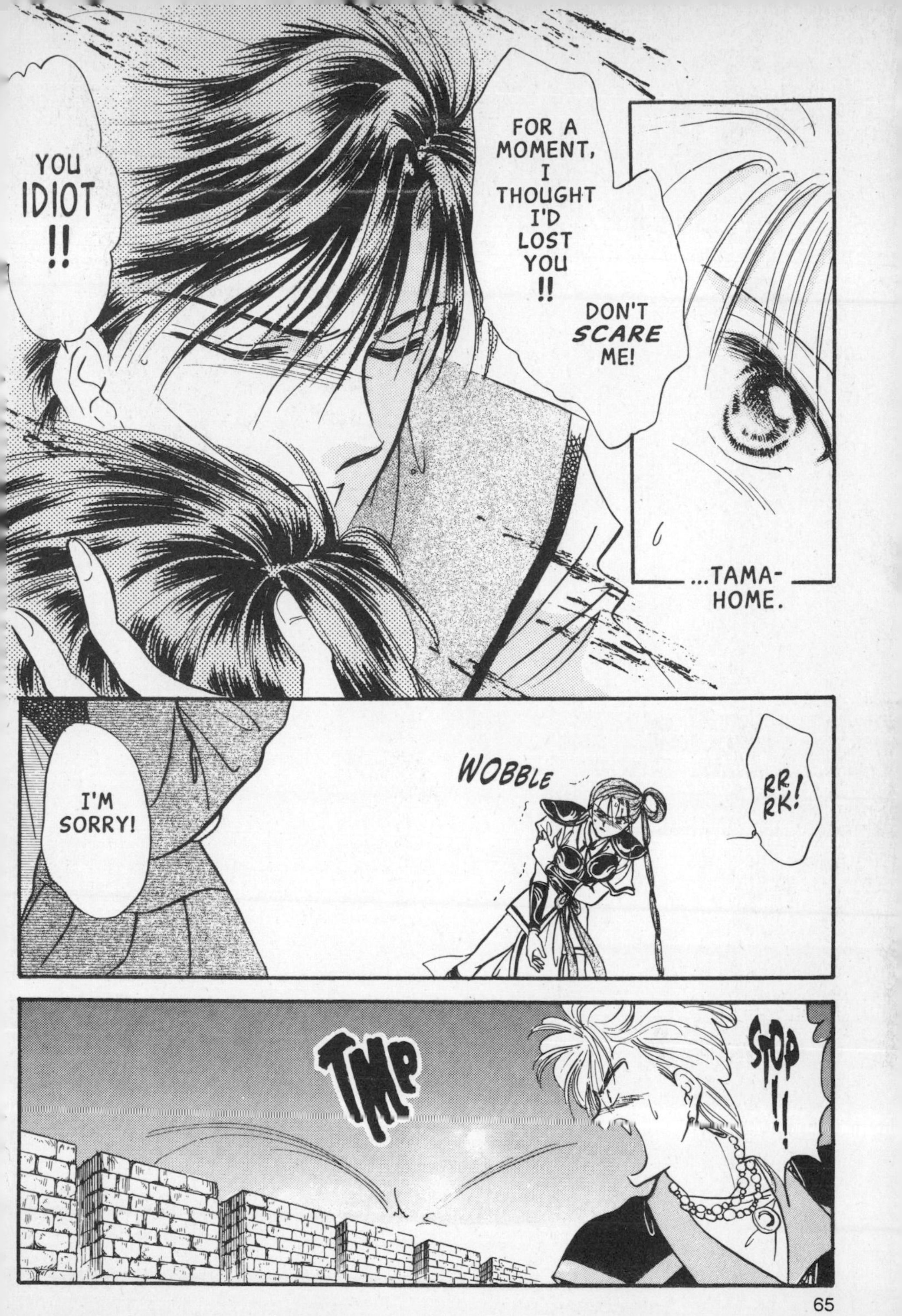
YOU IDIOT !!
FOR A MOMENT, I THOUGHT I'D LOST YOU !!
DON'T SCARE ME!
...TAMA-HOME.
I'M SORRY!
WOBBLE
RRRK!
TMP
STOP !!

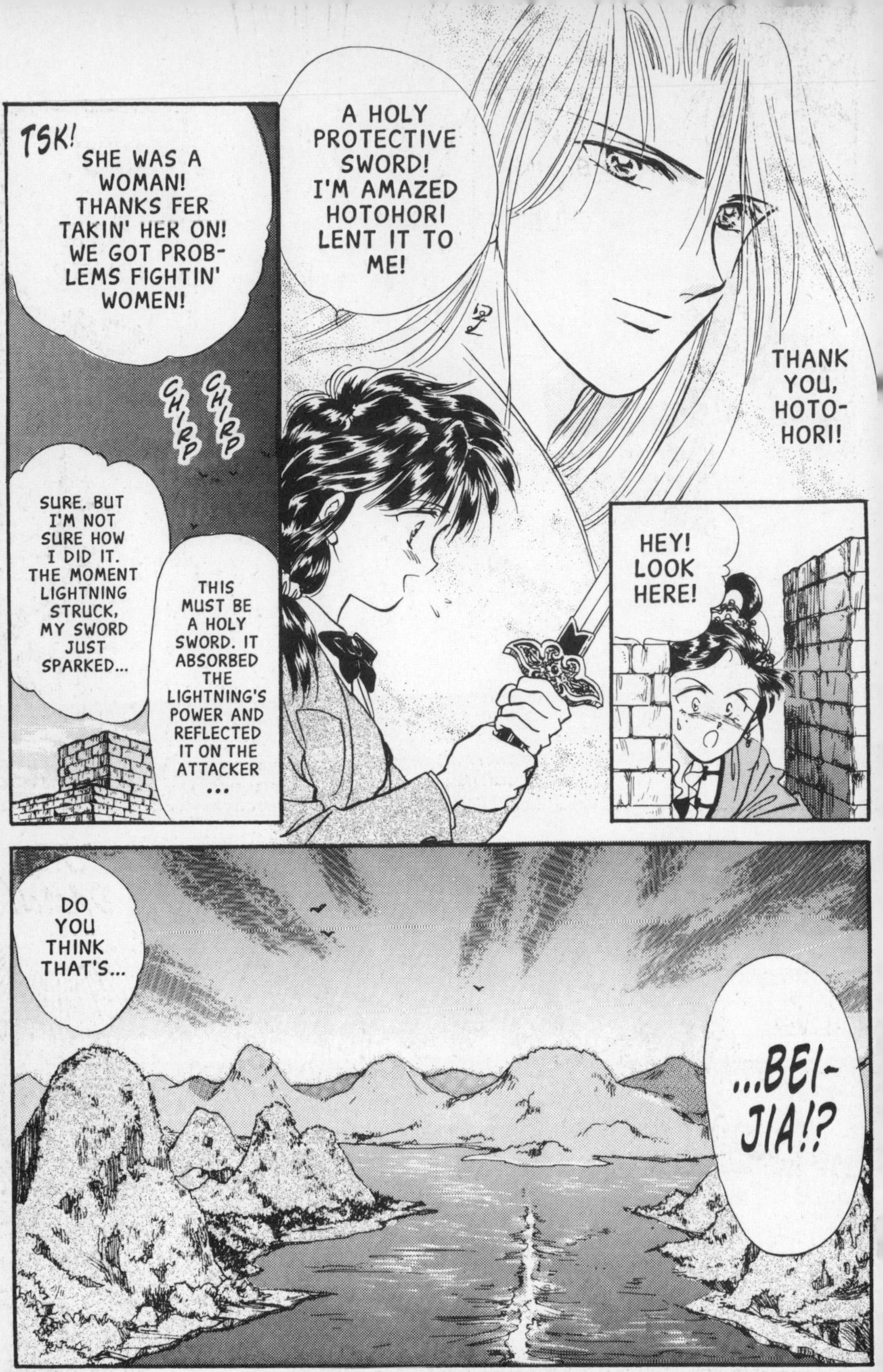
TSK!
SHE WAS A WOMAN! THANKS FER TAKIN' HER ON! WE GOT PROB-LEMS FIGHTIN' WOMEN!
CHIRP
CHIRP
SURE. BUT I'M NOT SURE HOW I DID IT. THE MOMENT LIGHTNING STRUCK, MY SWORD JUST SPARKED...
THIS MUST BE A HOLY SWORD. IT ABSORBED THE LIGHTNING'S POWER AND REFLECTED IT ON THE ATTACKER ...
A HOLY PROTECTIVE SWORD! I'M AMAZED HOTOHORI LENT IT TO ME!
THANK YOU, HOTO-HORI!
HEY! LOOK HERE!
DO YOU THINK THAT'S...
...BEI-JIA!?

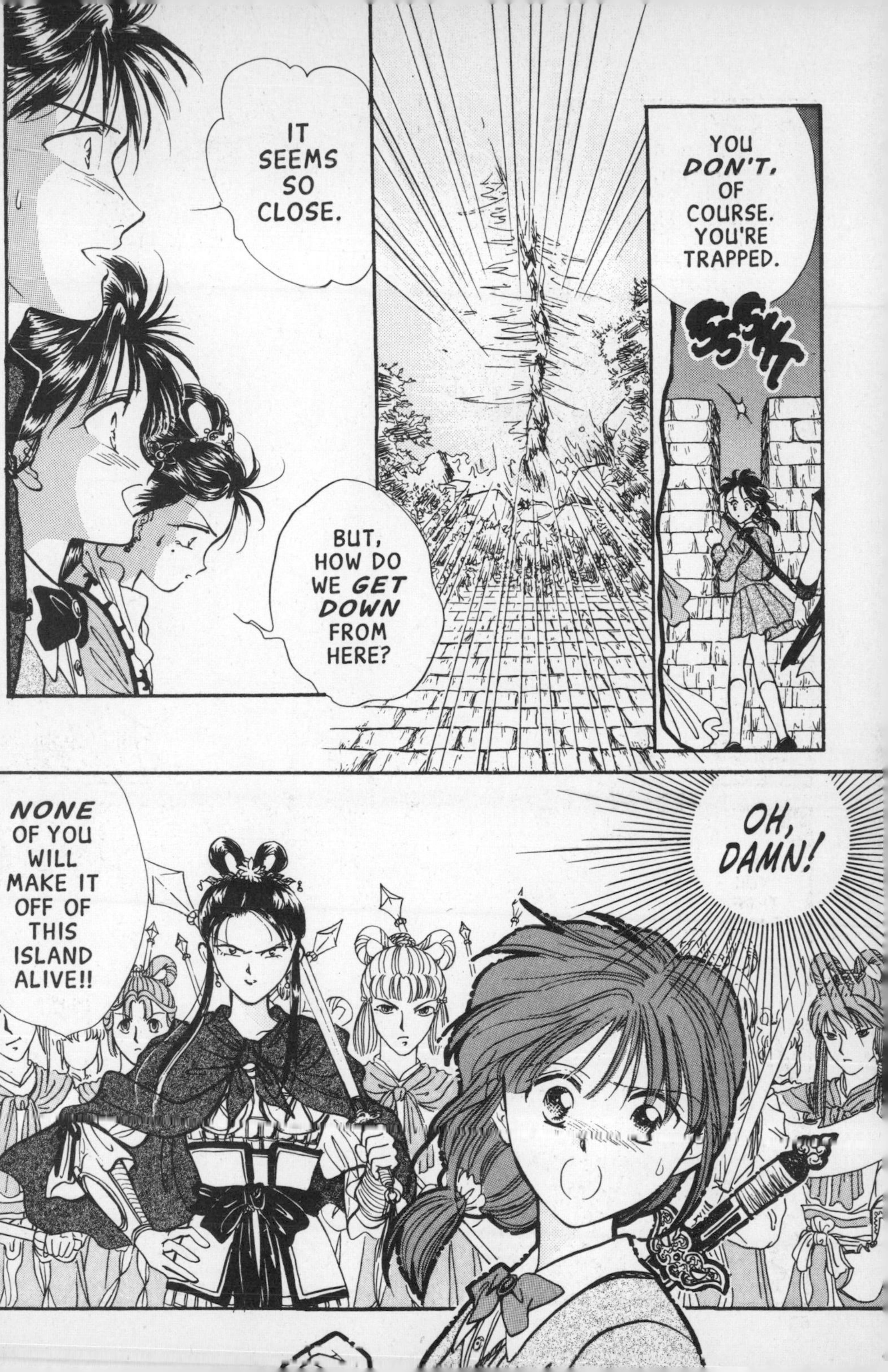
IT SEEMS SO CLOSE.
BUT, HOW DO WE *GET DOWN* FROM HERE?
YOU *DON'T*, OF COURSE. YOU'RE TRAPPED.
SSSHH
NONE OF YOU WILL MAKE IT OFF OF THIS ISLAND ALIVE!!
OH, DAMN!

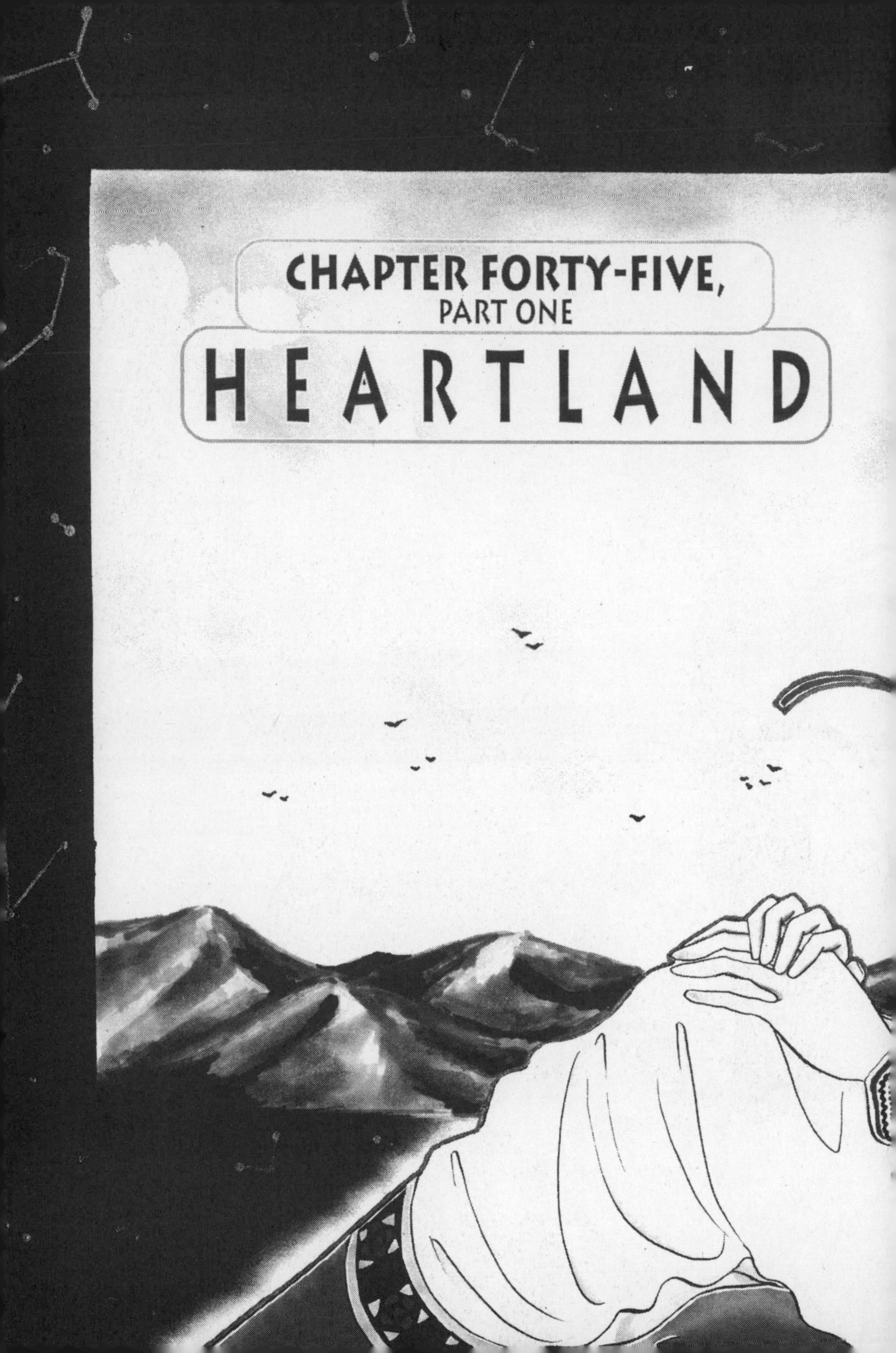
CHAPTER FORTY-FIVE,
PART ONE
HEARTLAND

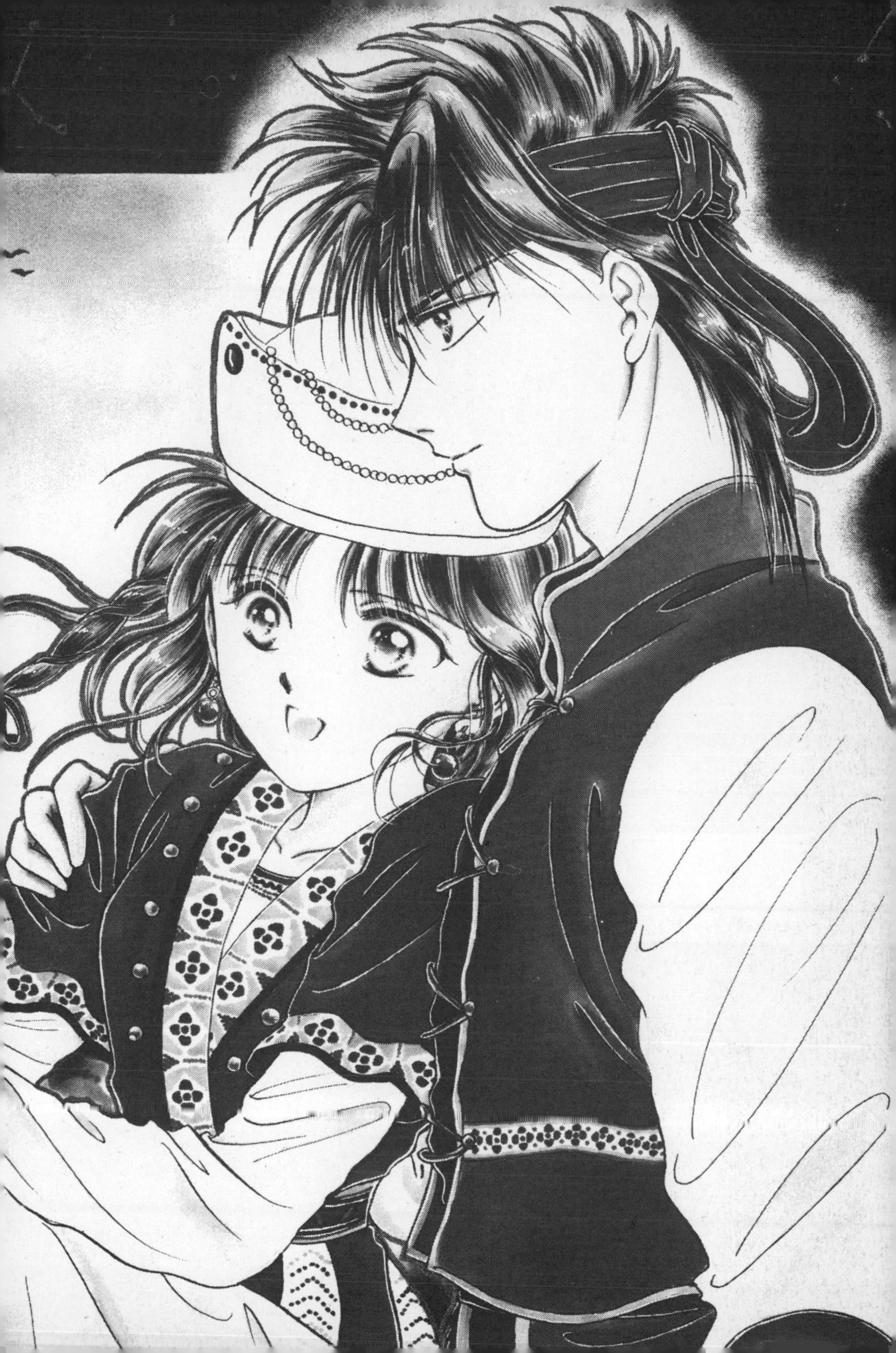

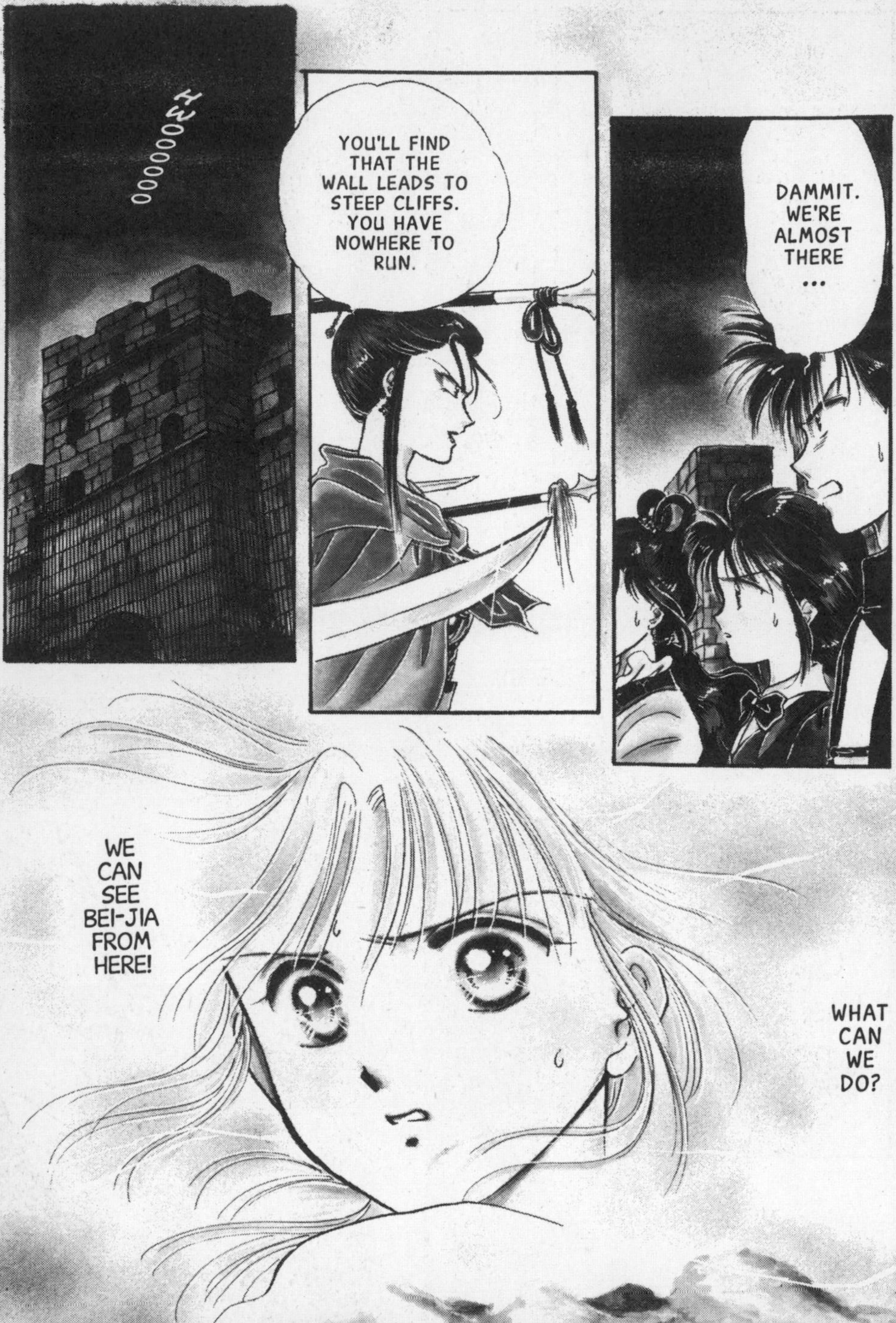
HWOOOOOOO
YOU'LL FIND THAT THE WALL LEADS TO STEEP CLIFFS. YOU HAVE NOWHERE TO RUN.
DAMMIT. WE'RE ALMOST THERE ...
WE CAN SEE BEI-JIA FROM HERE!
WHAT CAN WE DO?

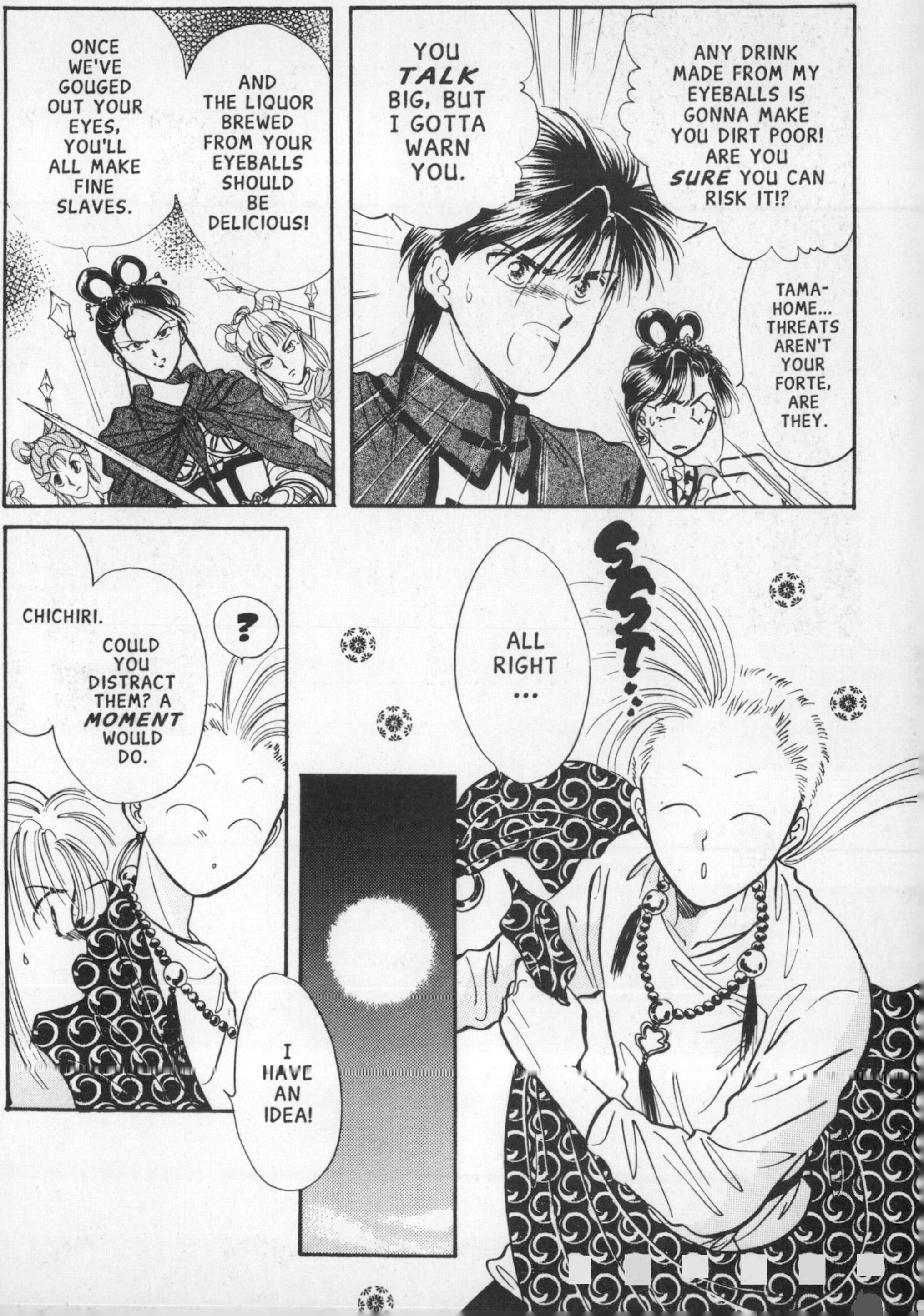
ONCE WE'VE GOUGED OUT YOUR EYES, YOU'LL ALL MAKE FINE SLAVES.
AND THE LIQUOR BREWED FROM YOUR EYEBALLS SHOULD BE DELICIOUS!
YOU *TALK* BIG, BUT I GOTTA WARN YOU.
ANY DRINK MADE FROM MY EYEBALLS IS GONNA MAKE YOU DIRT POOR! ARE YOU *SURE* YOU CAN RISK IT!?
TAMA-HOME... THREATS AREN'T YOUR FORTE, ARE THEY.
CHICHIRI.
COULD YOU DISTRACT THEM? A *MOMENT* WOULD DO.
?
ALL RIGHT ...
I HAVE AN IDEA!

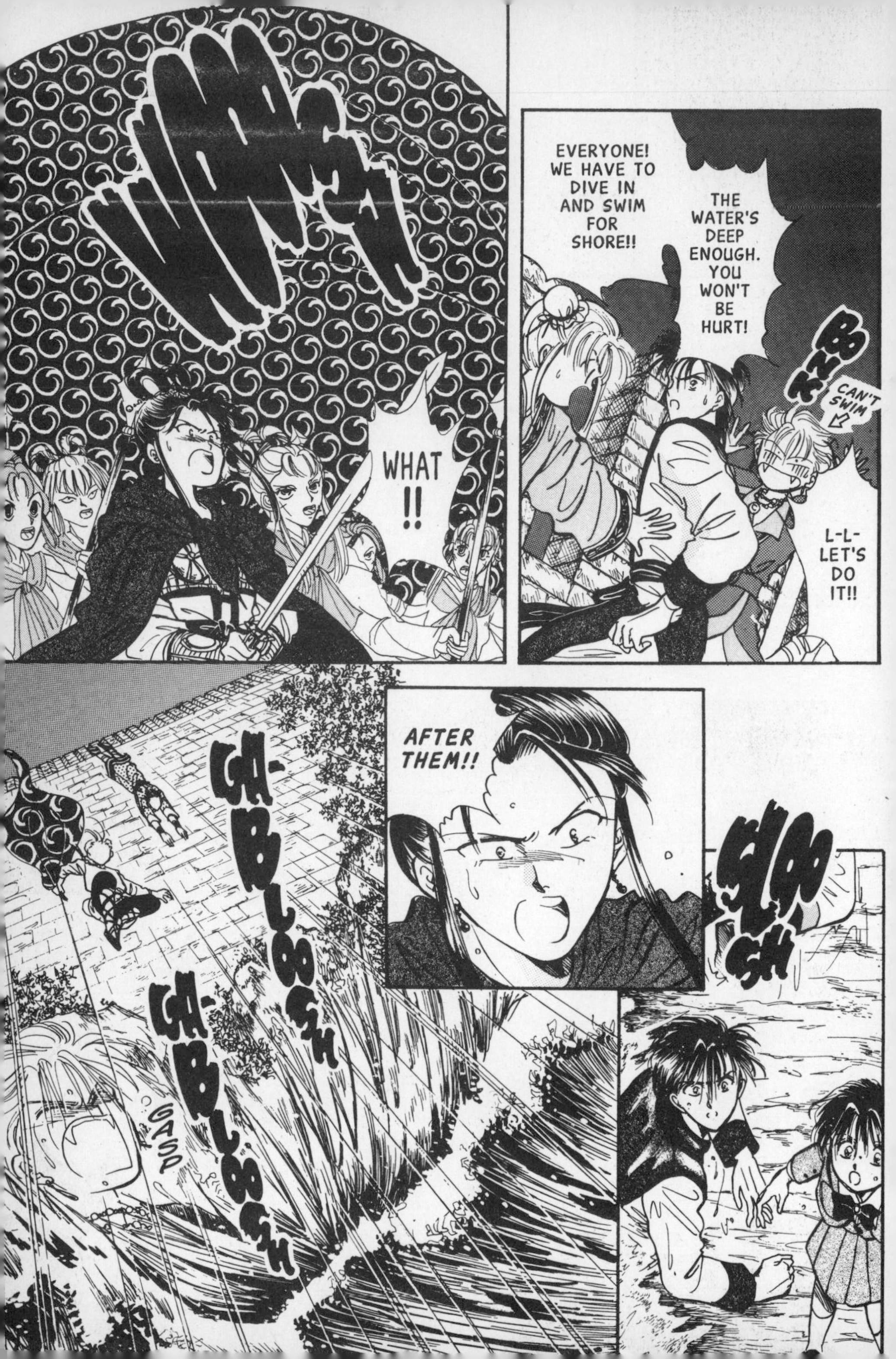
WHAT!!
EVERYONE! WE HAVE TO DIVE IN AND SWIM FOR SHORE!!
THE WATER'S DEEP ENOUGH. YOU WON'T BE HURT!
BONK
CAN'T SWIM
L-L-LET'S DO IT!!
GA-BLOOSH
GA-BLOOSH
GASP
AFTER THEM!!

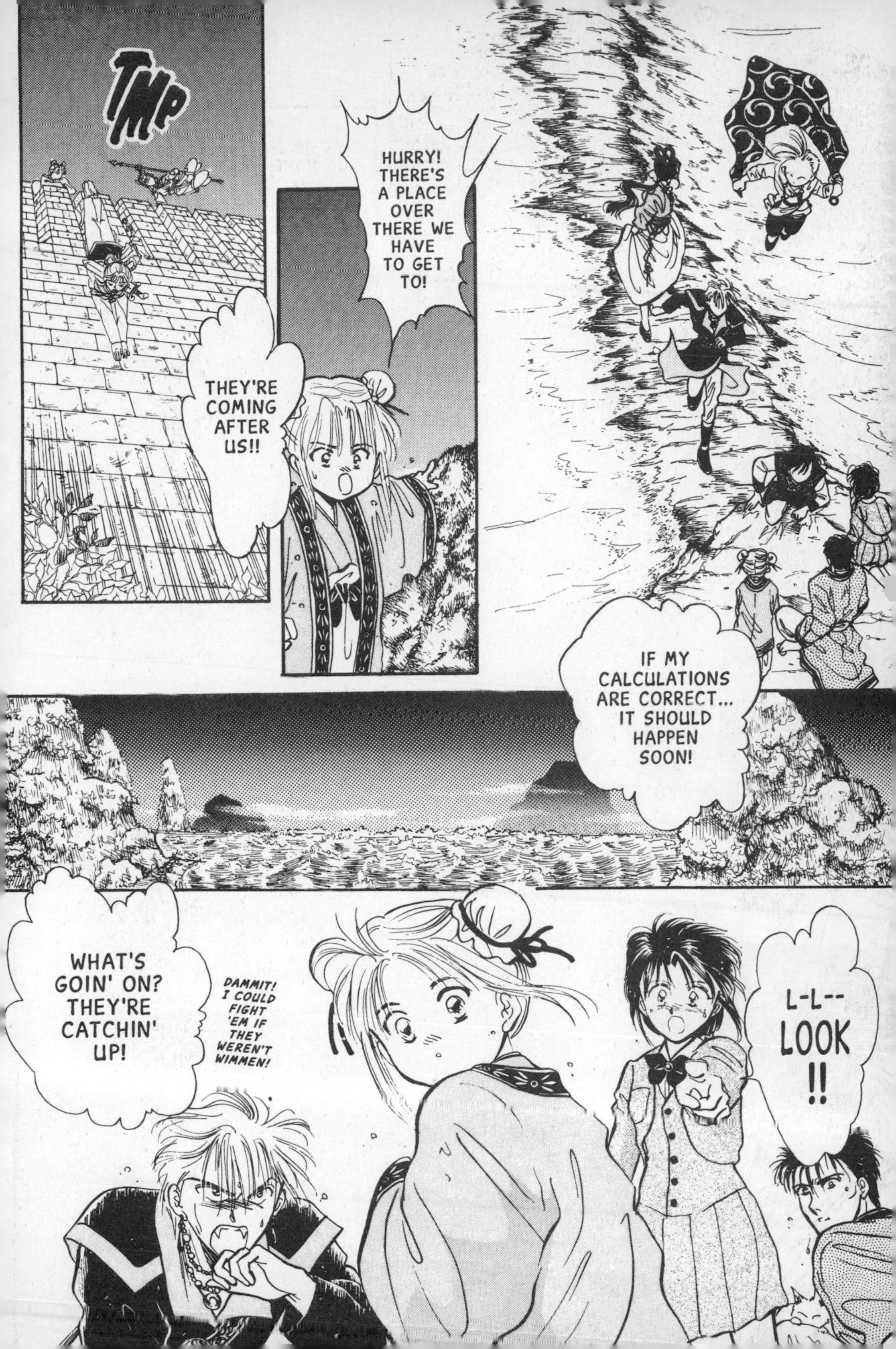
TMP
THEY'RE COMING AFTER US!!
HURRY! THERE'S A PLACE OVER THERE WE HAVE TO GET TO!
IF MY CALCULATIONS ARE CORRECT... IT SHOULD HAPPEN SOON!
WHAT'S GOIN' ON? THEY'RE CATCHIN' UP!
DAMMIT! I COULD FIGHT 'EM IF THEY WEREN'T WIMMEN!
L-L-- LOOK!!

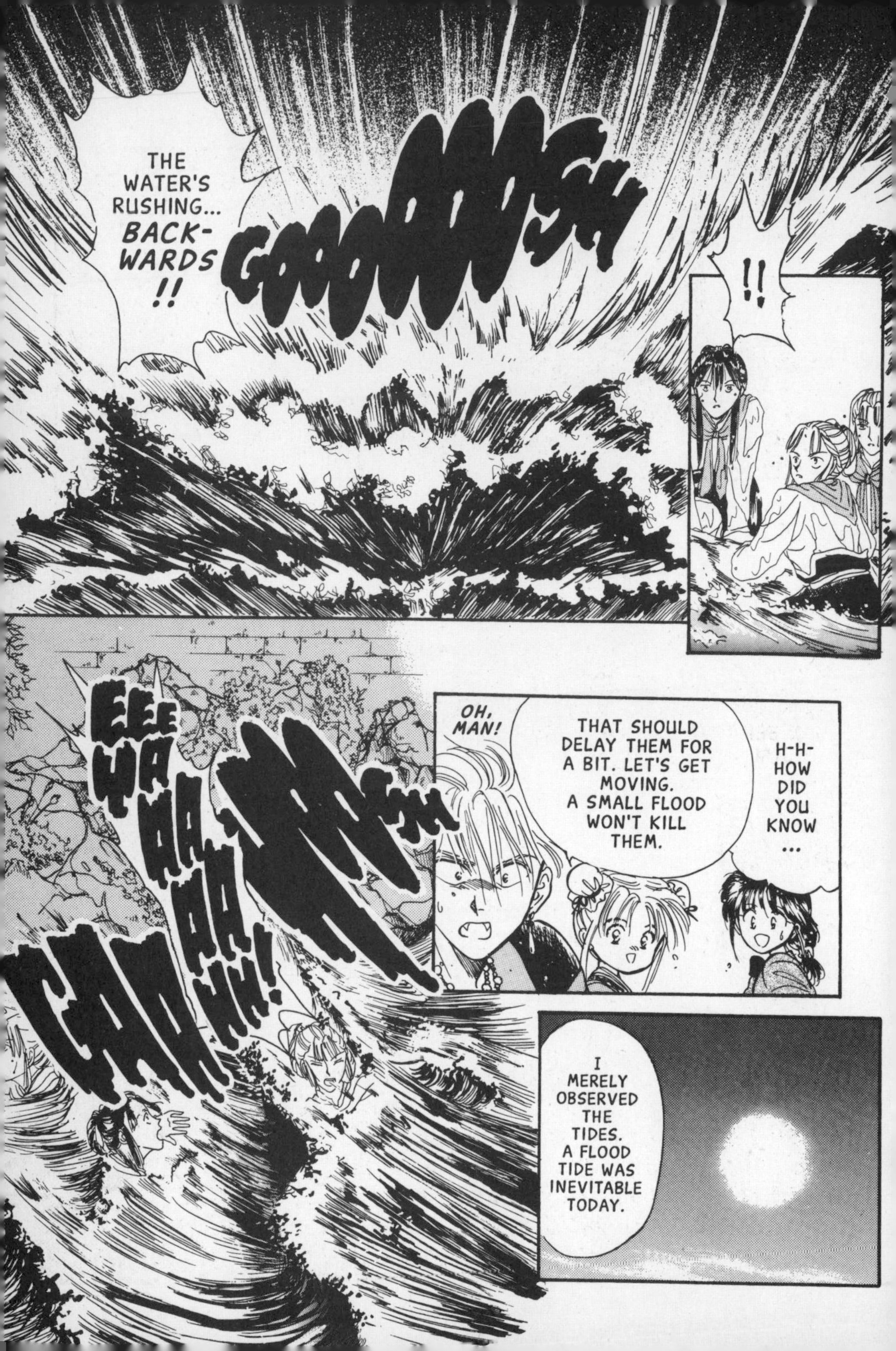
THE WATER'S RUSHING... BACK-WARDS !!
!!
OH, MAN!
THAT SHOULD DELAY THEM FOR A BIT. LET'S GET MOVING. A SMALL FLOOD WON'T KILL THEM.
H-H-HOW DID YOU KNOW ...
I MERELY OBSERVED THE TIDES. A FLOOD TIDE WAS INEVITABLE TODAY.

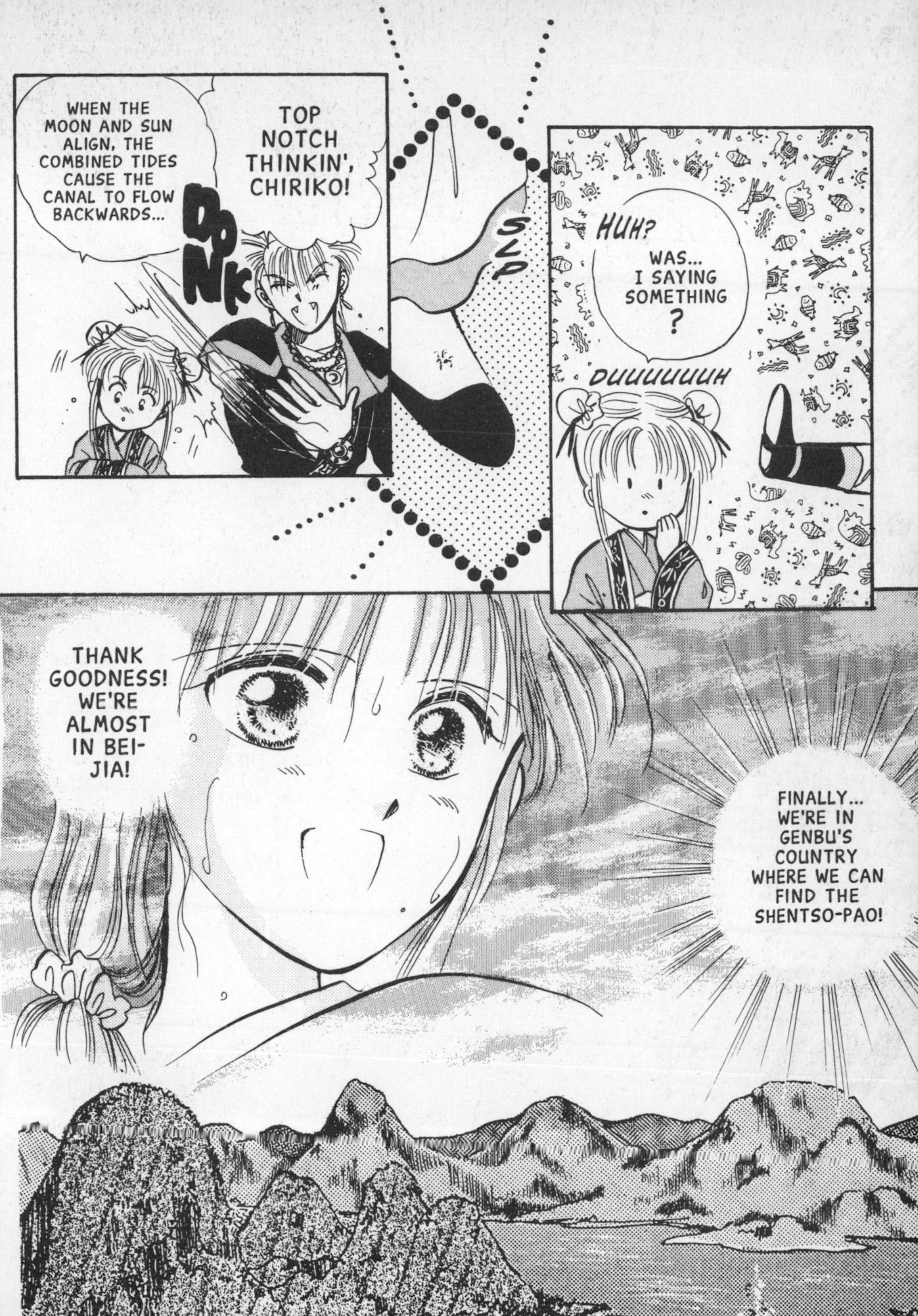
WHEN THE MOON AND SUN ALIGN, THE COMBINED TIDES CAUSE THE CANAL TO FLOW BACKWARDS...
TOP NOTCH THINKIN', CHIRIKO!
DONK
SLP
HUH?
WAS... I SAYING SOMETHING?
DUUUUUUH
THANK GOODNESS! WE'RE ALMOST IN BEI-JIA!
FINALLY... WE'RE IN GENBU'S COUNTRY WHERE WE CAN FIND THE SHENTSO-PAO!

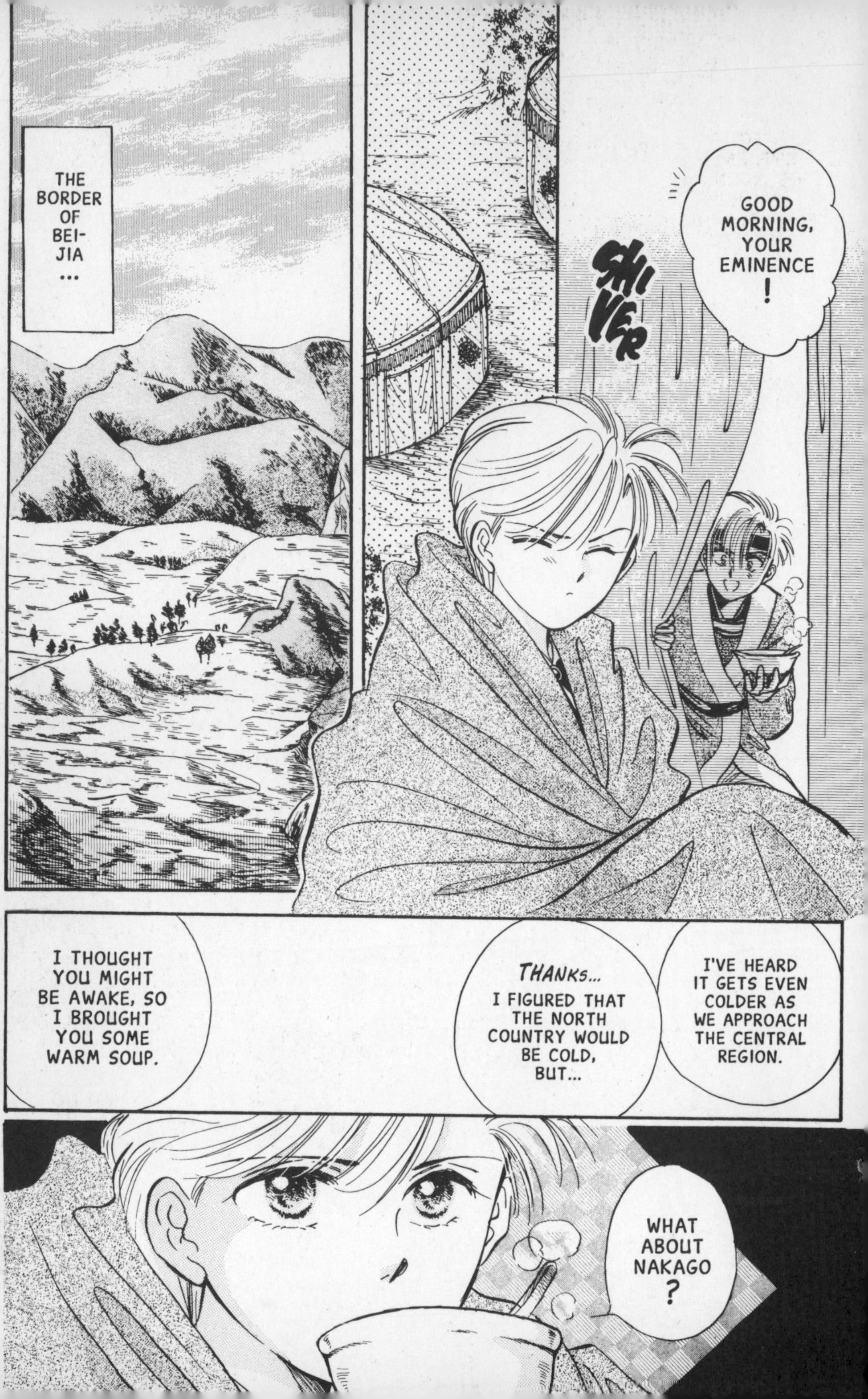
THE BORDER OF BEI-JIA ...
SHIVER
GOOD MORNING, YOUR EMINENCE!
I THOUGHT YOU MIGHT BE AWAKE, SO I BROUGHT YOU SOME WARM SOUP.
THANKS... I FIGURED THAT THE NORTH COUNTRY WOULD BE COLD, BUT...
I'VE HEARD IT GETS EVEN COLDER AS WE APPROACH THE CENTRAL REGION.
WHAT ABOUT NAKAGO?

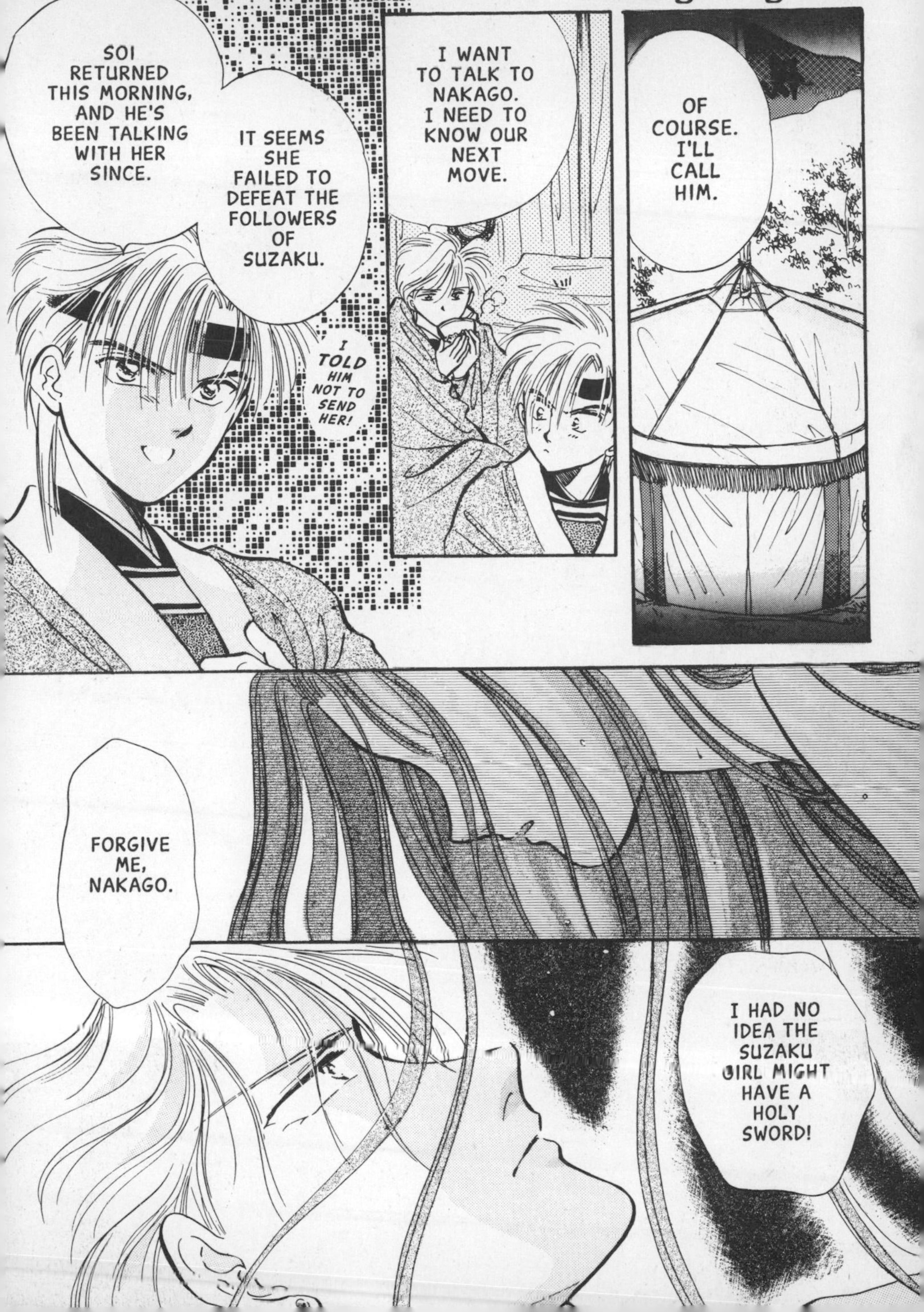
SOI RETURNED THIS MORNING, AND HE'S BEEN TALKING WITH HER SINCE.
IT SEEMS SHE FAILED TO DEFEAT THE FOLLOWERS OF SUZAKU.
I TOLD HIM NOT TO SEND HER!
I WANT TO TALK TO NAKAGO. I NEED TO KNOW OUR NEXT MOVE.
OF COURSE. I'LL CALL HIM.
FORGIVE ME, NAKAGO.
I HAD NO IDEA THE SUZAKU GIRL MIGHT HAVE A HOLY SWORD!

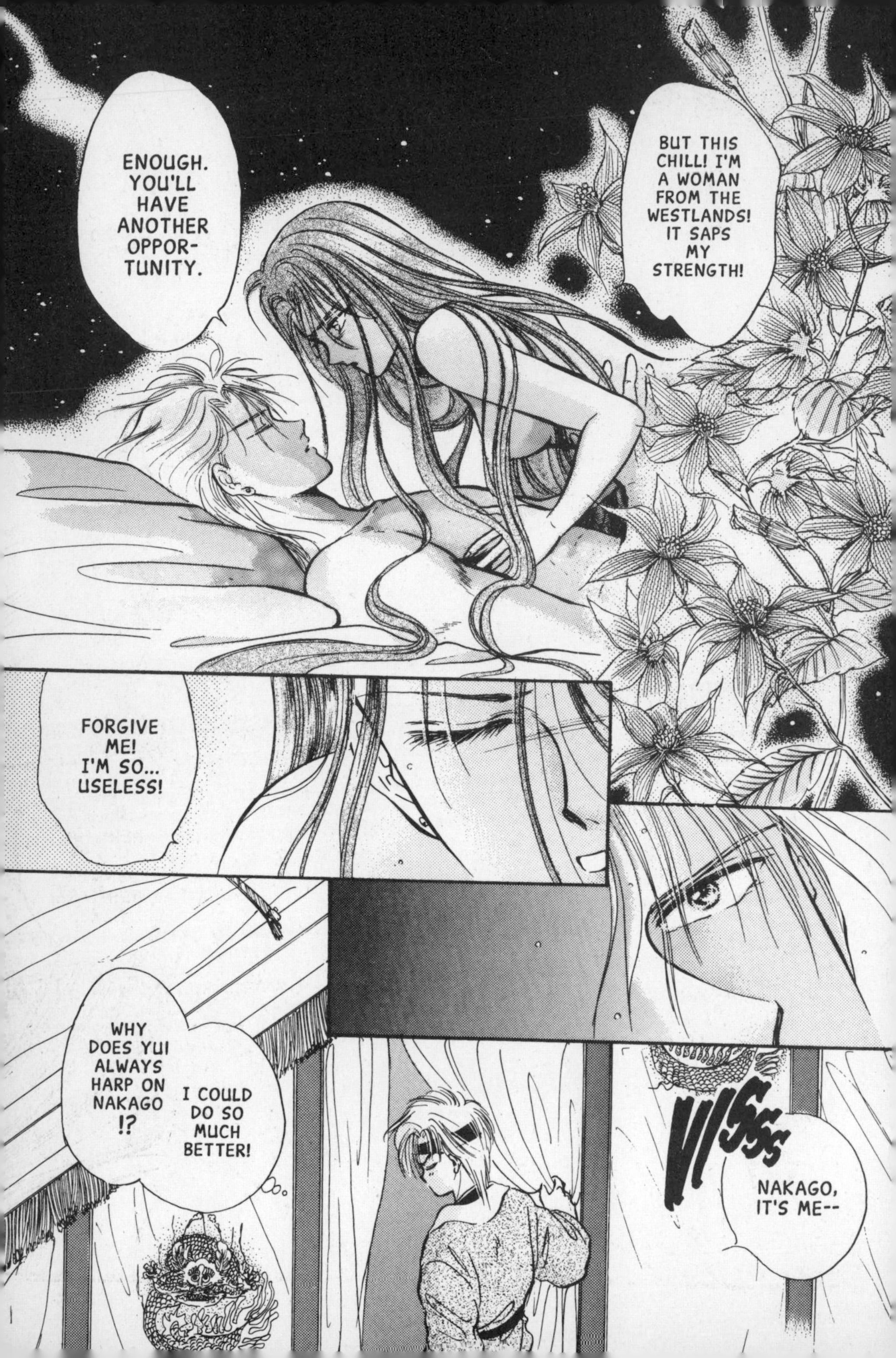
ENOUGH. YOU'LL HAVE ANOTHER OPPOR- TUNITY.
BUT THIS CHILL! I'M A WOMAN FROM THE WESTLANDS! IT SAPS MY STRENGTH!
FORGIVE ME! I'M SO... USELESS!
WHY DOES YUI ALWAYS HARP ON NAKAGO !?
I COULD DO SO MUCH BETTER!
VSSSS
NAKAGO, IT'S ME--

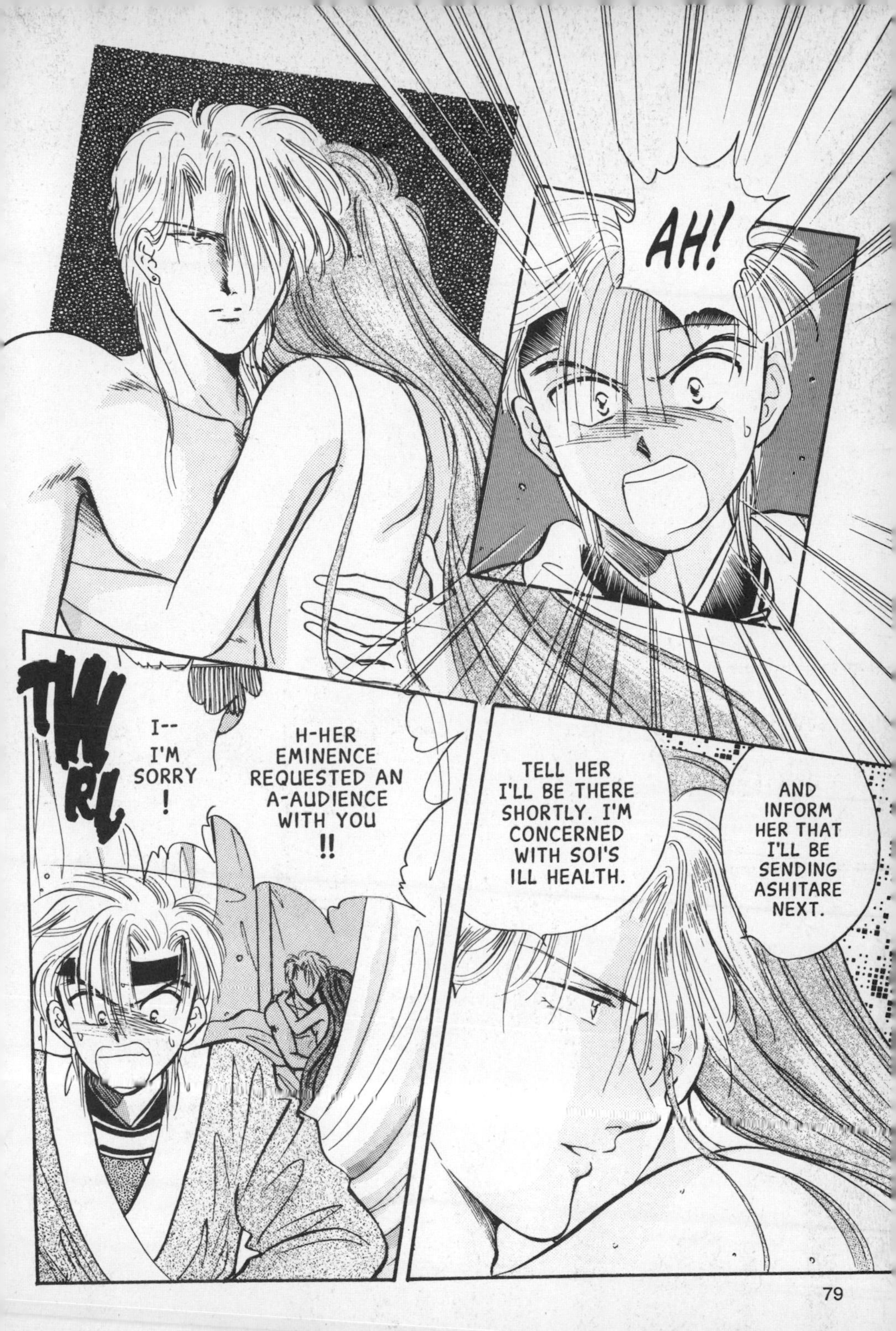
AH!
THWRL
I-- I'M SORRY!
H-HER EMINENCE REQUESTED AN A-AUDIENCE WITH YOU!!
TELL HER I'LL BE THERE SHORTLY. I'M CONCERNED WITH SOI'S ILL HEALTH.
AND INFORM HER THAT I'LL BE SENDING ASHITARE NEXT.

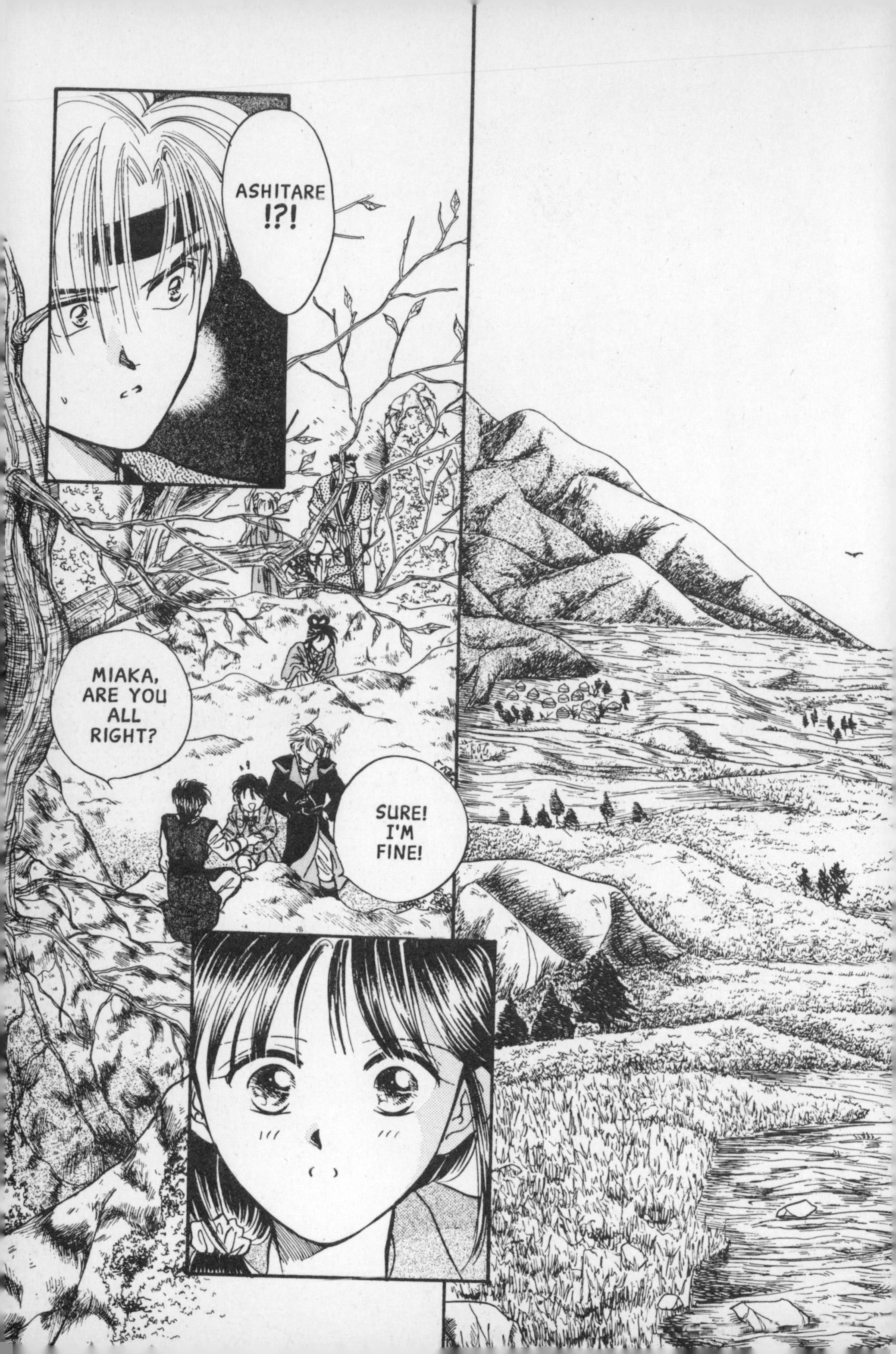
ASHITARE !?!
MIAKA, ARE YOU ALL RIGHT?
SURE! I'M FINE!

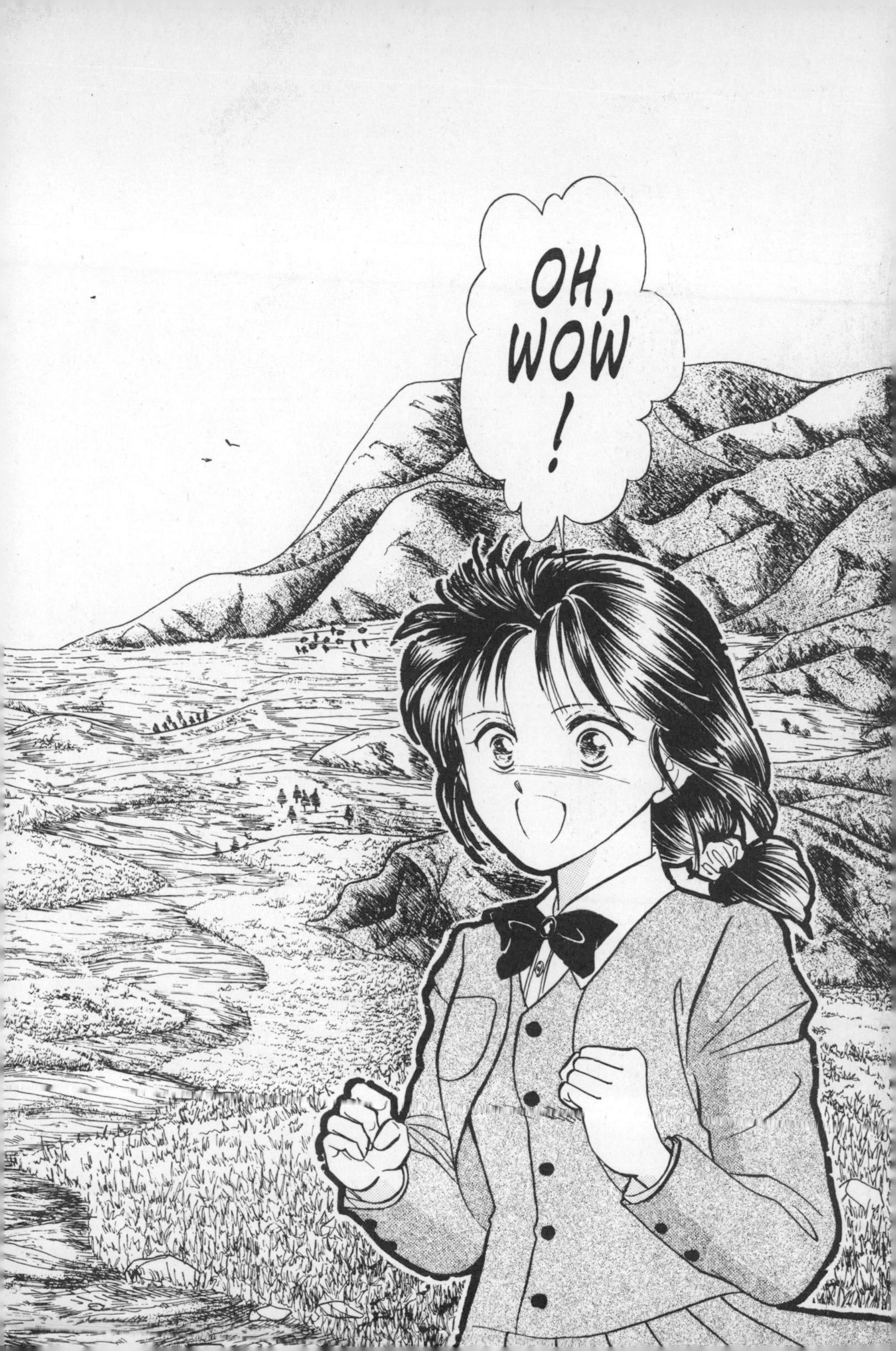
OH, WOW!

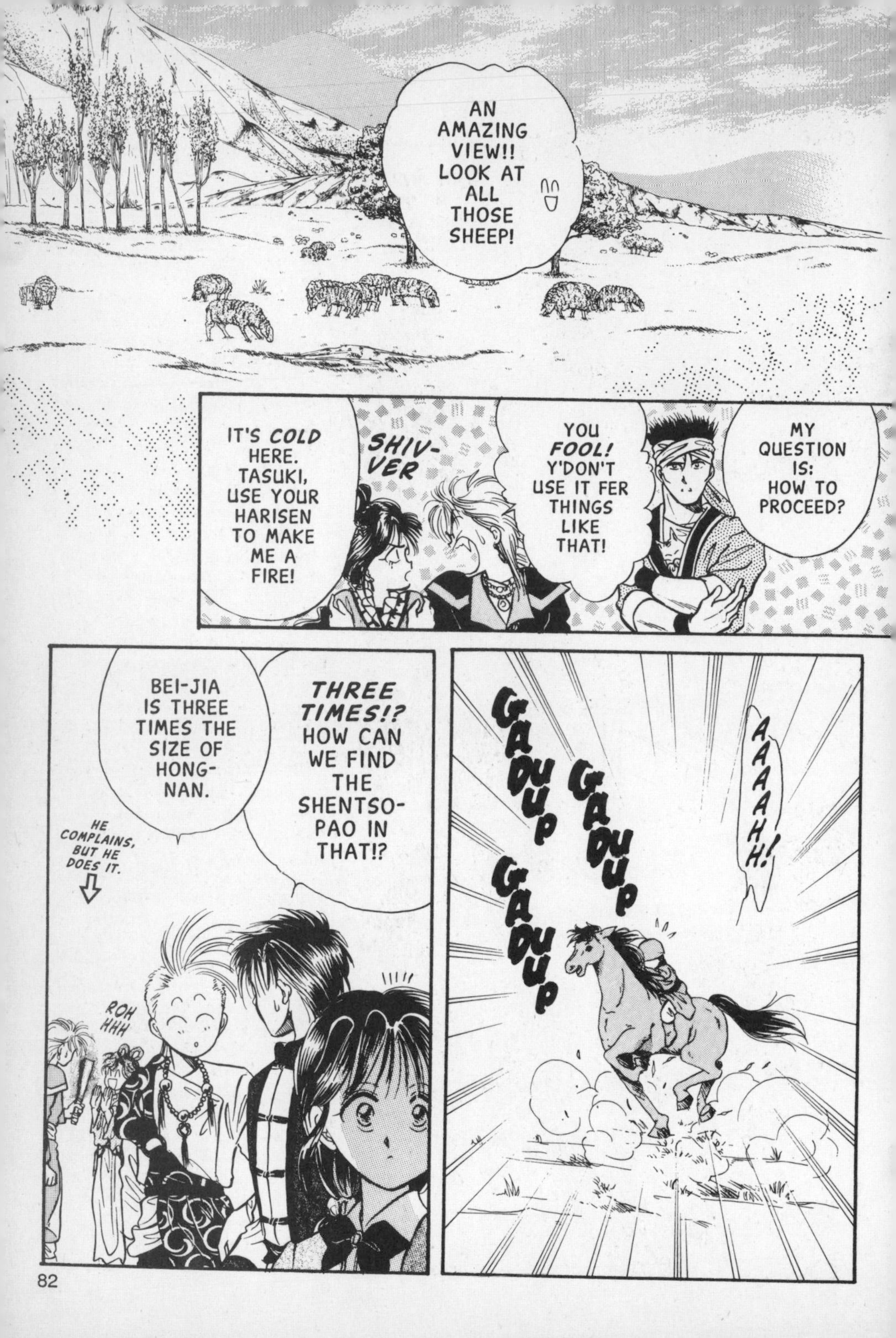
AN AMAZING VIEW!! LOOK AT ALL THOSE SHEEP!
IT'S *COLD* HERE. TASUKI, USE YOUR HARISEN TO MAKE ME A FIRE!
SHIV-VER
YOU *FOOL!* Y'DON'T USE IT FER THINGS LIKE THAT!
MY QUESTION IS: HOW TO PROCEED?
BEI-JIA IS THREE TIMES THE SIZE OF HONG-NAN.
THREE TIMES!? HOW CAN WE FIND THE SHENTSO-PAO IN THAT!?
HE COMPLAINS, BUT HE DOES IT.
ROHHHH
GADUP GADUP GADUP
AAAAAHH!

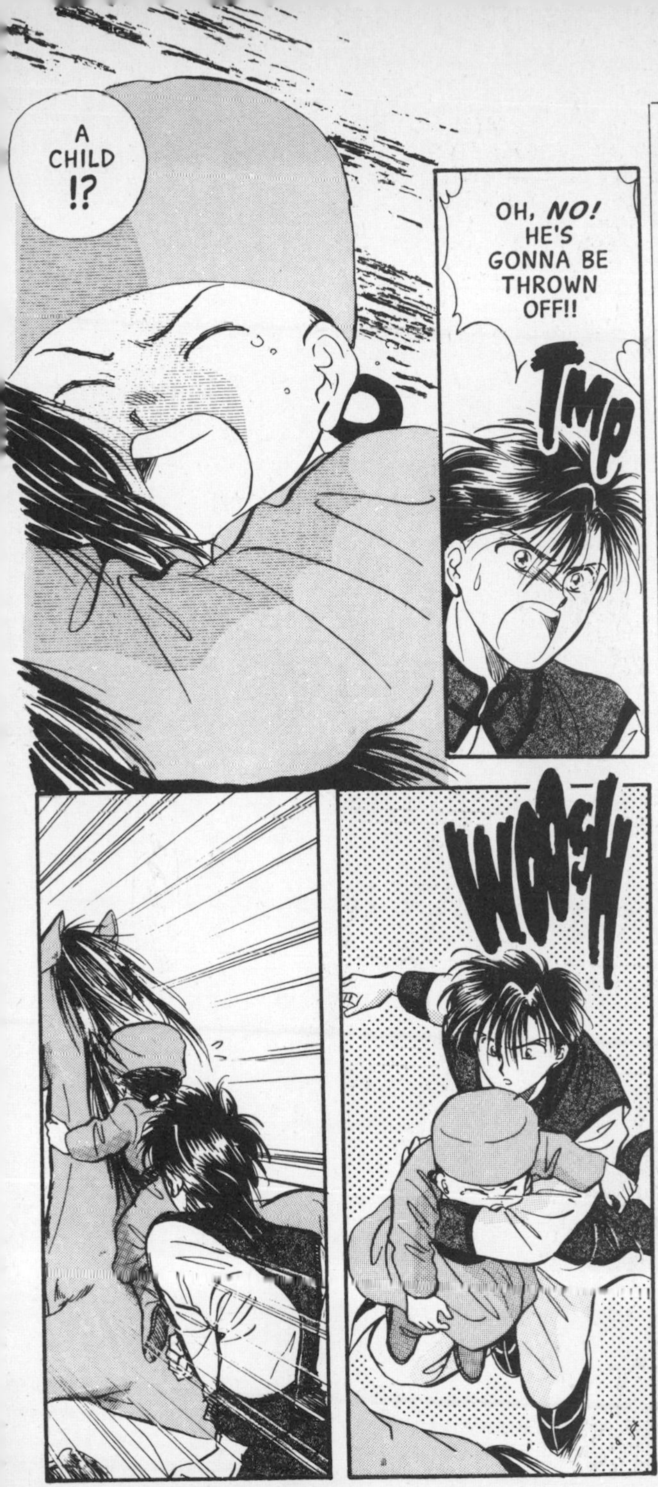
A CHILD !?
OH, NO! HE'S GONNA BE THROWN OFF!!
TMP
WOOSH

Friend

When I saw a hall, I thought, "Nuriko could be here!" Looking at the Emperor's throne, I'd think, "Hotohori would be sitting on that chair..." I'd see the roof and think, "Chichiri could be lying there, staring at the sky." My editor told me I was acting like an overzealous fangirl. But I think it was because I'd seen these sights so often (from research), that I almost felt at home. *Though I was far from it!* I bought the coffee-table photo book of course! Hong-Nan in FY is based on the Sung dynasty, so I should have gone to see the castle in Kaifeng, but it wasn't included in the tour. The Forbidden City was built in the Ming and Ch'eng dynasties, and that's a long time after the Sung. We passed by the HUGE walls where Pu Yi practiced riding his bike in the "Last Emperor."

I bought a Chinese man's outfit at a small shop. If Tamahome really existed, I'd want him to wear this awesome looking black outfit embroidered with a golden dragon and red ornamentation. *That night, wearing the outfit, the weird Ms. Yū burst into a smile.* The next place was the unforgettable Great Wall. At one point, we rode in a gondola car. It went up so high, I was terrified. Every time it shook, little Ms. Yū turned into which editor K ruthlessly captured on film. Our trusting relationship was called into question but we finally arrived. So it ended without the expected disaster. *What disaster did I expect?*

There was no one there, so the two of us walked around alone for a while, and that was it. The gondola ride was much more memorable. We also visited Tientan, which served as the basis for Suzaku's Temple. The altar is where the emperor prays to the heavens for a good harvest. People gathered around and prayed where the emperor used to stand.

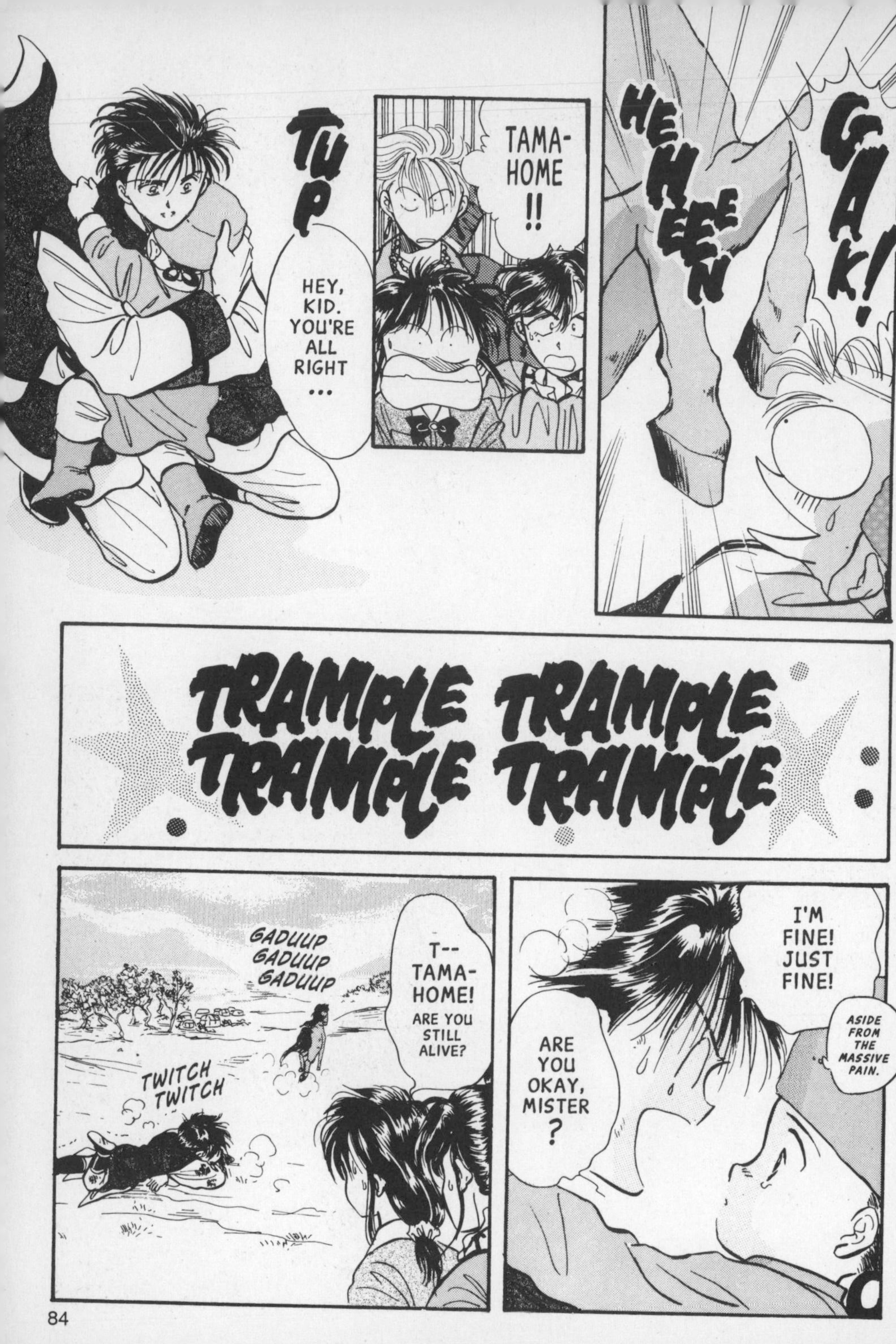
TUP
HEY, KID. YOU'RE ALL RIGHT ...
TAMA-HOME !!
HEHEEEN
GAK!
TRAMPLE TRAMPLE TRAMPLE TRAMPLE
GADUUP GADUUP GADUUP
T-- TAMA-HOME! ARE YOU STILL ALIVE?
TWITCH TWITCH
ARE YOU OKAY, MISTER ?
I'M FINE! JUST FINE!
ASIDE FROM THE MASSIVE PAIN.

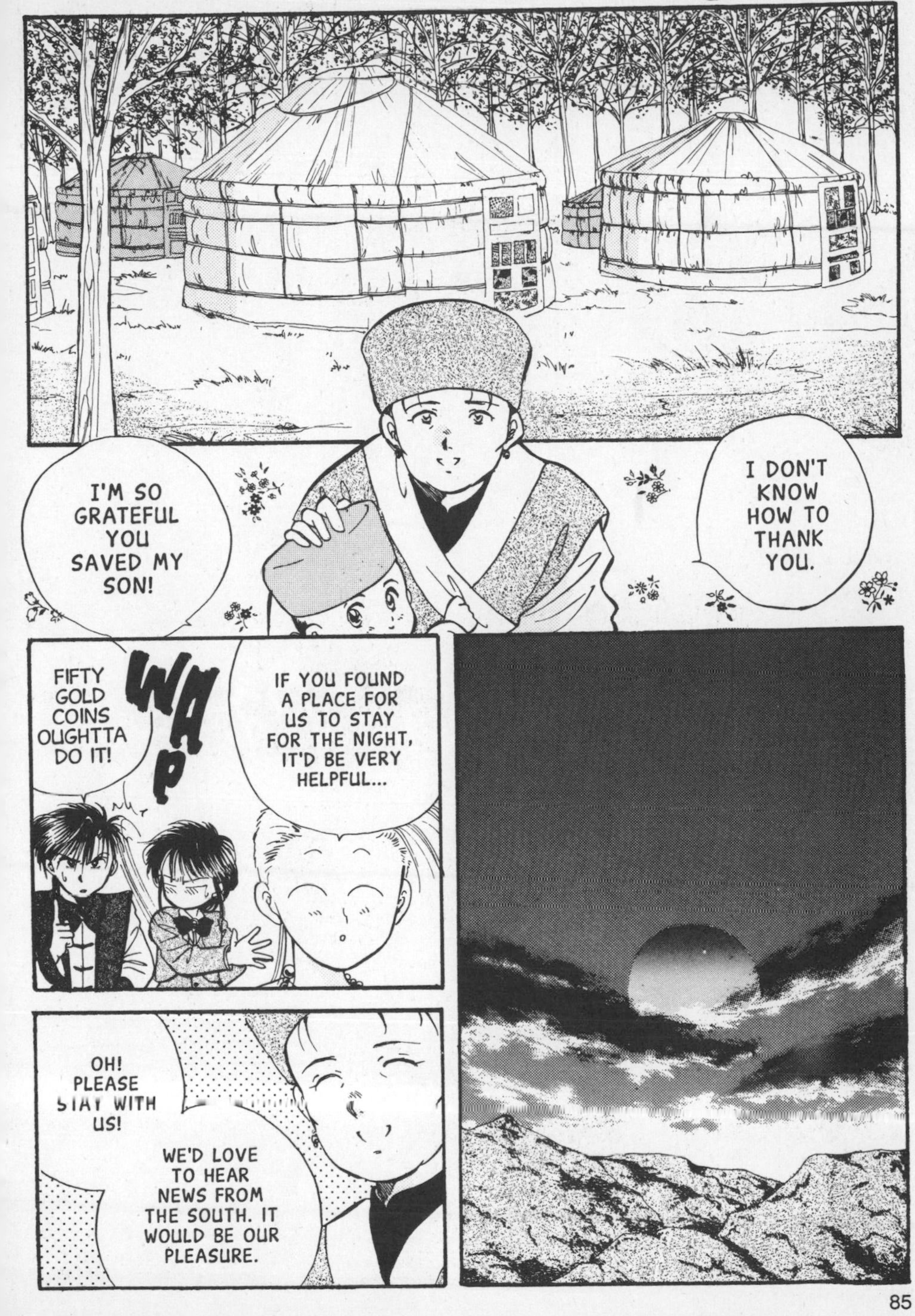
I'M SO GRATEFUL YOU SAVED MY SON!
I DON'T KNOW HOW TO THANK YOU.
FIFTY GOLD COINS OUGHTTA DO IT!
WAP
IF YOU FOUND A PLACE FOR US TO STAY FOR THE NIGHT, IT'D BE VERY HELPFUL...
OH! PLEASE STAY WITH US!
WE'D LOVE TO HEAR NEWS FROM THE SOUTH. IT WOULD BE OUR PLEASURE.

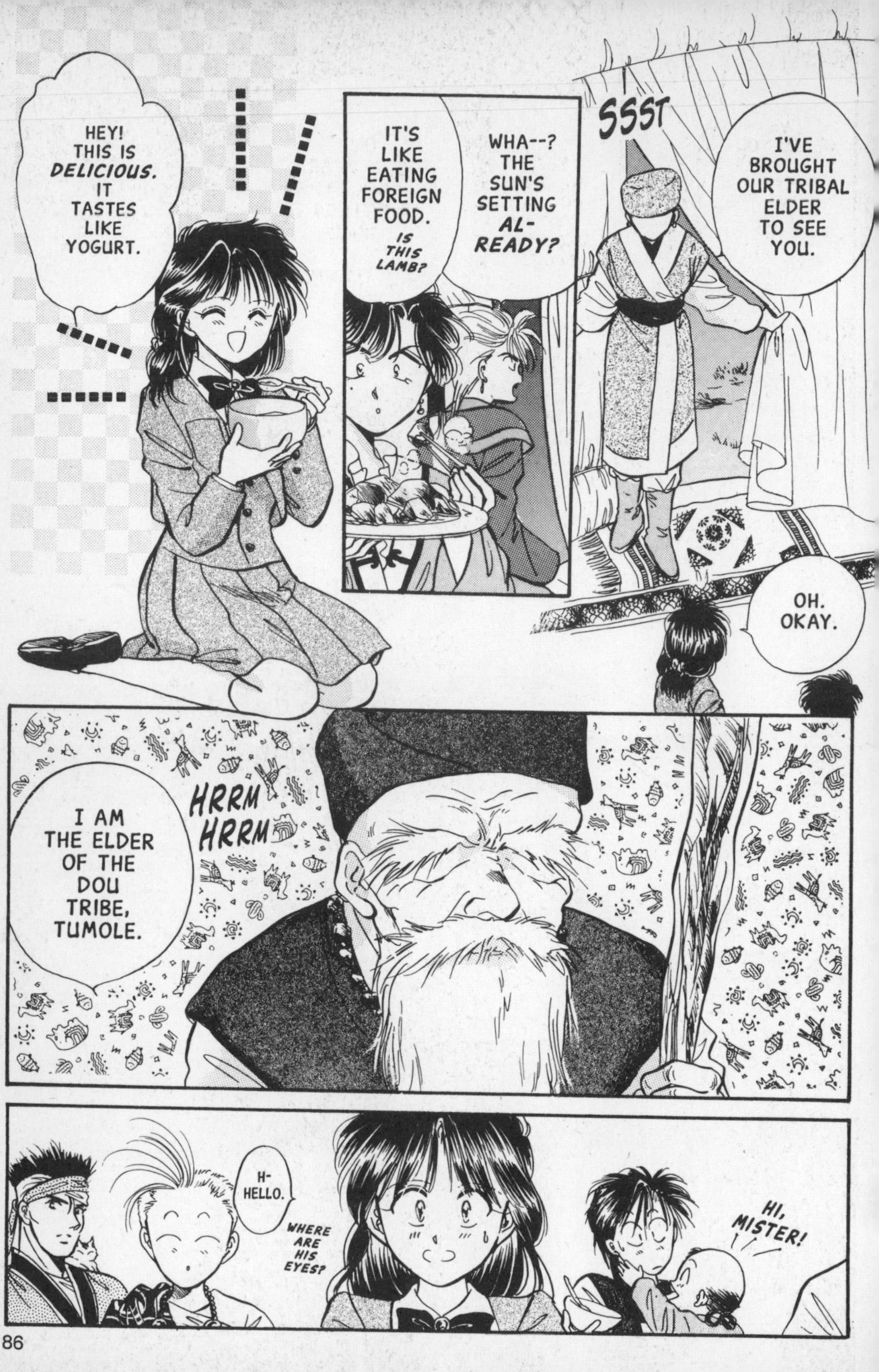
HEY! THIS IS *DELICIOUS.* IT TASTES LIKE YOGURT.
IT'S LIKE EATING FOREIGN FOOD.
IS THIS LAMB?
WHA--? THE SUN'S SETTING *AL-READY?*
SSST
I'VE BROUGHT OUR TRIBAL ELDER TO SEE YOU.
OH. OKAY.
I AM THE ELDER OF THE DOU TRIBE, TUMOLE.
HRRM HRRM
H-HELLO.
WHERE ARE HIS EYES?
HI, MISTER!

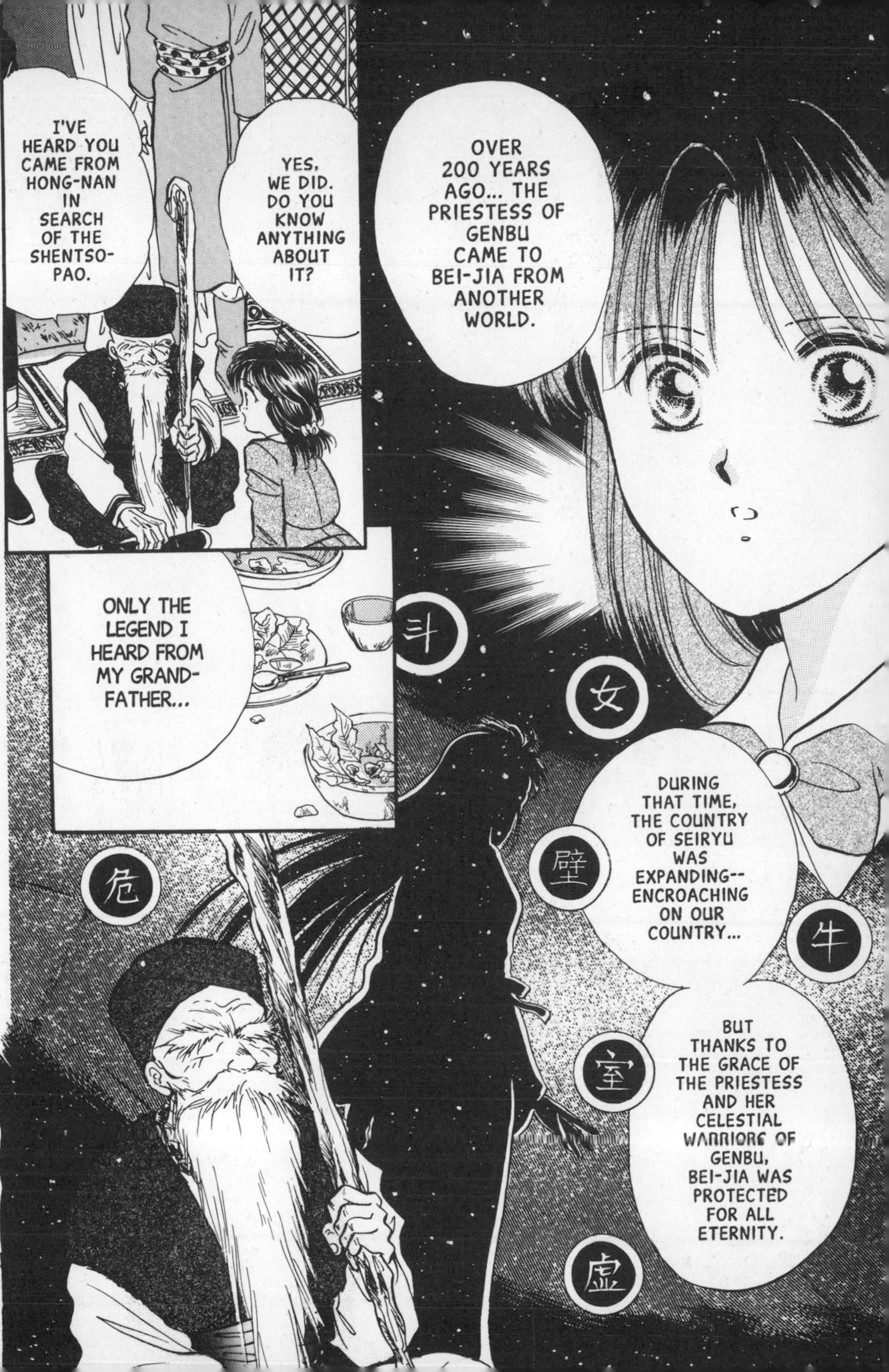
I'VE HEARD YOU CAME FROM HONG-NAN IN SEARCH OF THE SHENTSO-PAO.
YES, WE DID. DO YOU KNOW ANYTHING ABOUT IT?
ONLY THE LEGEND I HEARD FROM MY GRAND-FATHER...
OVER 200 YEARS AGO... THE PRIESTESS OF GENBU CAME TO BEI-JIA FROM ANOTHER WORLD.
斗
女
危
壁
牛
室
虚
DURING THAT TIME, THE COUNTRY OF SEIRYU WAS EXPANDING--ENCROACHING ON OUR COUNTRY...
BUT THANKS TO THE GRACE OF THE PRIESTESS AND HER CELESTIAL WARRIORS OF GENBU, BEI-JIA WAS PROTECTED FOR ALL ETERNITY.

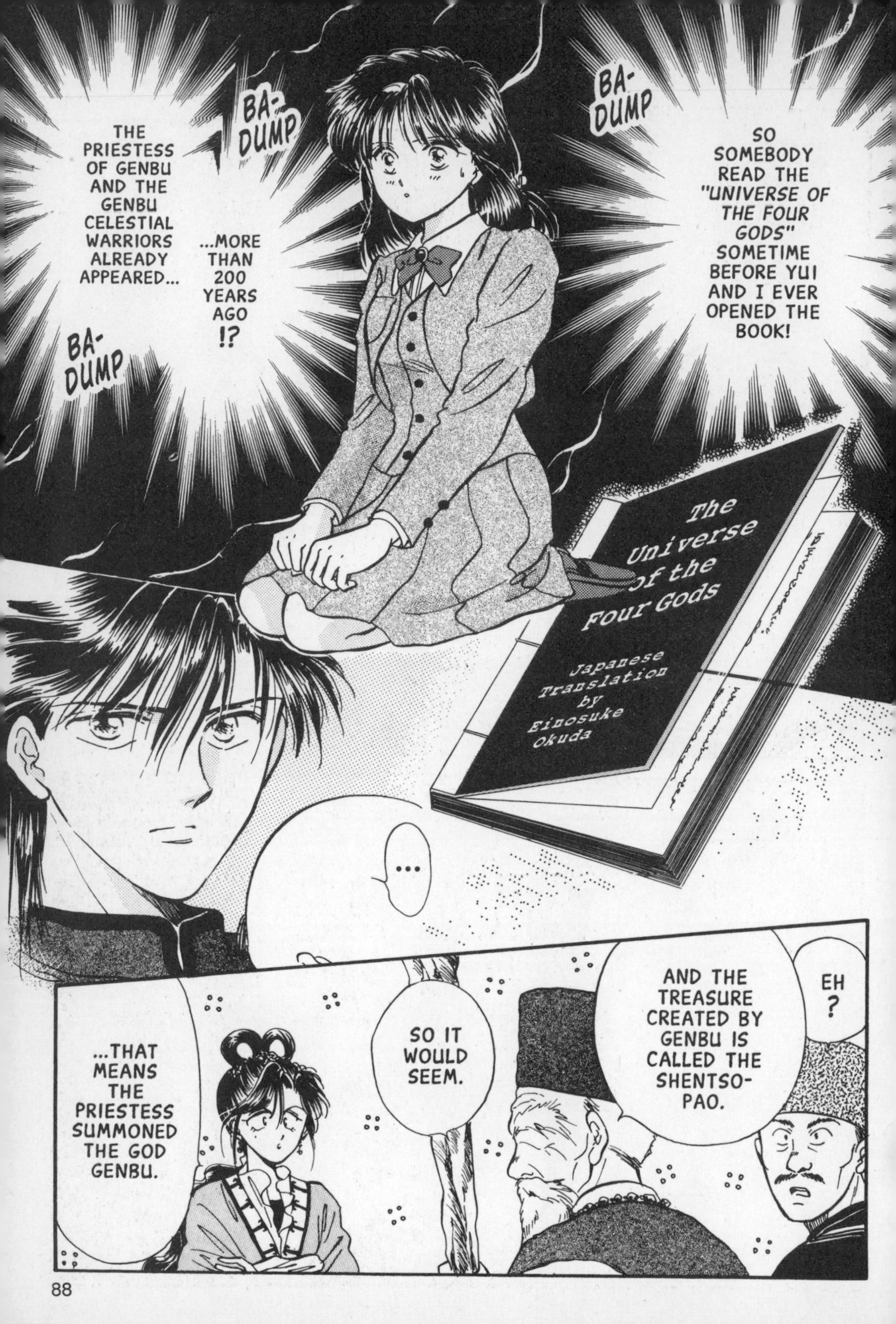
BA-DUMP
THE PRIESTESS OF GENBU AND THE GENBU CELESTIAL WARRIORS ALREADY APPEARED...
...MORE THAN 200 YEARS AGO !?
BA-DUMP
BA-DUMP
SO SOMEBODY READ THE "UNIVERSE OF THE FOUR GODS" SOMETIME BEFORE YUI AND I EVER OPENED THE BOOK!
The Universe of the Four Gods
Japanese Translation by Einosuke Okuda
...
...THAT MEANS THE PRIESTESS SUMMONED THE GOD GENBU.
SO IT WOULD SEEM.
AND THE TREASURE CREATED BY GENBU IS CALLED THE SHENTSO-PAO.
EH ?

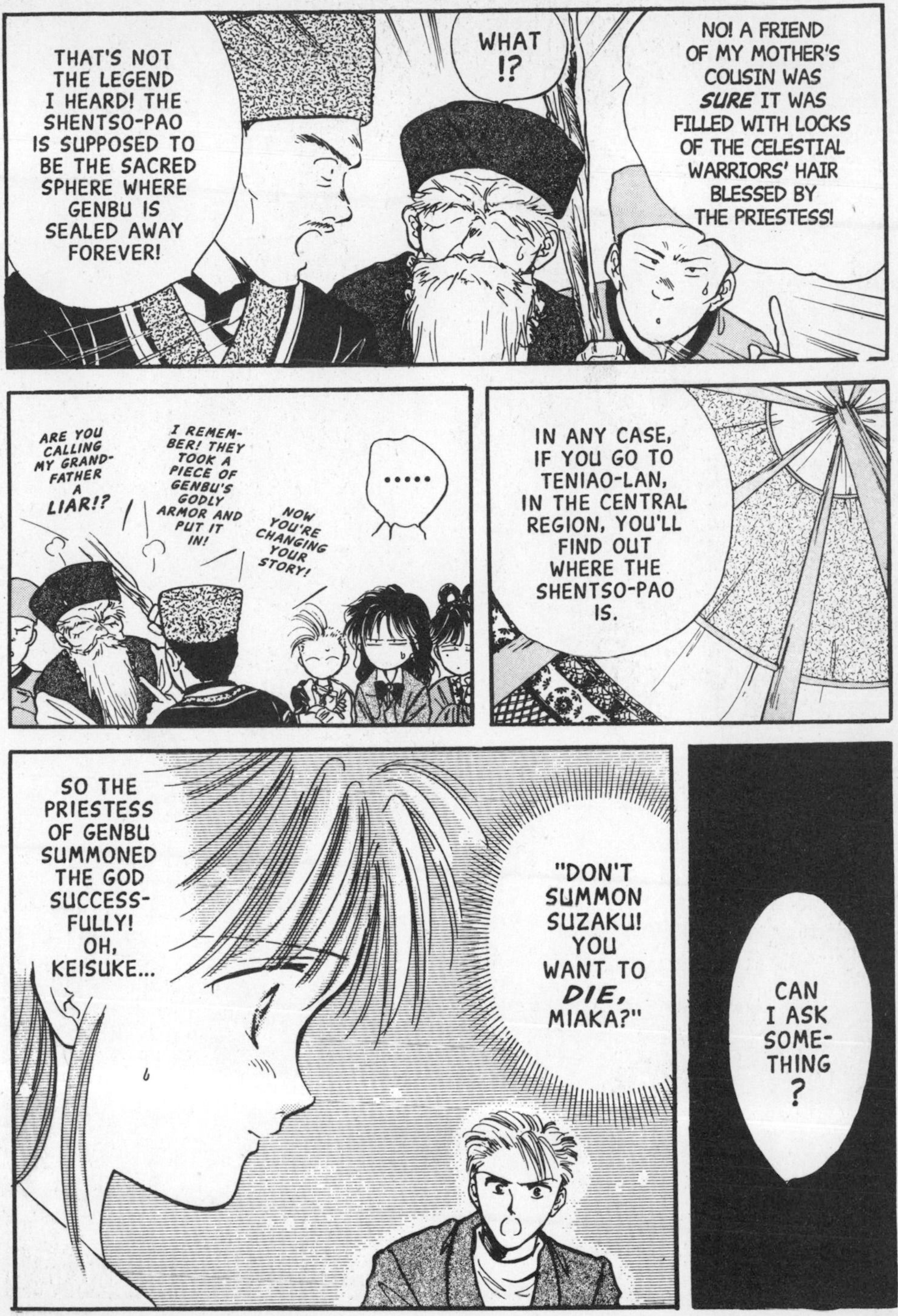
THAT'S NOT THE LEGEND I HEARD! THE SHENTSO-PAO IS SUPPOSED TO BE THE SACRED SPHERE WHERE GENBU IS SEALED AWAY FOREVER!
WHAT !?
NO! A FRIEND OF MY MOTHER'S COUSIN WAS *SURE* IT WAS FILLED WITH LOCKS OF THE CELESTIAL WARRIORS' HAIR BLESSED BY THE PRIESTESS!
ARE YOU CALLING MY GRAND-FATHER A *LIAR!?*
I REMEM-BER! THEY TOOK A PIECE OF GENBU'S GODLY ARMOR AND PUT IT IN!
NOW YOU'RE CHANGING YOUR STORY!
.....
IN ANY CASE, IF YOU GO TO TENIAO-LAN, IN THE CENTRAL REGION, YOU'LL FIND OUT WHERE THE SHENTSO-PAO IS.
SO THE PRIESTESS OF GENBU SUMMONED THE GOD SUCCESS-FULLY! OH, KEISUKE...
"DON'T SUMMON SUZAKU! YOU WANT TO *DIE,* MIAKA?"
CAN I ASK SOME-THING ?

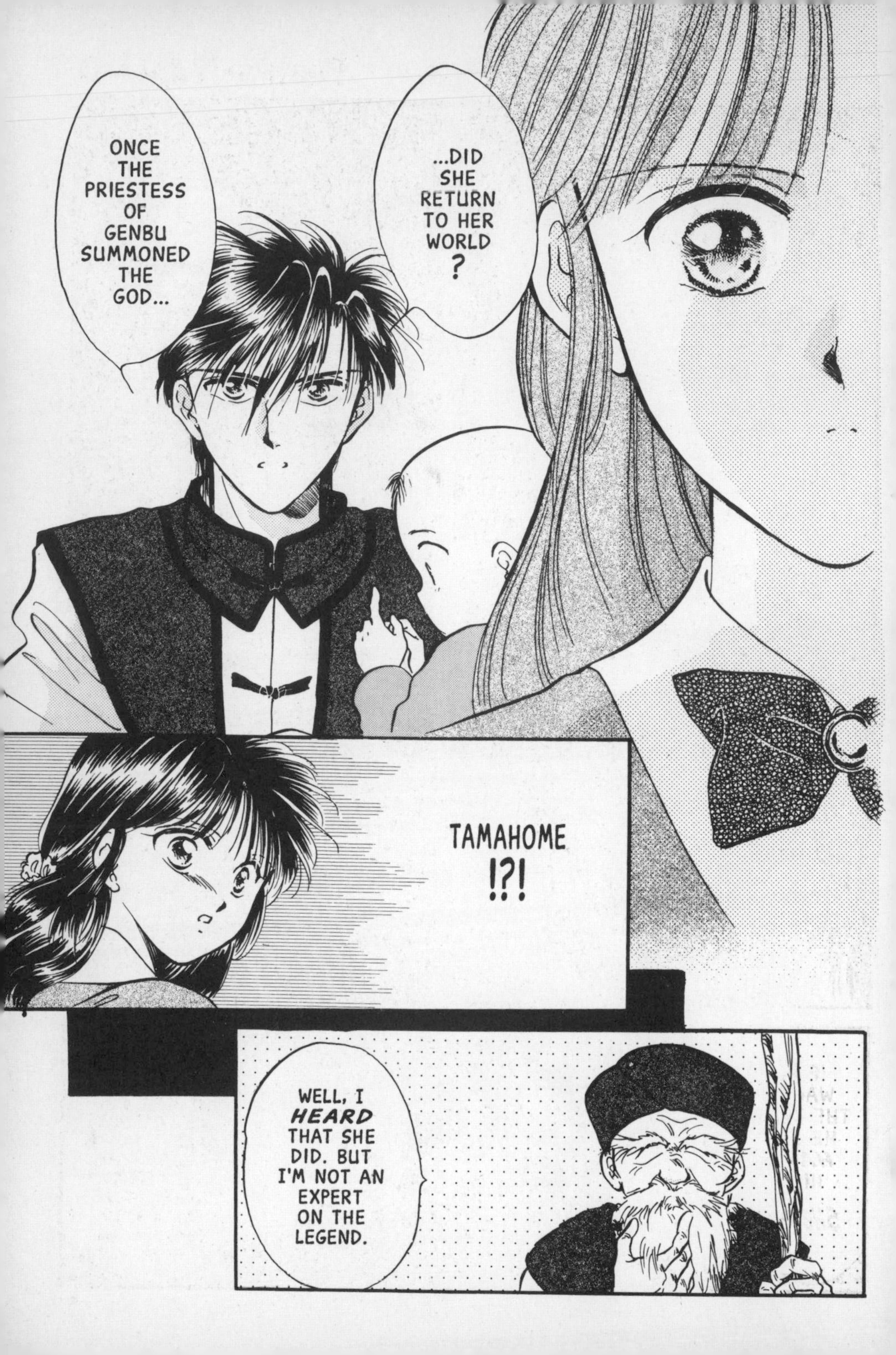
ONCE THE PRIESTESS OF GENBU SUMMONED THE GOD...
...DID SHE RETURN TO HER WORLD?
TAMAHOME !?!
WELL, I HEARD THAT SHE DID. BUT I'M NOT AN EXPERT ON THE LEGEND.

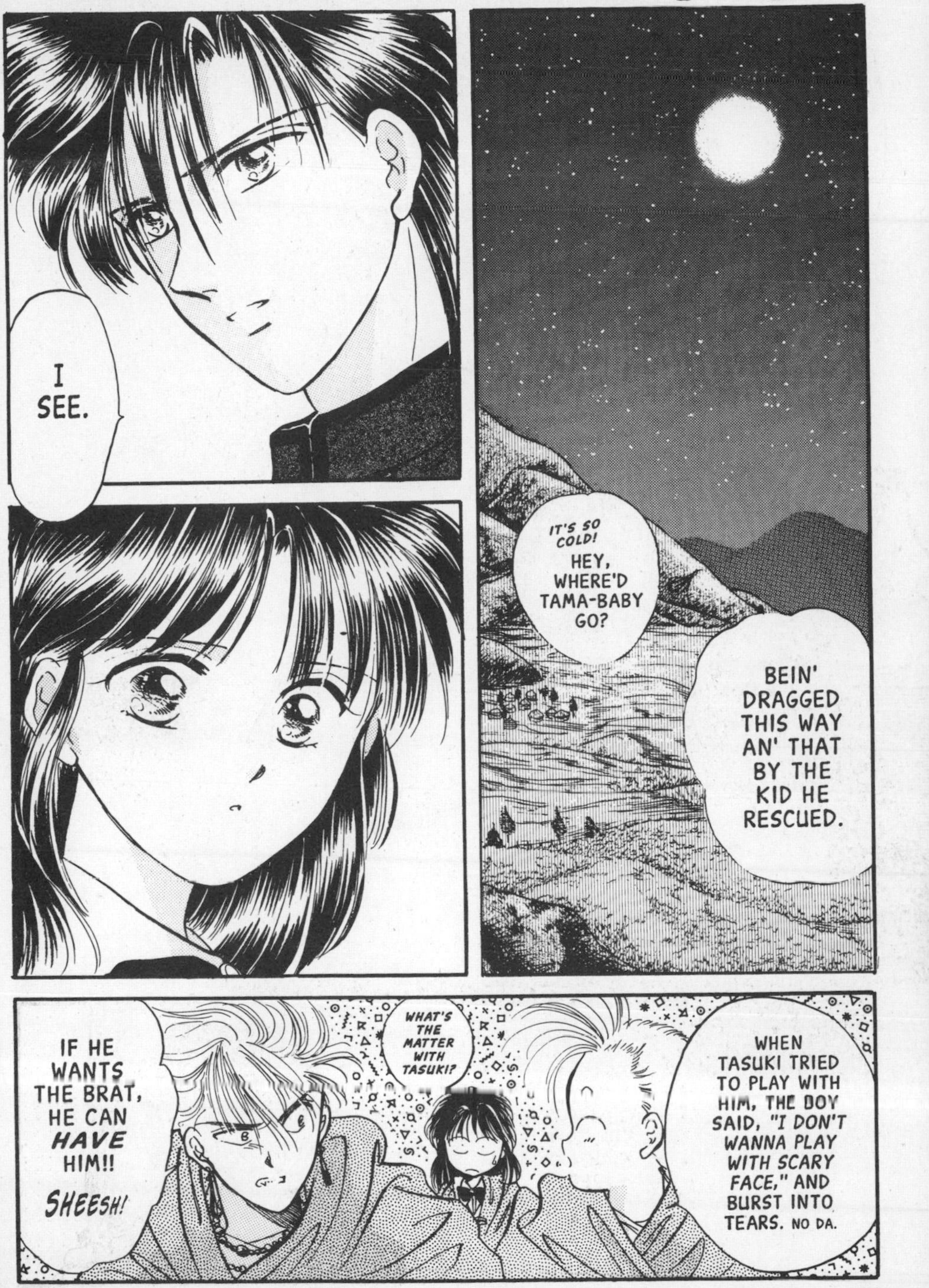
I SEE.
IT'S SO COLD!
HEY, WHERE'D TAMA-BABY GO?
BEIN' DRAGGED THIS WAY AN' THAT BY THE KID HE RESCUED.
IF HE WANTS THE BRAT, HE CAN HAVE HIM!! SHEESH!
WHAT'S THE MATTER WITH TASUKI?
WHEN TASUKI TRIED TO PLAY WITH HIM, THE BOY SAID, "I DON'T WANNA PLAY WITH SCARY FACE," AND BURST INTO TEARS. NO DA.

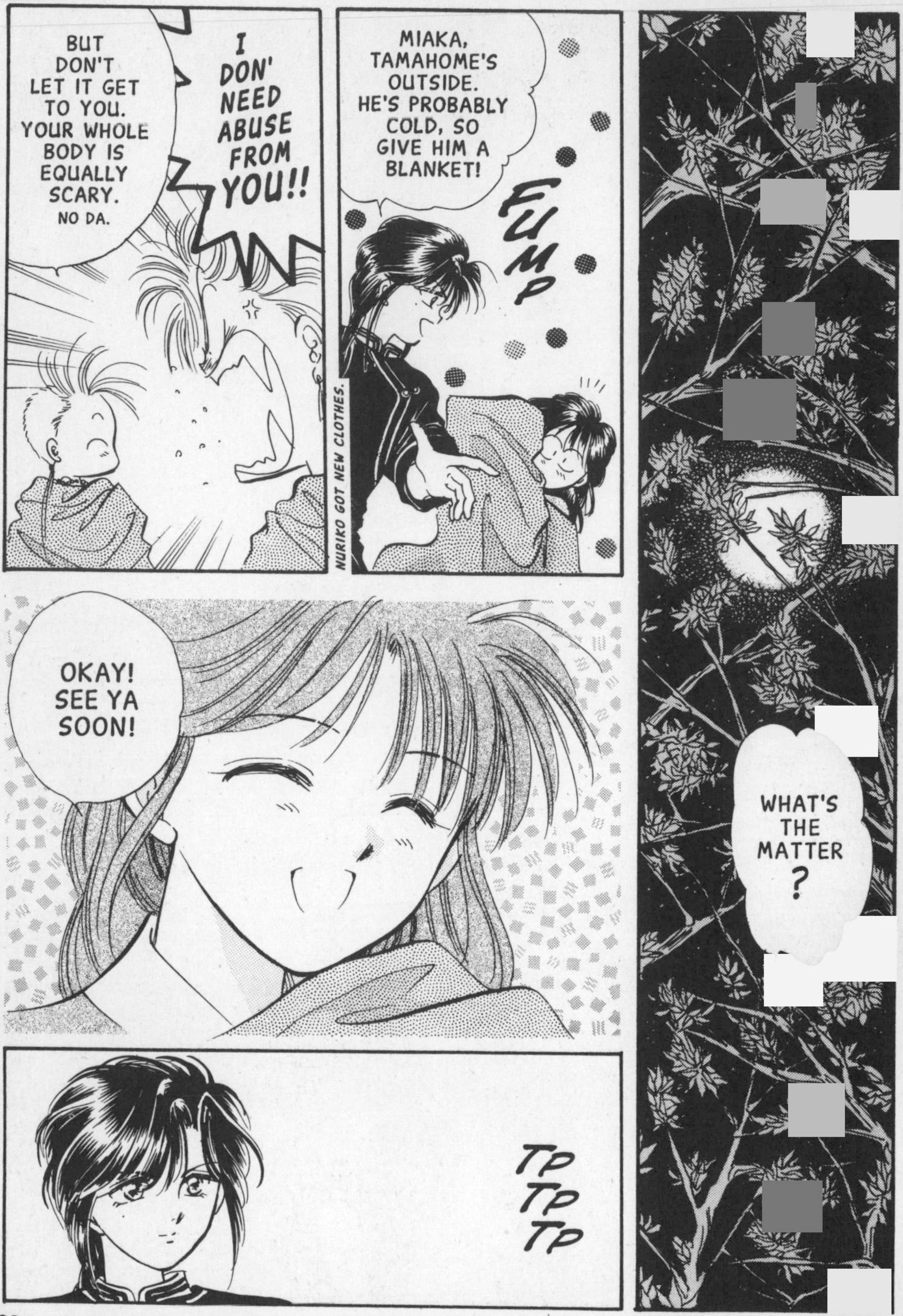
BUT DON'T LET IT GET TO YOU. YOUR WHOLE BODY IS EQUALLY SCARY. NO DA.
I DON' NEED ABUSE FROM YOU!!
MIAKA, TAMAHOME'S OUTSIDE. HE'S PROBABLY COLD, SO GIVE HIM A BLANKET!
FUMP
NURIKO GOT NEW CLOTHES.
OKAY! SEE YA SOON!
TP TP TP
WHAT'S THE MATTER ?

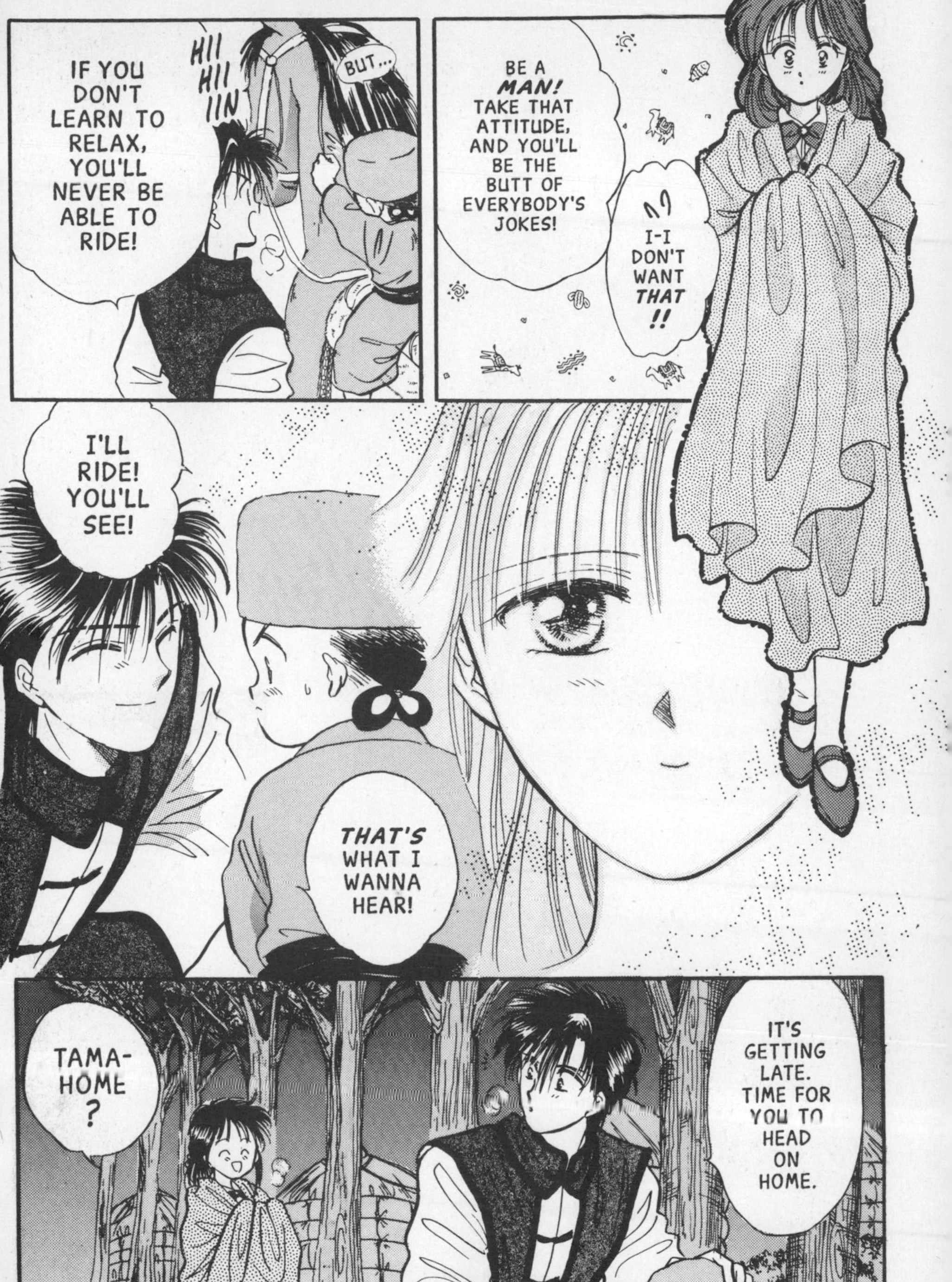
IF YOU DON'T LEARN TO RELAX, YOU'LL NEVER BE ABLE TO RIDE!
HII HII IIN
BUT...
BE A *MAN!* TAKE THAT ATTITUDE, AND YOU'LL BE THE BUTT OF EVERYBODY'S JOKES!
I-I DON'T WANT *THAT* !!
I'LL RIDE! YOU'LL SEE!
THAT'S WHAT I WANNA HEAR!
TAMA-HOME ?
IT'S GETTING LATE. TIME FOR YOU TO HEAD ON HOME.

SEE YOU!

YOU REALLY LIKE KIDS, DON'T YOU, TAMAHOME?

NOT ESPECIALLY. THEY JUST SEEM TO CROWD AROUND ME.

YOU WEREN'T ANY DIFFERENT.

GAK!

I'M NOT A CHILD!

IT WAS LIKE ANOTHER SISTER CAME OUTTA THE WOODWORK, DEPENDING ON ME FOR EVERYTHING!

MEMORIES OF THE PAST.

EXCUSE ME!!

AT FIRST, THAT'S HOW I FELT...

...THEN, AT SOME POINT, I REALIZED THAT I WAS IN LOVE WITH YOU.

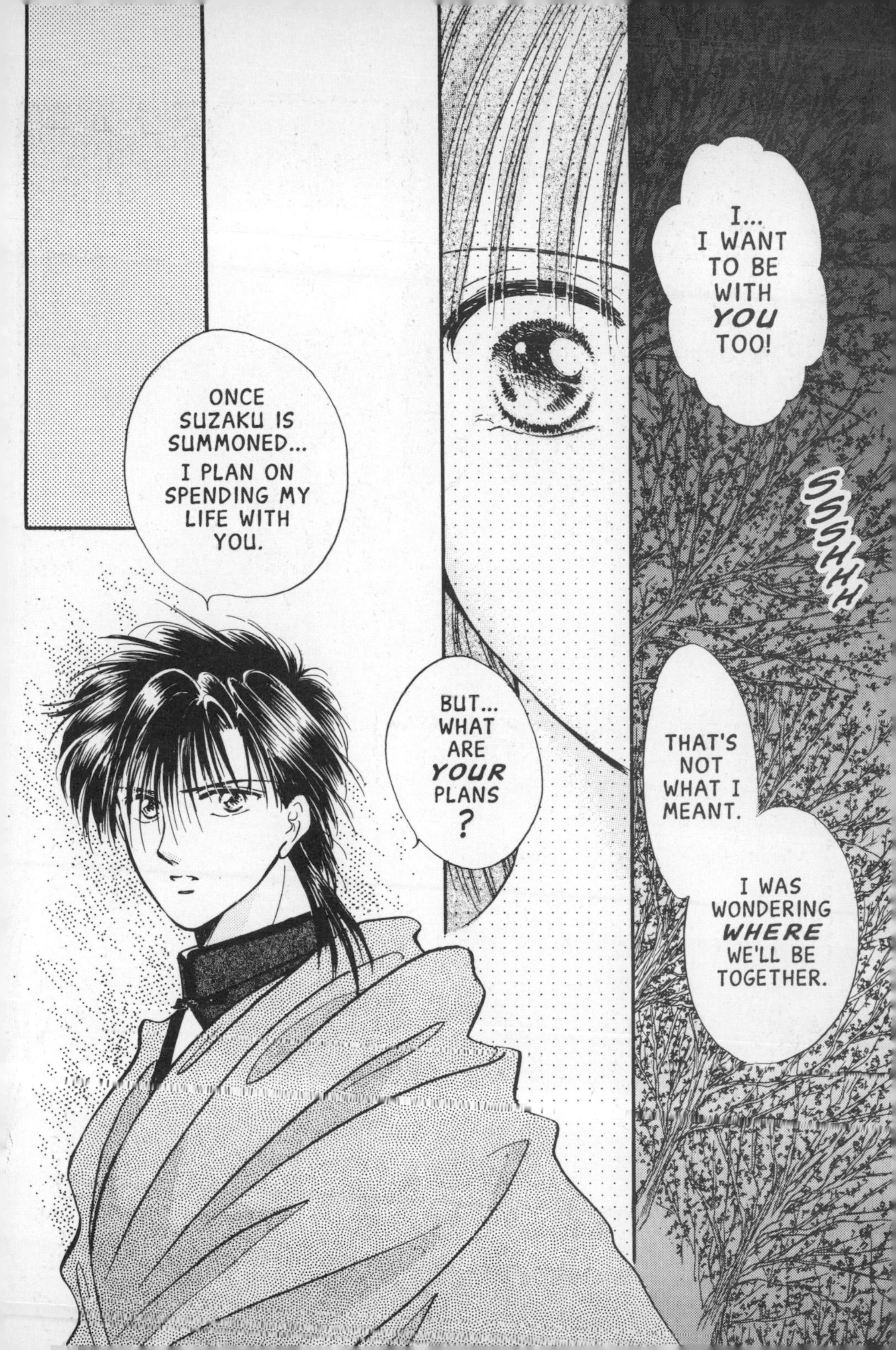
ONCE SUZAKU IS SUMMONED... I PLAN ON SPENDING MY LIFE WITH YOU.
BUT... WHAT ARE YOUR PLANS ?
I... I WANT TO BE WITH YOU TOO!
SSSHHH
THAT'S NOT WHAT I MEANT.
I WAS WONDERING WHERE WE'LL BE TOGETHER.

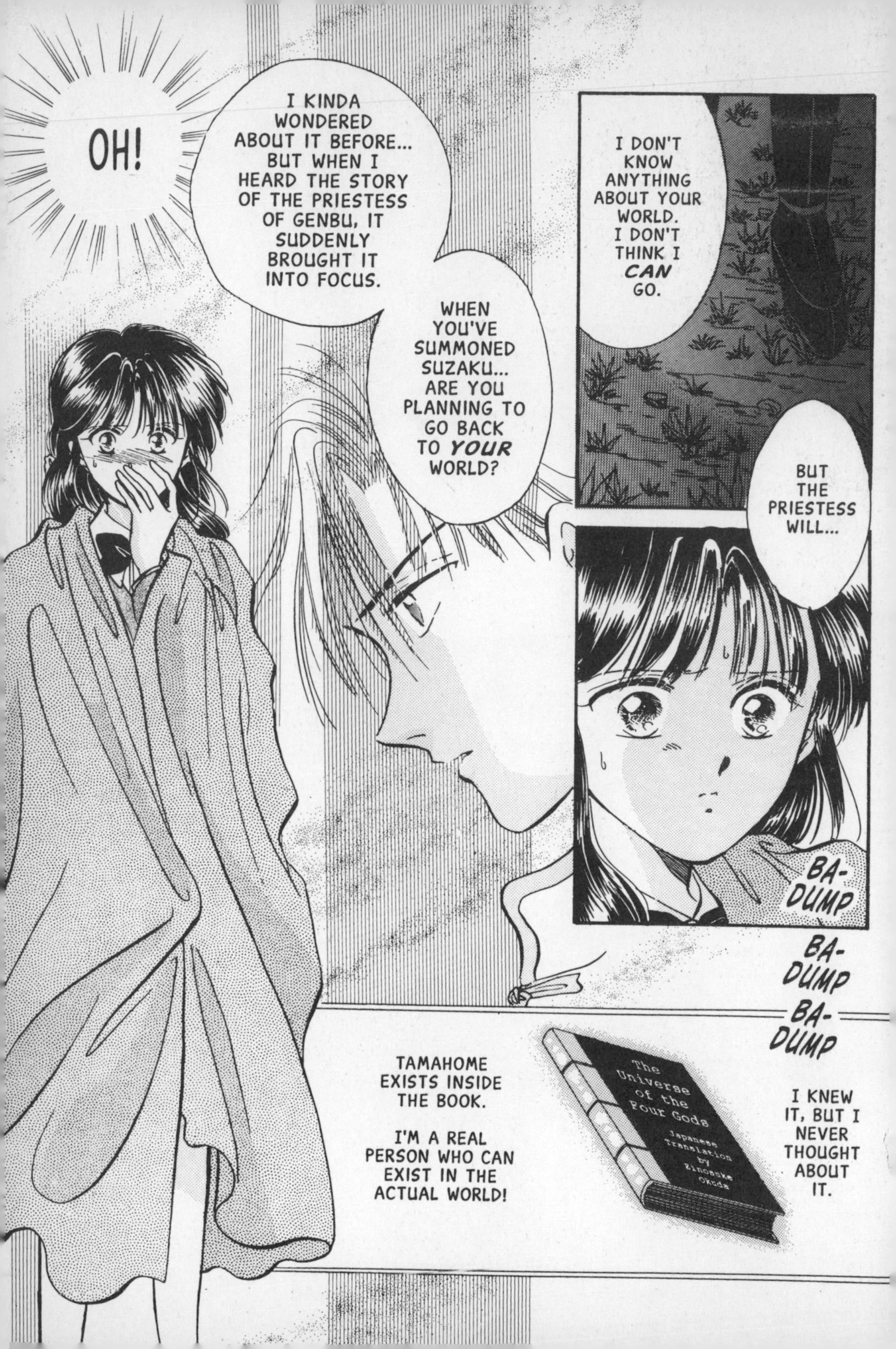
OH!
I KINDA WONDERED ABOUT IT BEFORE... BUT WHEN I HEARD THE STORY OF THE PRIESTESS OF GENBU, IT SUDDENLY BROUGHT IT INTO FOCUS.
WHEN YOU'VE SUMMONED SUZAKU... ARE YOU PLANNING TO GO BACK TO *YOUR* WORLD?
I DON'T KNOW ANYTHING ABOUT YOUR WORLD. I DON'T THINK I *CAN* GO.
BUT THE PRIESTESS WILL...
BA-DUMP
BA-DUMP
BA-DUMP
TAMAHOME EXISTS INSIDE THE BOOK.
I'M A REAL PERSON WHO CAN EXIST IN THE ACTUAL WORLD!
The Universe of the Four Gods
Japanese Translation by Einosuke Okuda
I KNEW IT, BUT I NEVER THOUGHT ABOUT IT.

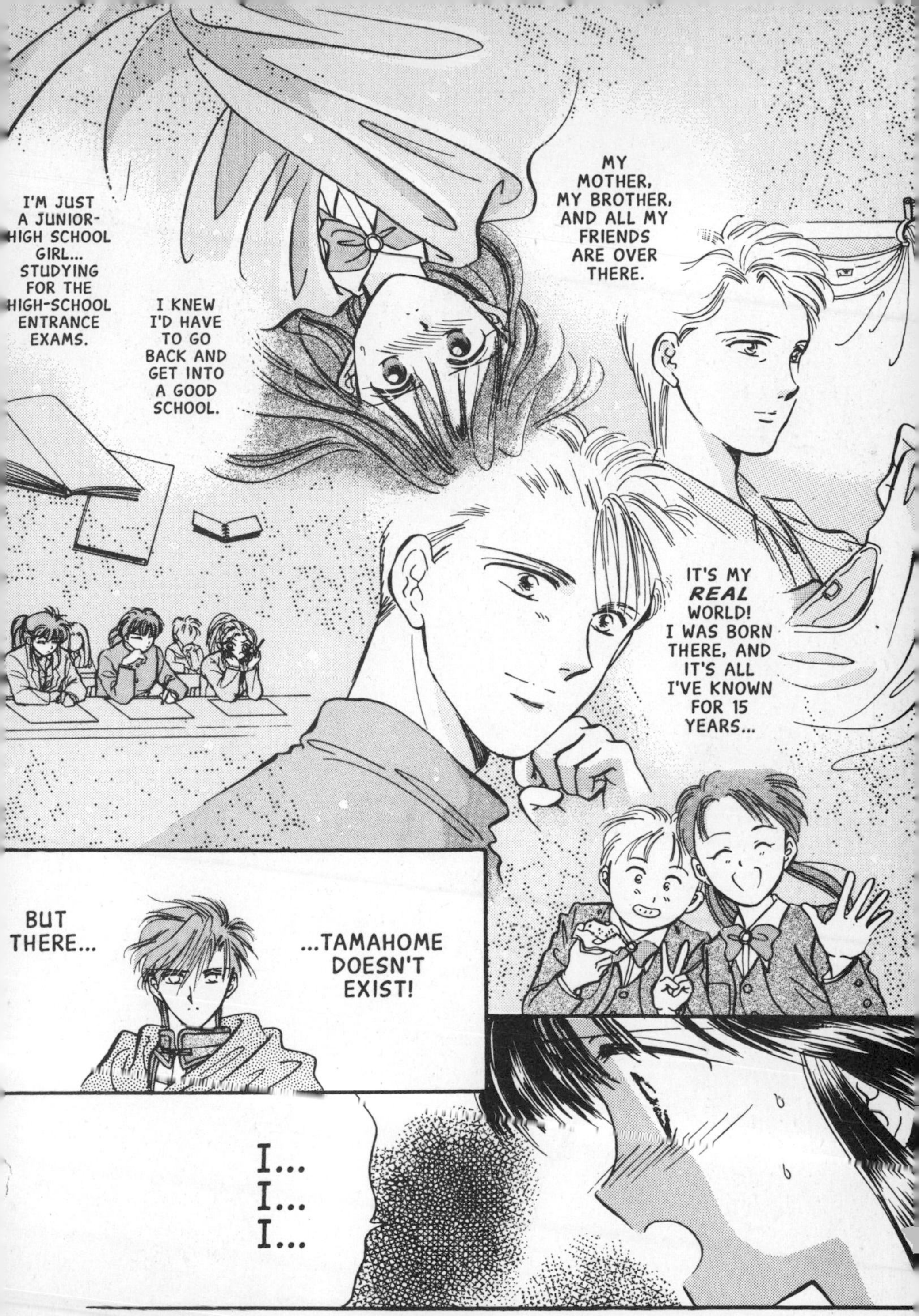
I'M JUST A JUNIOR-HIGH SCHOOL GIRL... STUDYING FOR THE HIGH-SCHOOL ENTRANCE EXAMS.
I KNEW I'D HAVE TO GO BACK AND GET INTO A GOOD SCHOOL.
MY MOTHER, MY BROTHER, AND ALL MY FRIENDS ARE OVER THERE.
IT'S MY *REAL* WORLD! I WAS BORN THERE, AND IT'S ALL I'VE KNOWN FOR 15 YEARS...
BUT THERE...
...TAMAHOME DOESN'T EXIST!
I... I... I...

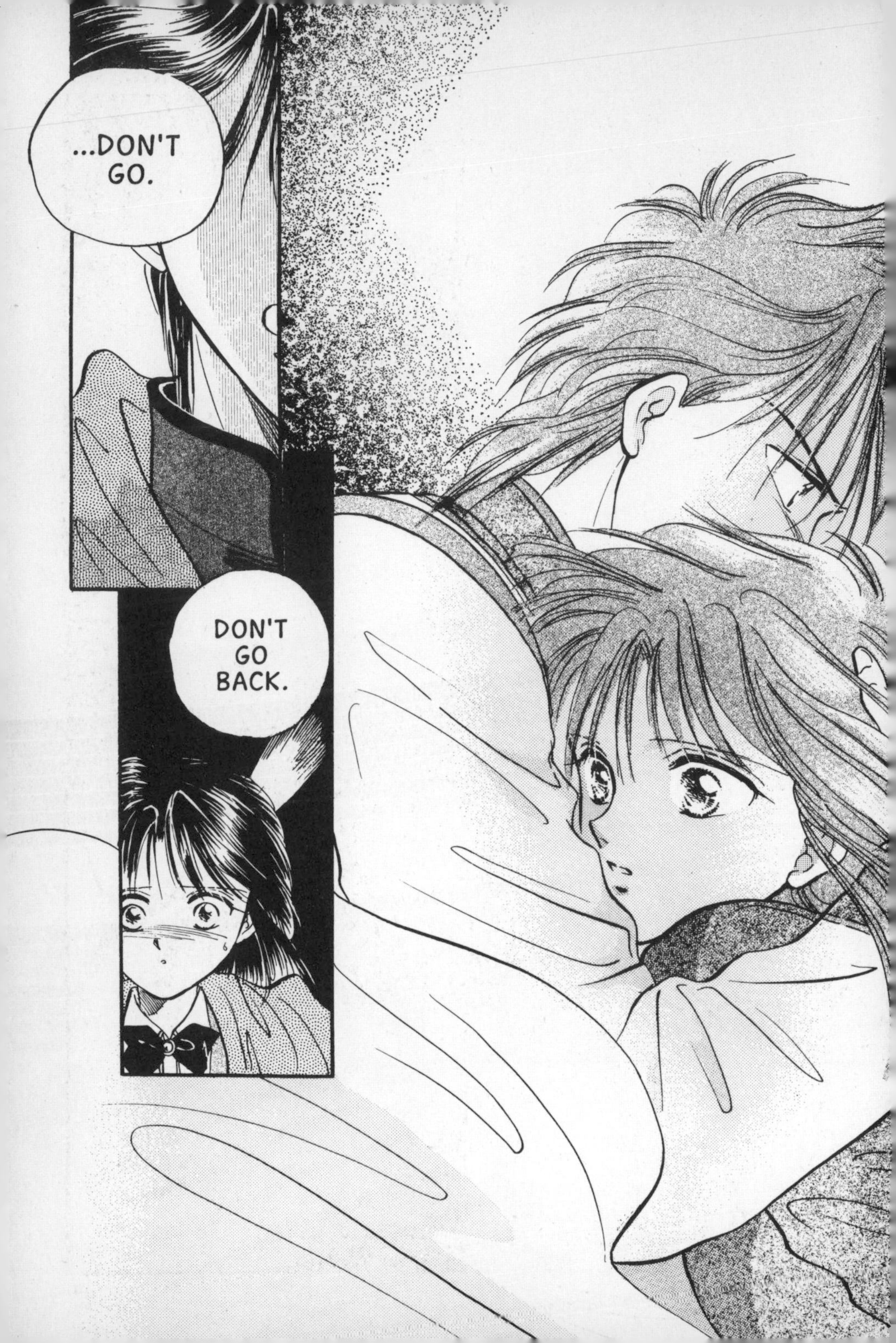
...DON'T GO.
DON'T GO BACK.

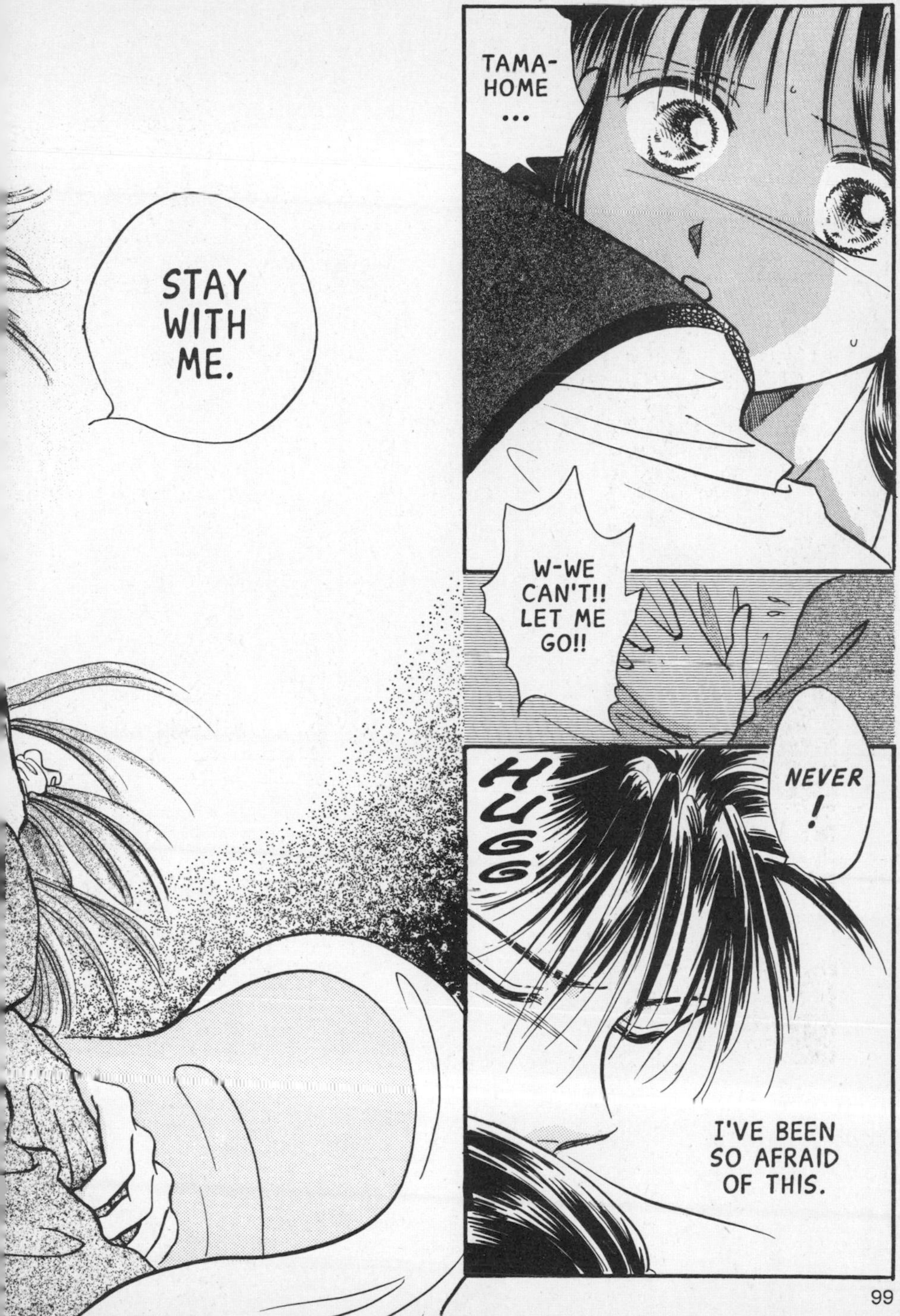
STAY WITH ME.
TAMA-HOME ...
W-WE CAN'T!! LET ME GO!!
HUGG
NEVER !
I'VE BEEN SO AFRAID OF THIS.

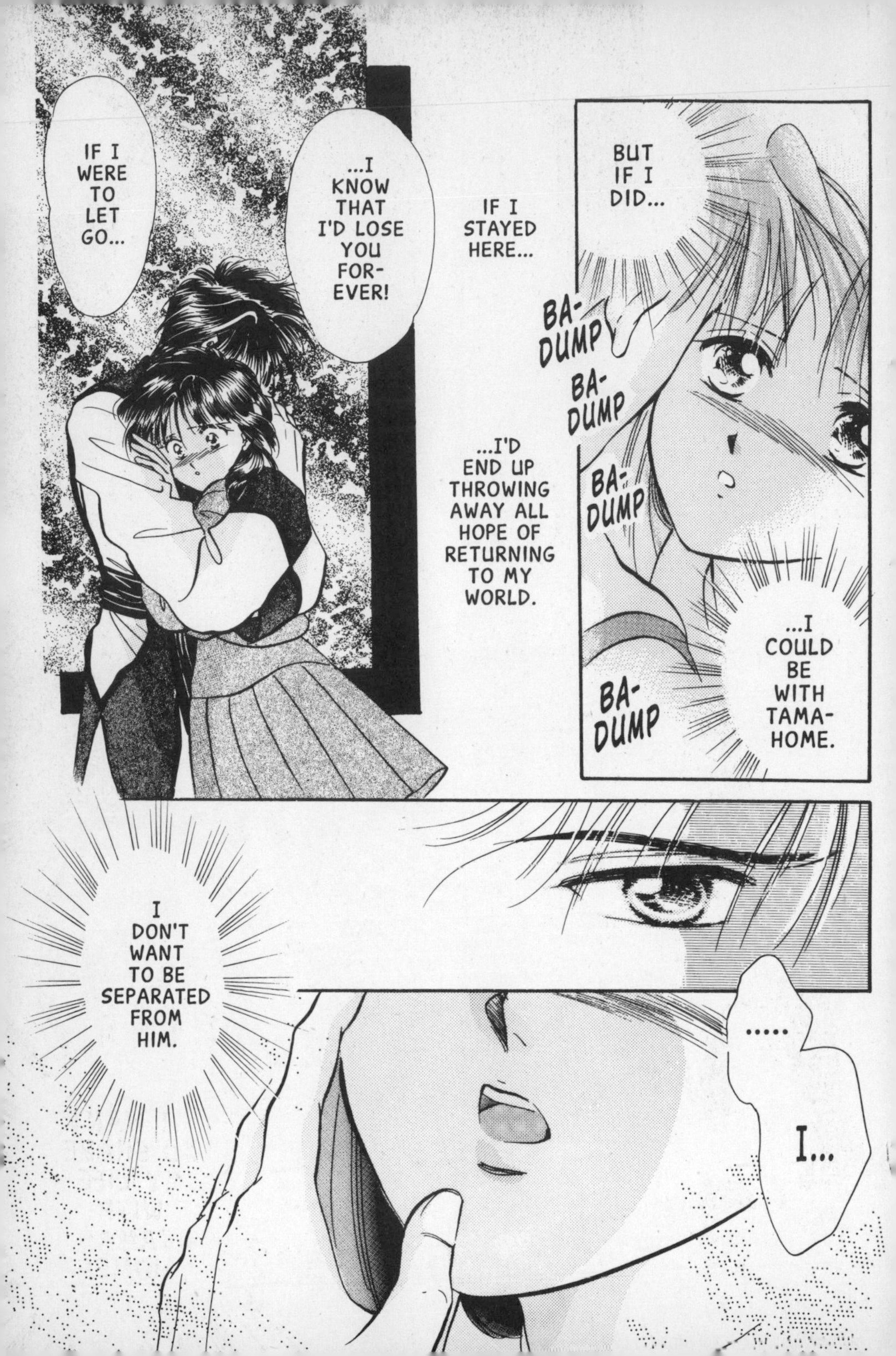
IF I WERE TO LET GO...
...I KNOW THAT I'D LOSE YOU FOR-EVER!
IF I STAYED HERE...
...I'D END UP THROWING AWAY ALL HOPE OF RETURNING TO MY WORLD.
BUT IF I DID...
BA-DUMP
BA-DUMP
BA-DUMP
BA-DUMP
...I COULD BE WITH TAMA-HOME.
I DON'T WANT TO BE SEPARATED FROM HIM.
.....
I...

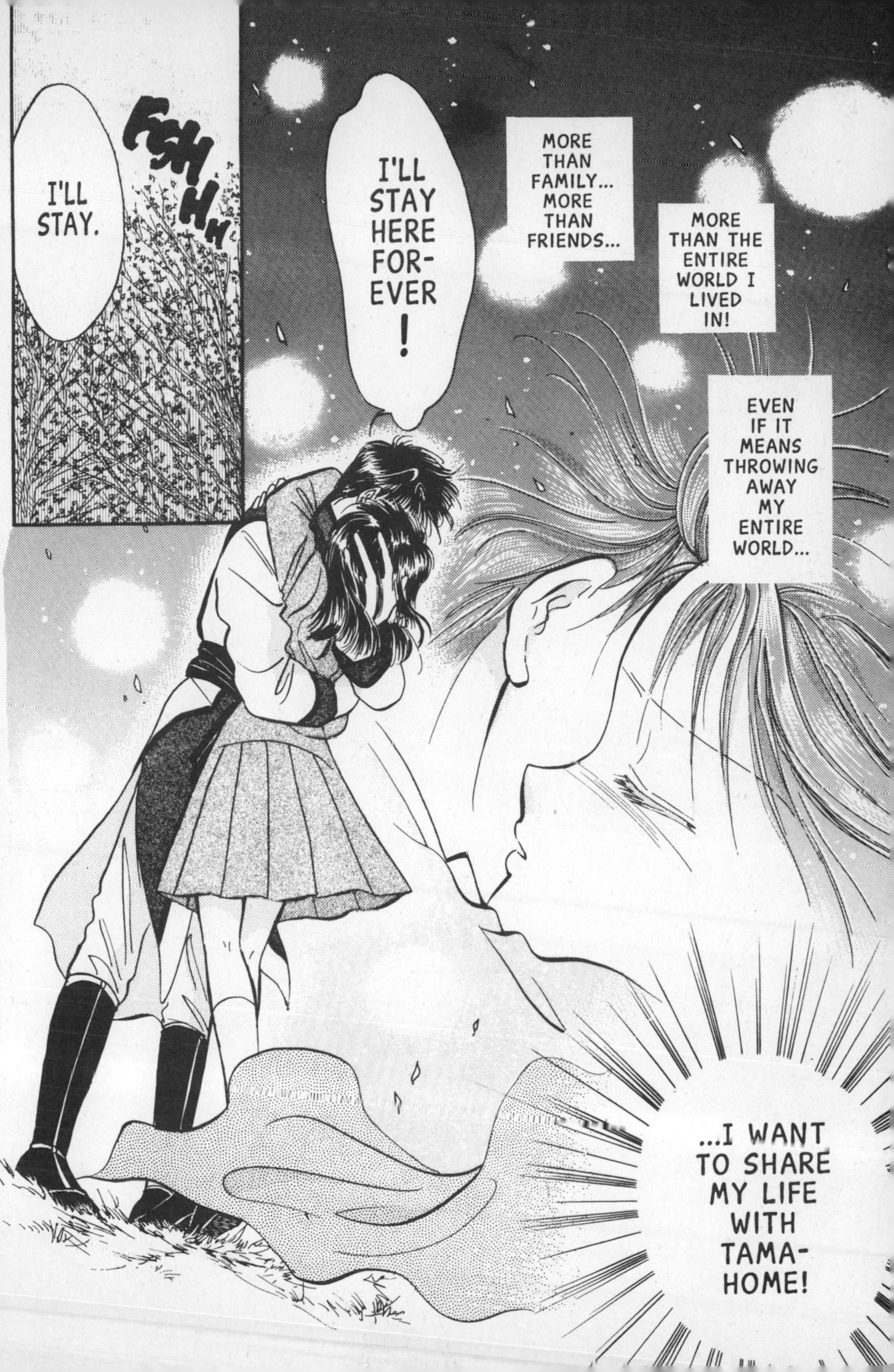
I'LL STAY.
FSHHM
I'LL STAY HERE FOR-EVER!
MORE THAN FAMILY... MORE THAN FRIENDS...
MORE THAN THE ENTIRE WORLD I LIVED IN!
EVEN IF IT MEANS THROWING AWAY MY ENTIRE WORLD...
...I WANT TO SHARE MY LIFE WITH TAMA-HOME!

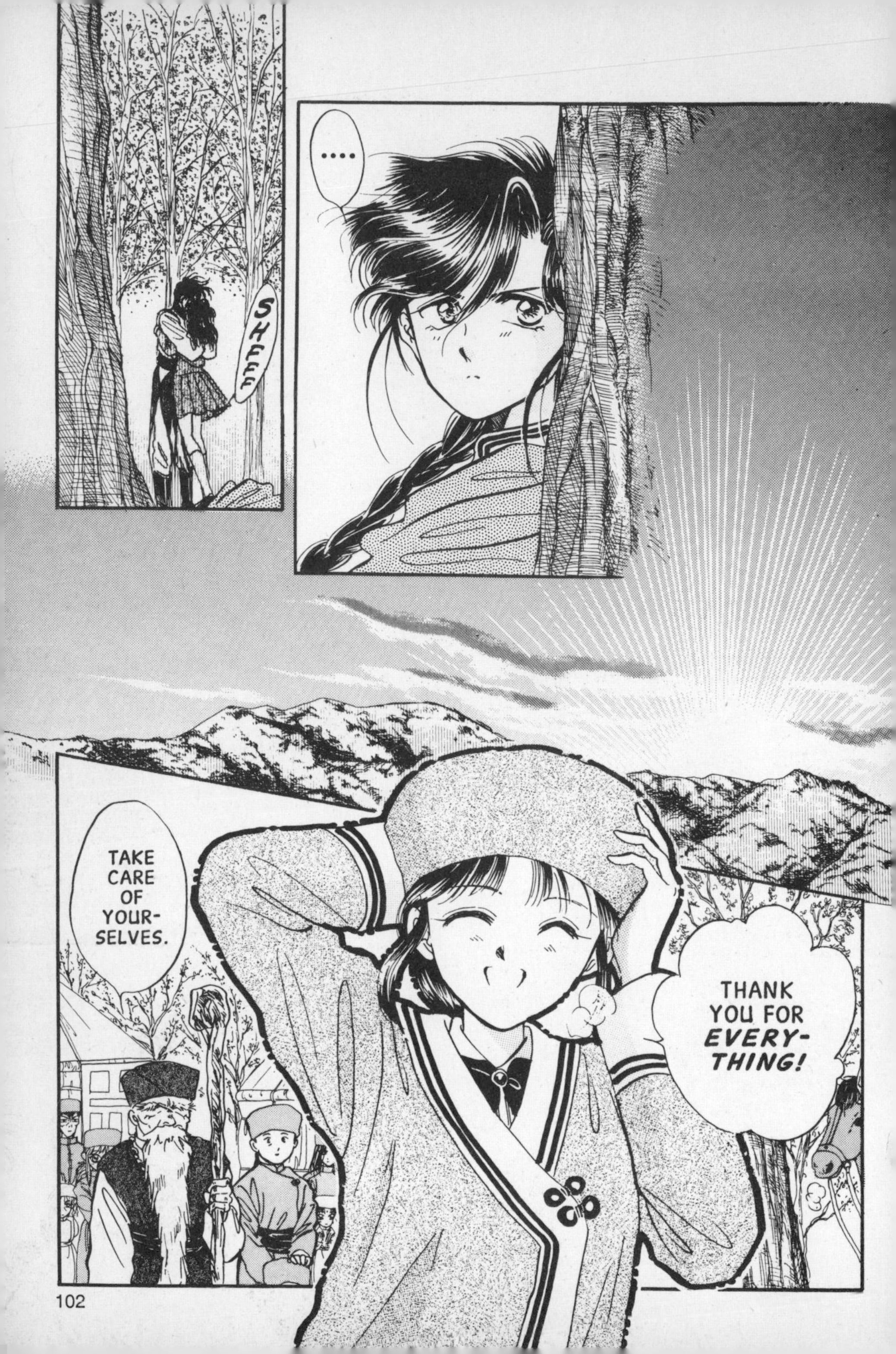
SHEEE
....
TAKE CARE OF YOURSELVES.
THANK YOU FOR EVERYTHING!

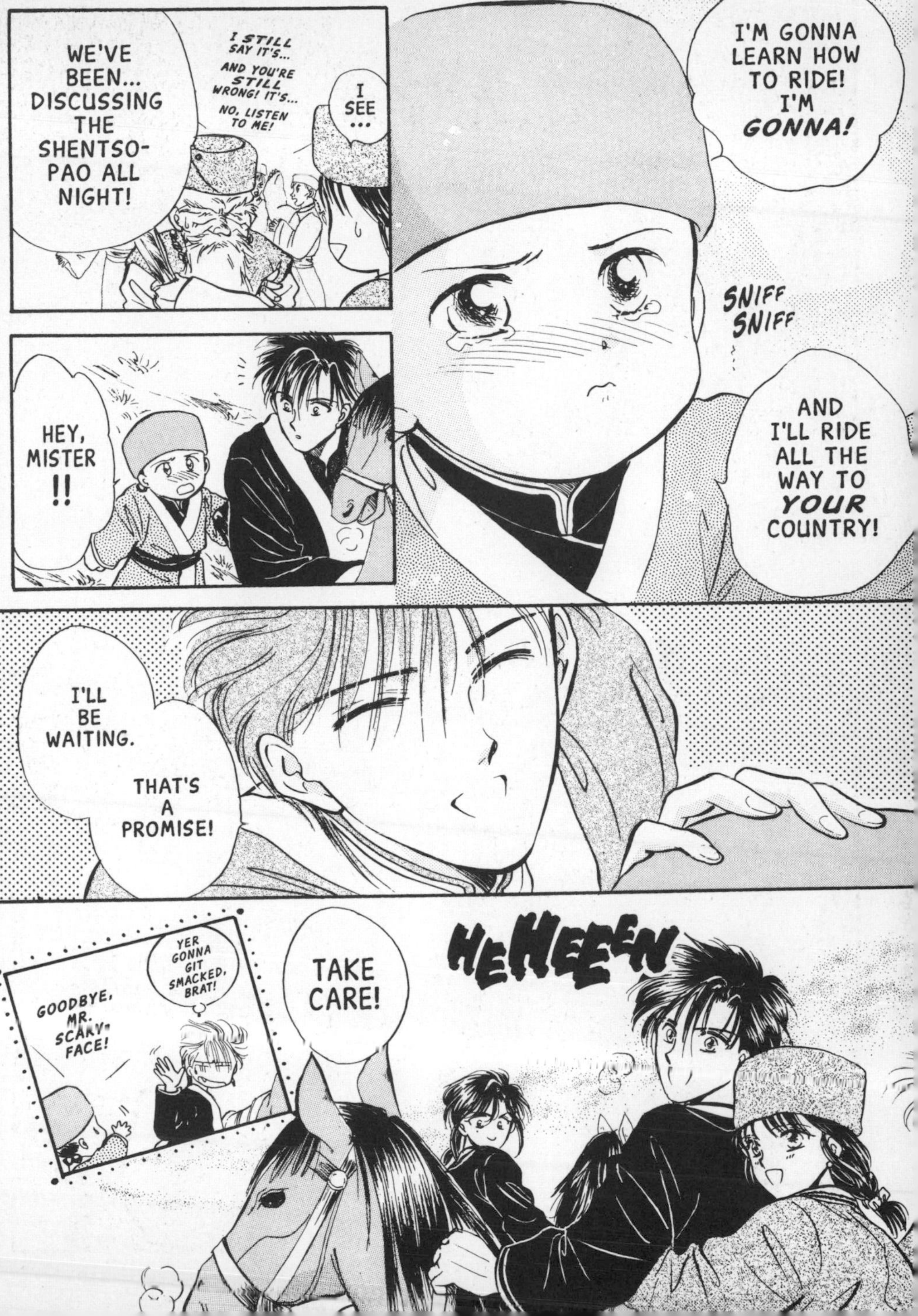
WE'VE BEEN... DISCUSSING THE SHENTSO-PAO ALL NIGHT!
I STILL SAY IT'S...
AND YOU'RE STILL WRONG! IT'S...
NO, LISTEN TO ME!
I SEE ...
HEY, MISTER !!
I'M GONNA LEARN HOW TO RIDE! I'M GONNA!
SNIFF SNIFF
AND I'LL RIDE ALL THE WAY TO YOUR COUNTRY!
I'LL BE WAITING.
THAT'S A PROMISE!
GOODBYE, MR. SCARY-FACE!
YER GONNA GIT SMACKED, BRAT!
TAKE CARE!
HEHEEEN

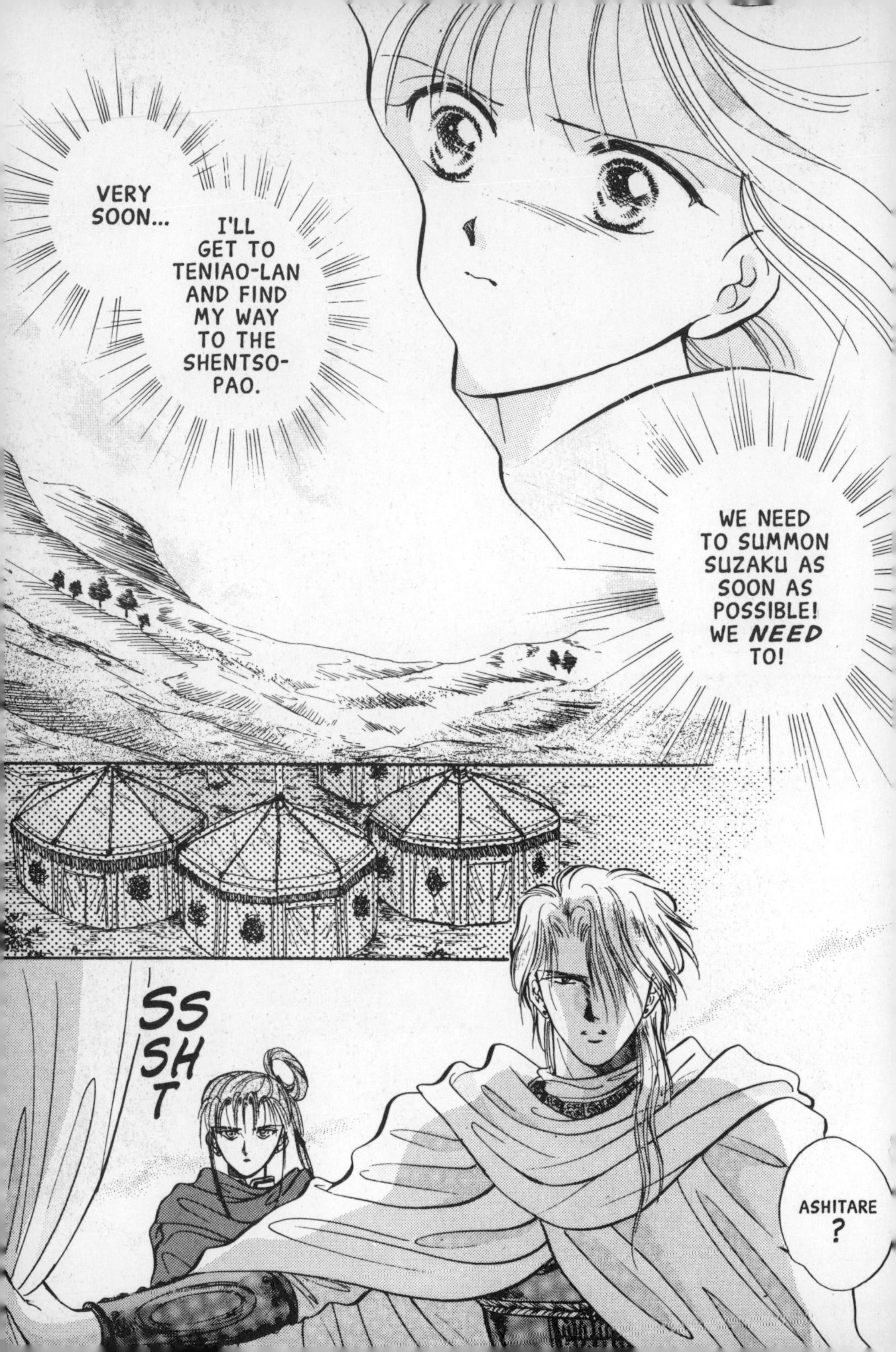
VERY SOON...
I'LL GET TO TENIAO-LAN AND FIND MY WAY TO THE SHENTSO-PAO.
WE NEED TO SUMMON SUZAKU AS SOON AS POSSIBLE! WE *NEED* TO!
SSSHT
ASHITARE ?

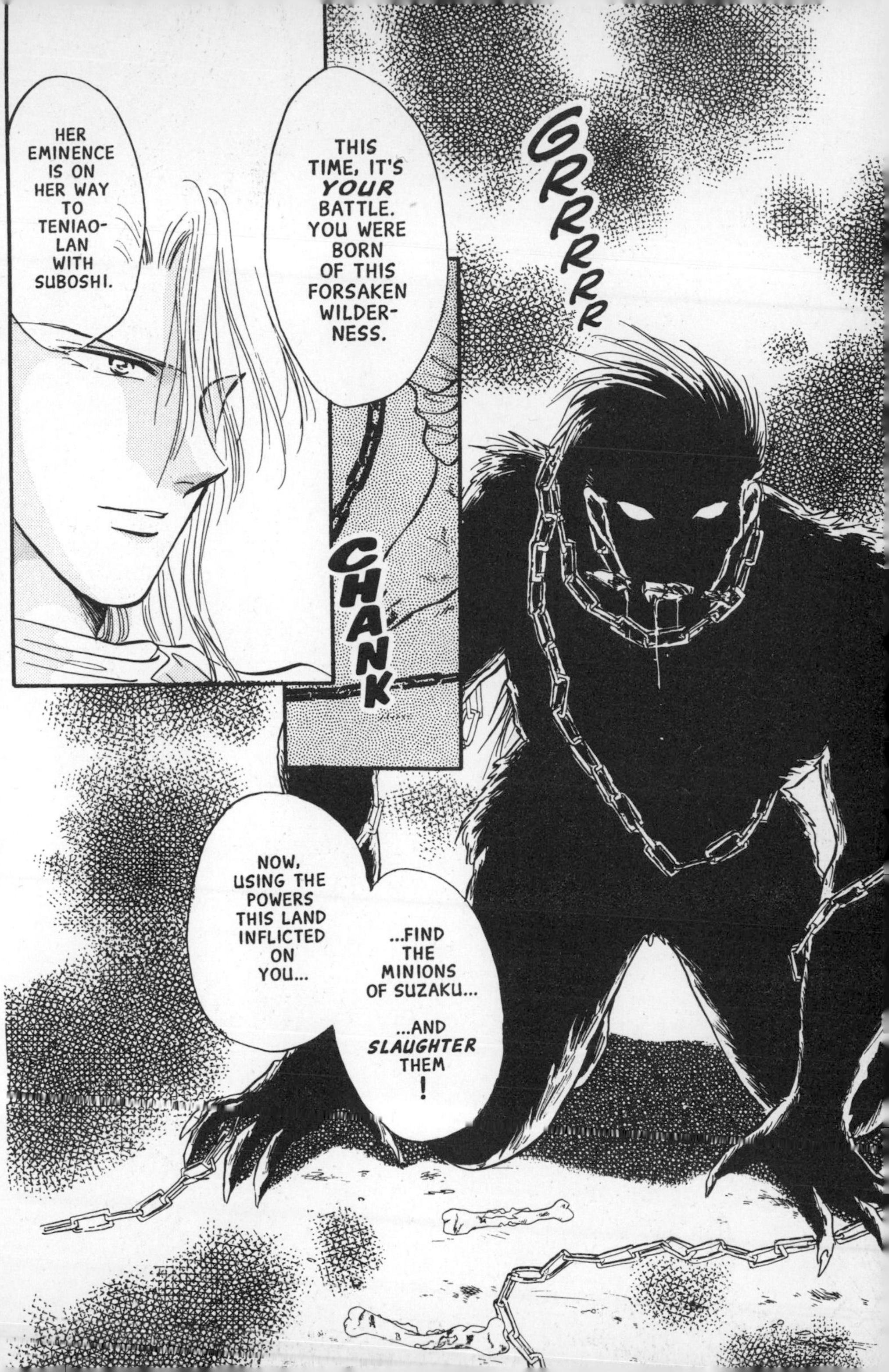
HER EMINENCE IS ON HER WAY TO TENIAO-LAN WITH SUBOSHI.
THIS TIME, IT'S *YOUR* BATTLE. YOU WERE BORN OF THIS FORSAKEN WILDER-NESS.
CHANK
GRRRRR
NOW, USING THE POWERS THIS LAND INFLICTED ON YOU...
...FIND THE MINIONS OF SUZAKU...
...AND *SLAUGHTER* THEM!

WONG   TAO   HUI

王   道   輝

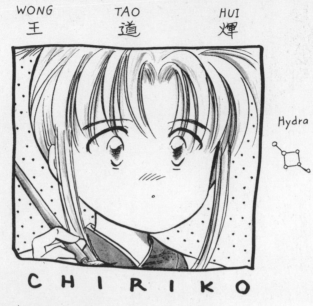

Hydra

C H I R I K O

- Birthplace: Zhuang-Yuan in western Hong-Nan
- Family: Elderly mother and older brother.
- Height: 4' 10"   • Bloodtype: A   • Age: 13
- Power: Heightened Intelligence
- Hobbies: Reading, Research

- He's a little small for his age, and that makes him look almost like a toddler. His incredible IQ gave him an interest in study from his earliest memories, and his major experiences in the world have mainly been through books and study.
On the other hand, his intelligence is tied to the appearance of the character on his foot, and when it disappears, he is even less mentally adept than a normal child his age. He also becomes something of a crybaby.
He's very sensitive about his height and peculiar intelligence, and that's what made him strive to grow up to be a "man of strength."
He's the nice, quiet, good-student type of kid.

Oh, in volume 7 on page 168, I said one of the words that had digital effects was "kiseki no hito" ("miraculous one"), but when I listened closer, it turned out to be "yume" ("dream").

CHAPTER FORTY-SIX
MAELSTROM OF FEAR

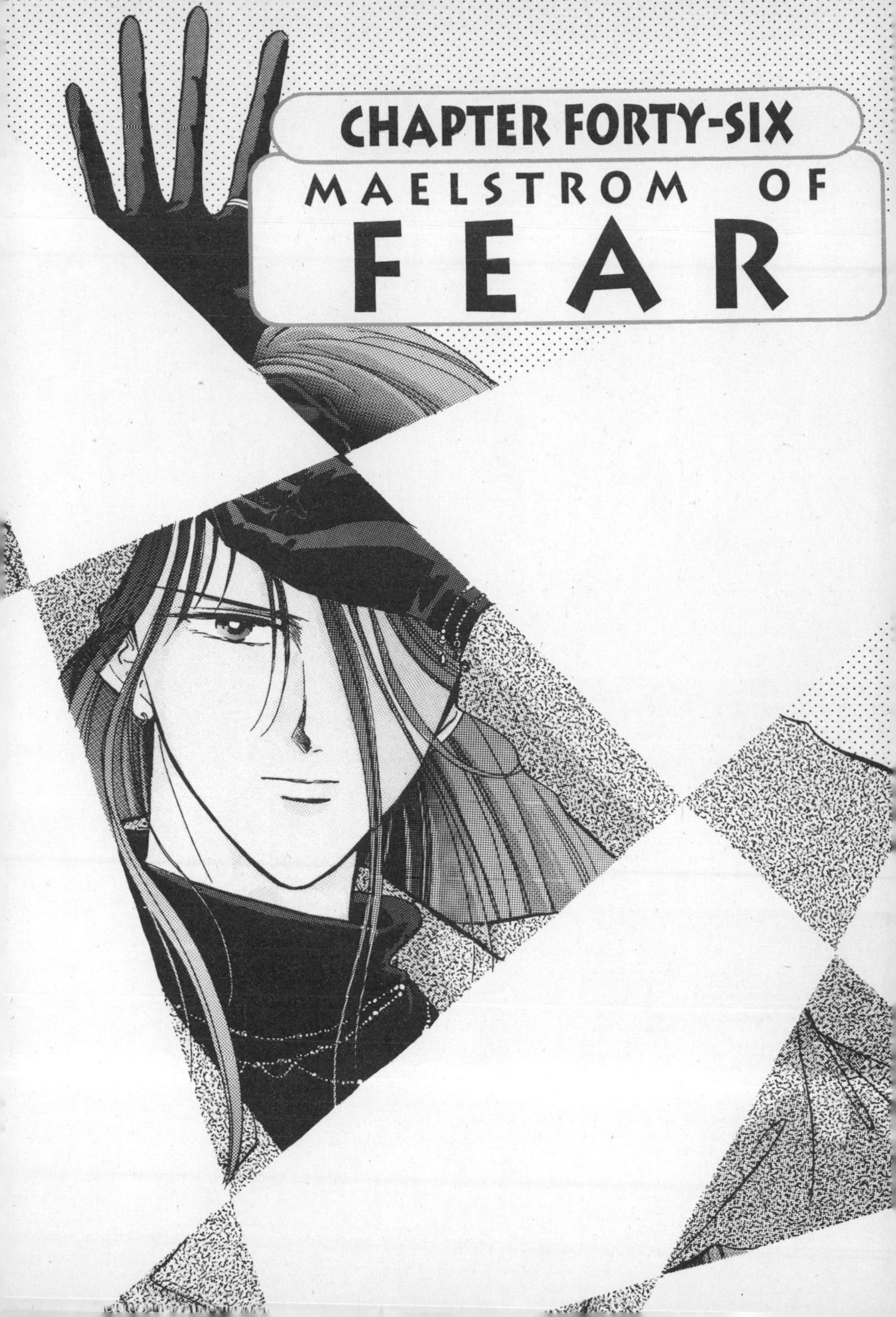

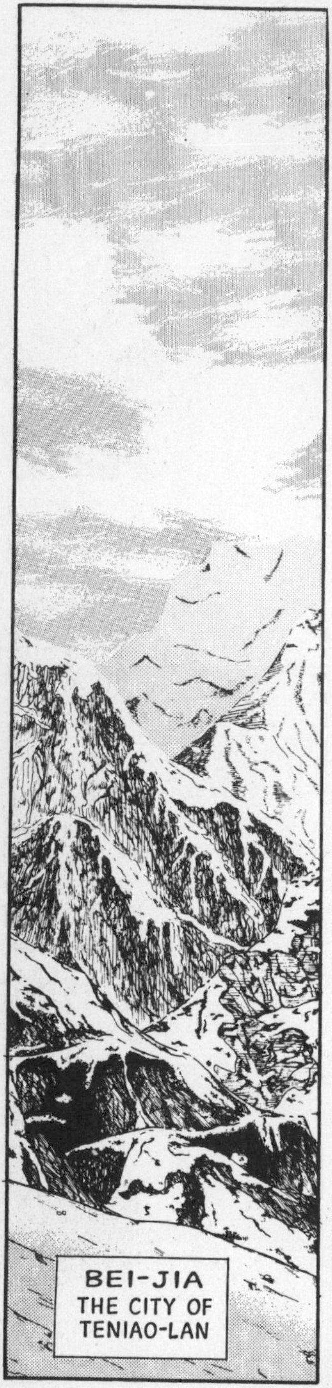
BEI-JIA
THE CITY OF TENIAO-LAN

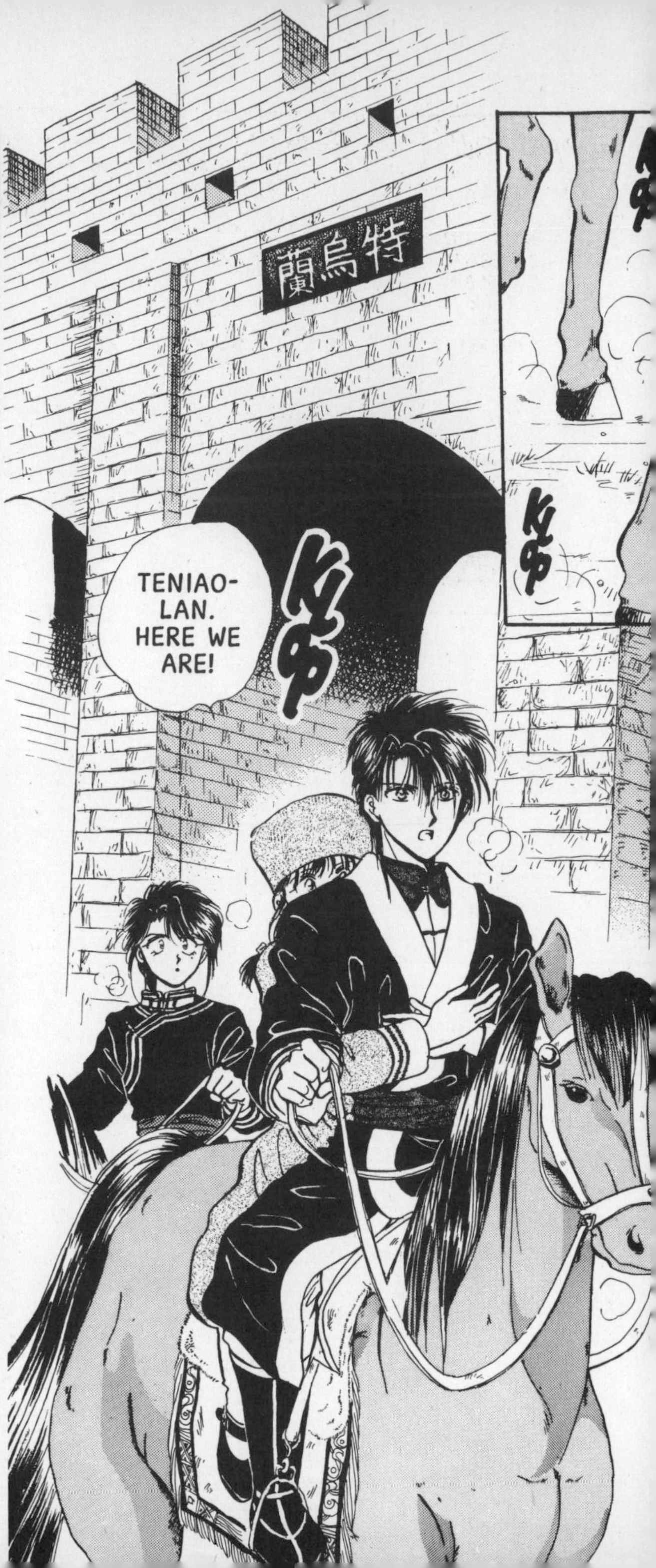
特烏蘭
TENIAO-LAN. HERE WE ARE!

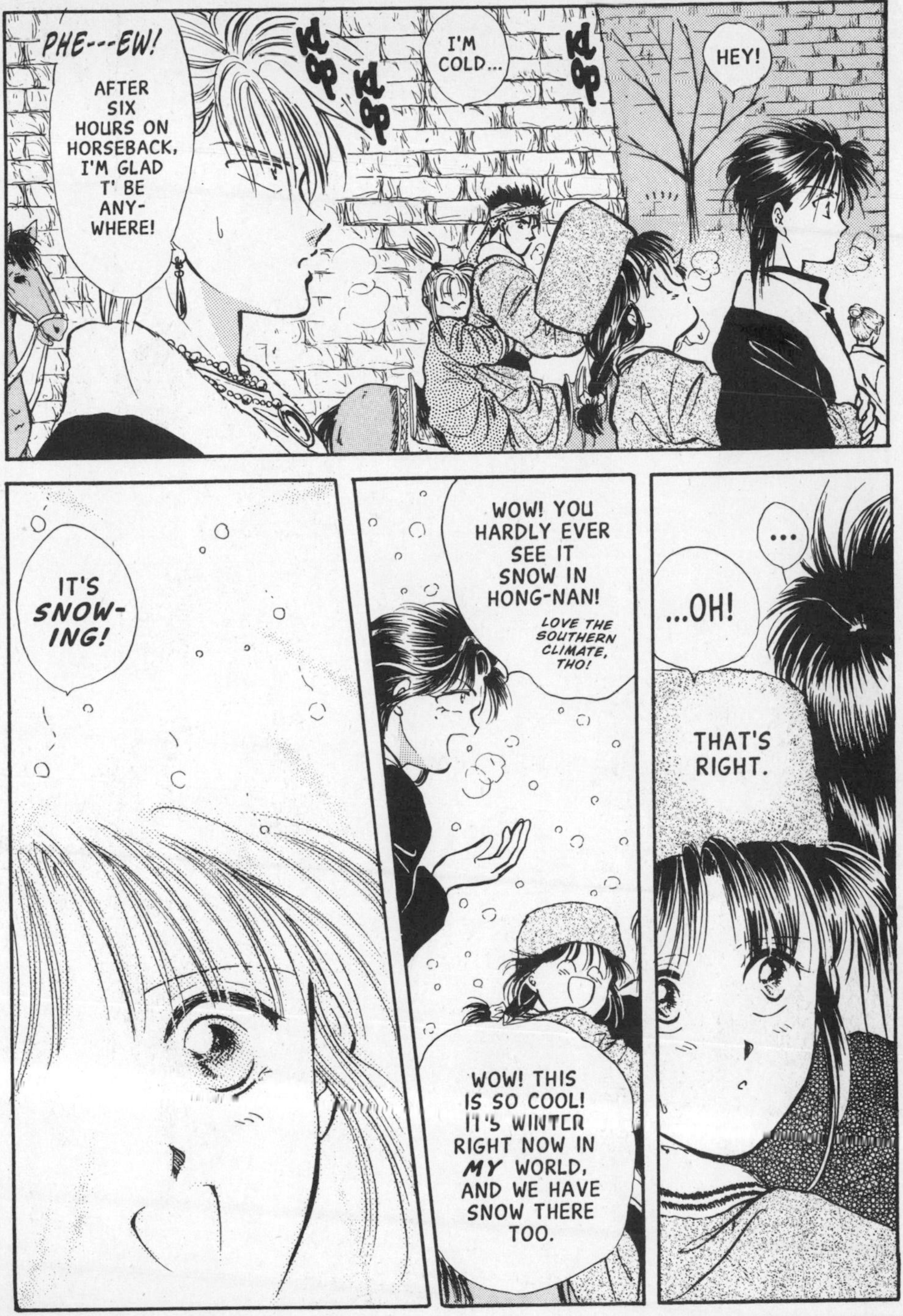
PHE---EW!
AFTER SIX HOURS ON HORSEBACK, I'M GLAD T' BE ANYWHERE!
KLOP
KLOP
I'M COLD...
KLOP
HEY!
IT'S SNOWING!
WOW! YOU HARDLY EVER SEE IT SNOW IN HONG-NAN!
LOVE THE SOUTHERN CLIMATE, THO!
WOW! THIS IS SO COOL! IT'S WINTER RIGHT NOW IN MY WORLD, AND WE HAVE SNOW THERE TOO.
...
...OH!
THAT'S RIGHT.

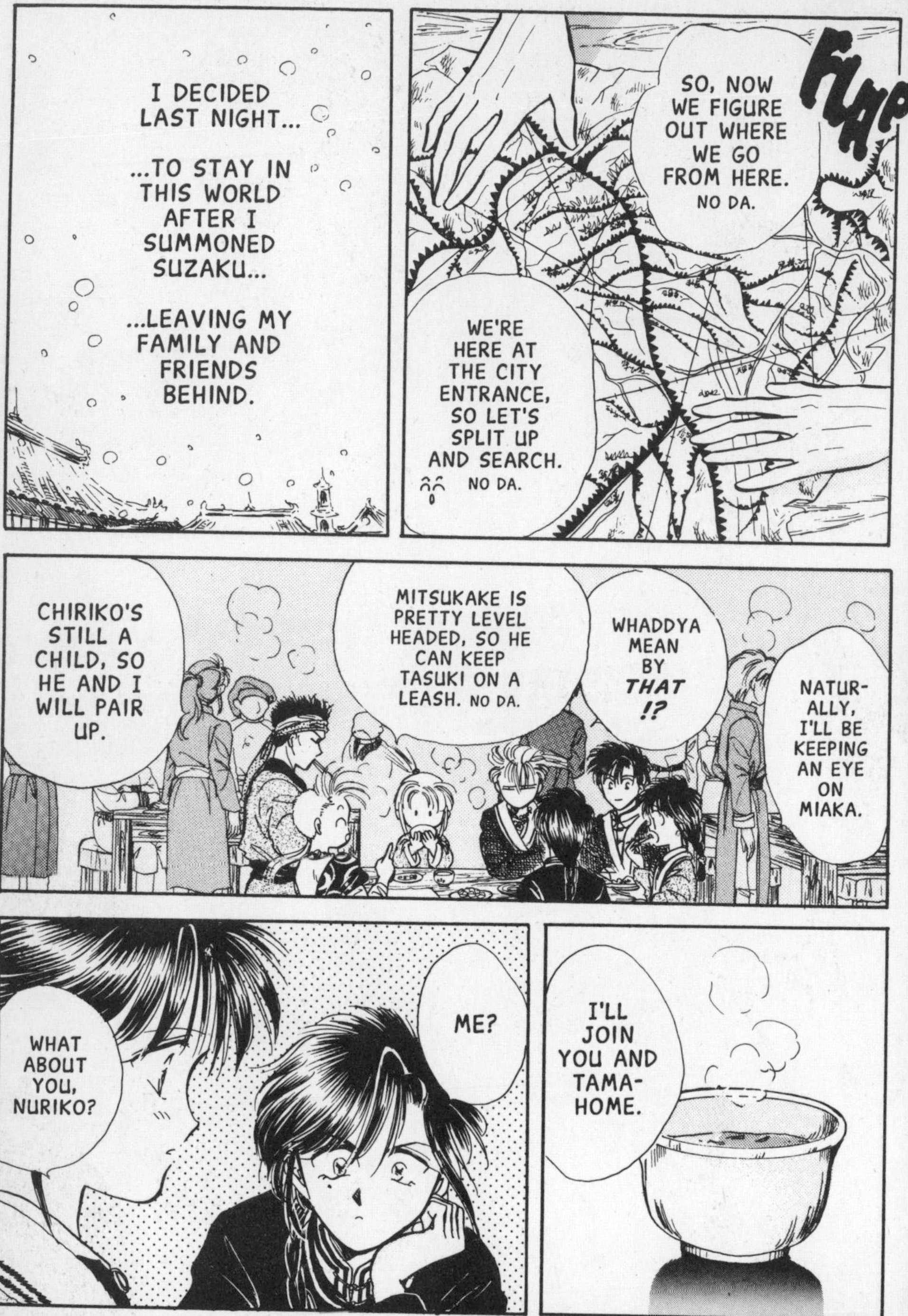
I DECIDED LAST NIGHT...
...TO STAY IN THIS WORLD AFTER I SUMMONED SUZAKU...
...LEAVING MY FAMILY AND FRIENDS BEHIND.
SO, NOW WE FIGURE OUT WHERE WE GO FROM HERE. NO DA.
FLAP
WE'RE HERE AT THE CITY ENTRANCE, SO LET'S SPLIT UP AND SEARCH. NO DA.
CHIRIKO'S STILL A CHILD, SO HE AND I WILL PAIR UP.
MITSUKAKE IS PRETTY LEVEL HEADED, SO HE CAN KEEP TASUKI ON A LEASH. NO DA.
WHADDYA MEAN BY *THAT !?*
NATURALLY, I'LL BE KEEPING AN EYE ON MIAKA.
WHAT ABOUT YOU, NURIKO?
ME?
I'LL JOIN YOU AND TAMAHOME.

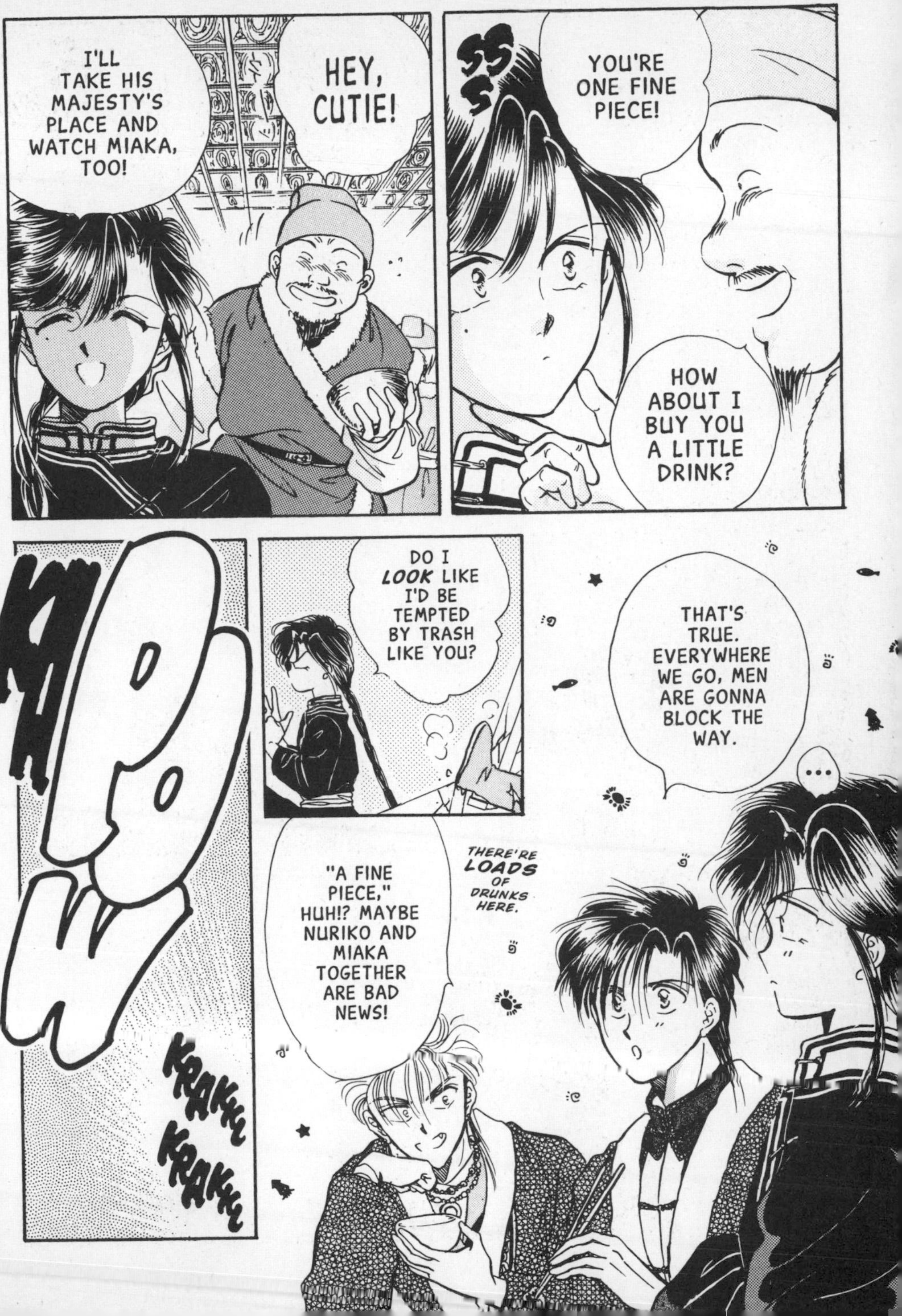
I'LL TAKE HIS MAJESTY'S PLACE AND WATCH MIAKA, TOO!
HEY, CUTIE!
YOU'RE ONE FINE PIECE!
HOW ABOUT I BUY YOU A LITTLE DRINK?
KRAKKK
KRAKKK
DO I *LOOK* LIKE I'D BE TEMPTED BY TRASH LIKE YOU?
THAT'S TRUE. EVERYWHERE WE GO, MEN ARE GONNA BLOCK THE WAY.
...
"A FINE PIECE," HUH!? MAYBE NURIKO AND MIAKA TOGETHER ARE BAD NEWS!
THERE'RE LOADS OF DRUNKS HERE.

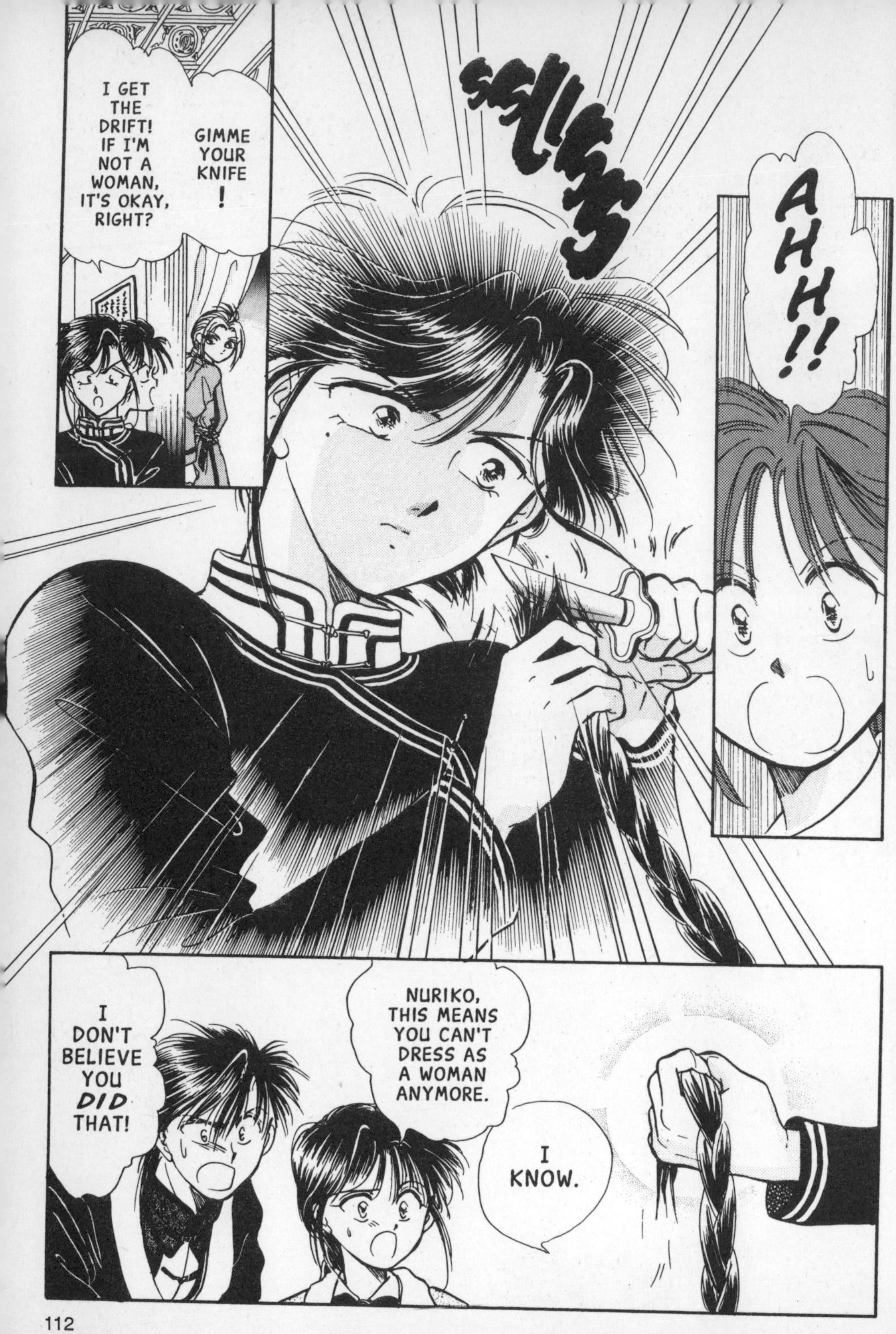
I GET THE DRIFT! IF I'M NOT A WOMAN, IT'S OKAY, RIGHT?
GIMME YOUR KNIFE!
AHH!!
I DON'T BELIEVE YOU *DID* THAT!
NURIKO, THIS MEANS YOU CAN'T DRESS AS A WOMAN ANYMORE.
I KNOW.

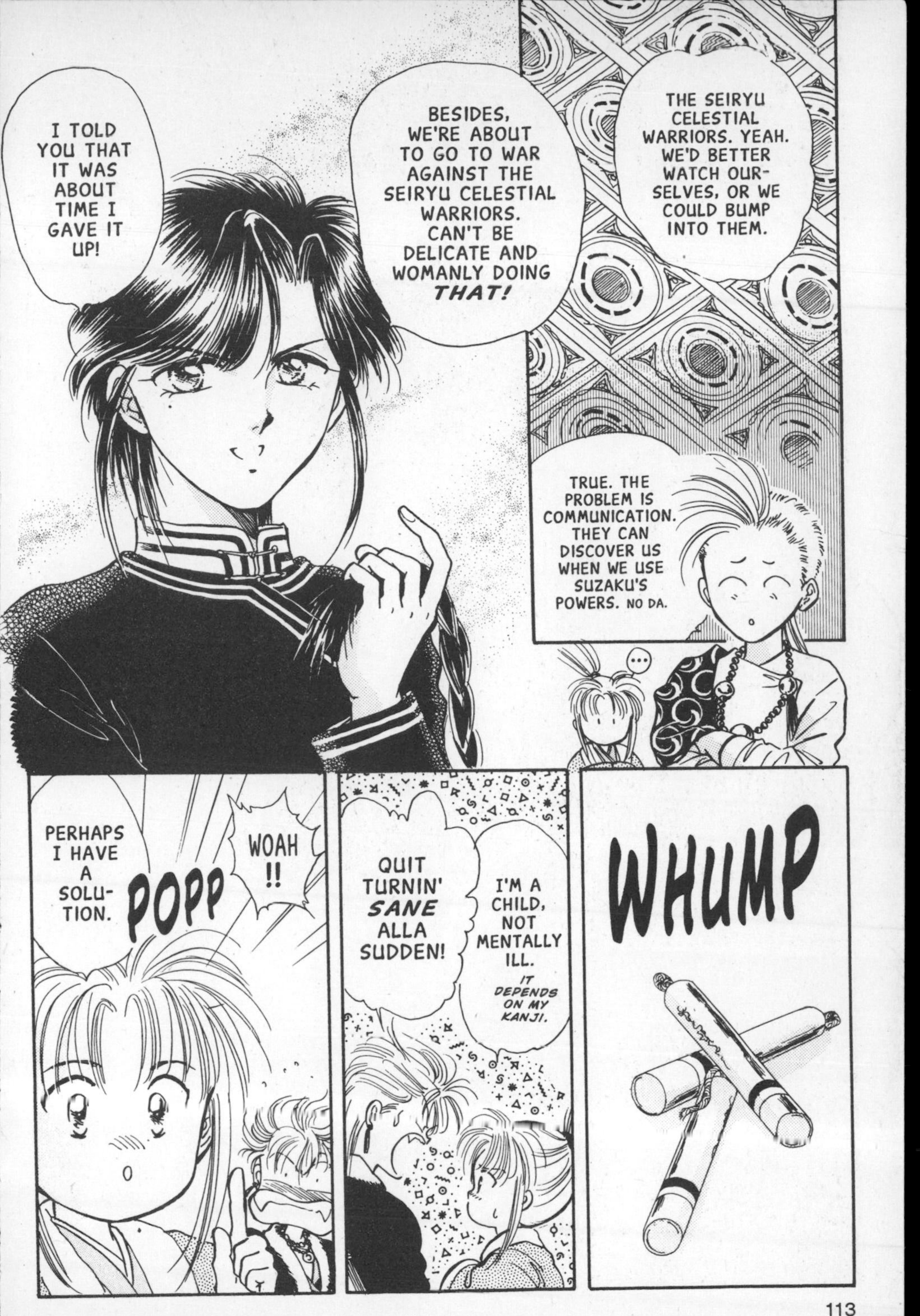

I TOLD YOU THAT IT WAS ABOUT TIME I GAVE IT UP!
BESIDES, WE'RE ABOUT TO GO TO WAR AGAINST THE SEIRYU CELESTIAL WARRIORS. CAN'T BE DELICATE AND WOMANLY DOING *THAT!*
THE SEIRYU CELESTIAL WARRIORS. YEAH. WE'D BETTER WATCH OUR-SELVES, OR WE COULD BUMP INTO THEM.
TRUE. THE PROBLEM IS COMMUNICATION. THEY CAN DISCOVER US WHEN WE USE SUZAKU'S POWERS. NO DA.
...
PERHAPS I HAVE A SOLU-TION.
POPP
WOAH !!
QUIT TURNIN' *SANE* ALLA SUDDEN!
I'M A CHILD, NOT MENTALLY ILL.
IT DEPENDS ON MY KANJI.
WHUMP

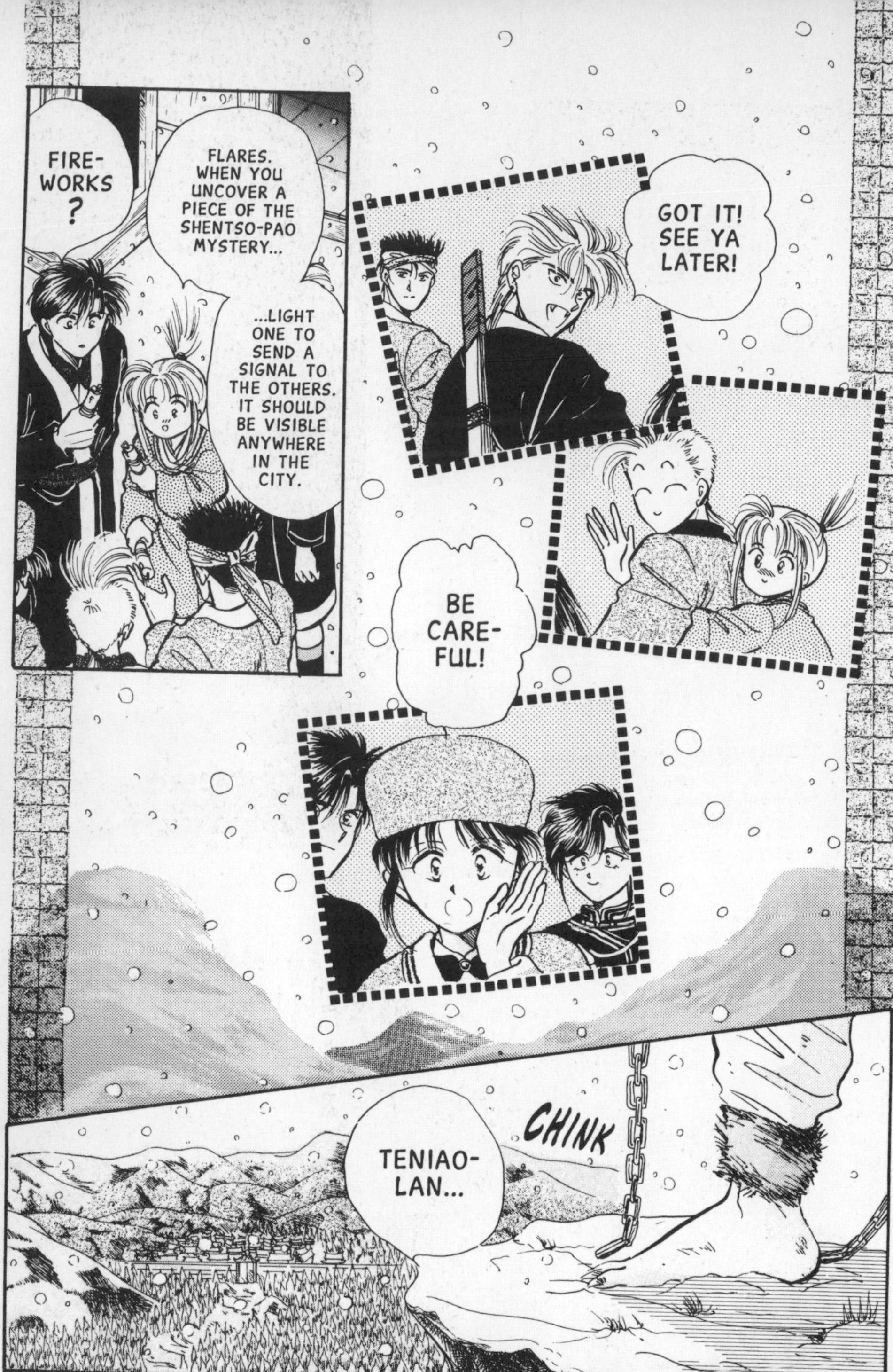
FIRE-WORKS ?
FLARES. WHEN YOU UNCOVER A PIECE OF THE SHENTSO-PAO MYSTERY...
...LIGHT ONE TO SEND A SIGNAL TO THE OTHERS. IT SHOULD BE VISIBLE ANYWHERE IN THE CITY.
GOT IT! SEE YA LATER!
BE CARE-FUL!
CHINK
TENIAO-LAN...

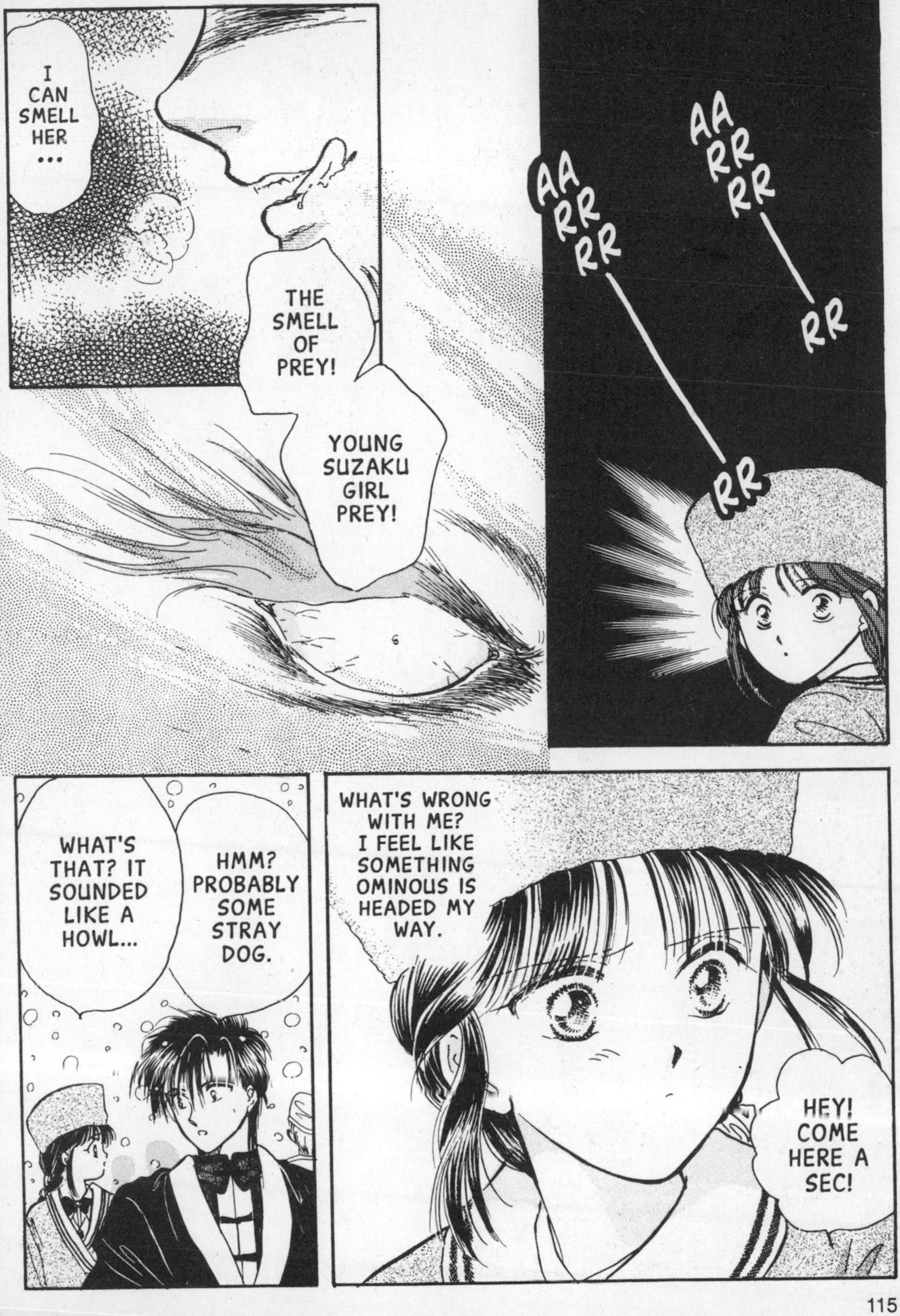

I CAN SMELL HER...
THE SMELL OF PREY!
YOUNG SUZAKU GIRL PREY!
AARRRR—RR
AARRRR—RR
WHAT'S THAT? IT SOUNDED LIKE A HOWL...
HMM? PROBABLY SOME STRAY DOG.
WHAT'S WRONG WITH ME? I FEEL LIKE SOMETHING OMINOUS IS HEADED MY WAY.
HEY! COME HERE A SEC!

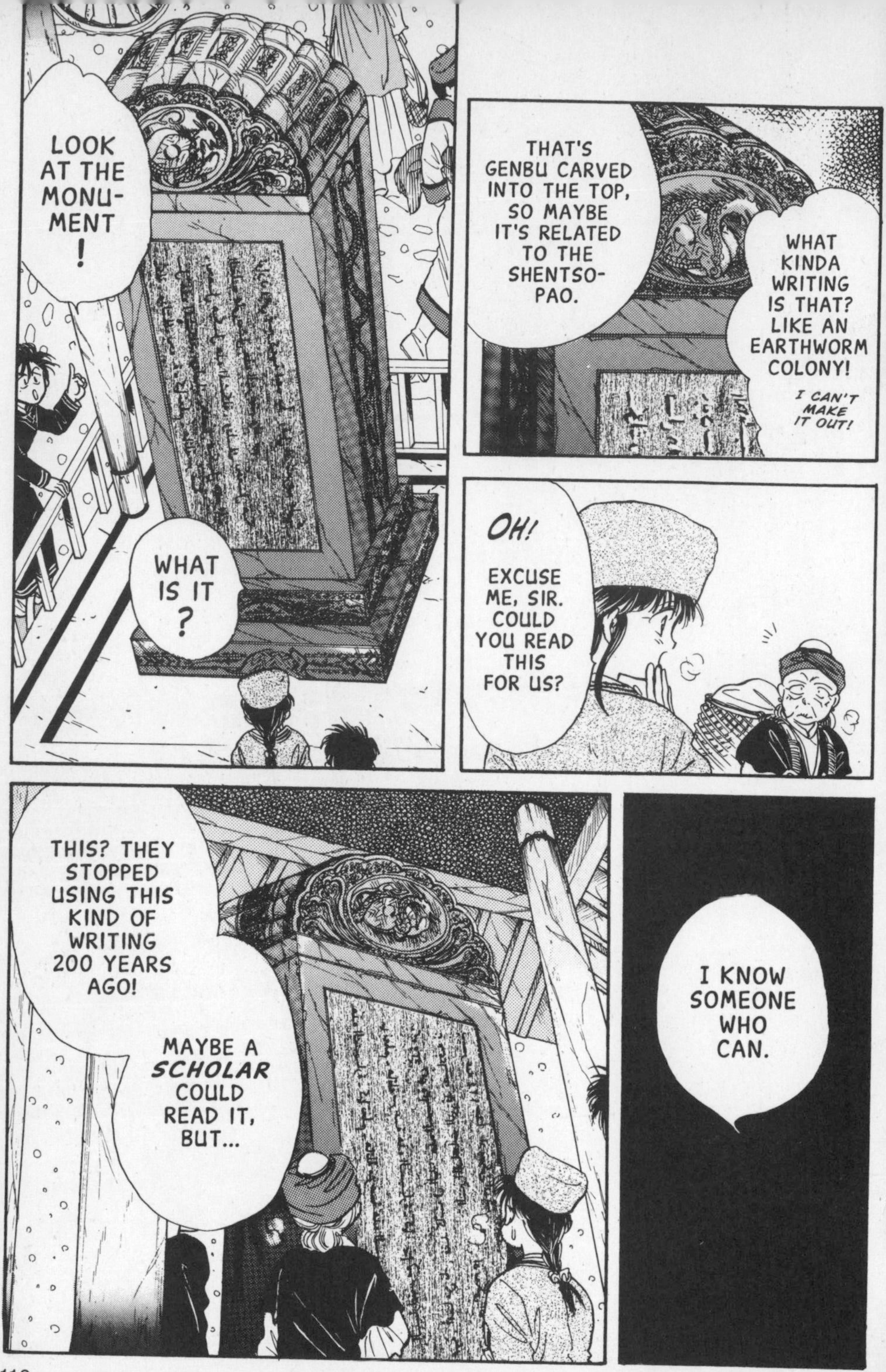
LOOK AT THE MONUMENT!
WHAT IS IT?
THAT'S GENBU CARVED INTO THE TOP, SO MAYBE IT'S RELATED TO THE SHENTSO-PAO.
WHAT KINDA WRITING IS THAT? LIKE AN EARTHWORM COLONY!
I CAN'T MAKE IT OUT!
OH!
EXCUSE ME, SIR. COULD YOU READ THIS FOR US?
THIS? THEY STOPPED USING THIS KIND OF WRITING 200 YEARS AGO!
MAYBE A SCHOLAR COULD READ IT, BUT...
I KNOW SOMEONE WHO CAN.

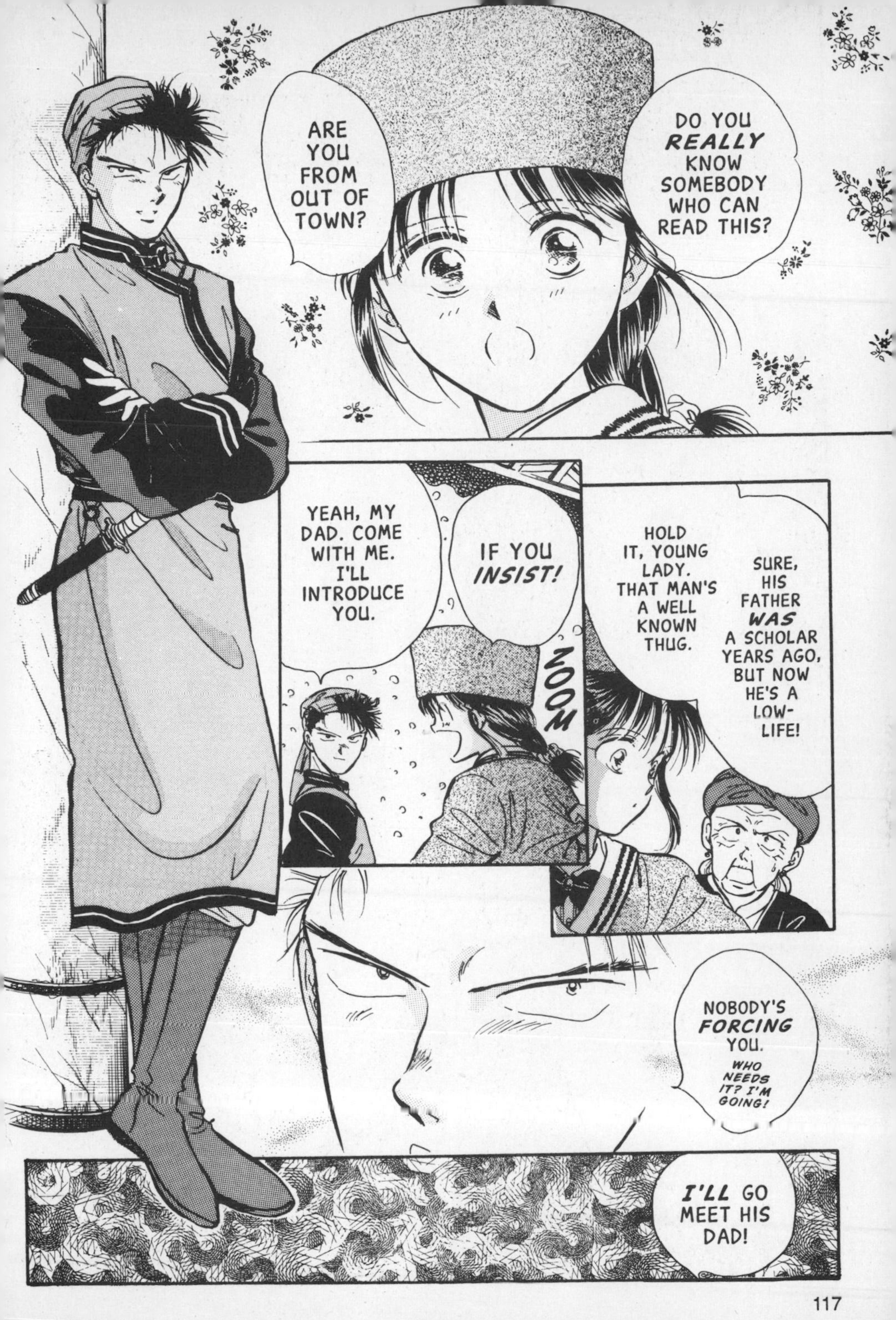
ARE YOU FROM OUT OF TOWN?
DO YOU REALLY KNOW SOMEBODY WHO CAN READ THIS?
YEAH, MY DAD. COME WITH ME. I'LL INTRODUCE YOU.
IF YOU INSIST!
ZOOM
HOLD IT, YOUNG LADY. THAT MAN'S A WELL KNOWN THUG.
SURE, HIS FATHER WAS A SCHOLAR YEARS AGO, BUT NOW HE'S A LOW-LIFE!
NOBODY'S FORCING YOU.
WHO NEEDS IT? I'M GOING!
I'LL GO MEET HIS DAD!

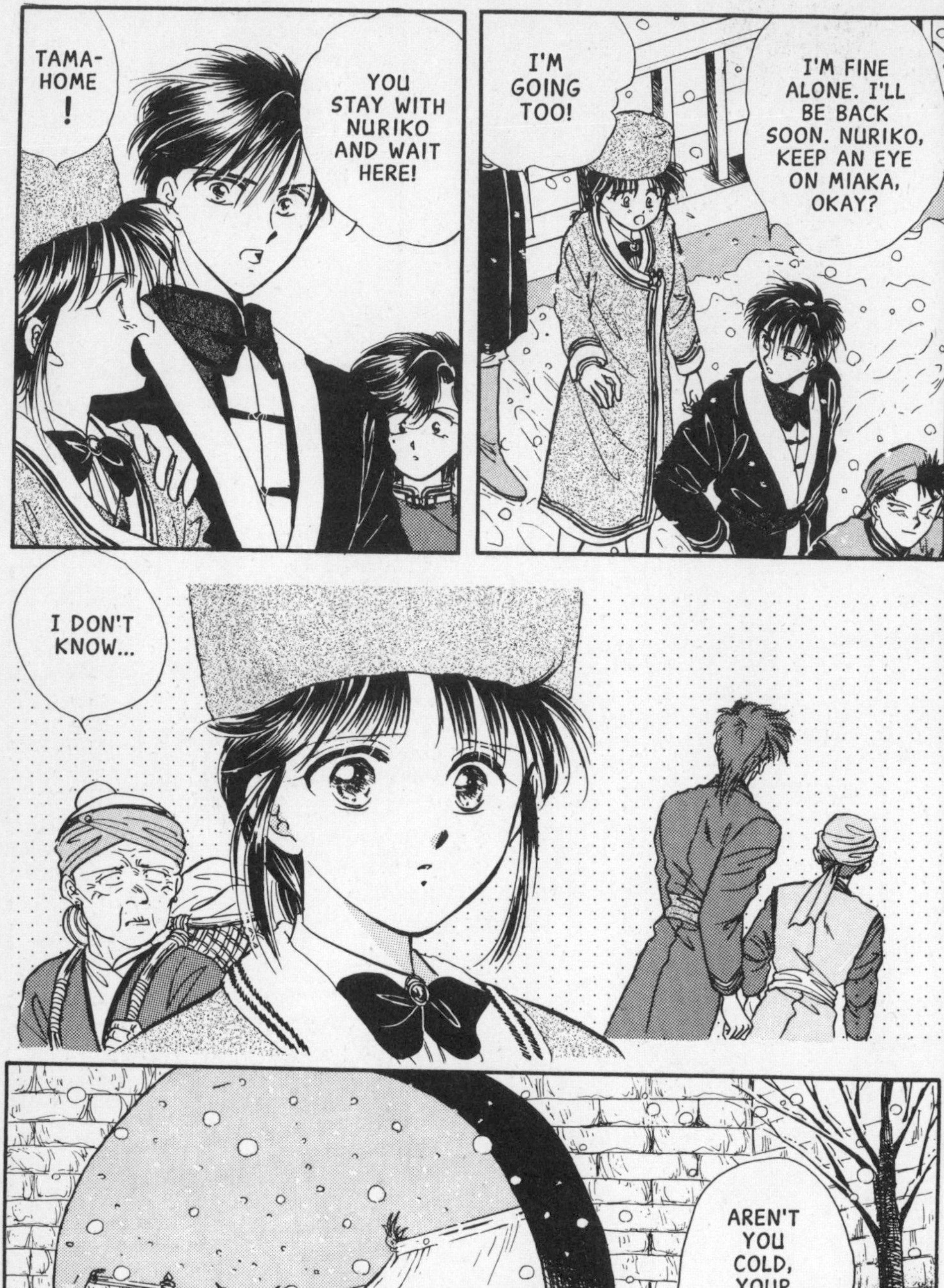
TAMA-HOME!
YOU STAY WITH NURIKO AND WAIT HERE!
I'M GOING TOO!
I'M FINE ALONE. I'LL BE BACK SOON. NURIKO, KEEP AN EYE ON MIAKA, OKAY?
I DON'T KNOW...
AREN'T YOU COLD, YOUR EMINENCE?

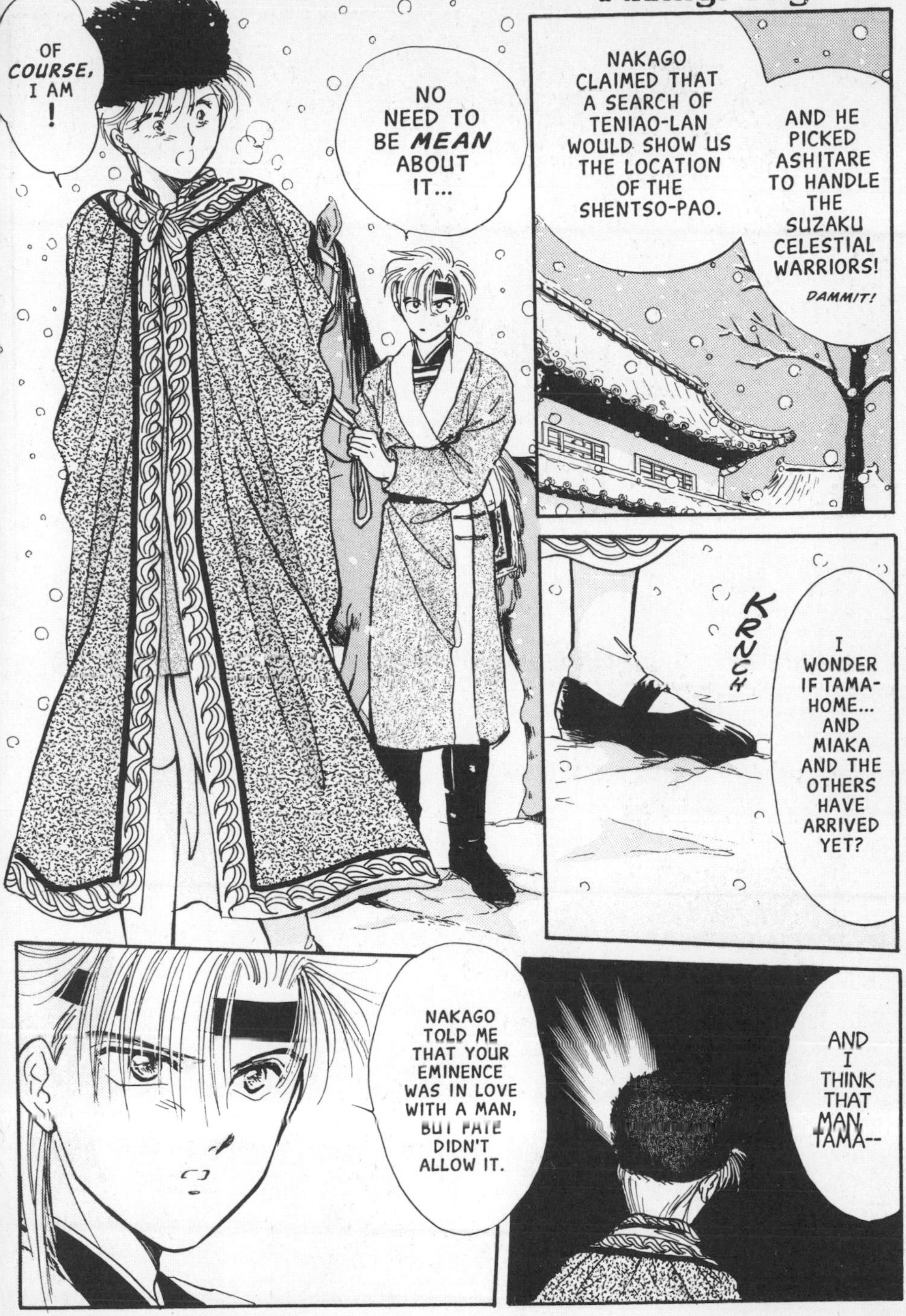
OF COURSE, I AM!
NO NEED TO BE MEAN ABOUT IT...
NAKAGO CLAIMED THAT A SEARCH OF TENIAO-LAN WOULD SHOW US THE LOCATION OF THE SHENTSO-PAO.
AND HE PICKED ASHITARE TO HANDLE THE SUZAKU CELESTIAL WARRIORS!
DAMMIT!
KRUNCH
I WONDER IF TAMA-HOME... AND MIAKA AND THE OTHERS HAVE ARRIVED YET?
NAKAGO TOLD ME THAT YOUR EMINENCE WAS IN LOVE WITH A MAN, BUT FATE DIDN'T ALLOW IT.
AND I THINK THAT MAN, TAMA--

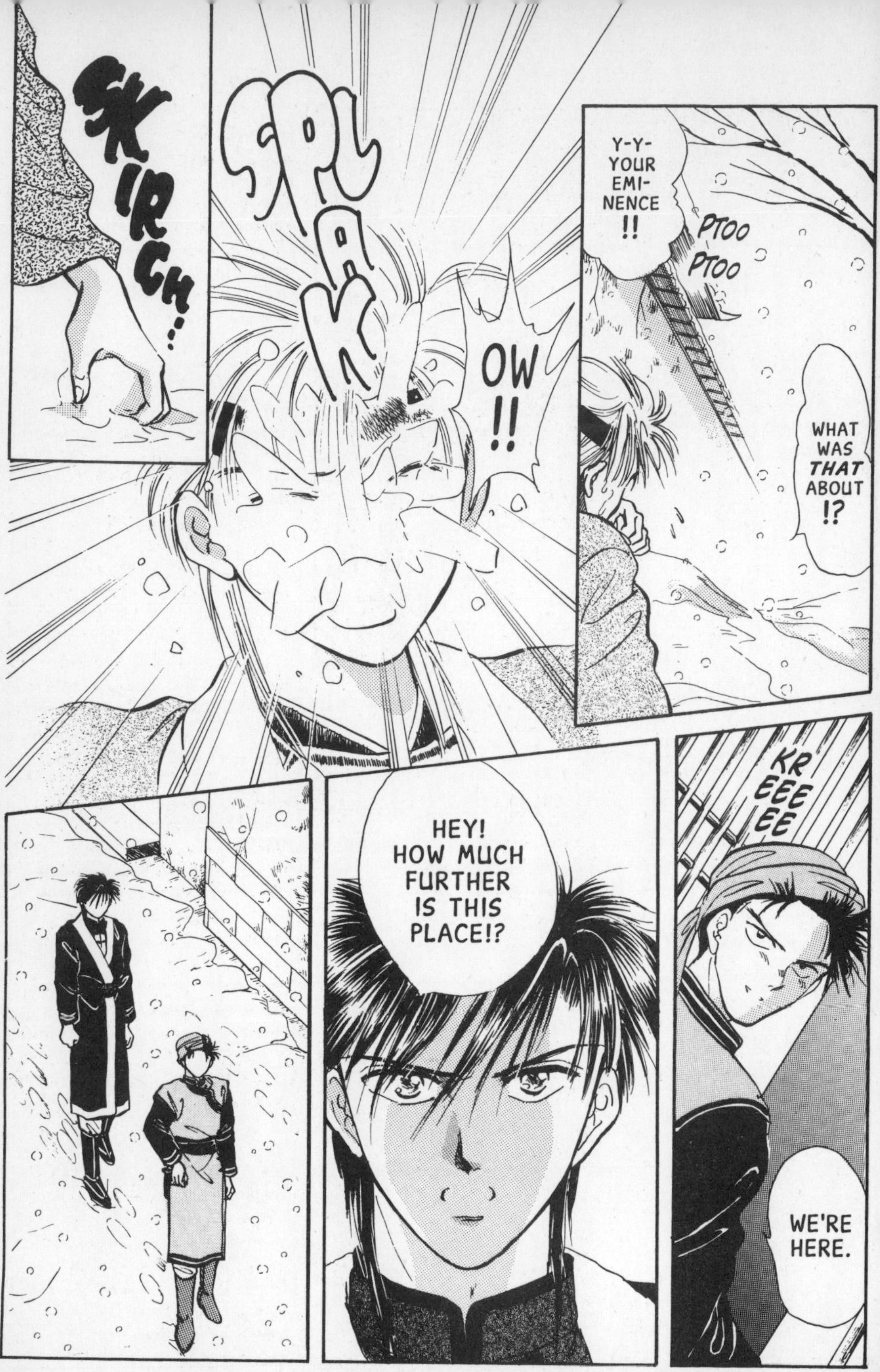
SKIRCH..
SPLAK
OW!!
Y-Y-YOUR EMINENCE!!
PTOO PTOO
WHAT WAS THAT ABOUT!?
HEY! HOW MUCH FURTHER IS THIS PLACE!?
KREEEEEE
WE'RE HERE.

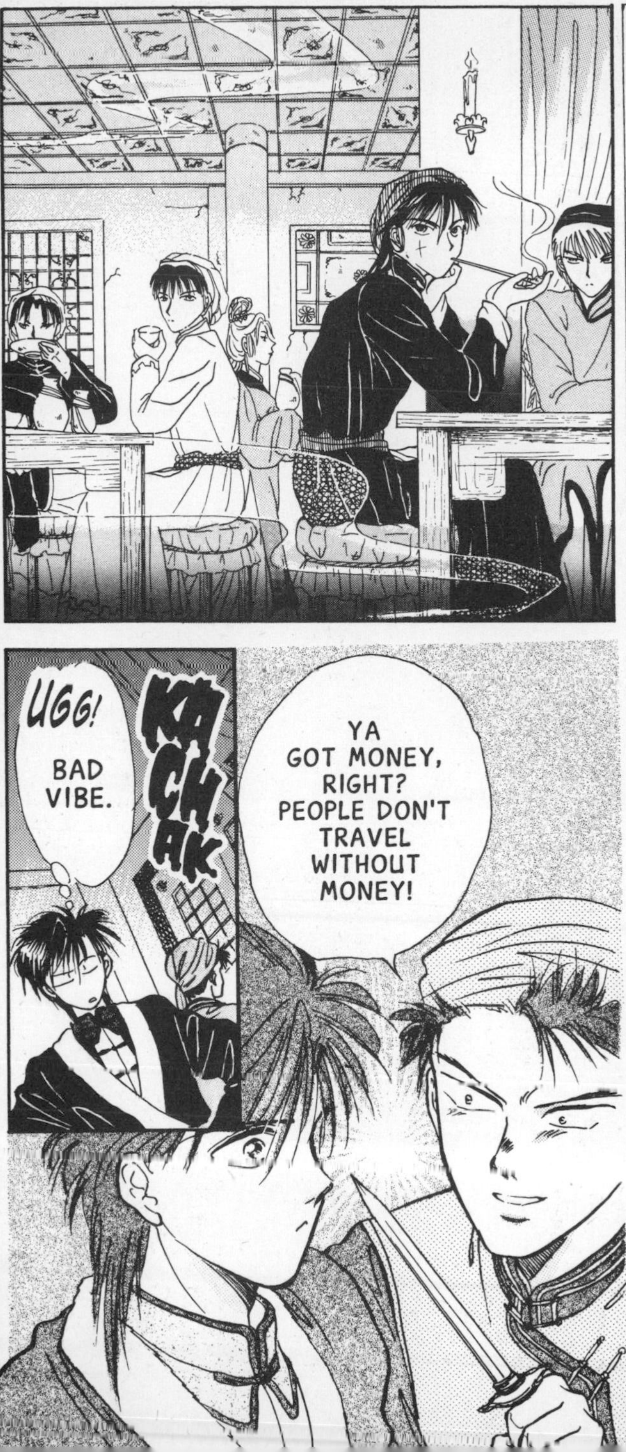
UGG!
BAD VIBE.
KACHAK
YA GOT MONEY, RIGHT? PEOPLE DON'T TRAVEL WITHOUT MONEY!

Next we went to Xian. By the way, Qu-Dong is based on Xian, aka, the ancient capital of China, Chang'an. A super gigantic city. Kaifeng doesn't even come close! (It gave me an idea of the difference in scale between Hong-Nan and Qu-Dong). Xian is a city of a million people with foreigners all over the place. The central "Suzaku Main Road" is supposed to have been 150 meters wide!! Narrow streets were 25 meters. *You're kidding!* Heijokyo (the capital of Nara-era Japan) was based on Chang'an, but it was about 4 times smaller. We're talking about a totally different scale here!
I wanted to see the old Imperial Palace... but it isn't there anymore. Instead, we went to the "West Gate" where Sanzo Genjo went off to Tenjiku (India). How romantic! The confrontation between Soi and Miaka was based on a photo of this area. It's not exactly the same, though. Let's see, then there's Emperor Xuanzang and Lady Yang-gui-fei. We went to the Huaqing Hot Springs where they bathed. It was there that Lady Yang's beauty won over Xuanzang! And we have another, "How romantic!" Which makes me think that Hotohori has rotten taste in women (I'm just kidding). It wasn't Miaka's beauty that attracted Hotohori. He fell for her innocence.
Another amazing sight was the famous Terra-Cotta Warriors and Horses Pits. One kilometer east of the Emperor Shi-huang's Mausoleum, it is an excavation site with life-size figures of soldiers. The surprising thing is that each one has a different face because they're all based on real people. They all have different bodies as well. The sight of row after row of these statues was really awesome.
They looked so real too!

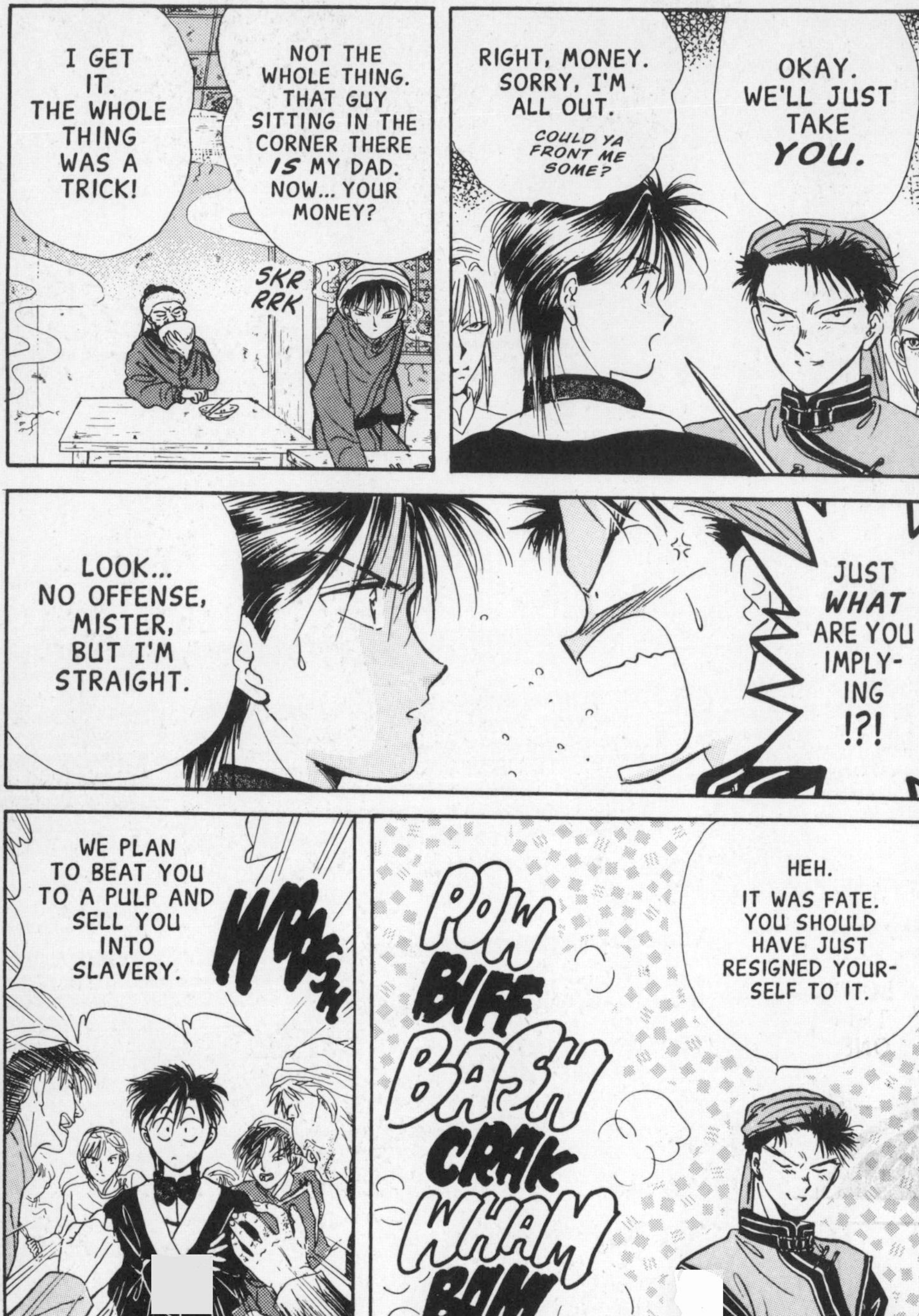
I GET IT. THE WHOLE THING WAS A TRICK!
NOT THE WHOLE THING. THAT GUY SITTING IN THE CORNER THERE *IS* MY DAD. NOW... YOUR MONEY?
SKR RRK
RIGHT, MONEY. SORRY, I'M ALL OUT.
COULD YA FRONT ME SOME?
OKAY. WE'LL JUST TAKE ***YOU.***
LOOK... NO OFFENSE, MISTER, BUT I'M STRAIGHT.
JUST ***WHAT*** ARE YOU IMPLY-ING!?!
WE PLAN TO BEAT YOU TO A PULP AND SELL YOU INTO SLAVERY.
POW BIFF BASH CRAK WHAM BAM
HEH. IT WAS FATE. YOU SHOULD HAVE JUST RESIGNED YOURSELF TO IT.

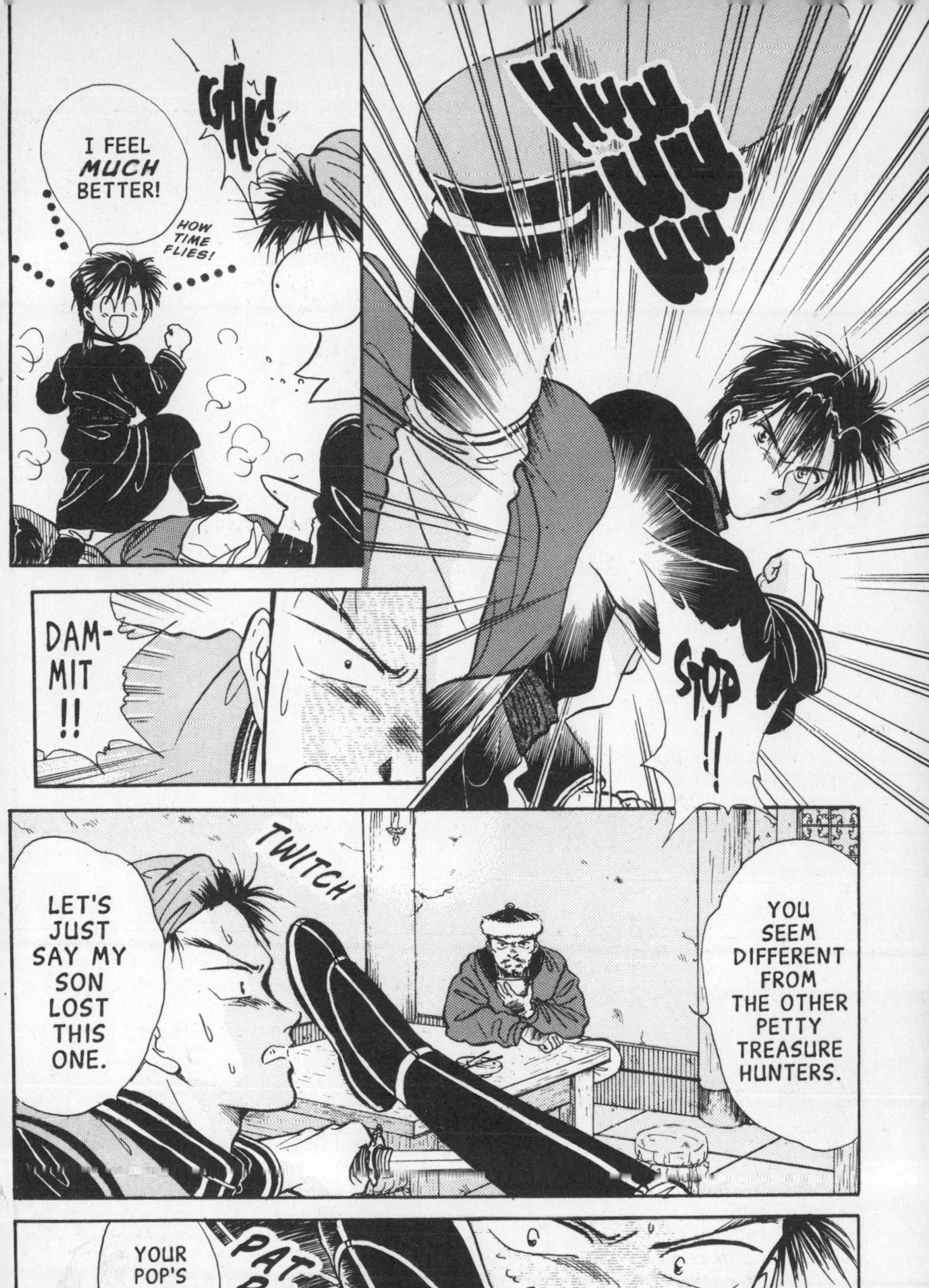
GAK!
I FEEL MUCH BETTER!
HOW TIME FLIES!
DAM-MIT!!
HYUUUUUUU
STOP!!
LET'S JUST SAY MY SON LOST THIS ONE.
TWITCH
YOU SEEM DIFFERENT FROM THE OTHER PETTY TREASURE HUNTERS.
YOUR POP'S TALKIN' HERE.
PAT PAT

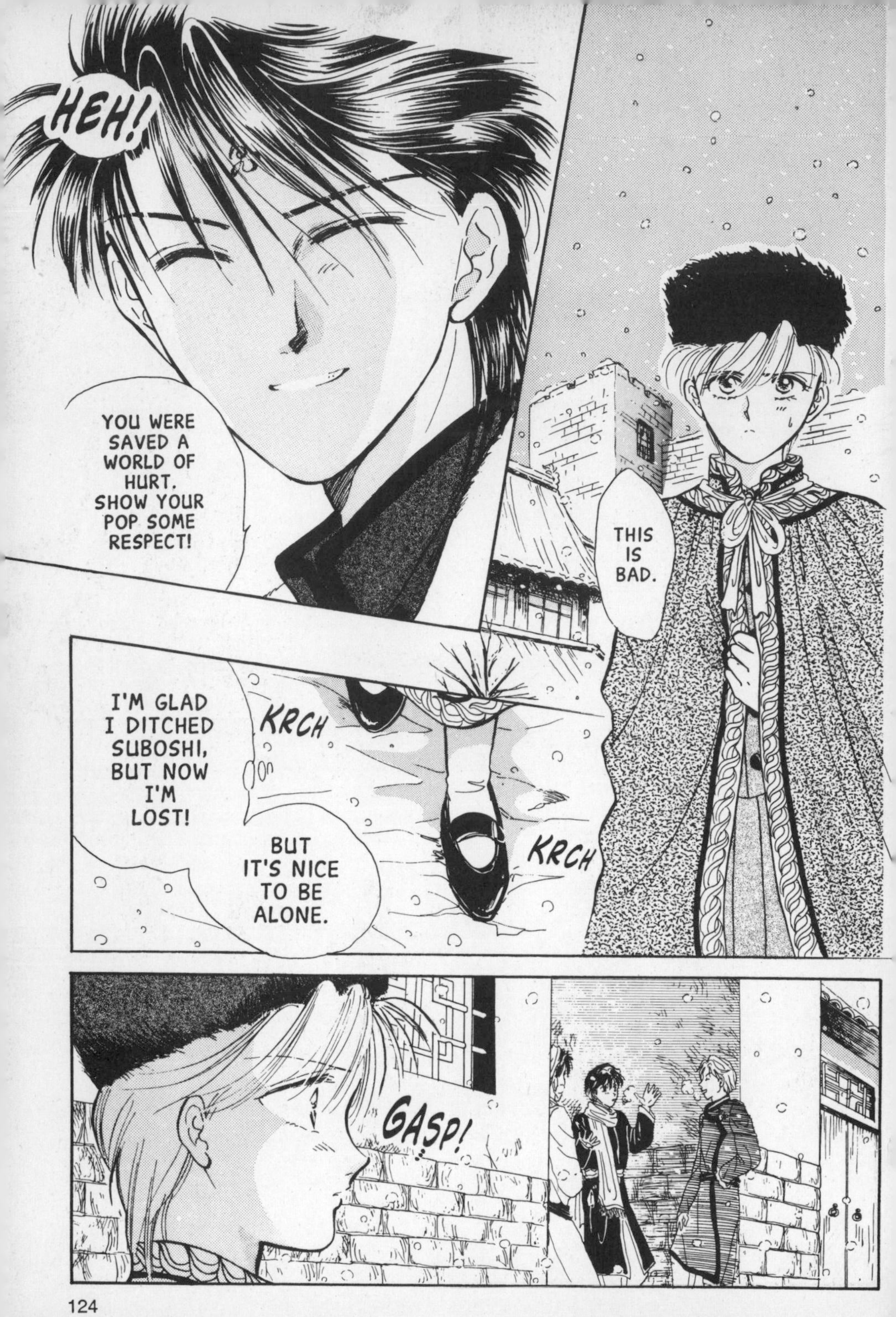
HEH!
YOU WERE SAVED A WORLD OF HURT. SHOW YOUR POP SOME RESPECT!
I'M GLAD I DITCHED SUBOSHI, BUT NOW I'M LOST!
KRCH
BUT IT'S NICE TO BE ALONE.
KRCH
THIS IS BAD.
GASP!

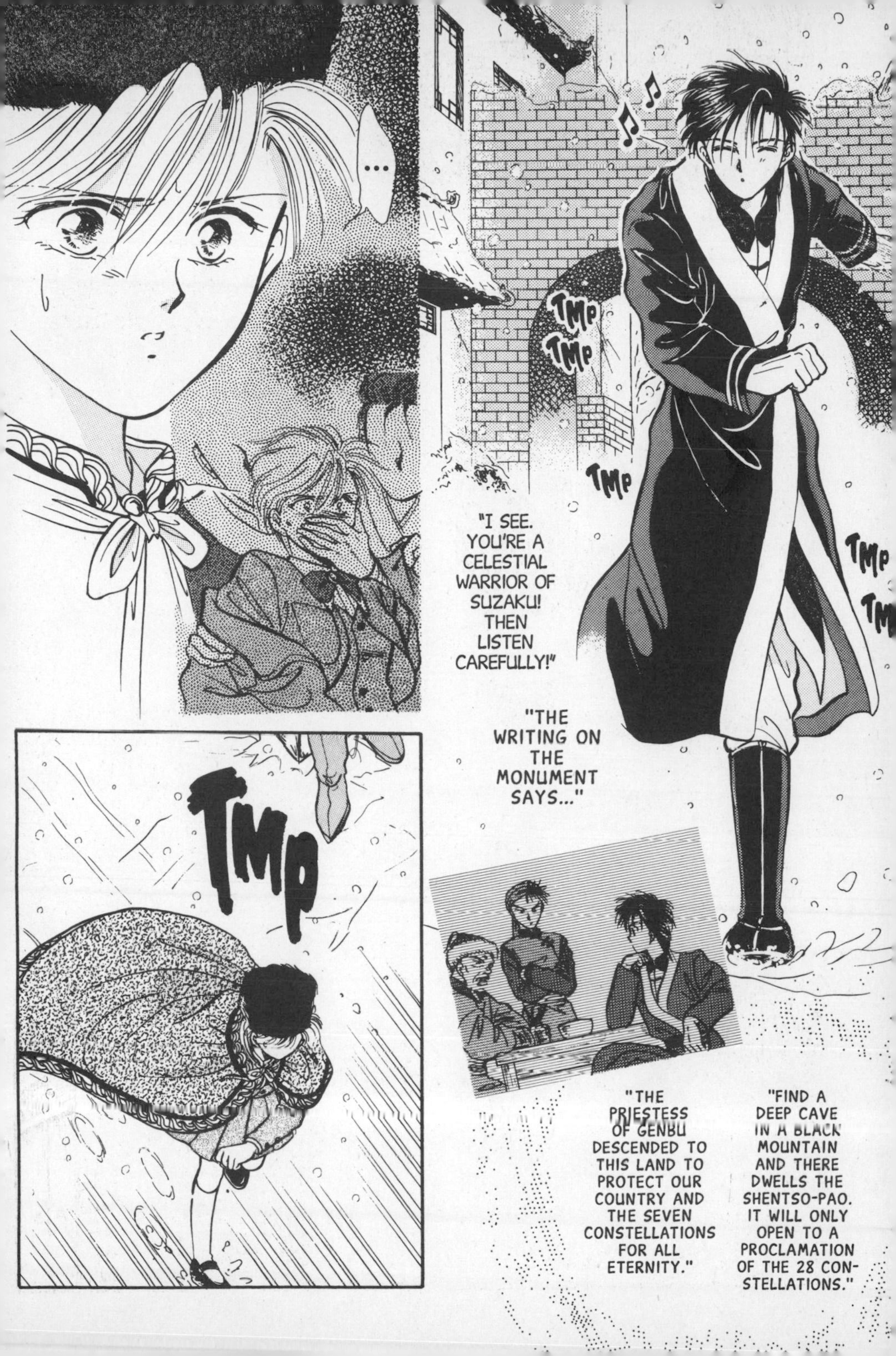
...
TMP
TMP
TMP
TMP
"I SEE. YOU'RE A CELESTIAL WARRIOR OF SUZAKU! THEN LISTEN CAREFULLY!"
TMP
TMP
"THE WRITING ON THE MONUMENT SAYS..."
"THE PRIESTESS OF GENBU DESCENDED TO THIS LAND TO PROTECT OUR COUNTRY AND THE SEVEN CONSTELLATIONS FOR ALL ETERNITY."
"FIND A DEEP CAVE IN A BLACK MOUNTAIN AND THERE DWELLS THE SHENTSO-PAO. IT WILL ONLY OPEN TO A PROCLAMATION OF THE 28 CONSTELLATIONS."

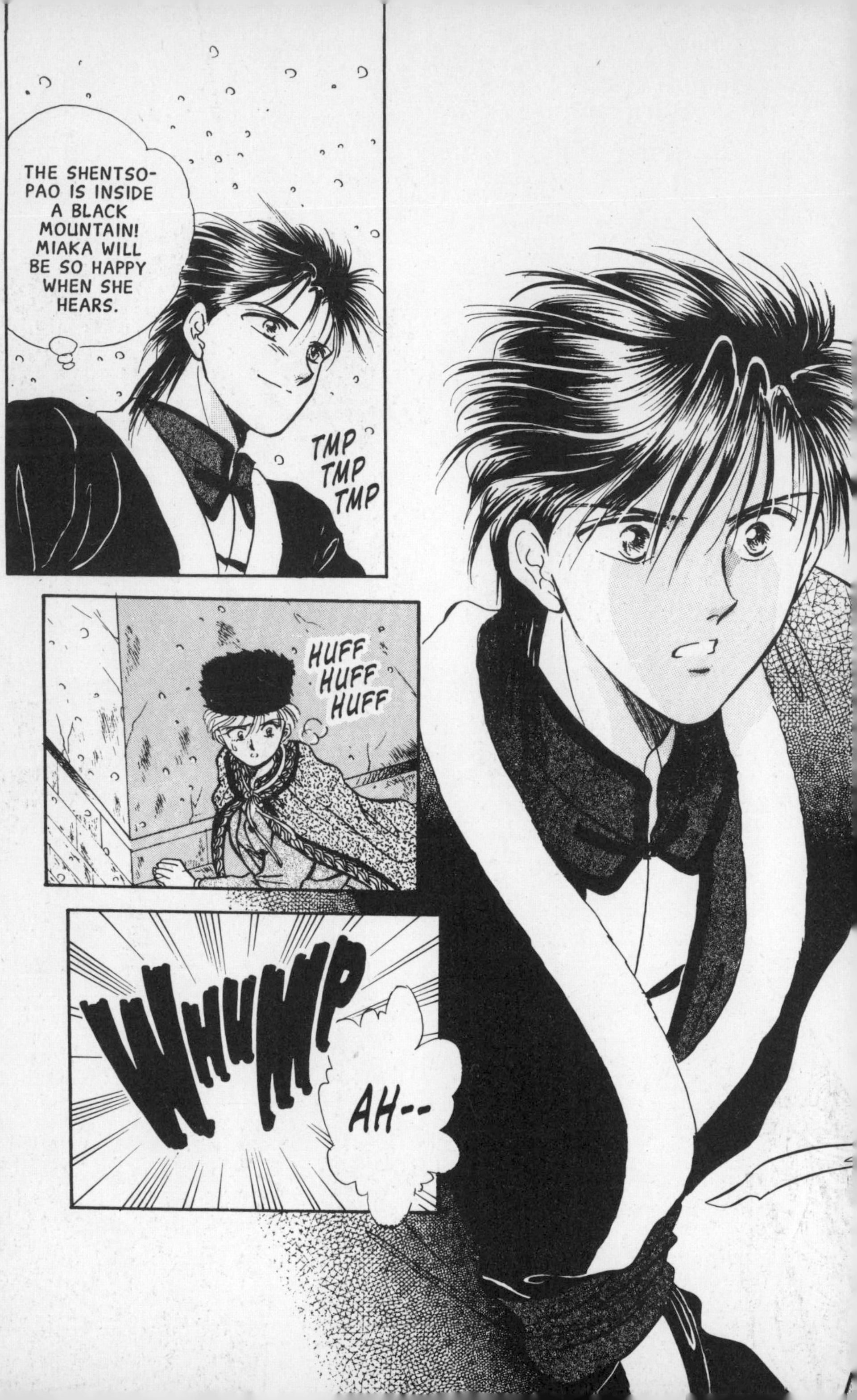
THE SHENTSO-PAO IS INSIDE A BLACK MOUNTAIN! MIAKA WILL BE SO HAPPY WHEN SHE HEARS.
TMP TMP TMP
HUFF HUFF HUFF
WHUMP
AH--

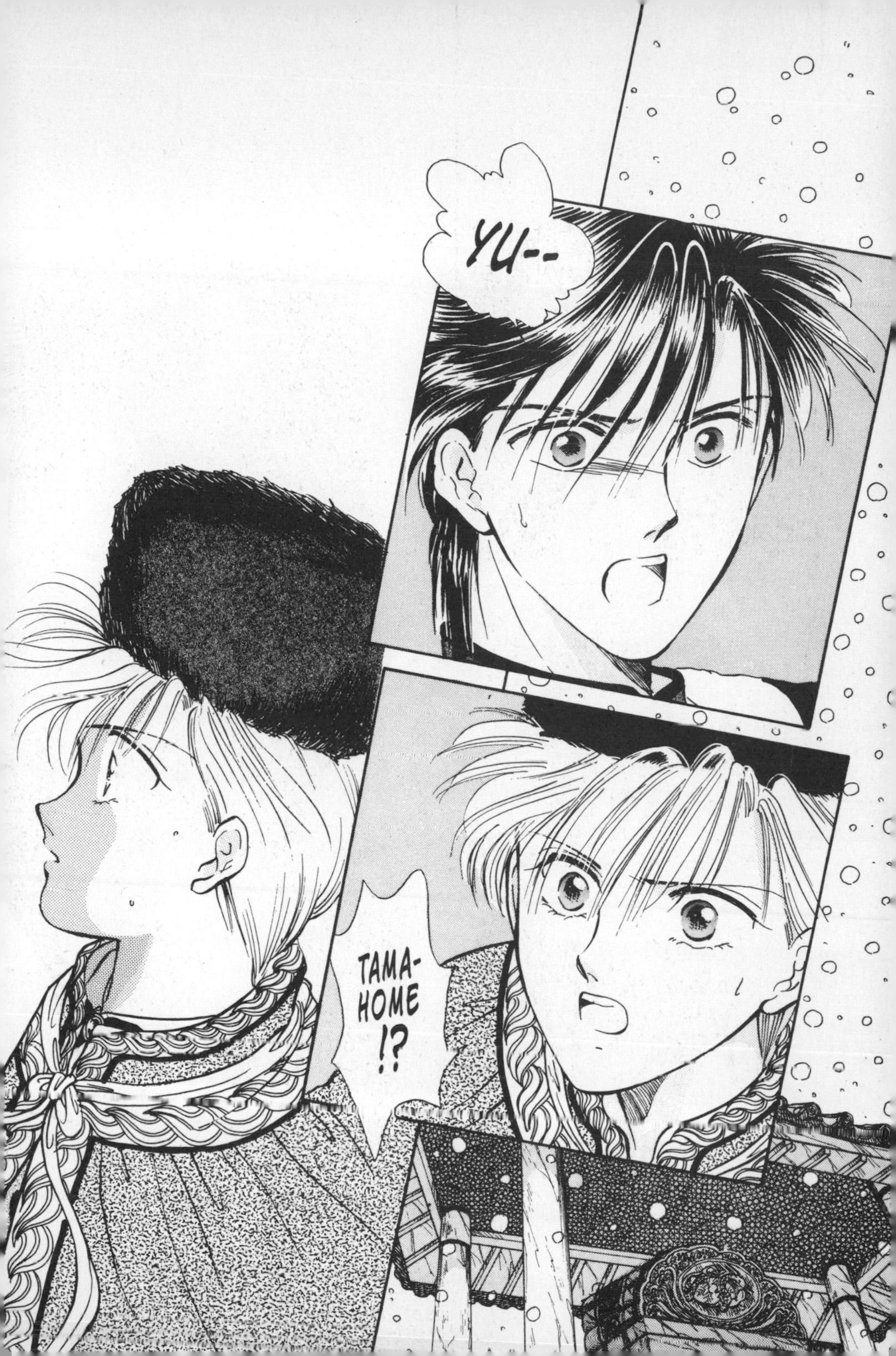
YU--
TAMA-
HOME
!?

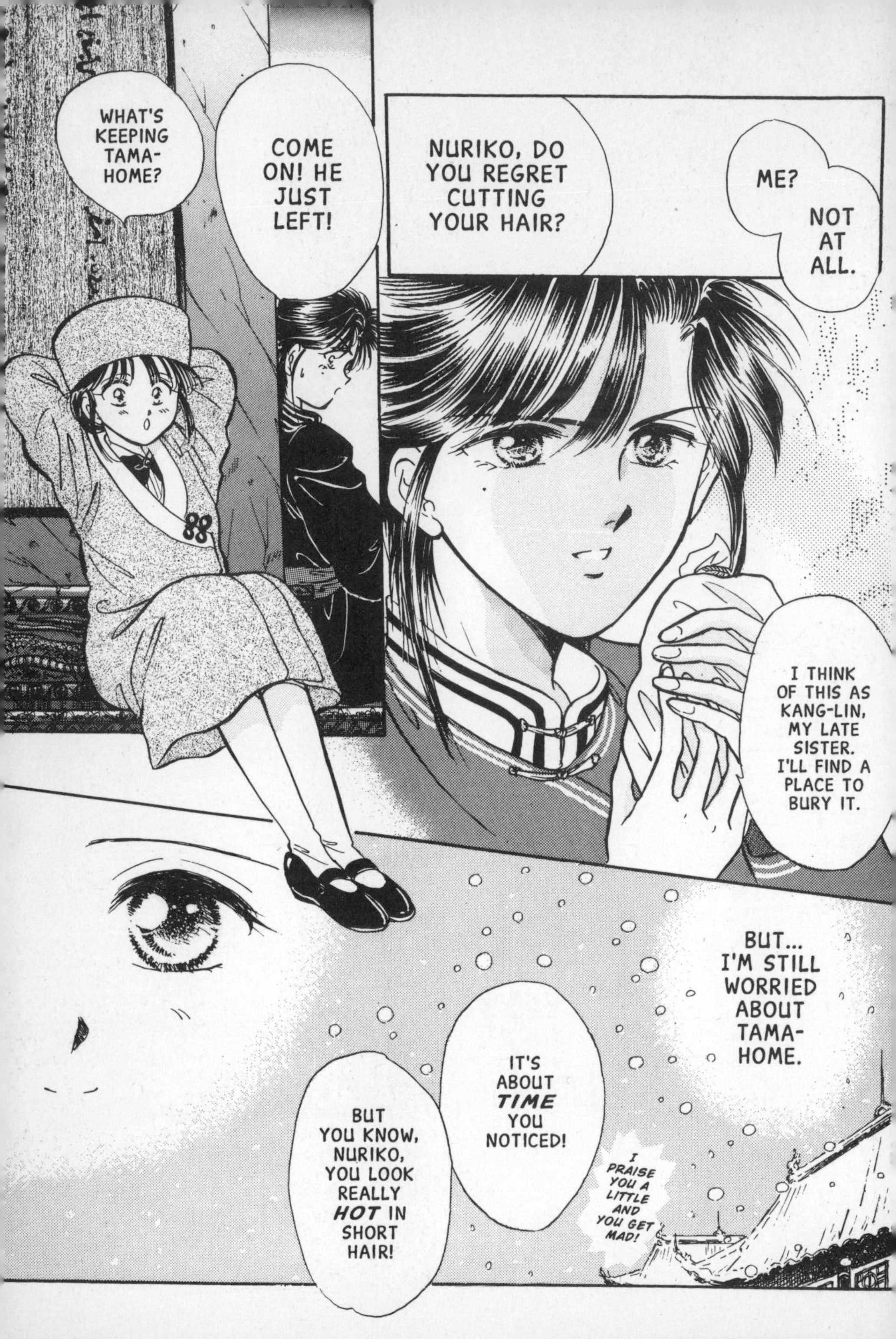
WHAT'S KEEPING TAMA-HOME?
COME ON! HE JUST LEFT!
NURIKO, DO YOU REGRET CUTTING YOUR HAIR?
ME? NOT AT ALL.
I THINK OF THIS AS KANG-LIN, MY LATE SISTER. I'LL FIND A PLACE TO BURY IT.
BUT... I'M STILL WORRIED ABOUT TAMA-HOME.
BUT YOU KNOW, NURIKO, YOU LOOK REALLY HOT IN SHORT HAIR!
IT'S ABOUT TIME YOU NOTICED!
I PRAISE YOU A LITTLE AND YOU GET MAD!

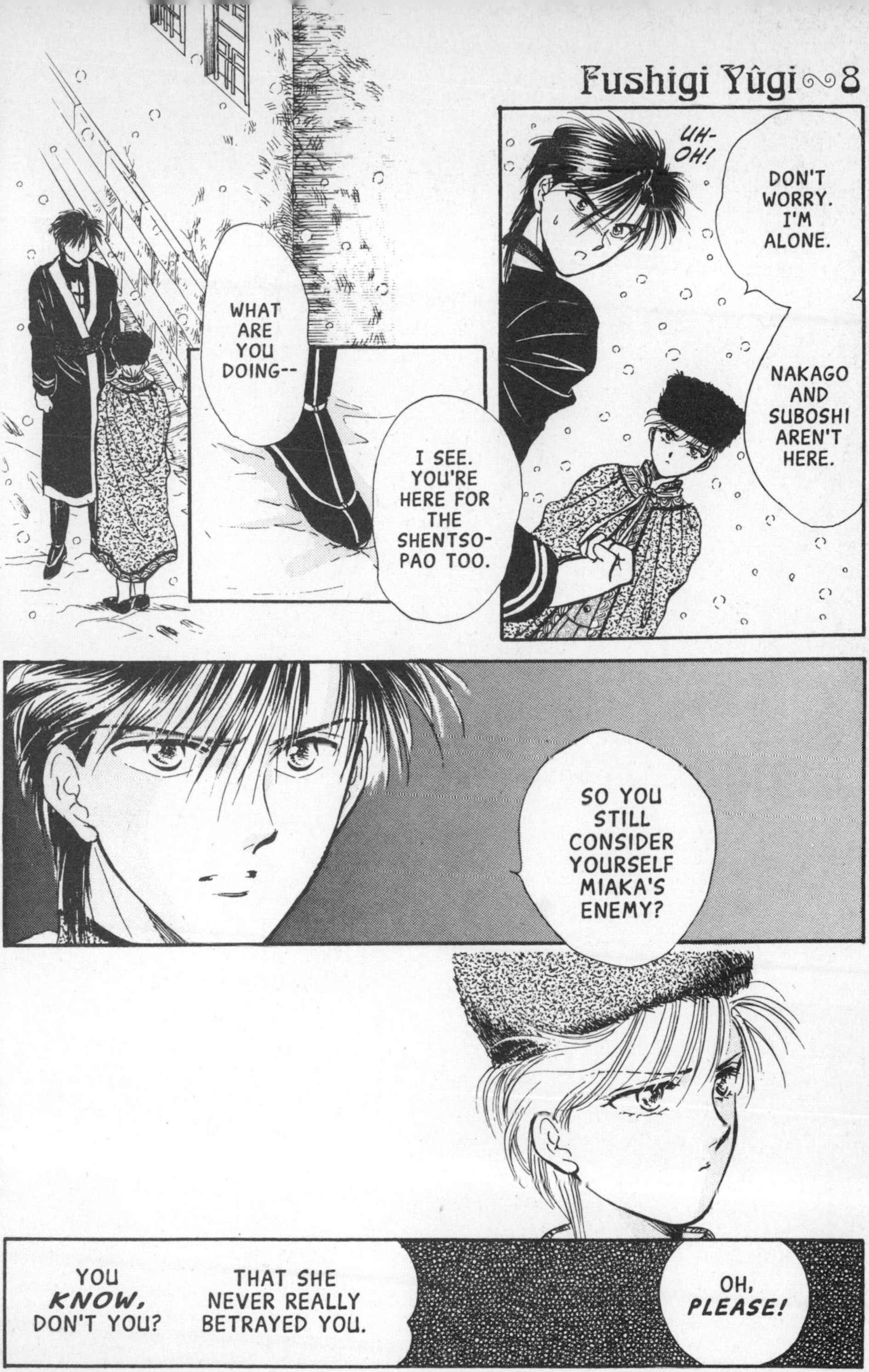
WHAT ARE YOU DOING--
I SEE. YOU'RE HERE FOR THE SHENTSO-PAO TOO.
UH-OH!
DON'T WORRY. I'M ALONE.
NAKAGO AND SUBOSHI AREN'T HERE.
SO YOU STILL CONSIDER YOURSELF MIAKA'S ENEMY?
YOU *KNOW,* DON'T YOU?
THAT SHE NEVER REALLY BETRAYED YOU.
OH, *PLEASE!*

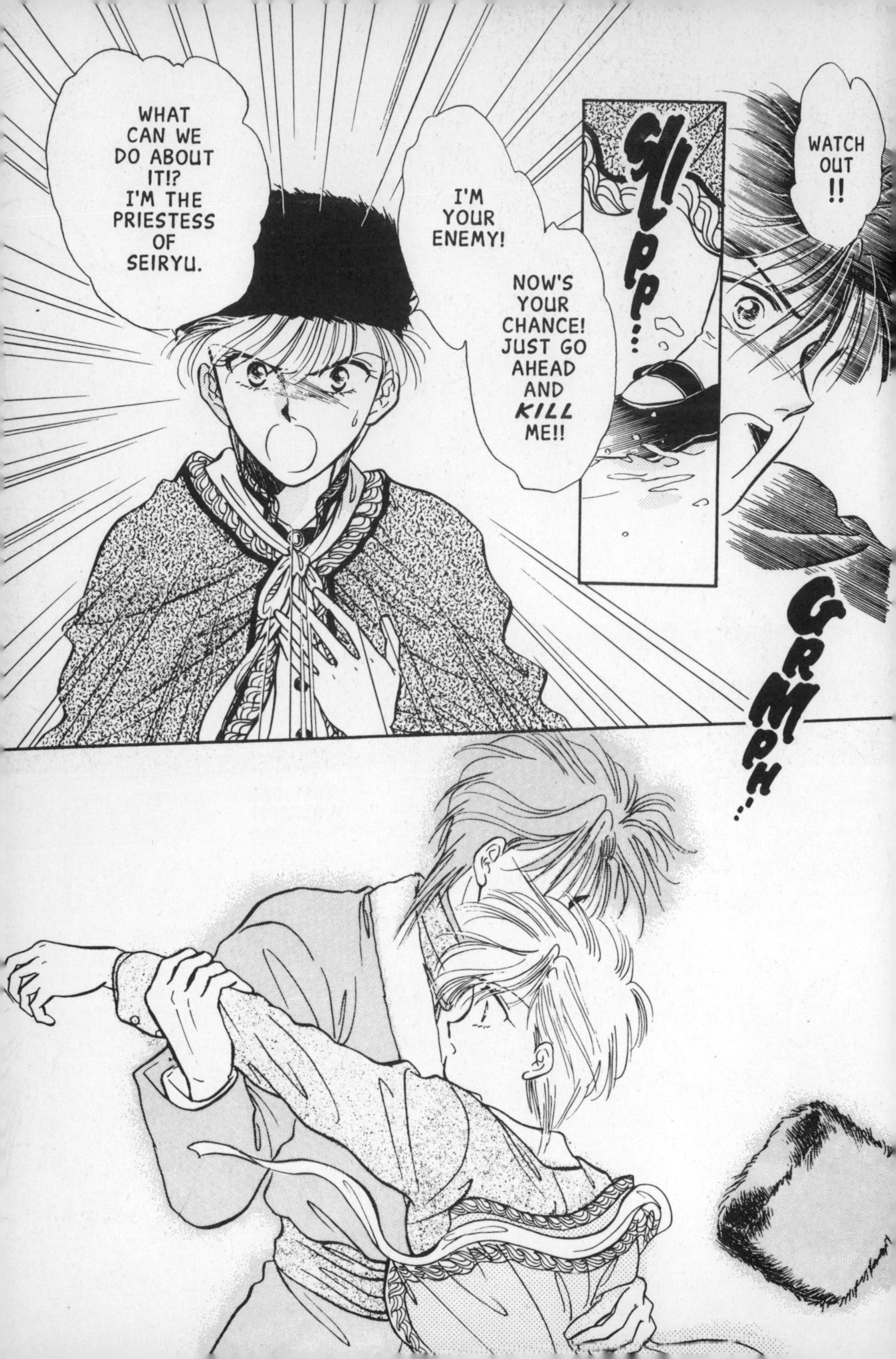
WHAT CAN WE DO ABOUT IT!? I'M THE PRIESTESS OF SEIRYU.
I'M YOUR ENEMY!
NOW'S YOUR CHANCE! JUST GO AHEAD AND *KILL* ME!!
SLIPP...
WATCH OUT !!
GRMPH...

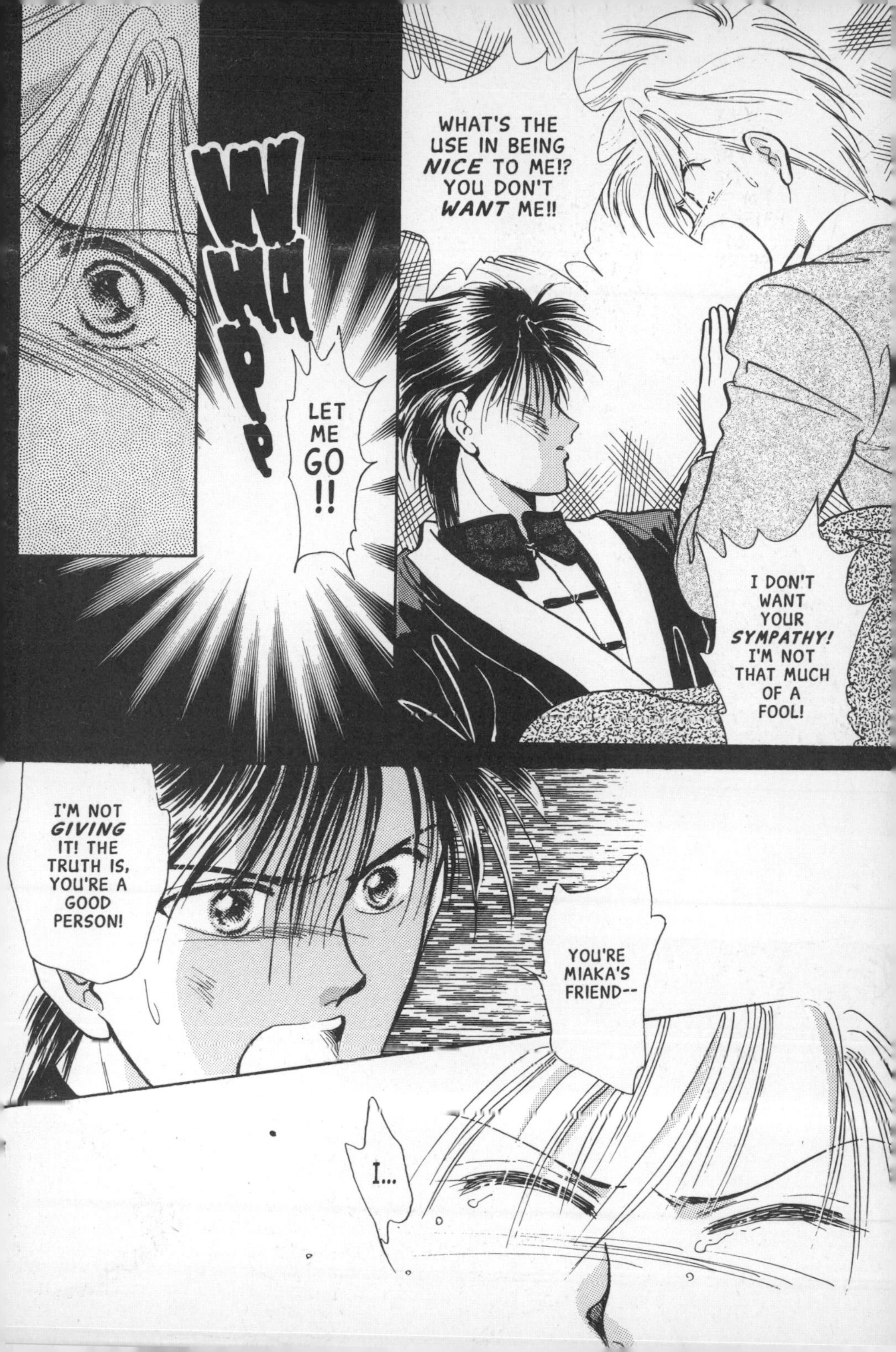
WHAPP
LET ME GO!!
WHAT'S THE USE IN BEING *NICE* TO ME!? YOU DON'T *WANT* ME!!
I DON'T WANT YOUR *SYMPATHY!* I'M NOT THAT MUCH OF A FOOL!
I'M NOT *GIVING* IT! THE TRUTH IS, YOU'RE A GOOD PERSON!
YOU'RE MIAKA'S FRIEND--
I...

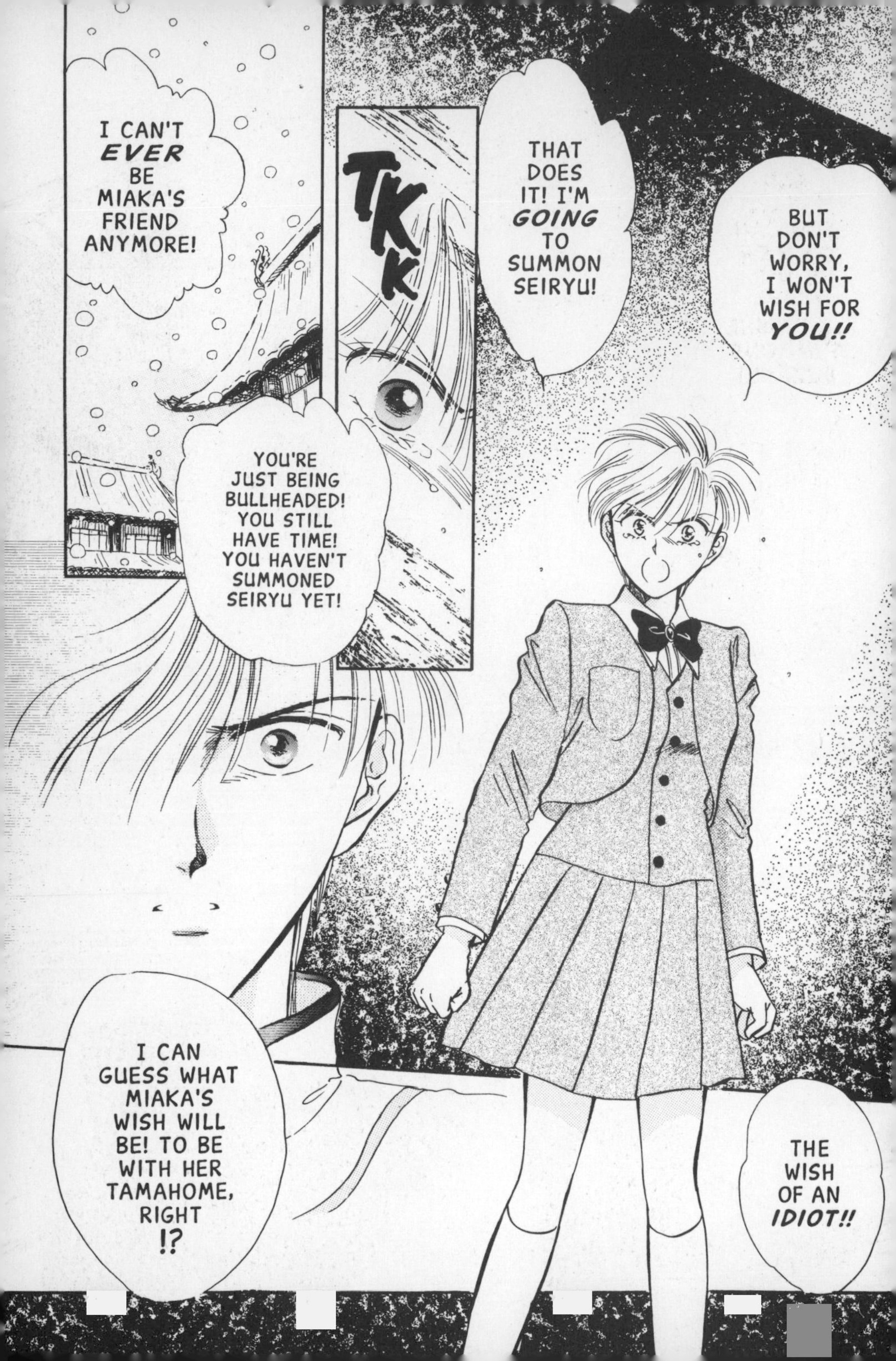
I CAN'T *EVER* BE MIAKA'S FRIEND ANYMORE!
TKK
YOU'RE JUST BEING BULLHEADED! YOU STILL HAVE TIME! YOU HAVEN'T SUMMONED SEIRYU YET!
THAT DOES IT! I'M *GOING* TO SUMMON SEIRYU!
BUT DON'T WORRY, I WON'T WISH FOR *YOU!!*
I CAN GUESS WHAT MIAKA'S WISH WILL BE! TO BE WITH HER TAMAHOME, RIGHT !?
THE WISH OF AN *IDIOT!!*

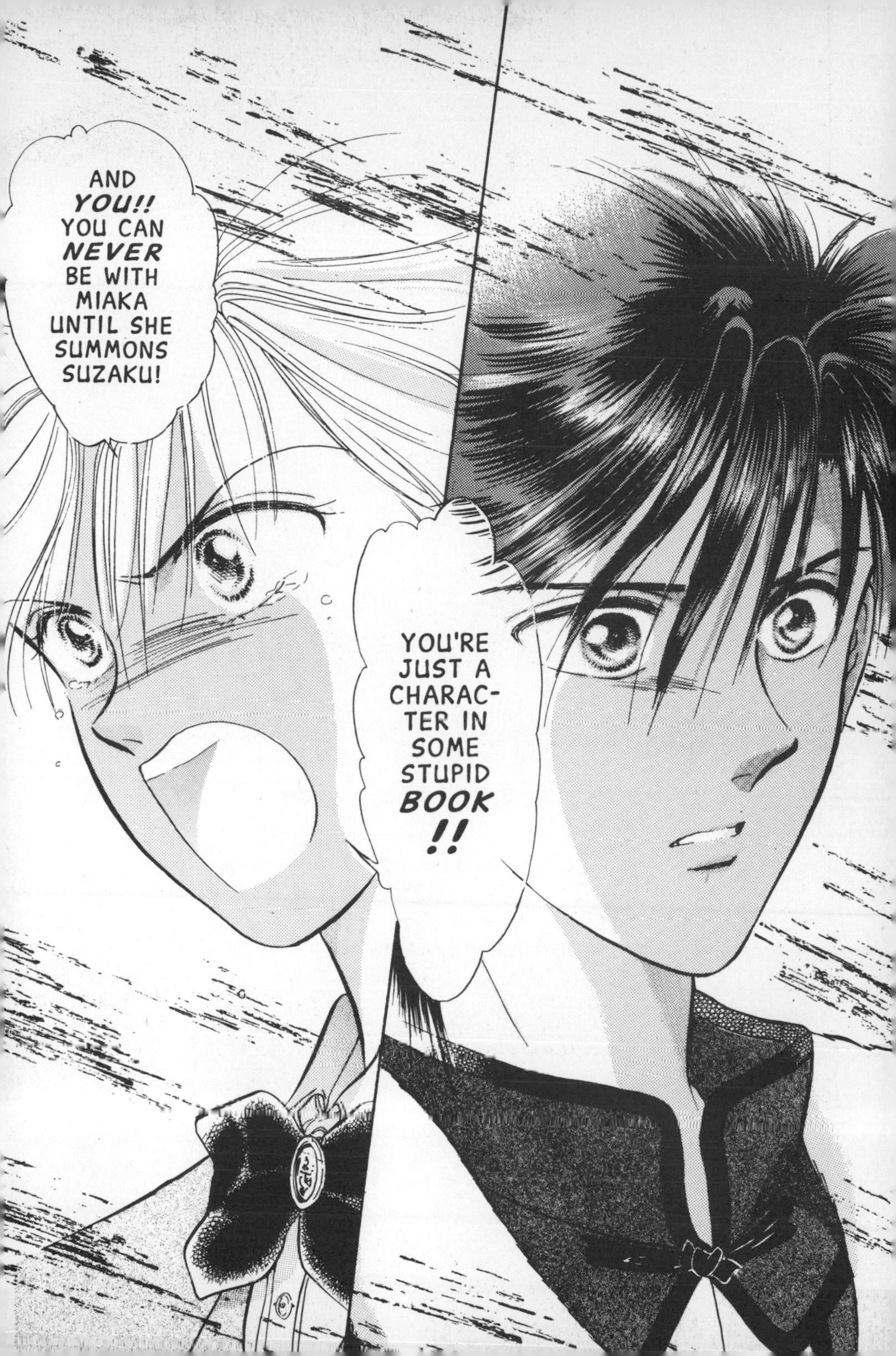
AND YOU!! YOU CAN NEVER BE WITH MIAKA UNTIL SHE SUMMONS SUZAKU!
YOU'RE JUST A CHARACTER IN SOME STUPID BOOK !!

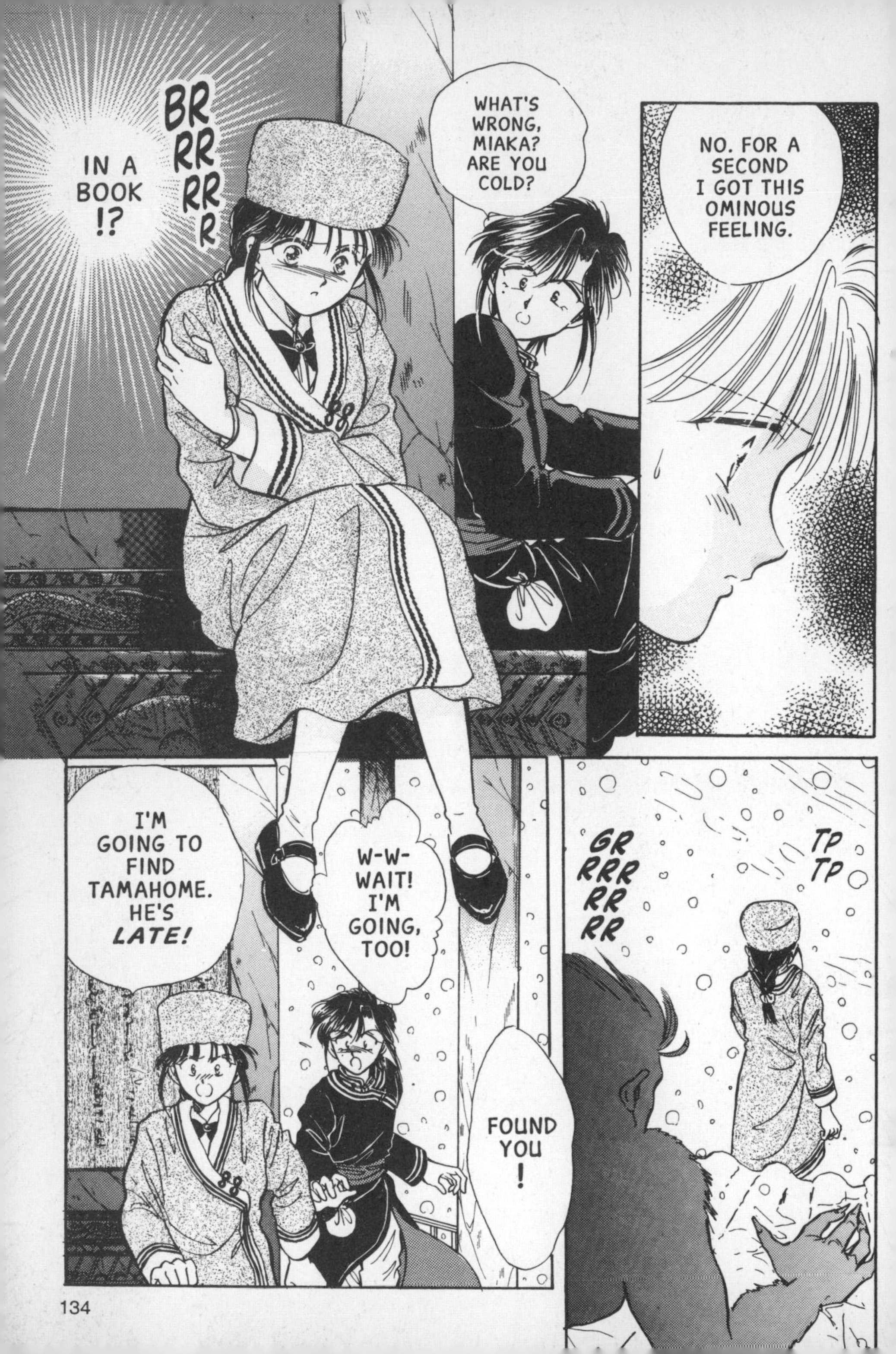
IN A BOOK !?
BRRRRRRR
WHAT'S WRONG, MIAKA? ARE YOU COLD?
NO. FOR A SECOND I GOT THIS OMINOUS FEELING.
I'M GOING TO FIND TAMAHOME. HE'S *LATE!*
W-W-WAIT! I'M GOING, TOO!
FOUND YOU !
GRRRRRRRRR
TP TP

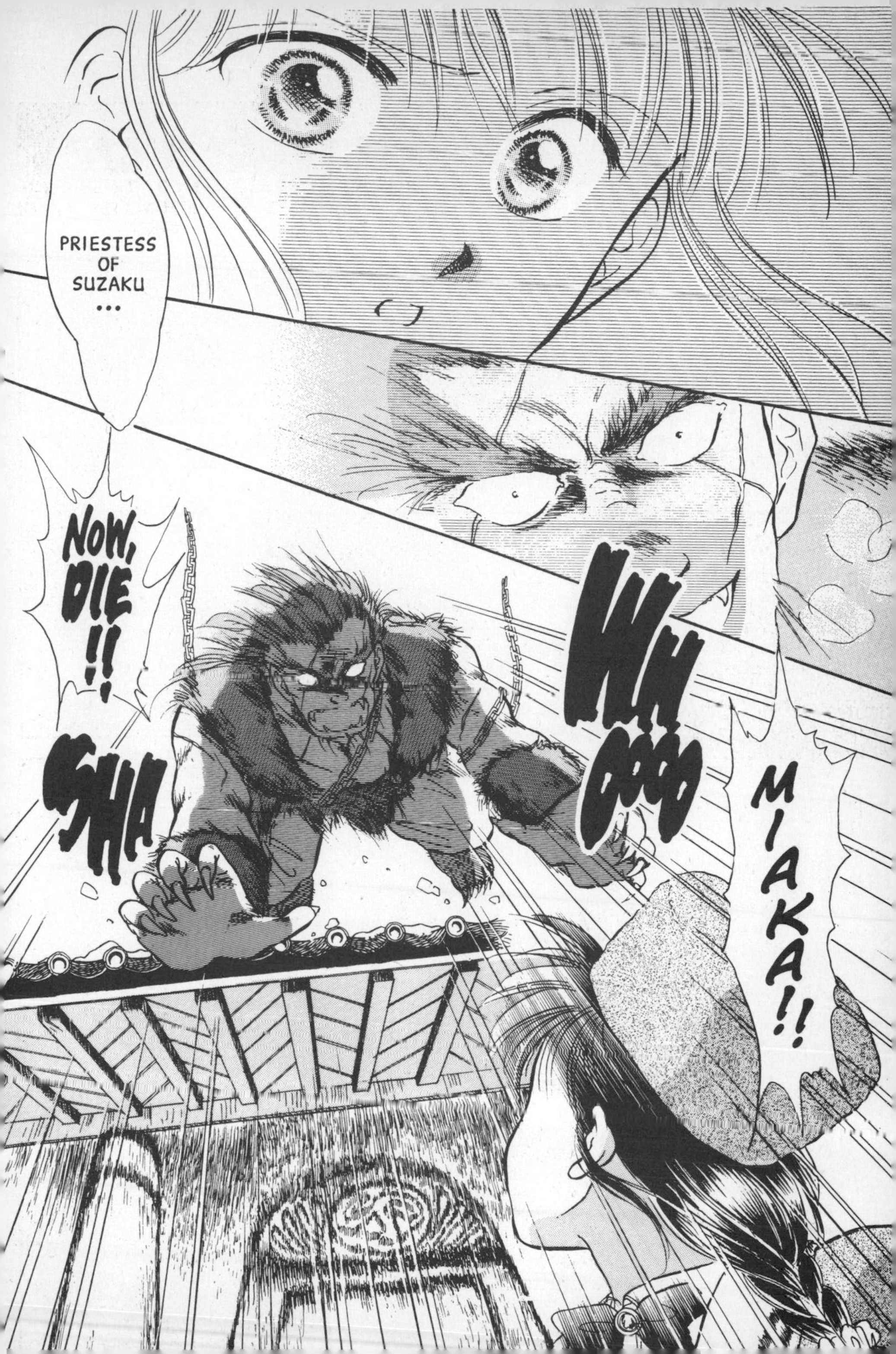
PRIESTESS OF SUZAKU ...
NOW, DIE !!
SHA
WHOOOO
MIAKA!!

SECRETS OF FUSHIGI YÛGI

This is a new corner that will explain the secrets and strange parts of Fushigi Yûgi to the fans!
When you say, "This sucks! Watase, this makes no sense, dammit!" I clear it up!

ITEM 1   **What is the time difference between the Universe of the Four Gods and the real world?**

Actually, several readers tried to calculate this. There are several periods such as "3 days," "1 year and 2 months," or "33 years" that characters have spent in the various worlds, and the true answer is: "There's no set rate." In chapter 11, Miaka spent about 2 hours in the real world while three months passed in the world of the book... And I think that most people took that as the standard rate, but here's the thing: If you read a book and one sentence reads, "and a month passed," it might only take a second or two while reading the book, but in the world of the book, that's a month!
This may seem like some kind of time warp, and in a worst case, it could warp up to 10 years or more, but since it takes the same few seconds to read "and 3 days passed" in the Universe of the Four Gods as it does for other time periods, there's no set rate of time passage.

ITEM 2   **When Amiboshi acted as the fake Chiriko, why was he able to enter the Shrine of Suzaku with no problem?**

Answer: There were no anti-Seiryu wards! Do you remember in chapter 16 when Chichiri said, "They've put up wards so none of Suzaku's chosen can get in! No da!" What really happened at the Seiryu Shrine was that Miaka went into the shrine, and Nakago quickly put up the wards. (That's why it took Miaka a few seconds before she started to feel pain.)
I'm sure that Qu-Dong has laws that forbid the entrance of the chosen ones of other Gods into the Seiryu Shrine during worship, but remember there are also Genbu and Byakko shrines as well, and I'm sure the practice isn't universal.
Over and above that, even if wards had been placed in the shrine, the breaking of wards is one of the powers and chi techniques that Seiryu Celestial Warriors practice. That's one place where Seiryu Warriors and Suzaku Warriors differ.

ITEM 3   **Why did Miaka have to go out and find her Celestial Warriors when Yui had them all come to her?**

This may seem like a similar answer to the one above, but this is a spot where the Seiryu chosen and the Suzaku chosen are very different. The Universe of the Four Gods (the scroll version) says that the Priestess has to find her Warriors, but in Yui's case, she used her chi to call her warriors to her. It could be thought of as Yui's power, but also remember that the Seiryu Celestial Warriors are very powerful! Their power to feel the presence of another's chi goes far beyond that of the Suzaku Celestial Warriors. It's even possible that Nakago could out power all of the Suzaku chosen by himself! The Seiryu chosen are quite a bit different from normal people (and that's how Nakago was able to locate Yui at the time). Compared to them, in power and way of life, the Suzaku chosen aren't all that different from normal people. They go around thinking, "Seven Warriors? Nothing to do with me!" (They even forget about it!) And they just live their lives. (That difference in attitude is also reflected in Qu-Dong which is rife with internal struggles, and Hong-Nan which is almost too peaceful.) That's one of the reasons why the Suzaku Warriors aren't very good at picking up Miaka's Priestess chi.
On the other hand...yes, Chichiri is the only warrior to actually pick our Miaka's chi and go to where she was (Chapter 13), but you may have noticed something. If you think about it, they were all pulled in by Miaka's chi anyway. Tamahome chose the time Miaka arrived to leave his home for work, and it was then that he got caught up in Miaka's adventures (until that day, he had never stepped foot outside his village). Hotohori chose that time for his parade. Miaka's chi was behind Nuriko's decision to enter the palace as a woman and suddenly appear before her. Tasuki had left the bandits, but it was the day Miaka arrived that he decided to come back to the bandit group...and so on. It all amounts to about the same thing. There are reasons behind why Chiriko took so long to appear.

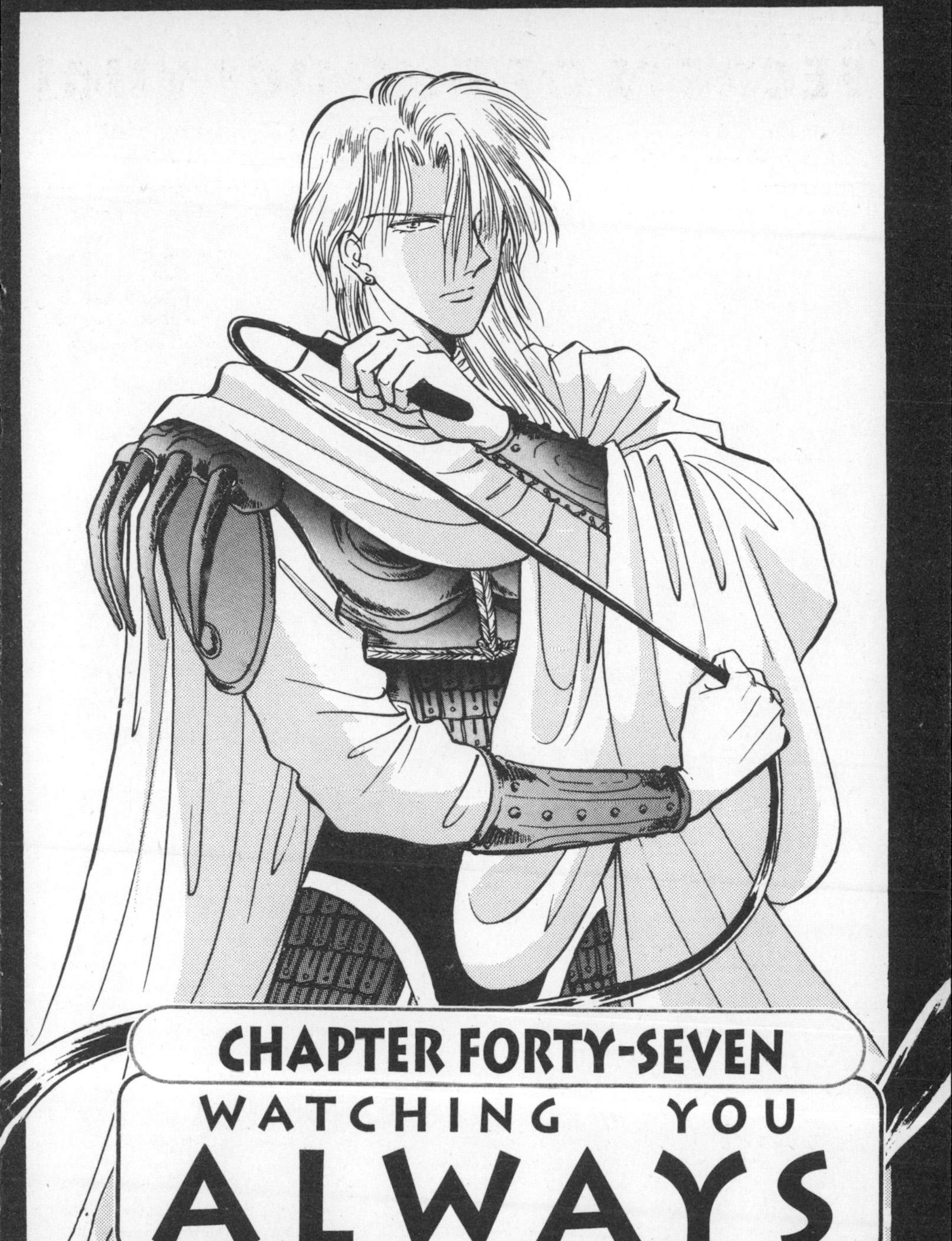
CHAPTER FORTY-SEVEN
WATCHING YOU
ALWAYS

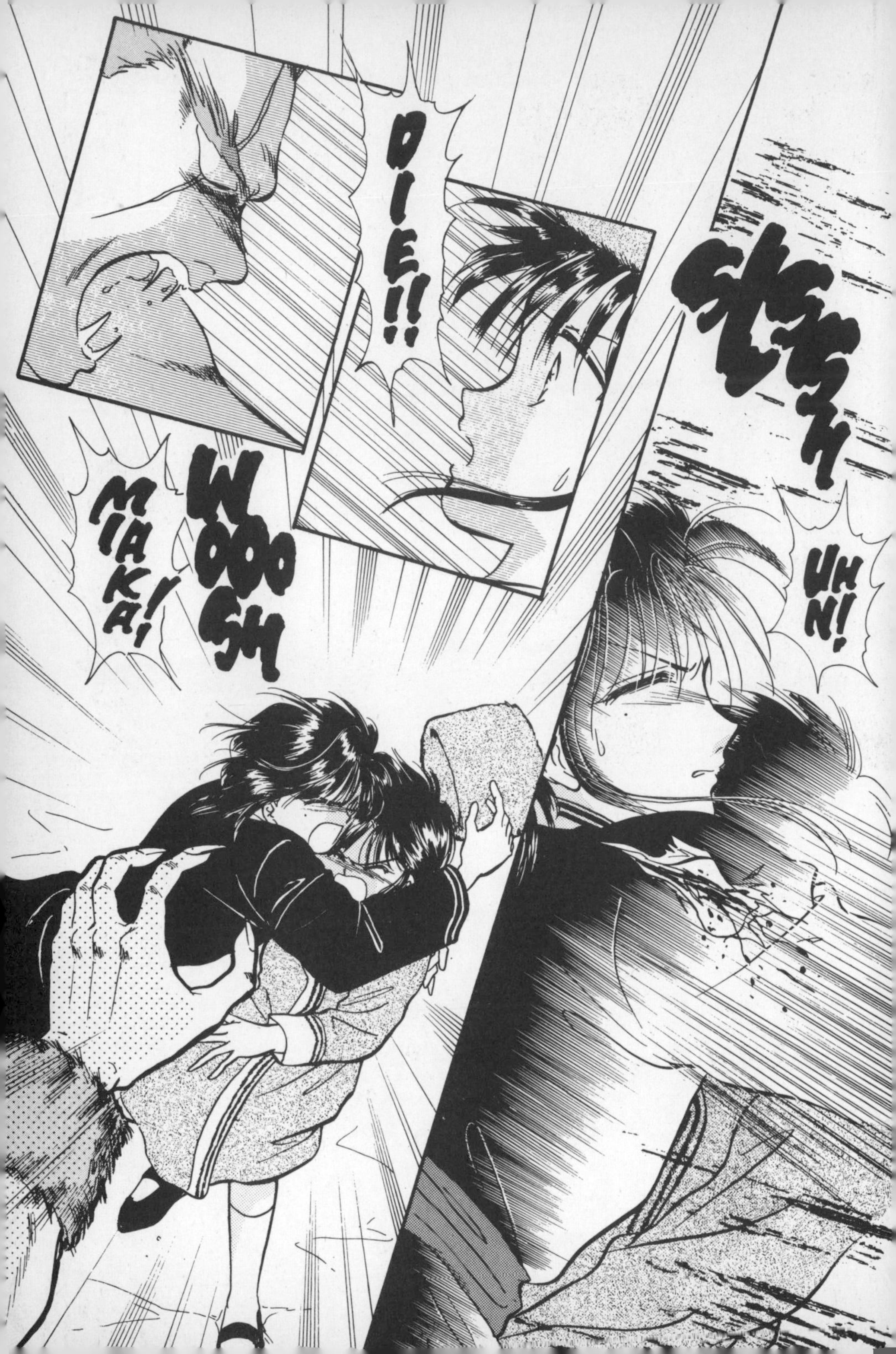
DIE!!
SLASH
MIAKA!
WHOOOSH
UHN!

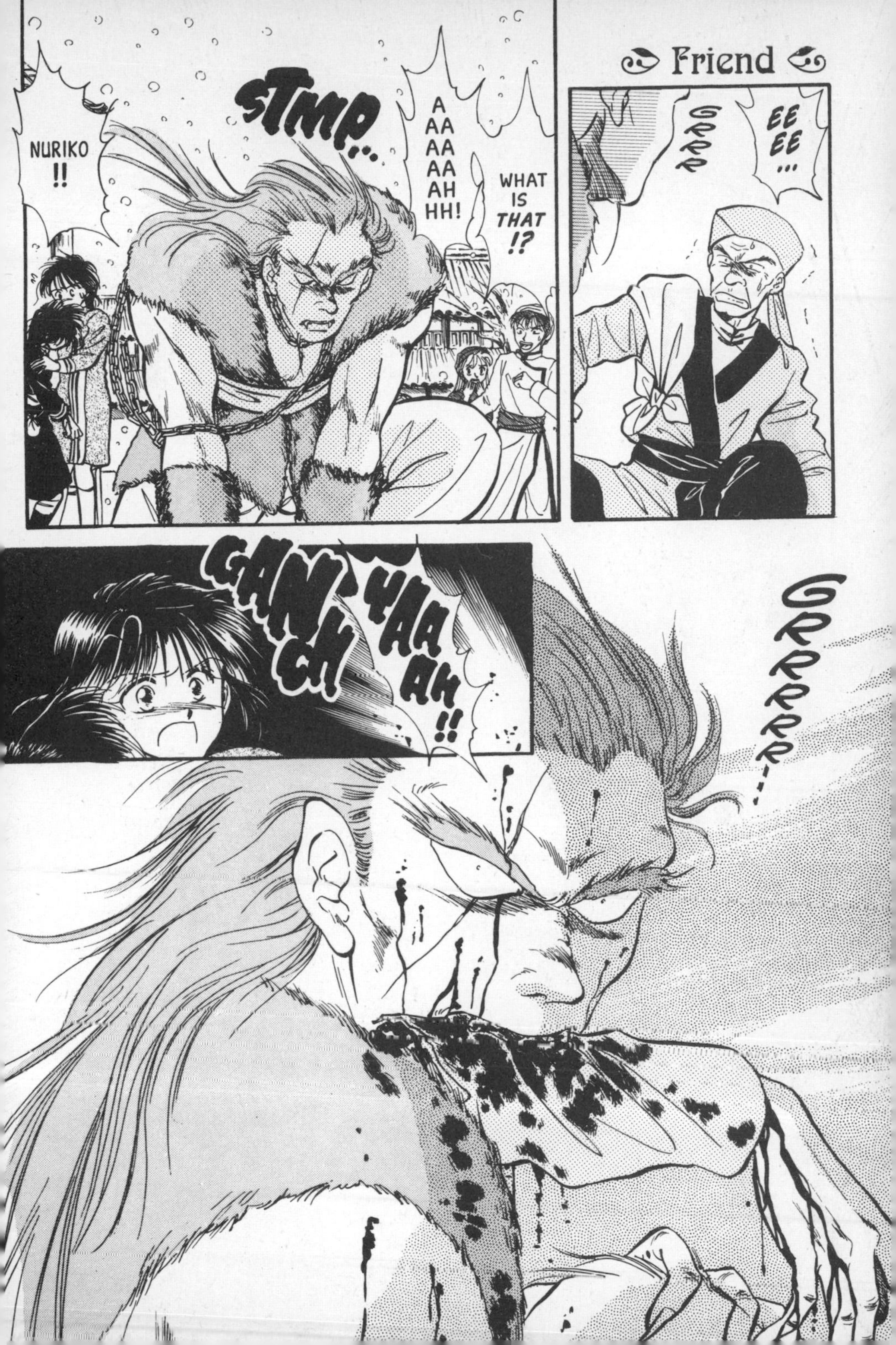
NURIKO !!
STMP...
A AA AA AA AH HH!
WHAT IS THAT !?
GRRR
EEEE...
GAN CH
WAAAAH !!
GRRRRR...

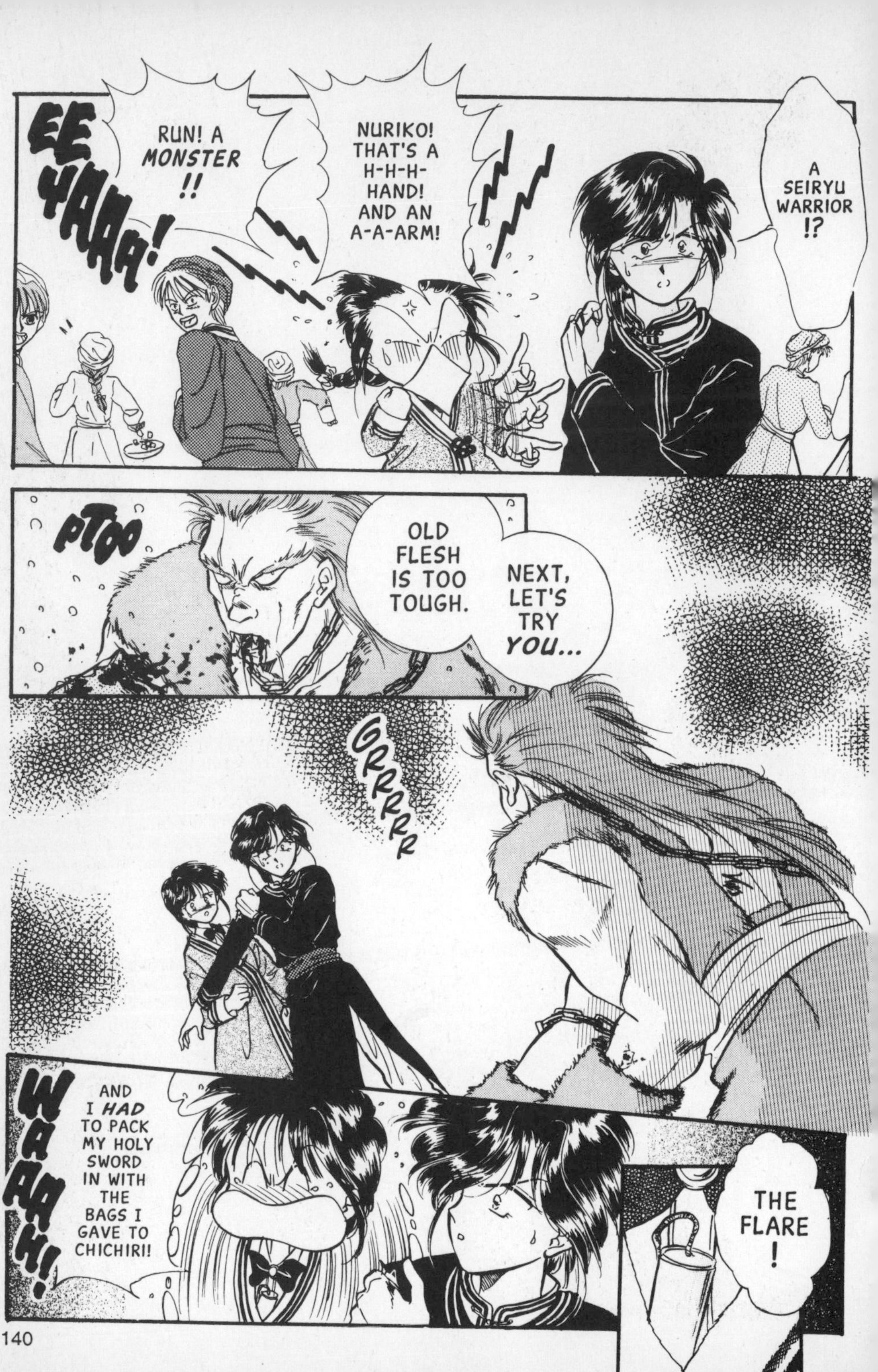
EE YAAAA!
RUN! A MONSTER !!
NURIKO! THAT'S A H-H-H-HAND! AND AN A-A-ARM!
A SEIRYU WARRIOR !?
PTOO
OLD FLESH IS TOO TOUGH.
NEXT, LET'S TRY YOU...
GRRRRR
WAAAH!
AND I HAD TO PACK MY HOLY SWORD IN WITH THE BAGS I GAVE TO CHICHIRI!
THE FLARE !

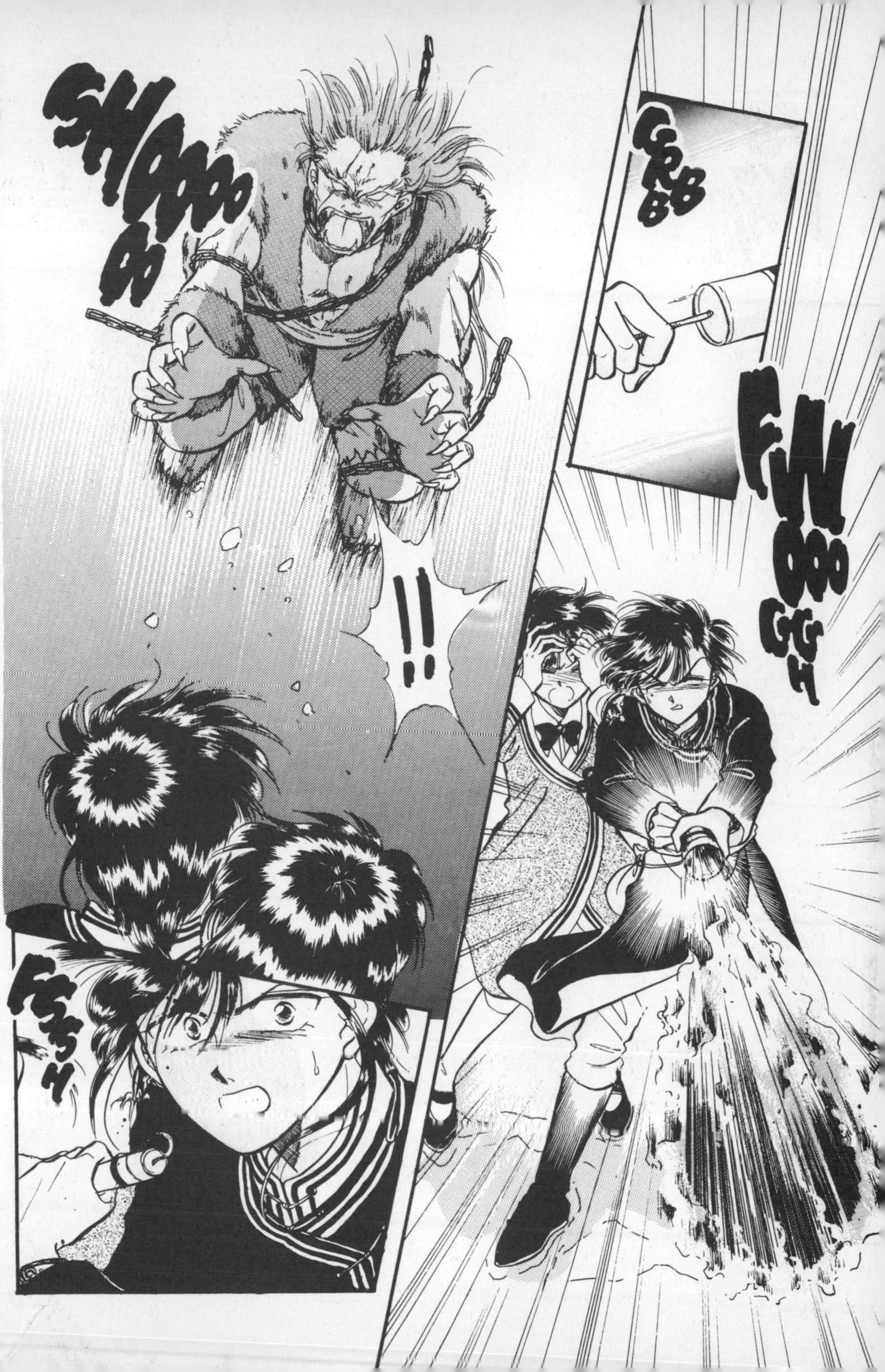
SHOOOOOOO
!!
FSSH
GRBBB
FWOOGGH

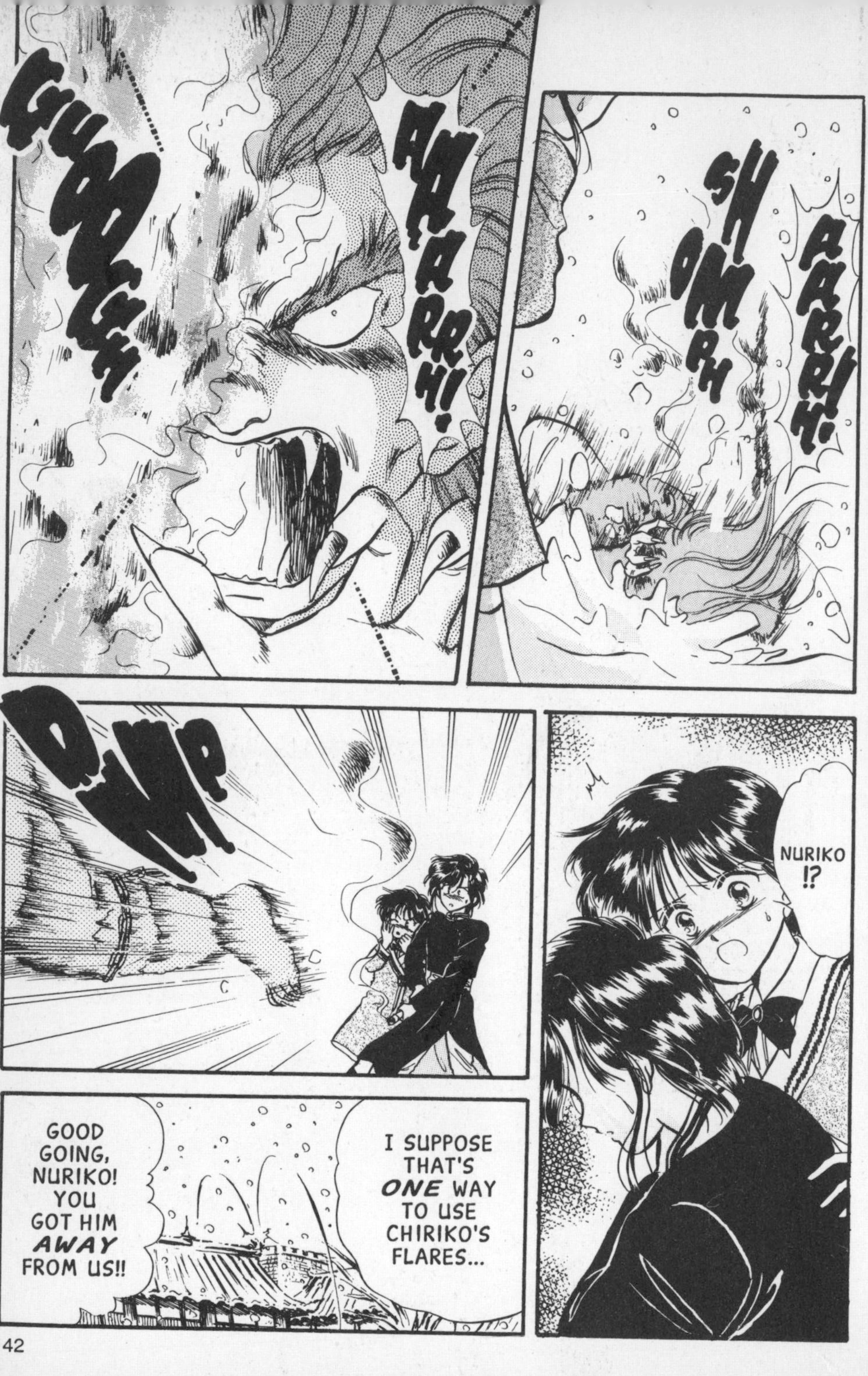
GWOOGH
AAAARRRH!
SHOMPH
AARRH!
DWHP
GOOD GOING, NURIKO! YOU GOT HIM *AWAY* FROM US!!
I SUPPOSE THAT'S *ONE* WAY TO USE CHIRIKO'S FLARES...
NURIKO !?

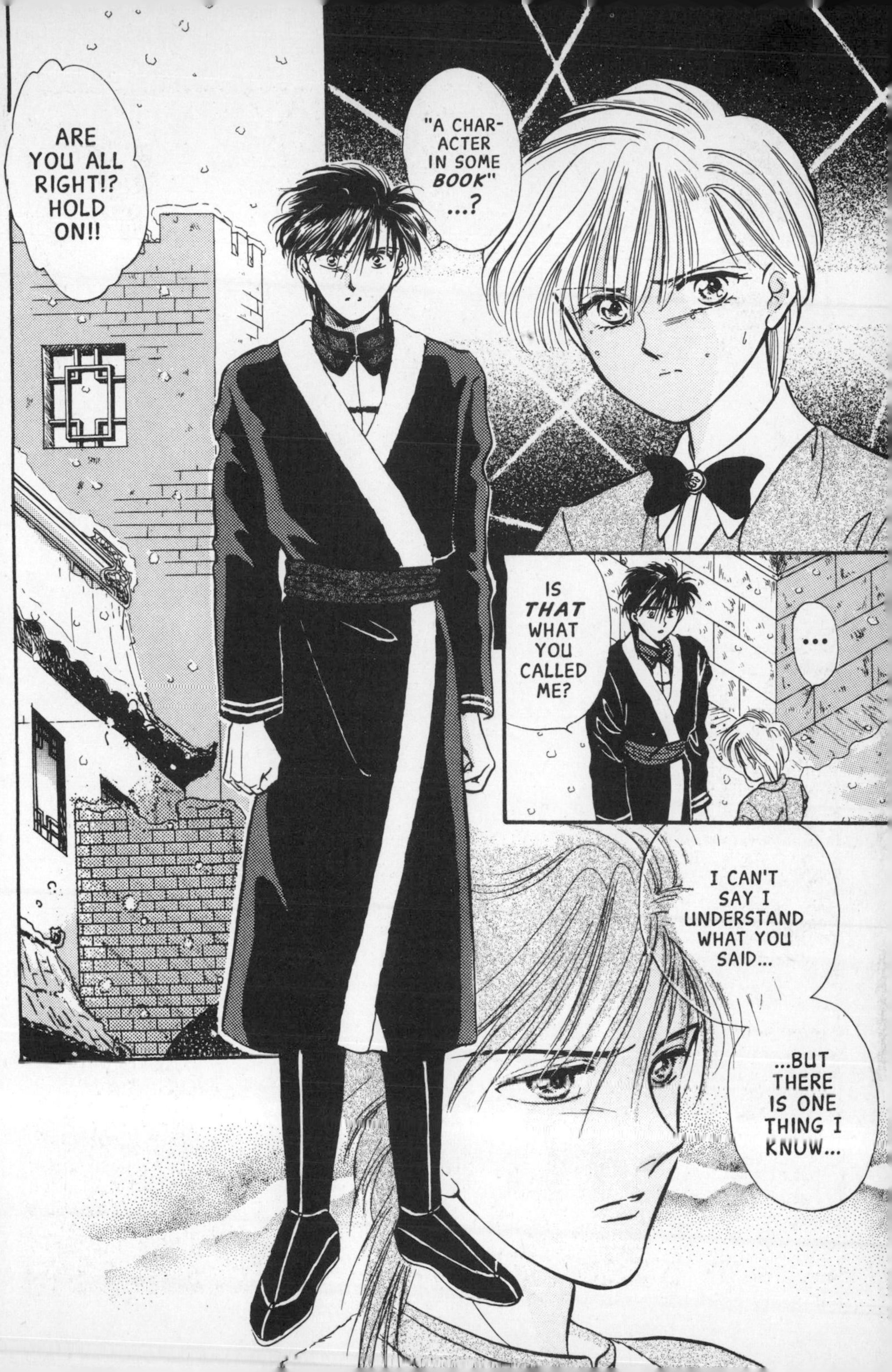
ARE YOU ALL RIGHT!? HOLD ON!!
"A CHARACTER IN SOME *BOOK*" ...?
IS *THAT* WHAT YOU CALLED ME?
...
I CAN'T SAY I UNDERSTAND WHAT YOU SAID...
...BUT THERE IS ONE THING I KNOW...

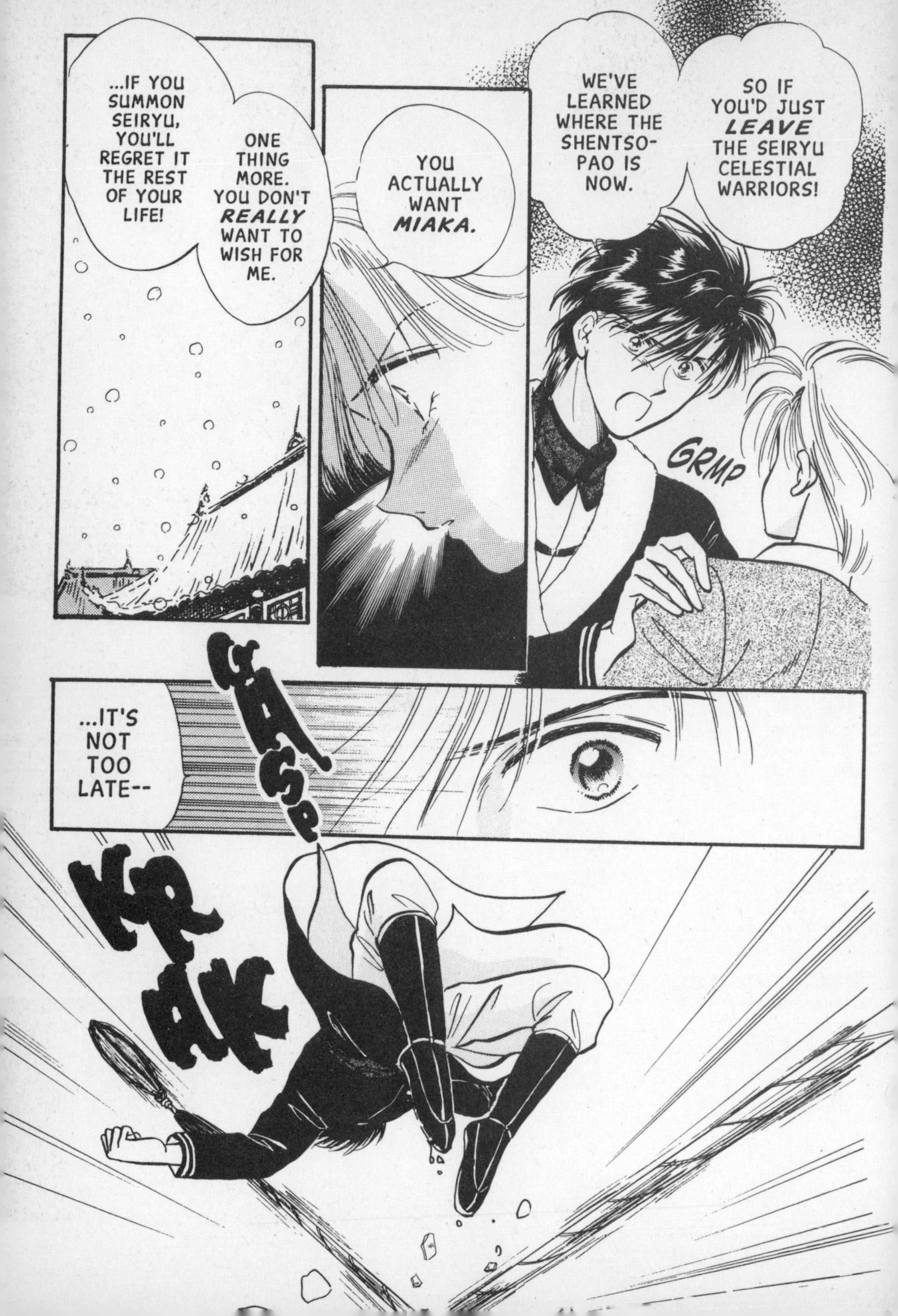

...IF YOU SUMMON SEIRYU, YOU'LL REGRET IT THE REST OF YOUR LIFE!
ONE THING MORE. YOU DON'T *REALLY* WANT TO WISH FOR ME.
YOU ACTUALLY WANT *MIAKA.*
WE'VE LEARNED WHERE THE SHENTSO-PAO IS NOW.
SO IF YOU'D JUST *LEAVE* THE SEIRYU CELESTIAL WARRIORS!
GRMP
...IT'S NOT TOO LATE--
GASP
KRAK

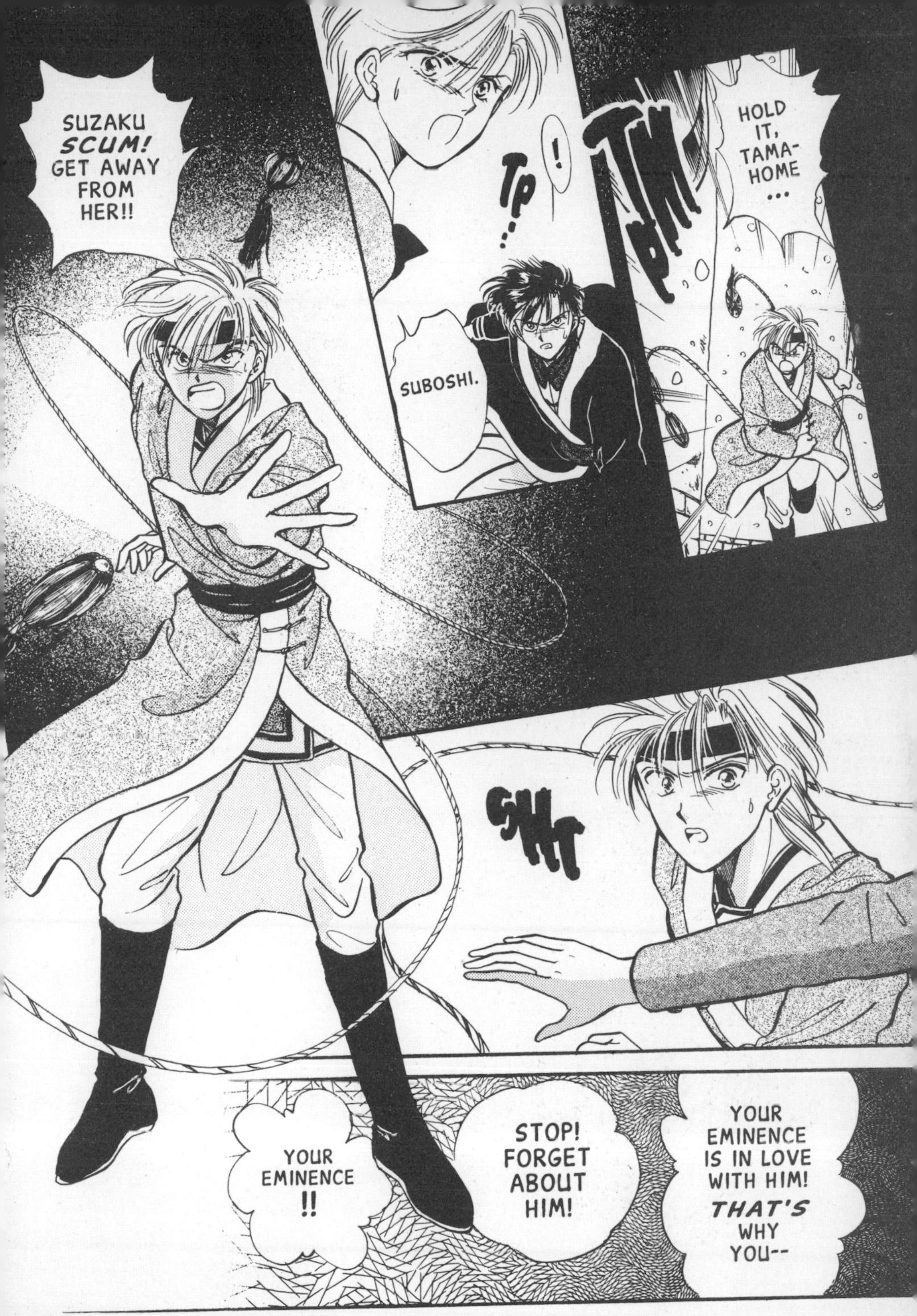

SUZAKU SCUM! GET AWAY FROM HER!!
!
TP..
SUBOSHI.
TMP
HOLD IT, TAMA-HOME ...
SHT
YOUR EMINENCE !!
STOP! FORGET ABOUT HIM!
YOUR EMINENCE IS IN LOVE WITH HIM! THAT'S WHY YOU--

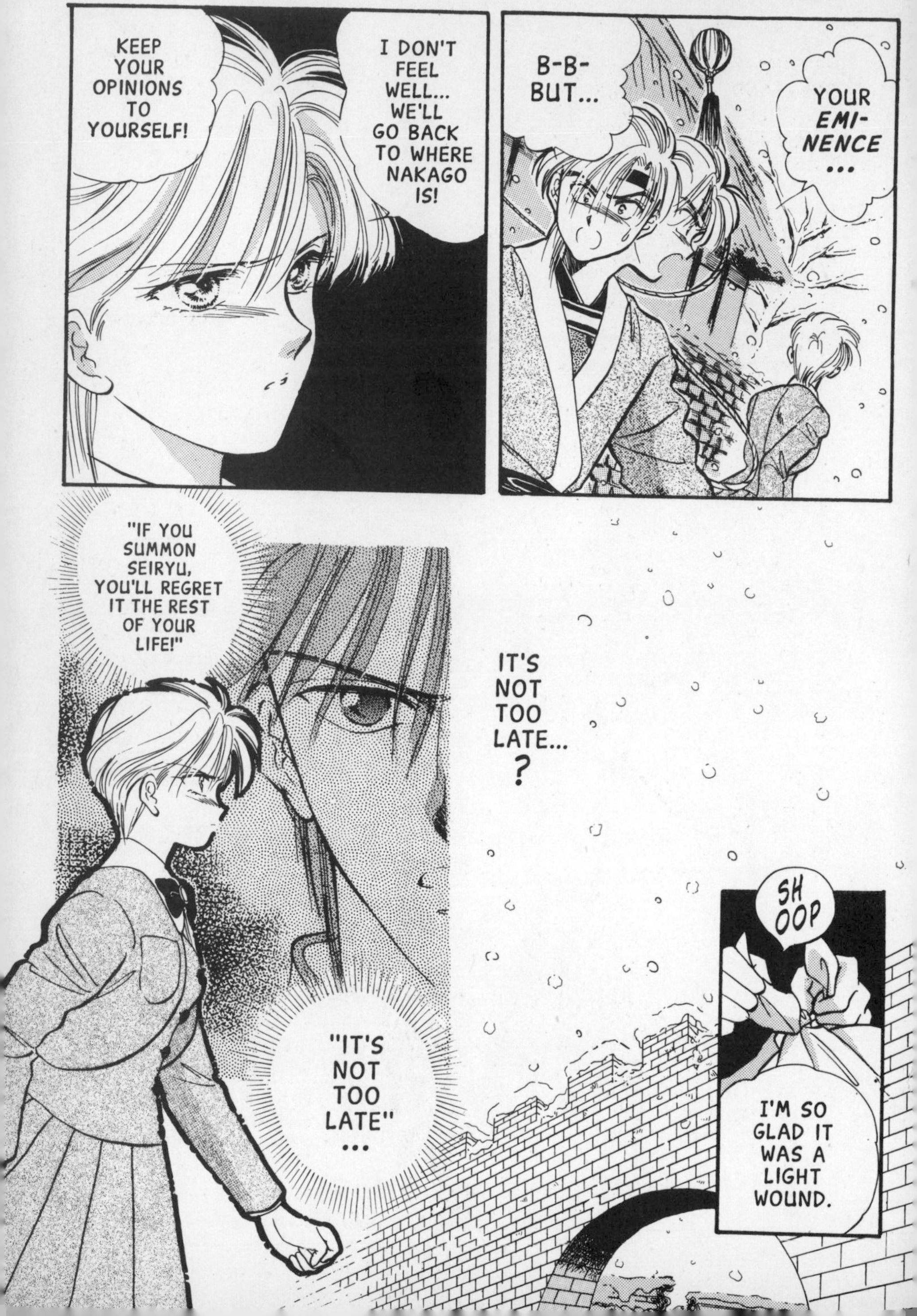
KEEP YOUR OPINIONS TO YOURSELF!
I DON'T FEEL WELL... WE'LL GO BACK TO WHERE NAKAGO IS!
B-B-BUT...
YOUR *EMINENCE* ...
"IF YOU SUMMON SEIRYU, YOU'LL REGRET IT THE REST OF YOUR LIFE!"
IT'S NOT TOO LATE... ?
"IT'S NOT TOO LATE" ...
SHOOP
I'M SO GLAD IT WAS A LIGHT WOUND.

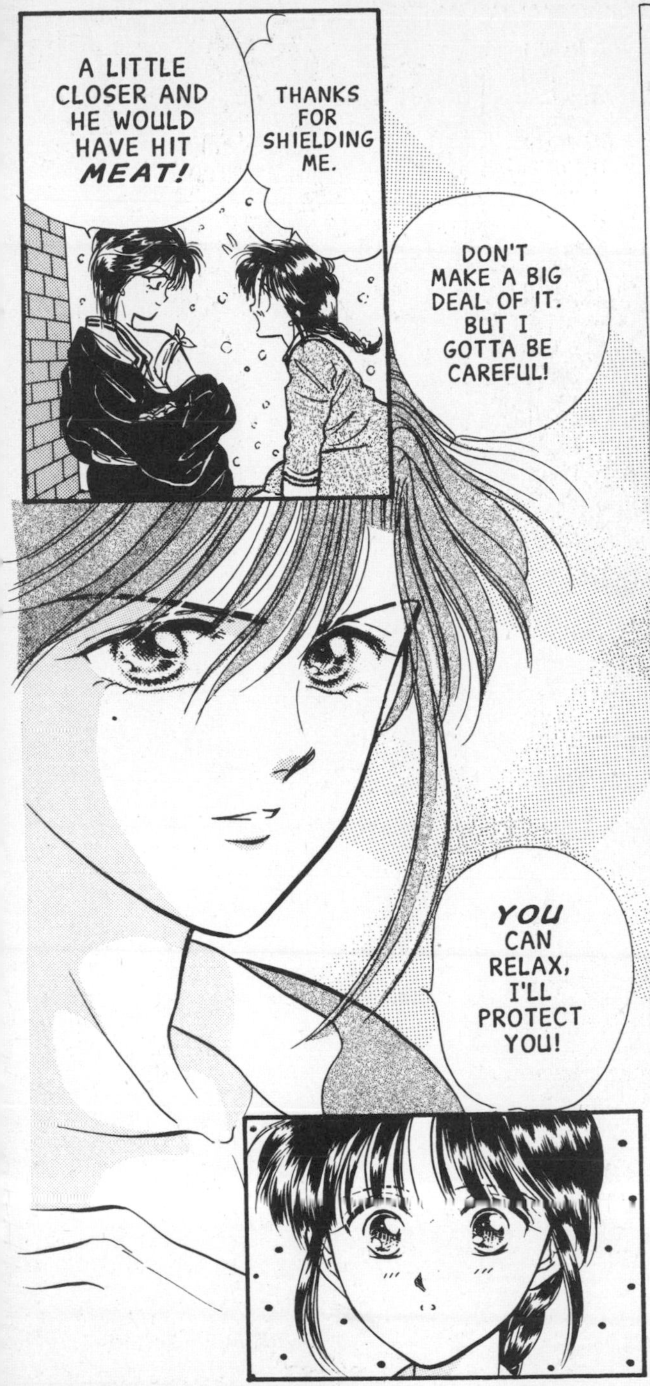
A LITTLE CLOSER AND HE WOULD HAVE HIT *MEAT!*
THANKS FOR SHIELDING ME.
DON'T MAKE A BIG DEAL OF IT. BUT I GOTTA BE CAREFUL!
YOU CAN RELAX, I'LL PROTECT YOU!

These statues are 180-185 cm tall. I guess people were taller back then. I heard something about how the more civilization advances and the smarter we are, the shorter we get. *Really?* Which would mean there were men as tall as Tasuki and Tamahome. That's thousands of years ago! And guys like them were walking the Earth! *Ba-dump! Ba-dump!* But before these statues were made, living soldiers were buried alive in the emperor's tomb. I'll bet it was awful! Or did their loyalty numb the pain? The Chinese are supposed to be very loyal. Once they've committed, they go all the way, even risking their lives. On the other hand, they have a reputation of being merciless and wily. I'll bet most readers (myself included) have a notion of China that's based on the clothes they wear in the Hong Kong Kung Fu movies. A "Pseudo-Chinese" man. (Do you have any idea what I'm trying to say? ()) But the real China seems more Earthy and alive!
It's a land where you get the feeling that a lot of people have given their blood and tears in endless wars. It's not to be taken lightly. A man's country! And the tough women who survived in their shadows. "Fushigi Yûgi" has gradually evolved from "Pseudo-Chinese" to a more "Real Chinese" feel. I'd like to draw a story that's both sweet and serious.
Oops, I got side tracked.
I'll continue with my travels next time...

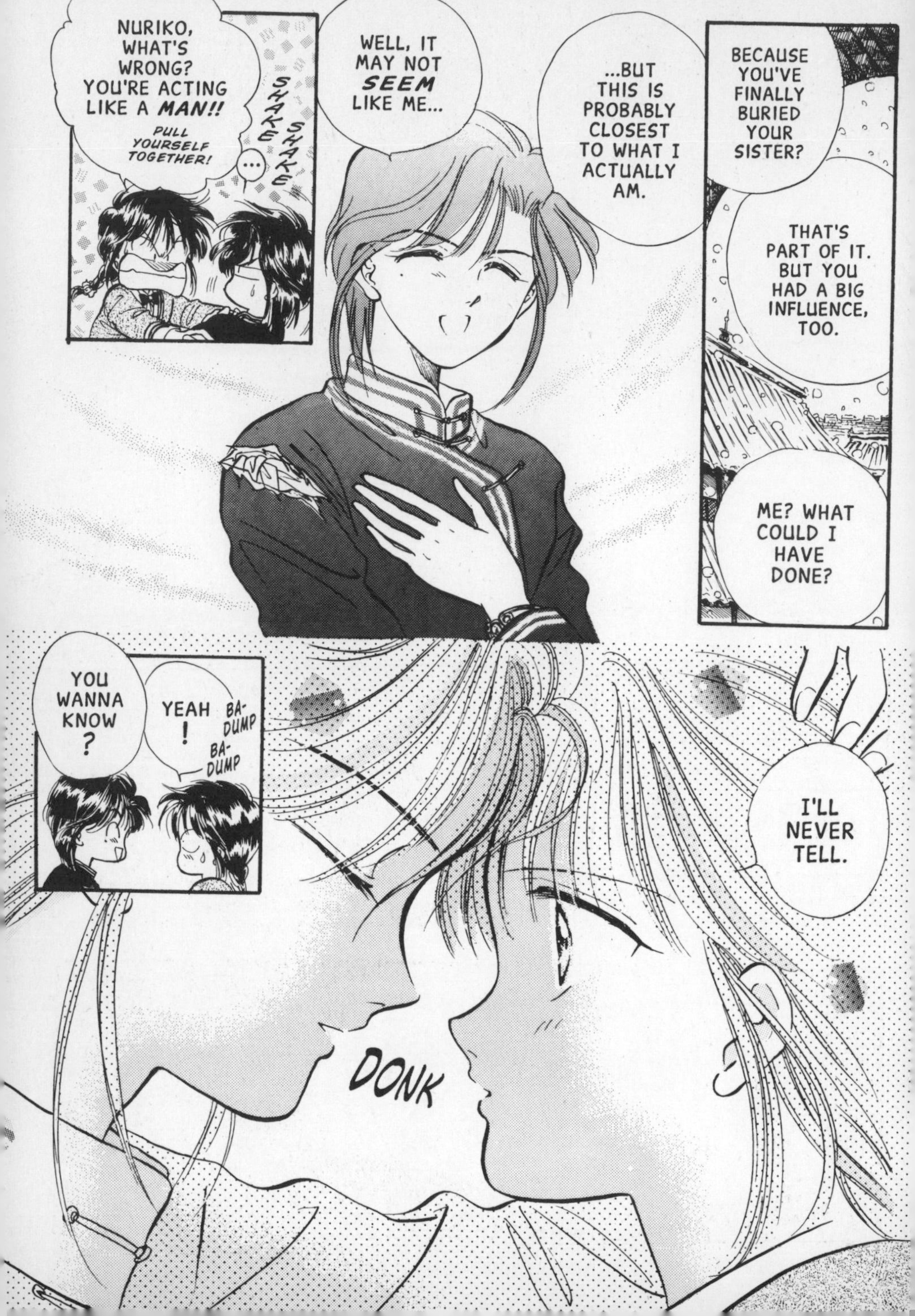
NURIKO, WHAT'S WRONG? YOU'RE ACTING LIKE A MAN!!
PULL YOURSELF TOGETHER!
SHAKE SHAKE
...
WELL, IT MAY NOT SEEM LIKE ME...
...BUT THIS IS PROBABLY CLOSEST TO WHAT I ACTUALLY AM.
BECAUSE YOU'VE FINALLY BURIED YOUR SISTER?
THAT'S PART OF IT. BUT YOU HAD A BIG INFLUENCE, TOO.
ME? WHAT COULD I HAVE DONE?
YOU WANNA KNOW?
YEAH!
BA-DUMP BA-DUMP
I'LL NEVER TELL.
DONK

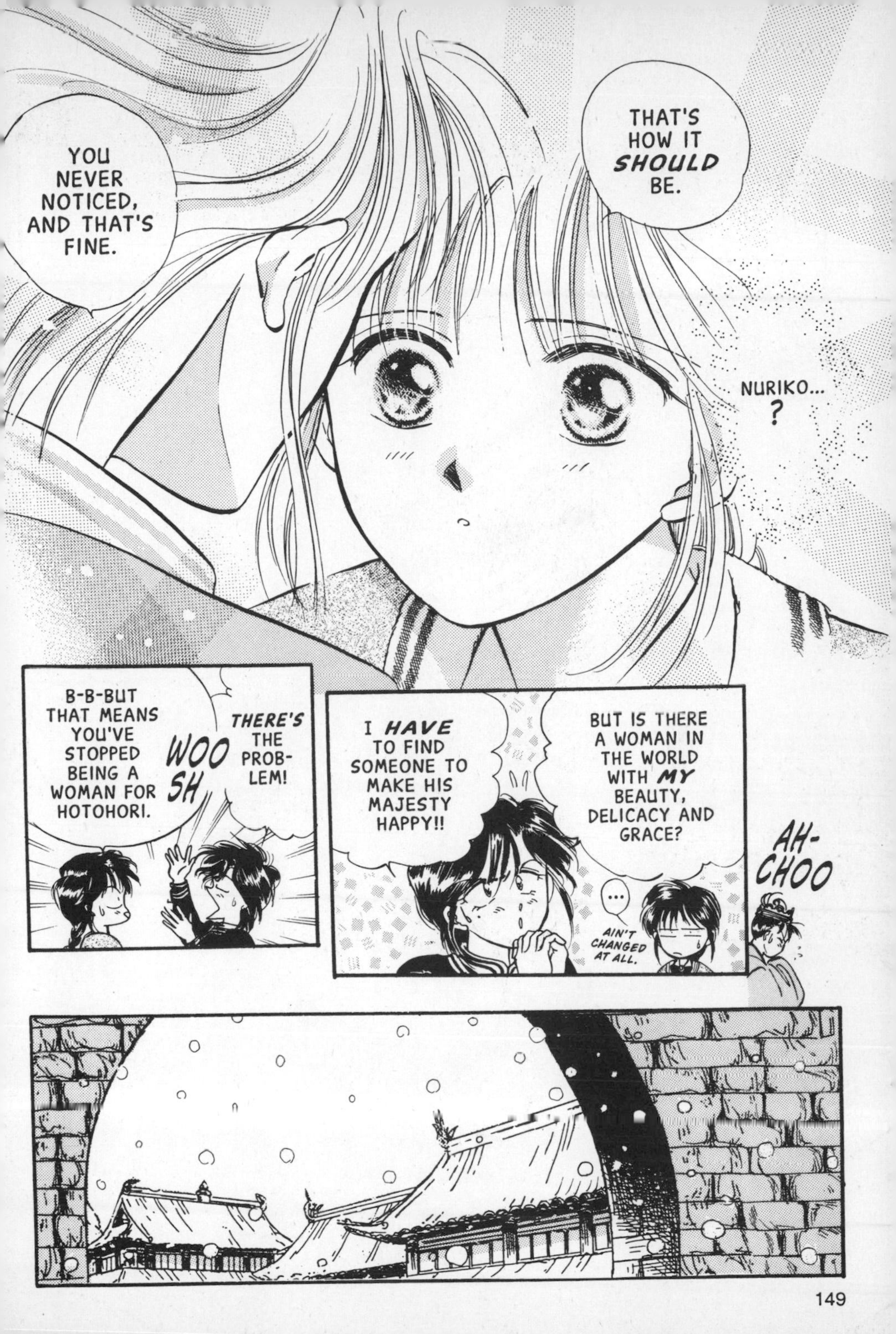

YOU NEVER NOTICED, AND THAT'S FINE.
THAT'S HOW IT SHOULD BE.
NURIKO...?
B-B-BUT THAT MEANS YOU'VE STOPPED BEING A WOMAN FOR HOTOHORI.
WOOSH
THERE'S THE PROB-LEM!
I HAVE TO FIND SOMEONE TO MAKE HIS MAJESTY HAPPY!!
BUT IS THERE A WOMAN IN THE WORLD WITH MY BEAUTY, DELICACY AND GRACE?
...
AIN'T CHANGED AT ALL.
AH-CHOO

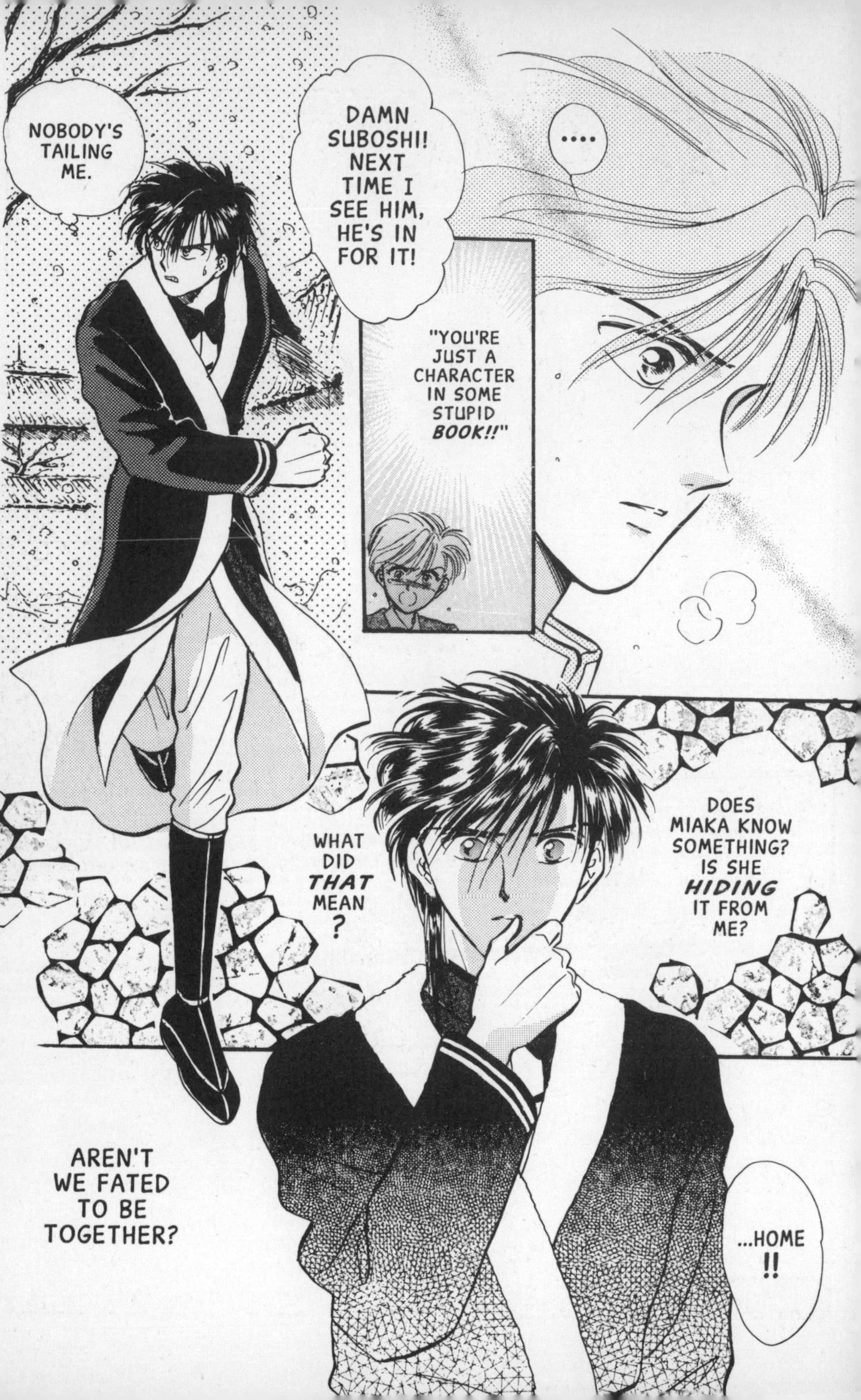
NOBODY'S TAILING ME.
DAMN SUBOSHI! NEXT TIME I SEE HIM, HE'S IN FOR IT!
....
"YOU'RE JUST A CHARACTER IN SOME STUPID BOOK!!"
WHAT DID THAT MEAN ?
DOES MIAKA KNOW SOMETHING? IS SHE HIDING IT FROM ME?
AREN'T WE FATED TO BE TOGETHER?
...HOME !!

TAMA-HOME!!

SHUNK

MAYBE MY SNOWBALL WAS A LITTLE TOO BIG.

TAMA-HOME!

OW...

NURIKO!! CAN'T YOU TELL WHEN A GUY'S LOST IN THOUGHT!?!

I'M SO *GLAD* TO SEE THAT YOU'RE SAFE! DID YOU LEARN ANY-THING ABOUT THE SHENTSO-PAO?

WELL?

"YOU CAN *NEVER* BE WITH MIAKA UNTIL SHE SUMMONS SUZAKU!"

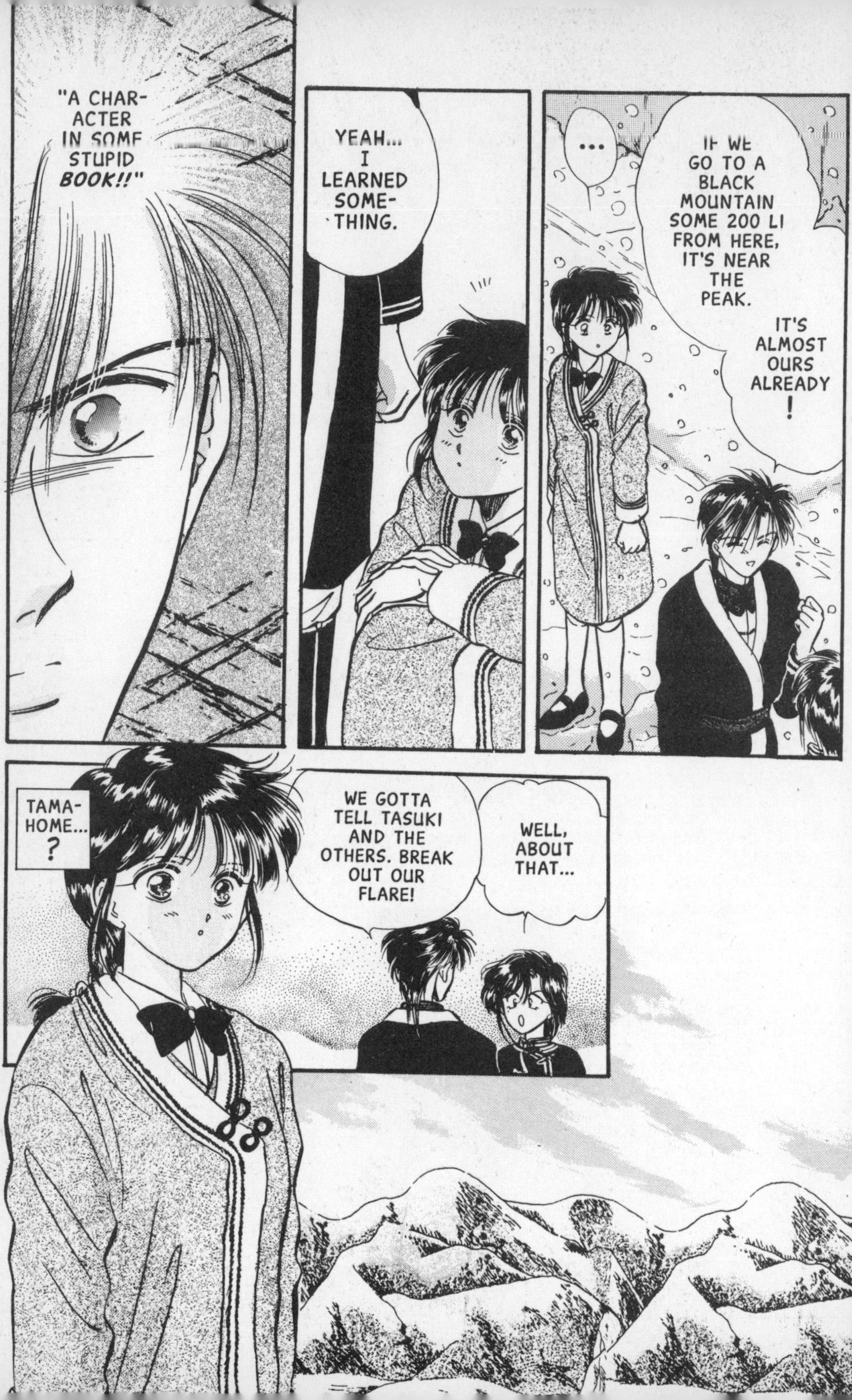
"A CHARACTER IN SOME STUPID BOOK!!"
YEAH... I LEARNED SOMETHING.
...
IF WE GO TO A BLACK MOUNTAIN SOME 200 LI FROM HERE, IT'S NEAR THE PEAK.
IT'S ALMOST OURS ALREADY!
TAMAHOME...?
WE GOTTA TELL TASUKI AND THE OTHERS. BREAK OUT OUR FLARE!
WELL, ABOUT THAT...

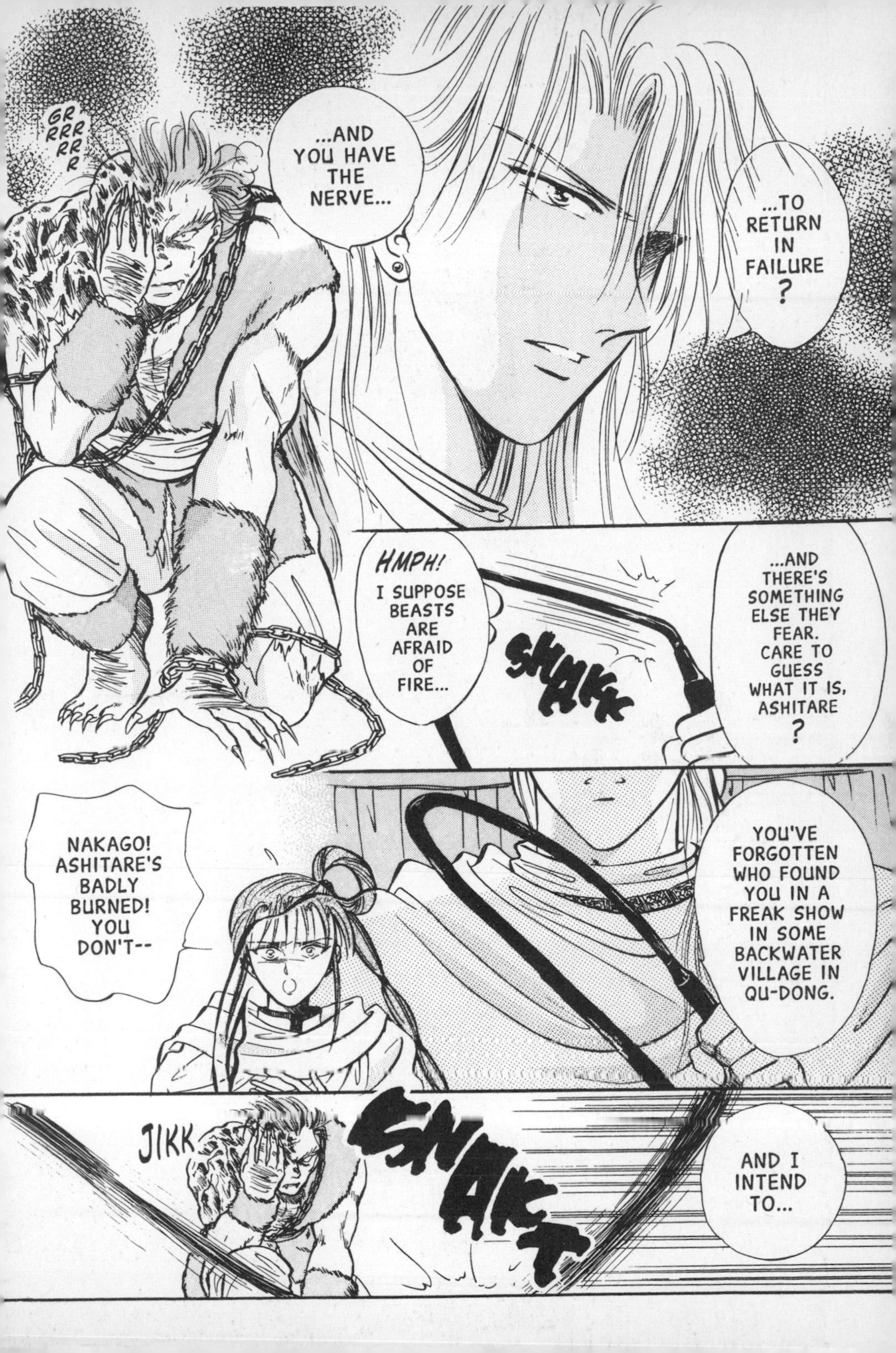
GRRRRRRR
...AND YOU HAVE THE NERVE...
...TO RETURN IN FAILURE?
HMPH! I SUPPOSE BEASTS ARE AFRAID OF FIRE...
SHIKK
...AND THERE'S SOMETHING ELSE THEY FEAR. CARE TO GUESS WHAT IT IS, ASHITARE?
NAKAGO! ASHITARE'S BADLY BURNED! YOU DON'T--
YOU'VE FORGOTTEN WHO FOUND YOU IN A FREAK SHOW IN SOME BACKWATER VILLAGE IN QU-DONG.
JIKK
SNAKT
AND I INTEND TO...

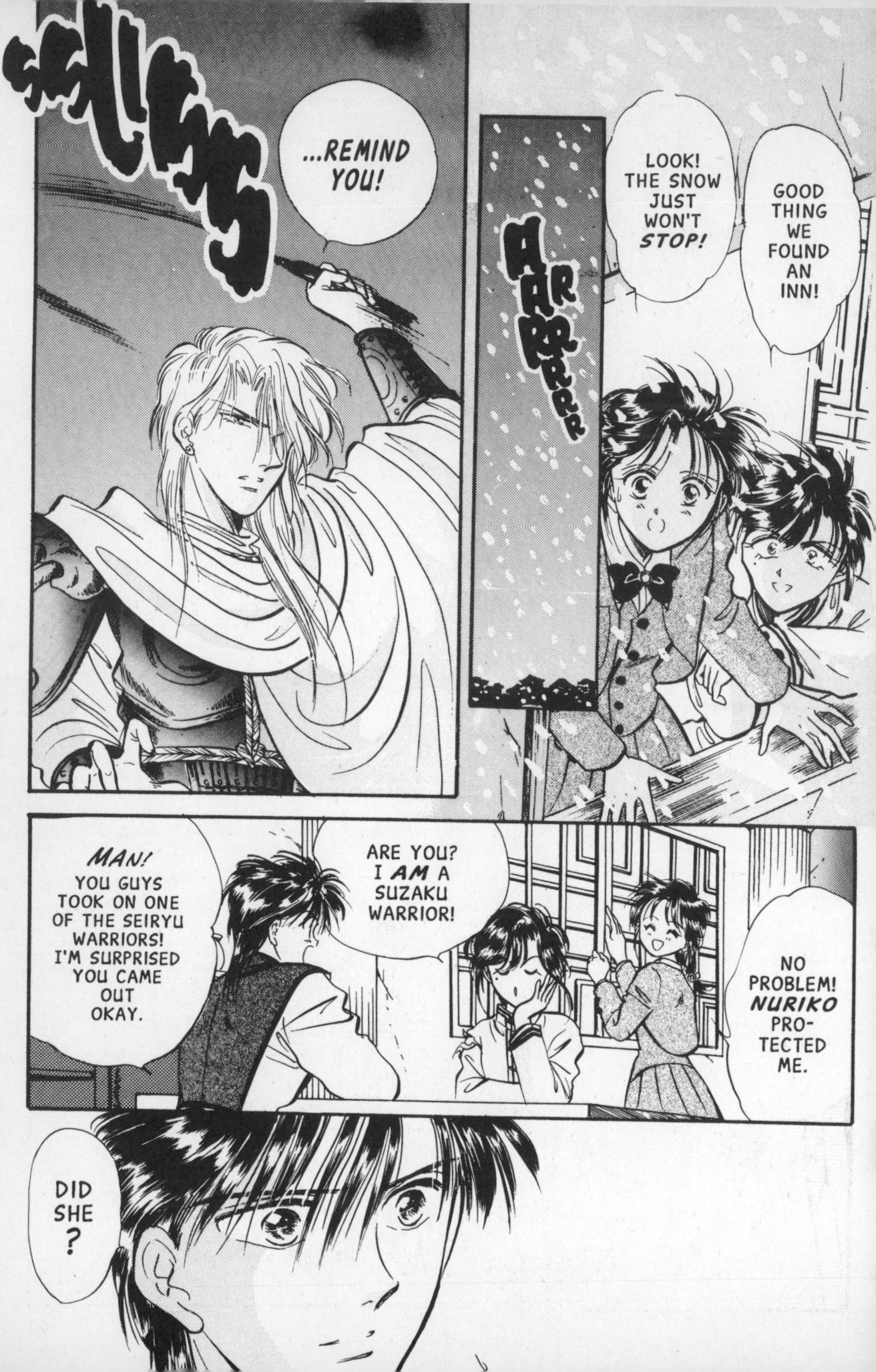

...REMIND YOU!
LOOK! THE SNOW JUST WON'T *STOP!*
GOOD THING WE FOUND AN INN!
MAN! YOU GUYS TOOK ON ONE OF THE SEIRYU WARRIORS! I'M SURPRISED YOU CAME OUT OKAY.
ARE YOU? I *AM* A SUZAKU WARRIOR!
NO PROBLEM! *NURIKO* PRO-TECTED ME.
DID SHE ?

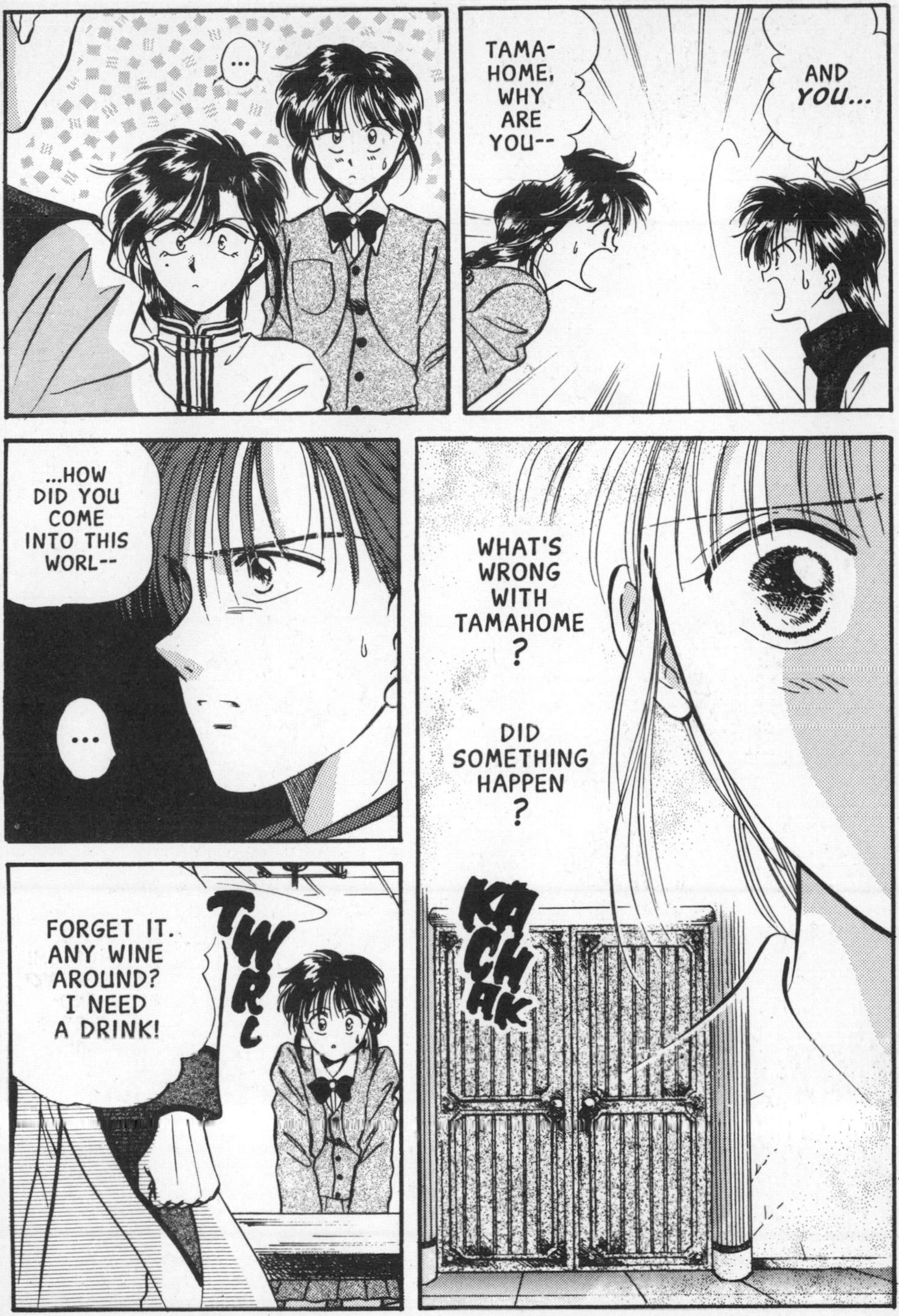
...
TAMA-HOME, WHY ARE YOU--
AND *YOU...*
...HOW DID YOU COME INTO THIS WORL--
...
FORGET IT. ANY WINE AROUND? I NEED A DRINK!
TWRL
WHAT'S WRONG WITH TAMAHOME?
DID SOMETHING HAPPEN?
KACHAK

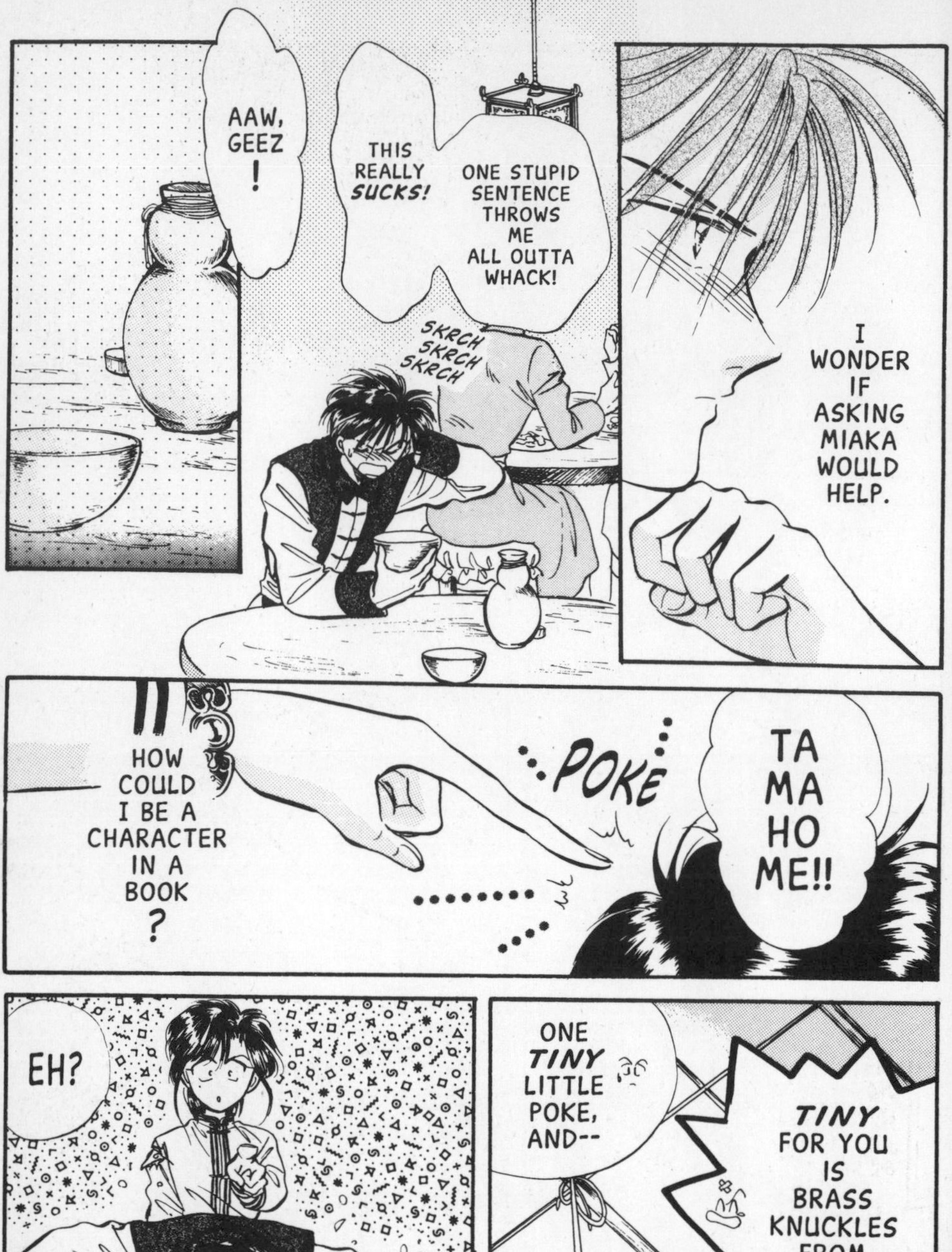
AAW, GEEZ!
THIS REALLY SUCKS!
ONE STUPID SENTENCE THROWS ME ALL OUTTA WHACK!
SKRCH SKRCH SKRCH
I WONDER IF ASKING MIAKA WOULD HELP.
HOW COULD I BE A CHARACTER IN A BOOK?
POKE
....
TAMAHOME!!
EH?
ONE TINY LITTLE POKE, AND--
TINY FOR YOU IS BRASS KNUCKLES FROM ANYBODY HUMAN!

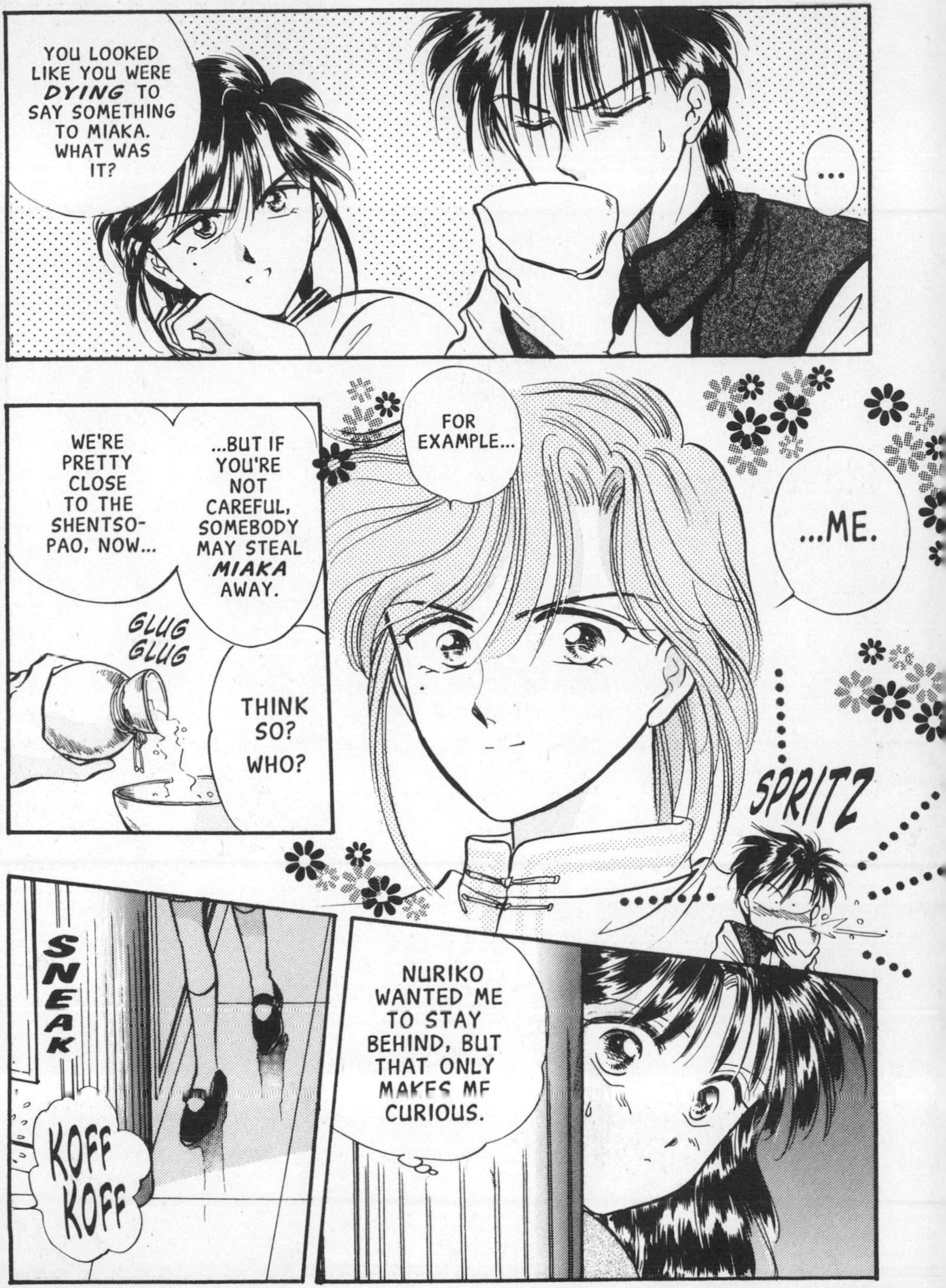
YOU LOOKED LIKE YOU WERE *DYING* TO SAY SOMETHING TO MIAKA. WHAT WAS IT?
...
WE'RE PRETTY CLOSE TO THE SHENTSO-PAO, NOW...
...BUT IF YOU'RE NOT CAREFUL, SOMEBODY MAY STEAL *MIAKA* AWAY.
GLUG GLUG
THINK SO? WHO?
FOR EXAMPLE...
...ME.
SPRITZ
SNEAK
KOFF KOFF
NURIKO WANTED ME TO STAY BEHIND, BUT THAT ONLY MAKES ME CURIOUS.

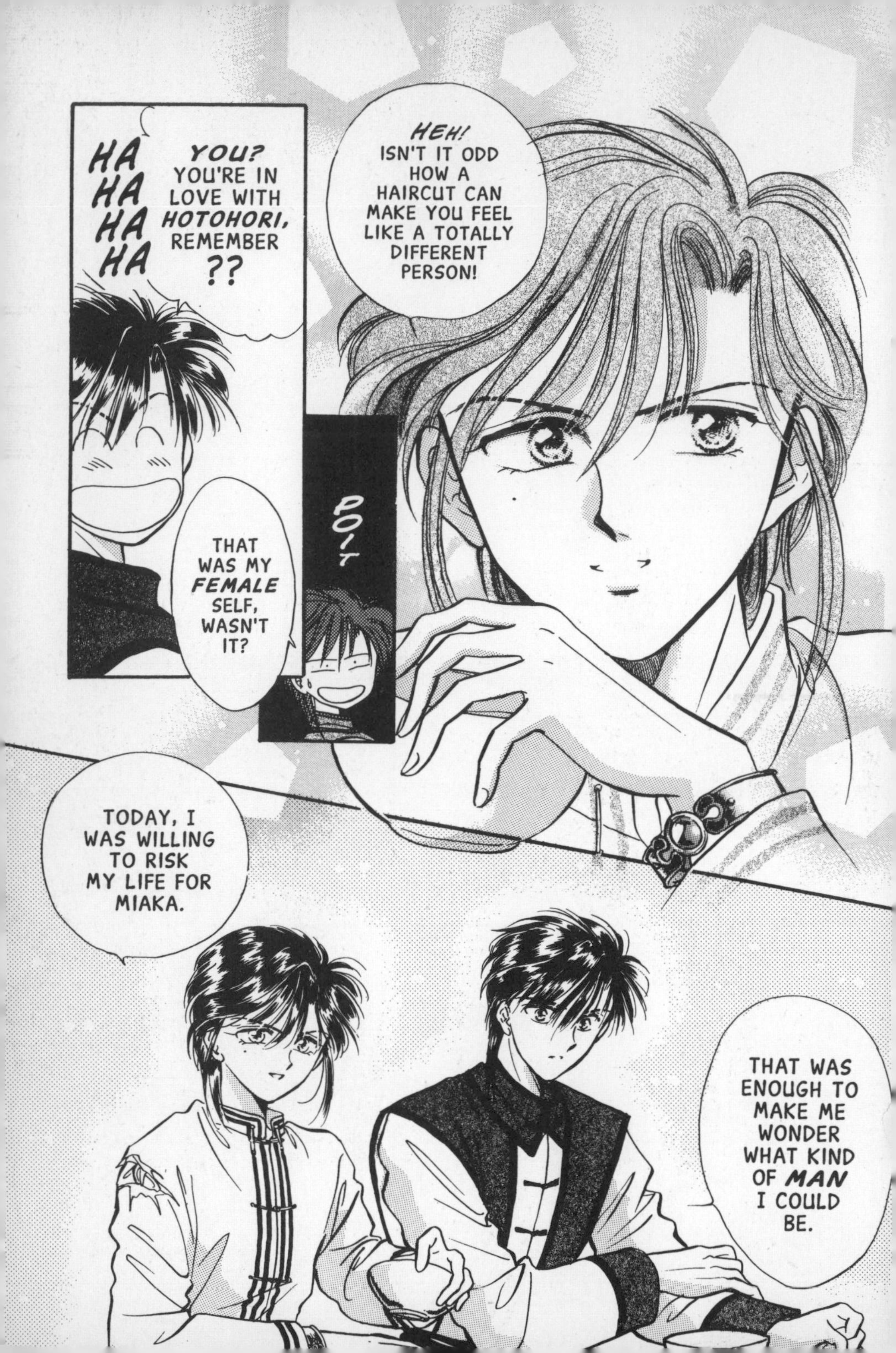
HA HA HA HA
YOU? YOU'RE IN LOVE WITH HOTOHORI, REMEMBER ??
POIT
THAT WAS MY FEMALE SELF, WASN'T IT?
HEH! ISN'T IT ODD HOW A HAIRCUT CAN MAKE YOU FEEL LIKE A TOTALLY DIFFERENT PERSON!
TODAY, I WAS WILLING TO RISK MY LIFE FOR MIAKA.
THAT WAS ENOUGH TO MAKE ME WONDER WHAT KIND OF MAN I COULD BE.

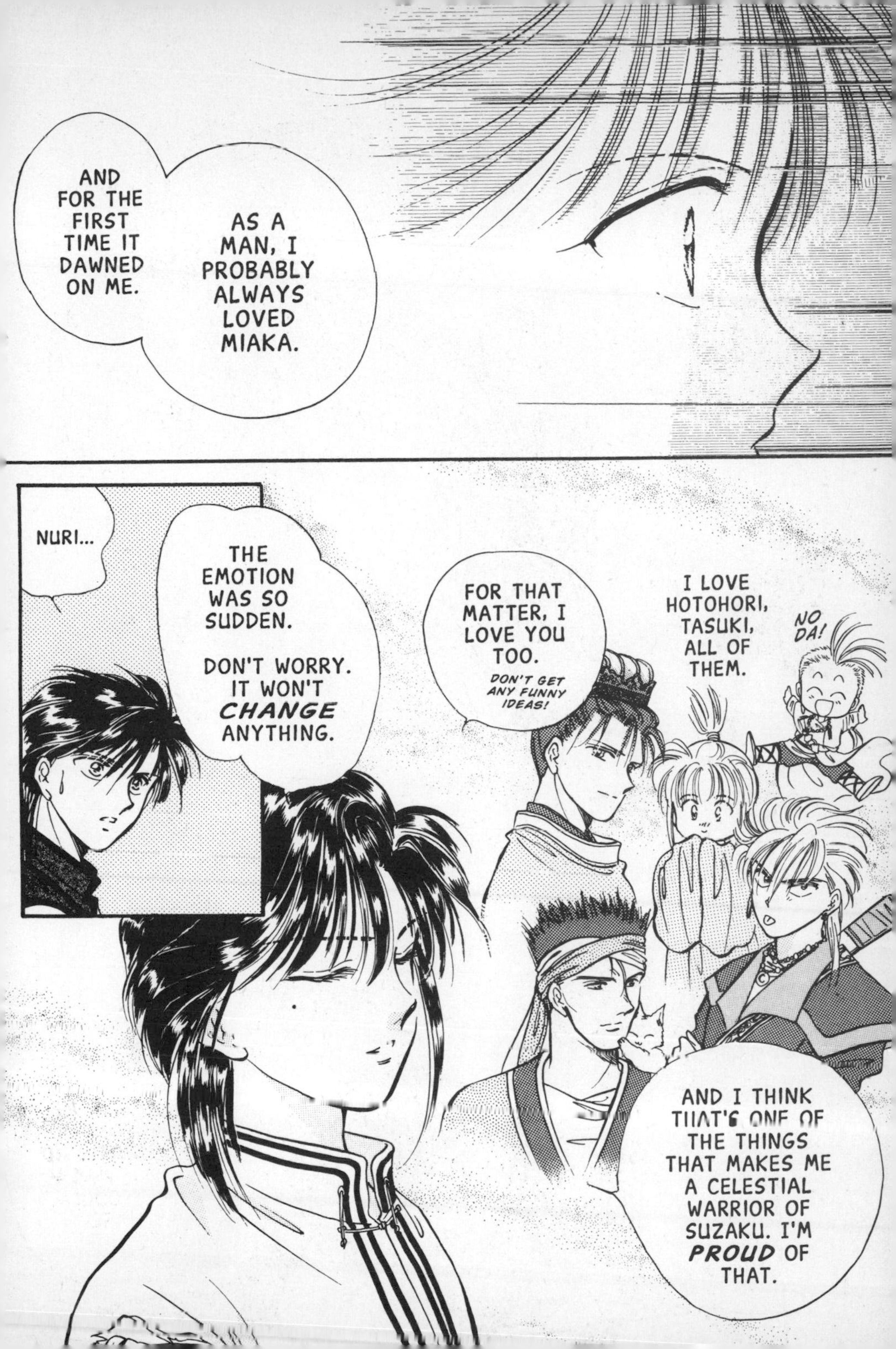
AND FOR THE FIRST TIME IT DAWNED ON ME.
AS A MAN, I PROBABLY ALWAYS LOVED MIAKA.
NURI...
THE EMOTION WAS SO SUDDEN.
DON'T WORRY. IT WON'T *CHANGE* ANYTHING.
FOR THAT MATTER, I LOVE YOU TOO.
DON'T GET ANY FUNNY IDEAS!
I LOVE HOTOHORI, TASUKI, ALL OF THEM.
NO DA!
AND I THINK THAT'S ONE OF THE THINGS THAT MAKES ME A CELESTIAL WARRIOR OF SUZAKU. I'M *PROUD* OF THAT.

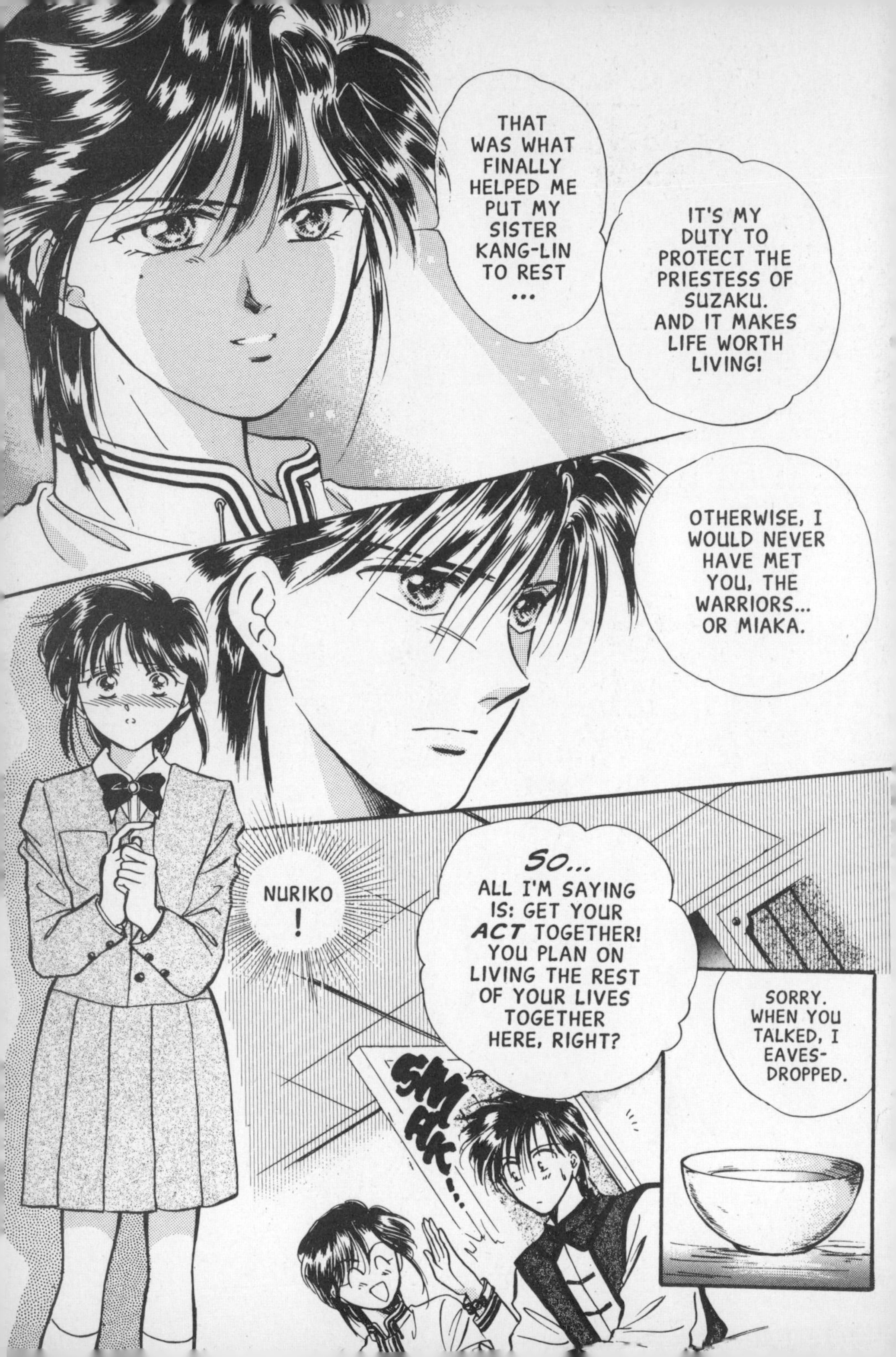
THAT WAS WHAT FINALLY HELPED ME PUT MY SISTER KANG-LIN TO REST ...
IT'S MY DUTY TO PROTECT THE PRIESTESS OF SUZAKU. AND IT MAKES LIFE WORTH LIVING!
OTHERWISE, I WOULD NEVER HAVE MET YOU, THE WARRIORS... OR MIAKA.
NURIKO !
SO... ALL I'M SAYING IS: GET YOUR *ACT* TOGETHER! YOU PLAN ON LIVING THE REST OF YOUR LIVES TOGETHER HERE, RIGHT?
SMAK...
SORRY. WHEN YOU TALKED, I EAVES-DROPPED.

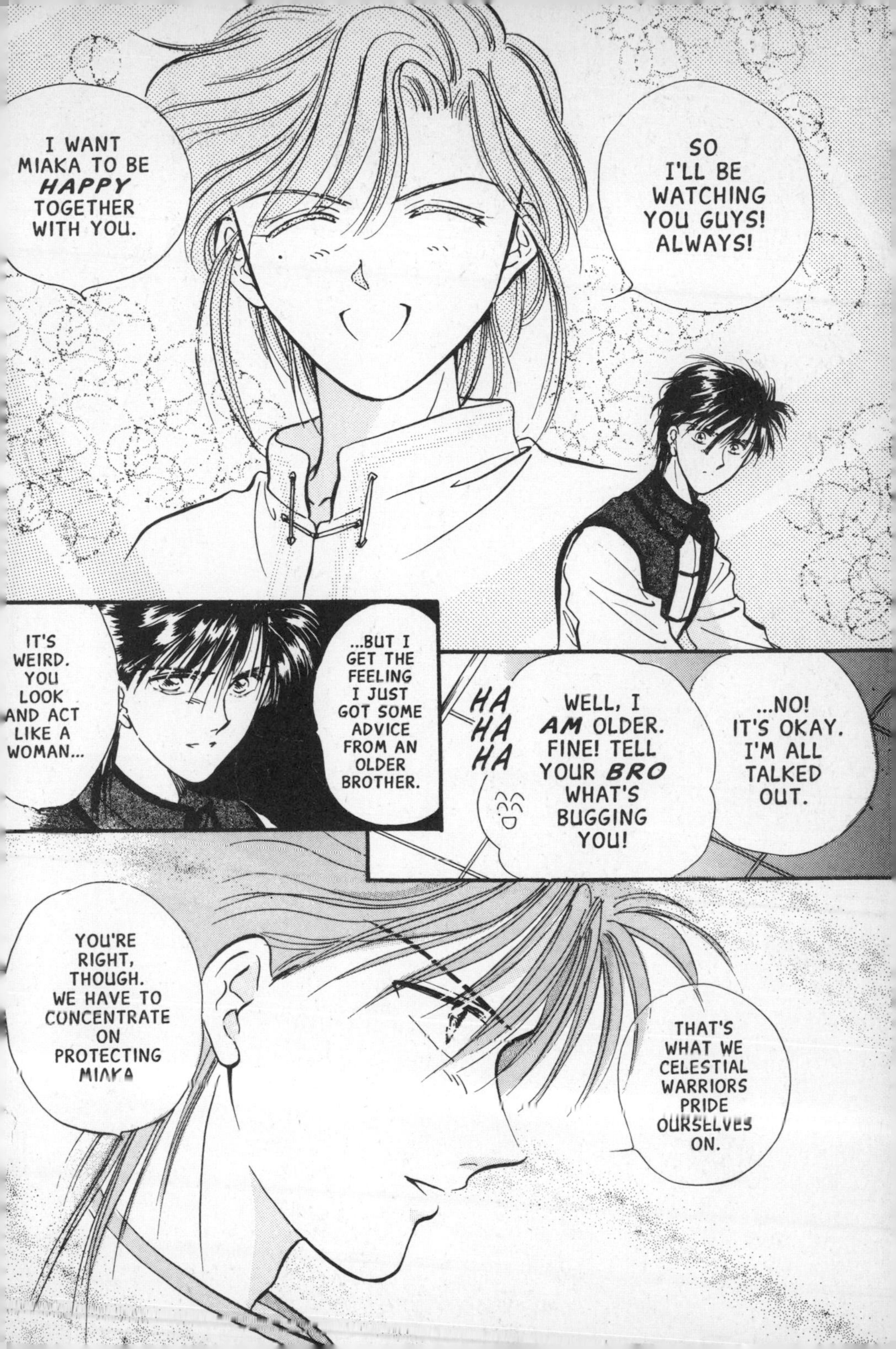
I WANT MIAKA TO BE HAPPY TOGETHER WITH YOU.
SO I'LL BE WATCHING YOU GUYS! ALWAYS!
IT'S WEIRD. YOU LOOK AND ACT LIKE A WOMAN...
...BUT I GET THE FEELING I JUST GOT SOME ADVICE FROM AN OLDER BROTHER.
HA HA HA
WELL, I AM OLDER. FINE! TELL YOUR BRO WHAT'S BUGGING YOU!
...NO! IT'S OKAY. I'M ALL TALKED OUT.
YOU'RE RIGHT, THOUGH. WE HAVE TO CONCENTRATE ON PROTECTING MIAKA
THAT'S WHAT WE CELESTIAL WARRIORS PRIDE OURSELVES ON.

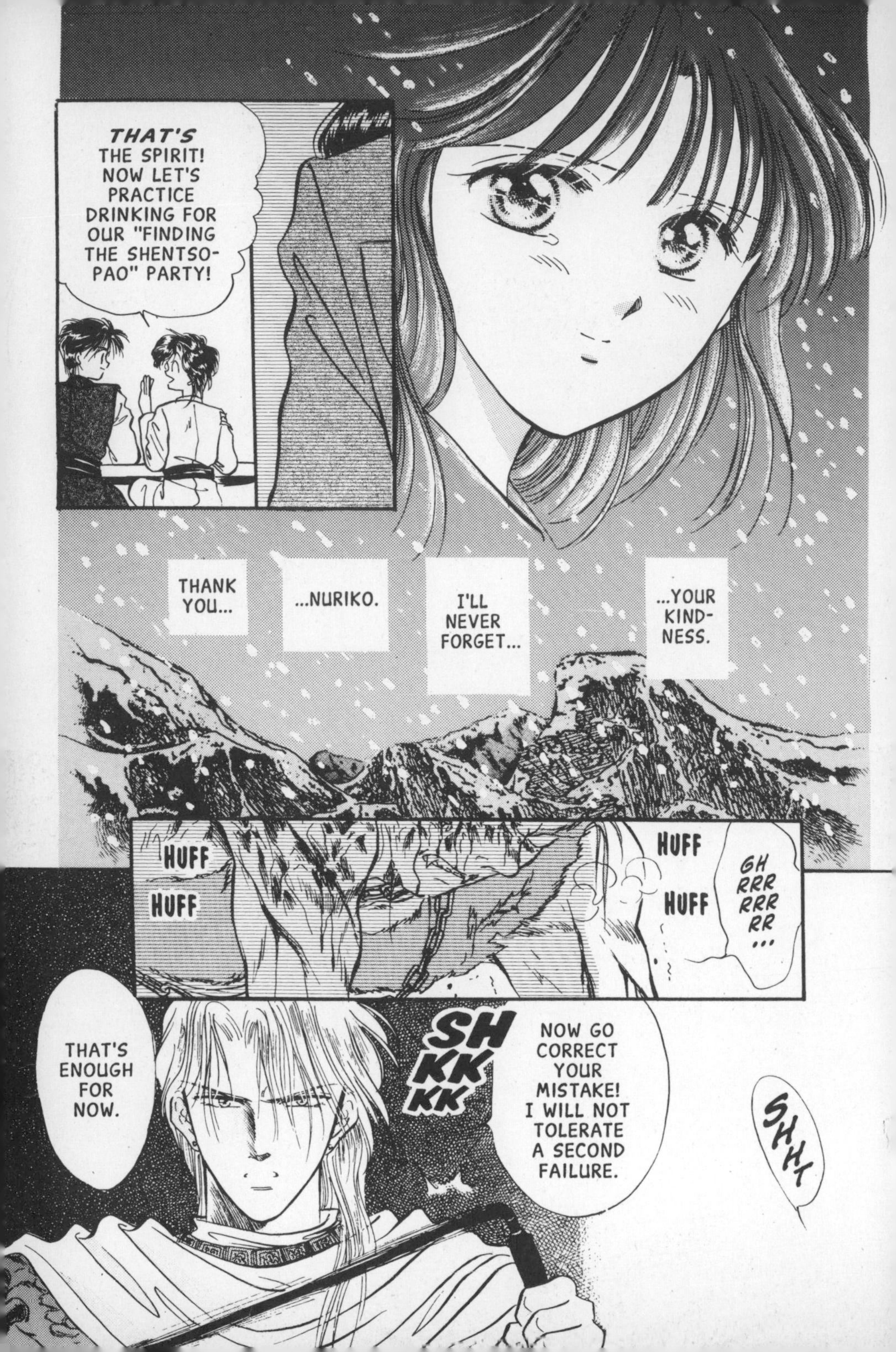
THAT'S THE SPIRIT! NOW LET'S PRACTICE DRINKING FOR OUR "FINDING THE SHENTSO-PAO" PARTY!
THANK YOU...
...NURIKO.
I'LL NEVER FORGET...
...YOUR KINDNESS.
HUFF
HUFF
HUFF
HUFF
GHRRRRRRRR...
THAT'S ENOUGH FOR NOW.
SHKKKK
NOW GO CORRECT YOUR MISTAKE! I WILL NOT TOLERATE A SECOND FAILURE.
SHHH

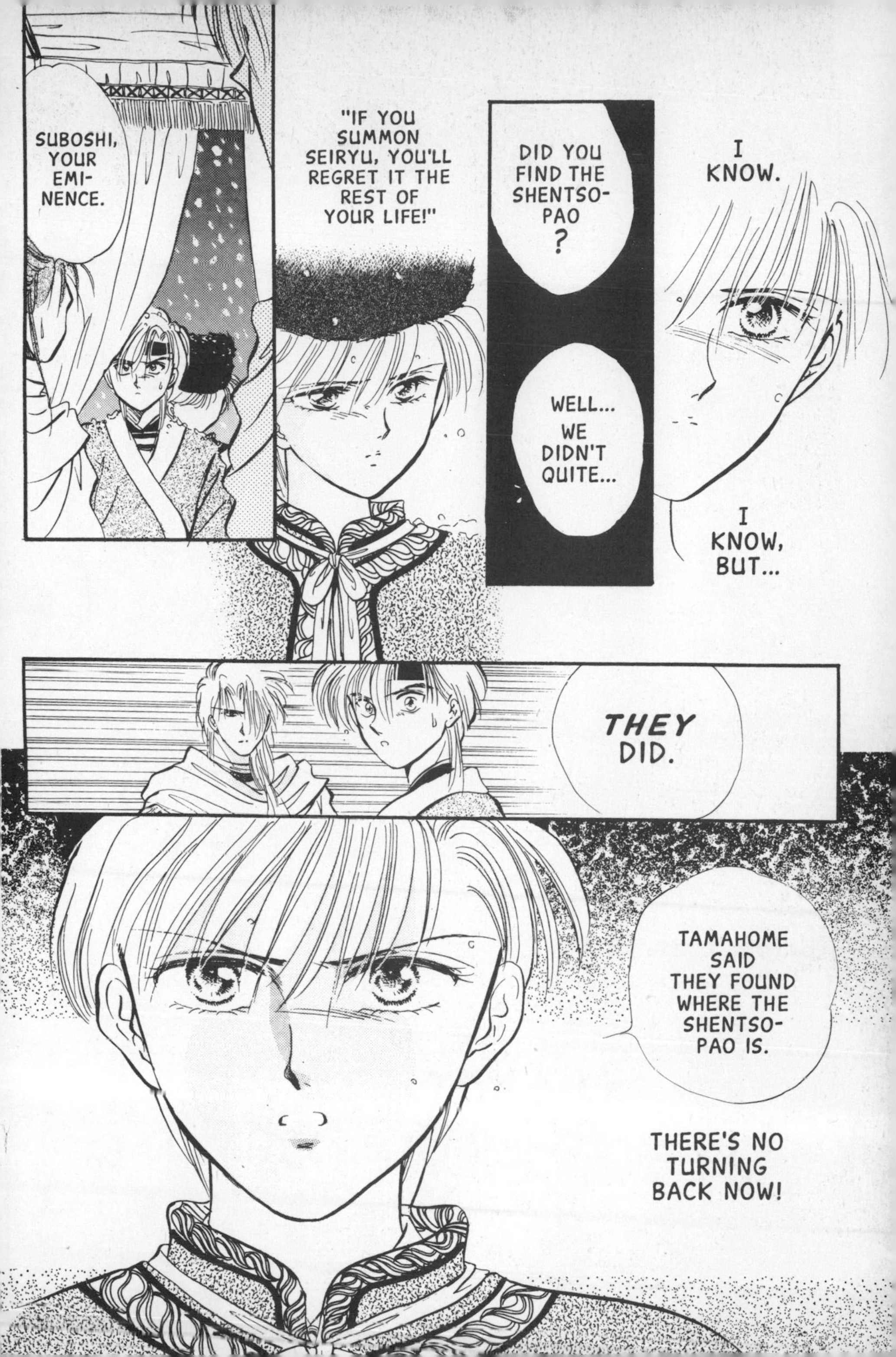
SUBOSHI, YOUR EMINENCE.
"IF YOU SUMMON SEIRYU, YOU'LL REGRET IT THE REST OF YOUR LIFE!"
DID YOU FIND THE SHENTSO-PAO ?
WELL... WE DIDN'T QUITE...
I KNOW.
I KNOW, BUT...
THEY DID.
TAMAHOME SAID THEY FOUND WHERE THE SHENTSO-PAO IS.
THERE'S NO TURNING BACK NOW!

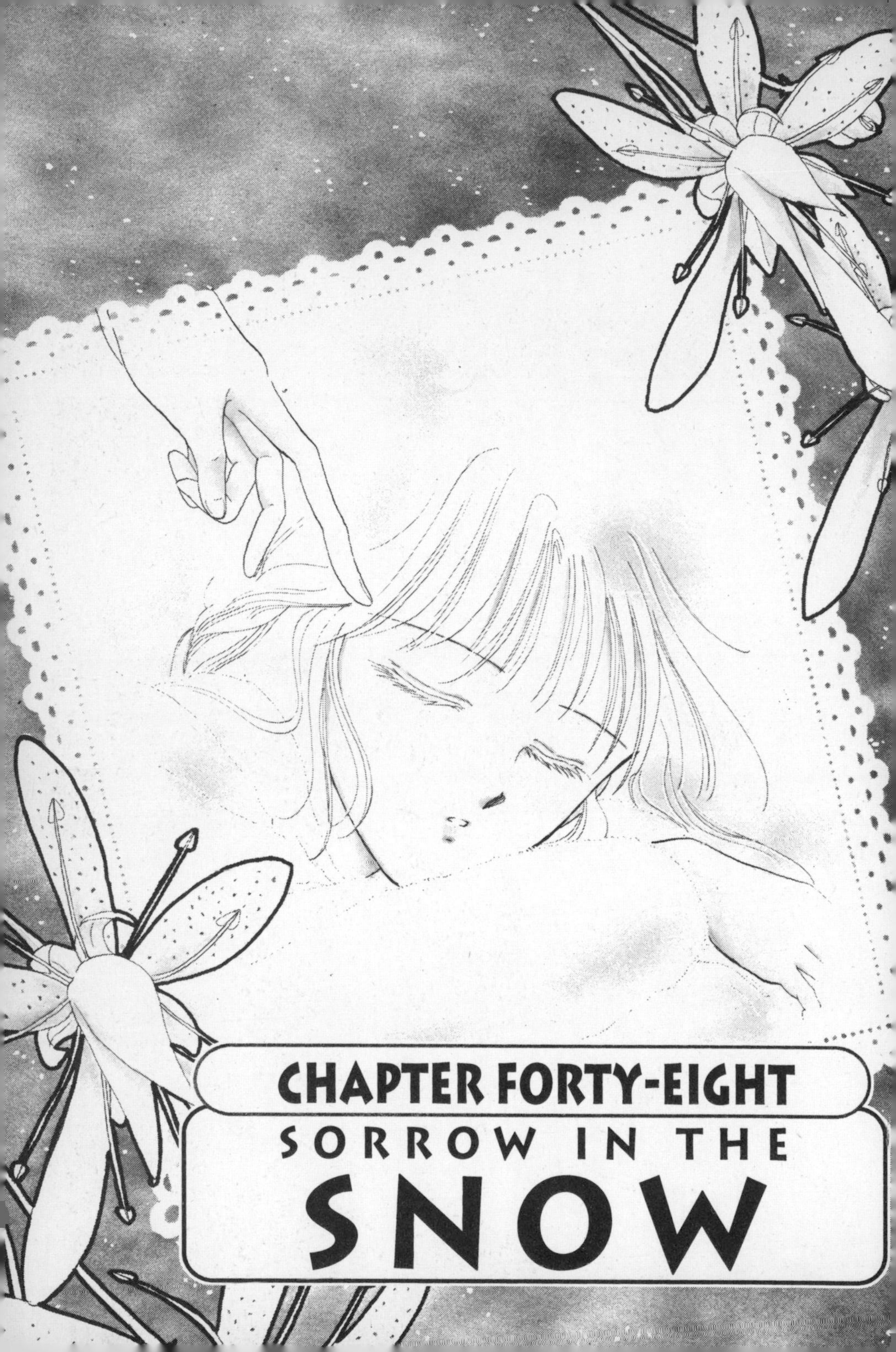
CHAPTER FORTY-EIGHT
SORROW IN THE
SNOW

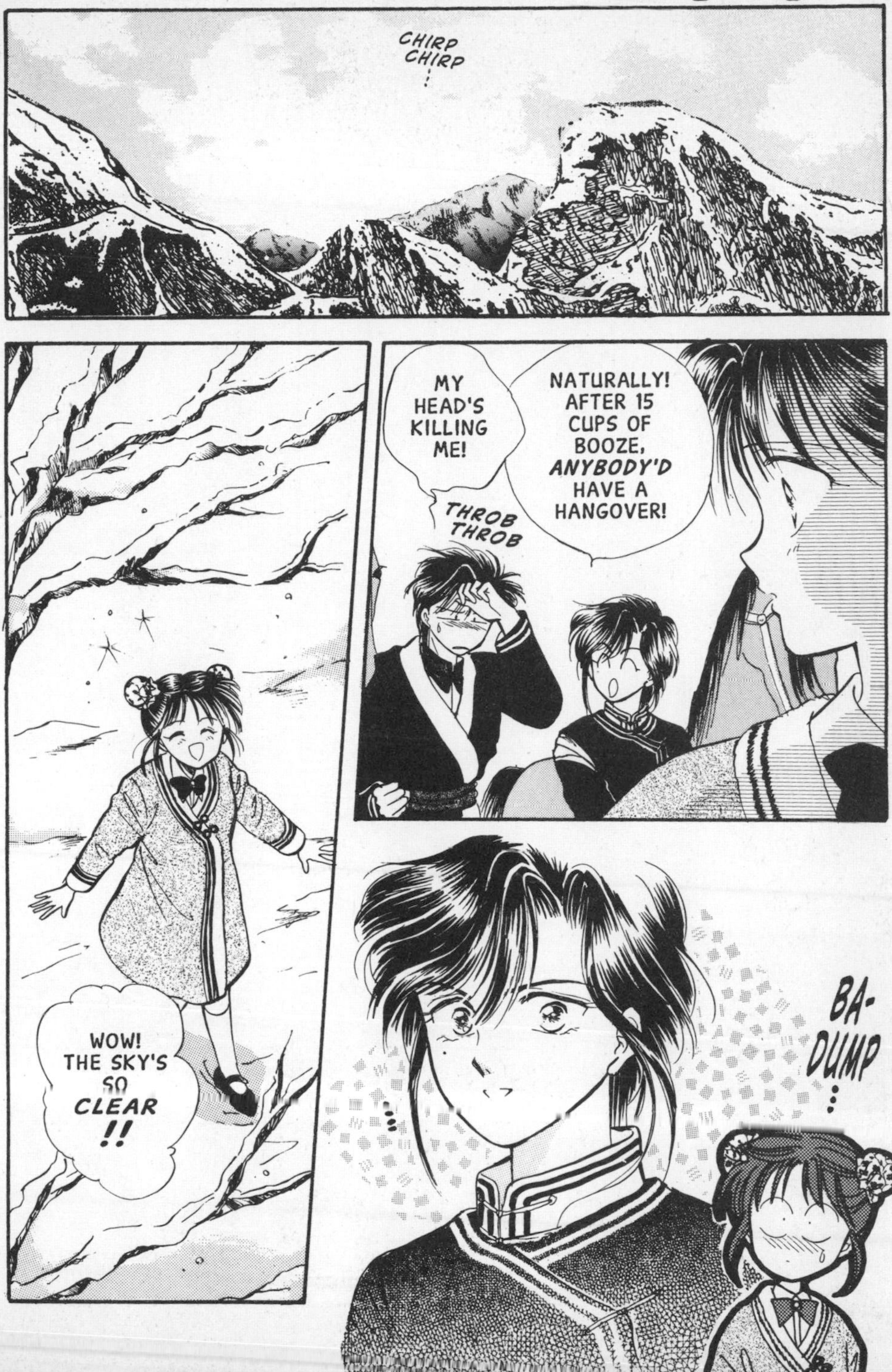
CHIRP CHIRP
WOW! THE SKY'S SO CLEAR!!
MY HEAD'S KILLING ME!
THROB THROB
NATURALLY! AFTER 15 CUPS OF BOOZE, ANYBODY'D HAVE A HANGOVER!
BA-DUMP

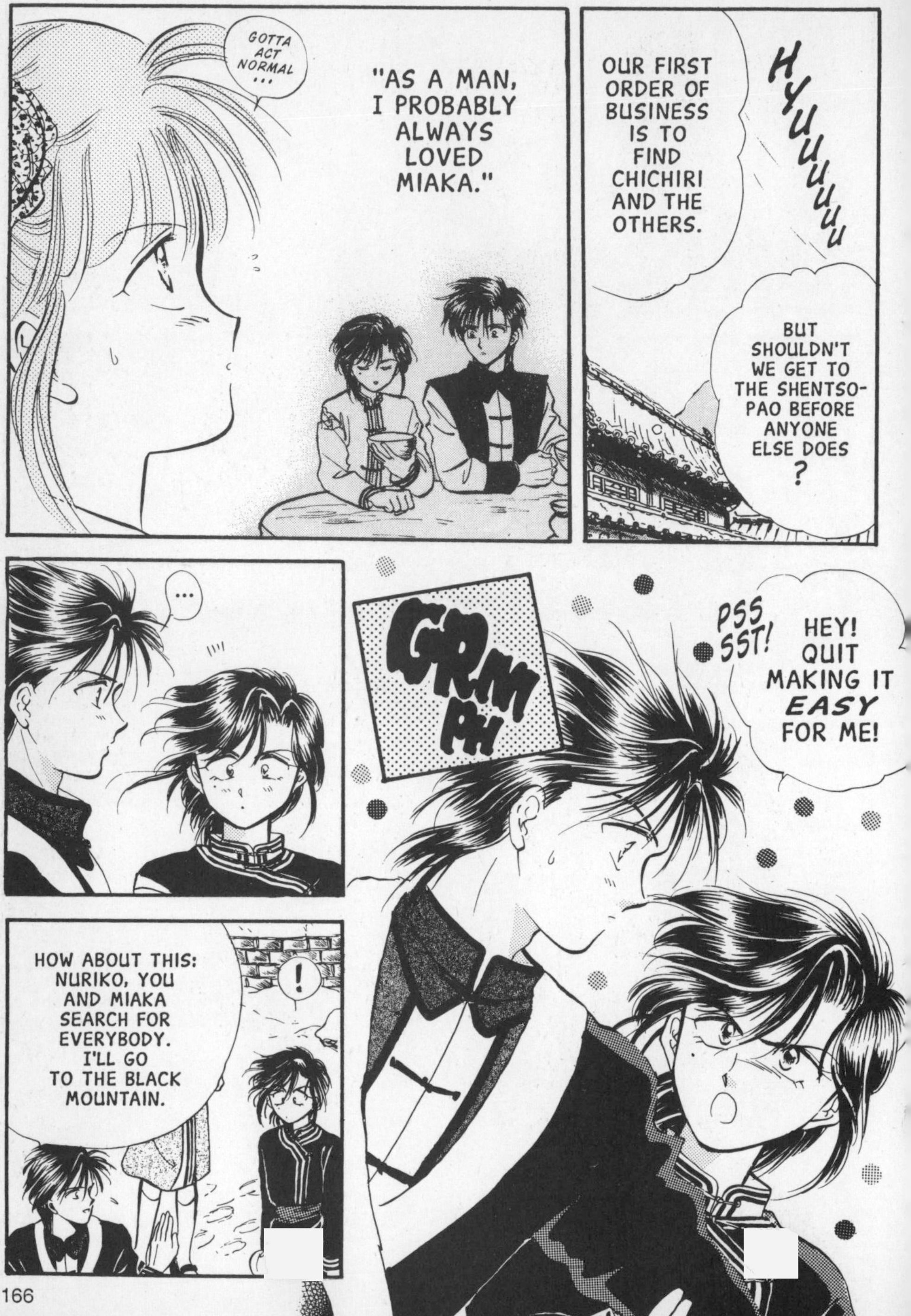
GOTTA ACT NORMAL ...
"AS A MAN, I PROBABLY ALWAYS LOVED MIAKA."
OUR FIRST ORDER OF BUSINESS IS TO FIND CHICHIRI AND THE OTHERS.
HYUUUUUU
BUT SHOULDN'T WE GET TO THE SHENTSO-PAO BEFORE ANYONE ELSE DOES ?
...
HOW ABOUT THIS: NURIKO, YOU AND MIAKA SEARCH FOR EVERYBODY. I'LL GO TO THE BLACK MOUNTAIN.
!
GRMPH
PSS SST!
HEY! QUIT MAKING IT *EASY* FOR ME!

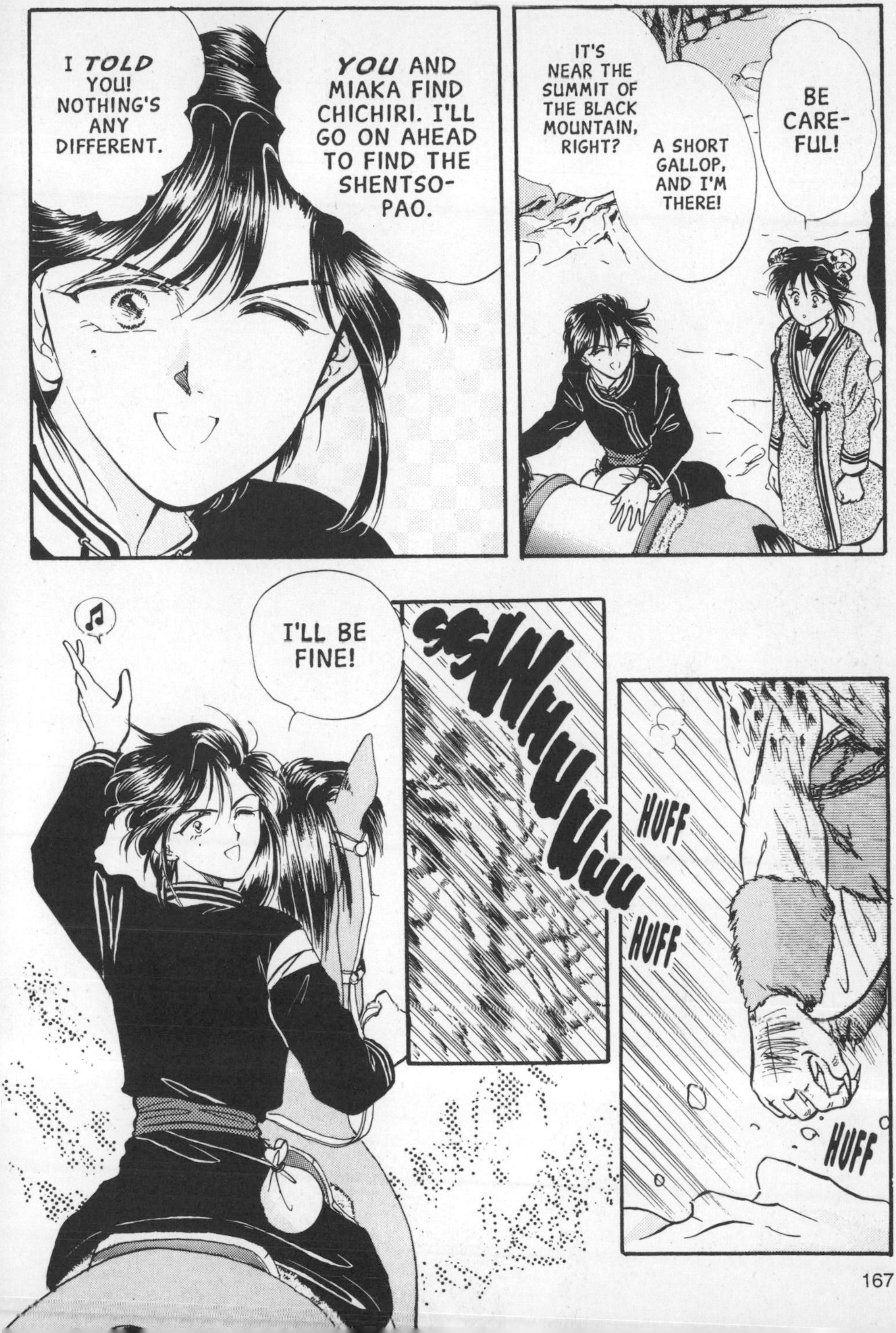
I TOLD YOU! NOTHING'S ANY DIFFERENT.
YOU AND MIAKA FIND CHICHIRI. I'LL GO ON AHEAD TO FIND THE SHENTSO-PAO.
IT'S NEAR THE SUMMIT OF THE BLACK MOUNTAIN, RIGHT?
A SHORT GALLOP, AND I'M THERE!
BE CARE-FUL!
♫
I'LL BE FINE!
SSSWHHUUUUUUuuu
HUFF
HUFF
HUFF

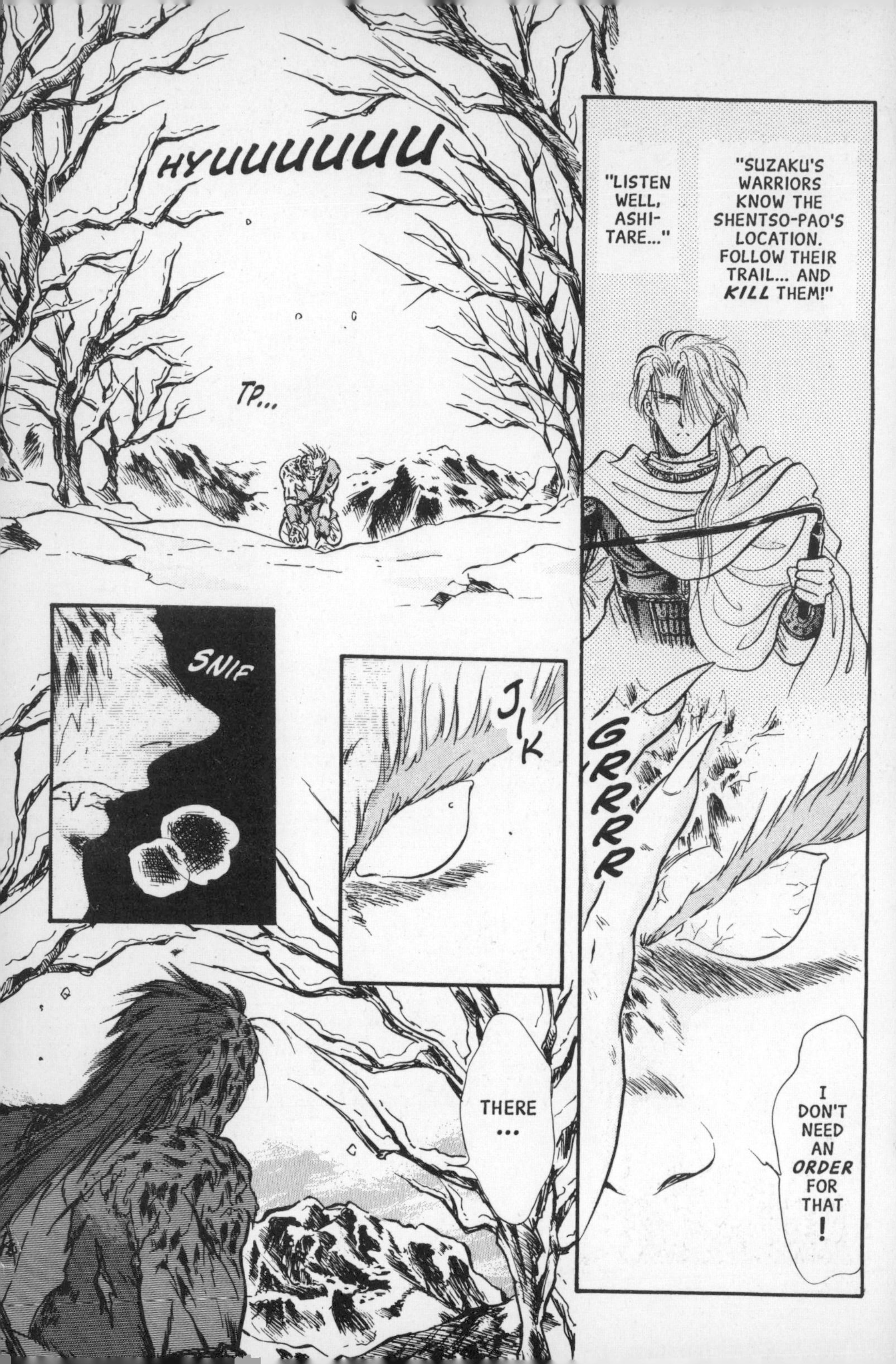
HYUUUUUUU
TP...
SNIF
JIK
THERE...
"LISTEN WELL, ASHI-TARE..."
"SUZAKU'S WARRIORS KNOW THE SHENTSO-PAO'S LOCATION. FOLLOW THEIR TRAIL... AND KILL THEM!"
GRRRR
I DON'T NEED AN ORDER FOR THAT!

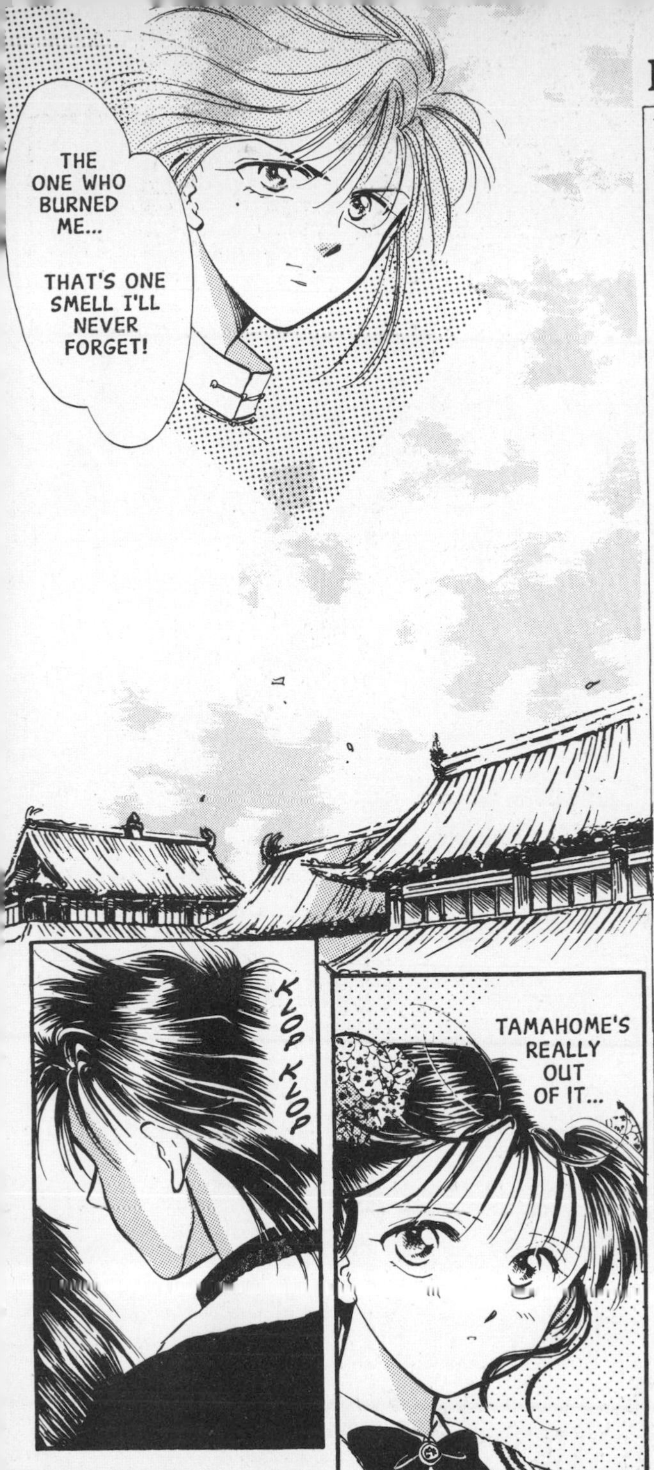
THE ONE WHO BURNED ME...
THAT'S ONE SMELL I'LL NEVER FORGET!
KLOP KLOP
TAMAHOME'S REALLY OUT OF IT...

Fushigi Yûgi ∾ 8

This is the last chat section of this volume. I'll share some recent letters that surprised me. One writer observed, "Doesn't Ashitare look like Blanka from Street Fighter II?" I just burst out laughing! I didn't do it on purpose! But maybe in my subconscious, I wanted revenge for all the fights where Blanka beat me! However, Ashitare had nothing at all to do with that! Bei-Jia is based on Mongolia. Mongolia put me in mind of Ghengis Khan, which put me in mind of his nickname "Blue Wolf," and from there to WOLF!! It's a pretty simple idea. What if I based a human character on a wolf? HA HA HA! Next time I'll play Ashitare and defeat Blanka!
The next letter was more serious. It mentioned that the cover of my graphic novel Suna no Tiara ("Tiara of Sand") looked just like an anime calendar!! That was a total coincidence! The cover for the graphic novel was simply taken from the cover of the Shōjo Comic anthology magazine that Suna no Tiara was printed in...two years ago! I usually draw new art for each graphic novel, but back then, I was just too busy (I mean it was already early August), so my editor came up with the idea of using the magazine cover for the the graphic novel. (I had them wait for the back cover illustration which was an original.) But I'm not implying that the guys who made the animation calendar stole my idea. Given how much manga and anime there is in the world, it's only a matter of time before two people come up with the same design independently.
So don't let it phase you!
Besides, I don't have the guts to plagiarize! I'm too much of a coward to lie. And I'm such a terrible writer, I'll bet I'm giving you wrong impressions in a 1/3 page chat section!
Thank you for all your letters and presents! To the fan from Aomori, I know it's a little late, but thank you! Your gift was delicious! Geez! I got it more than half a year ago! And I'll try to keep my stress to a minimum, but I'll still be working hard!!
See you next time!!

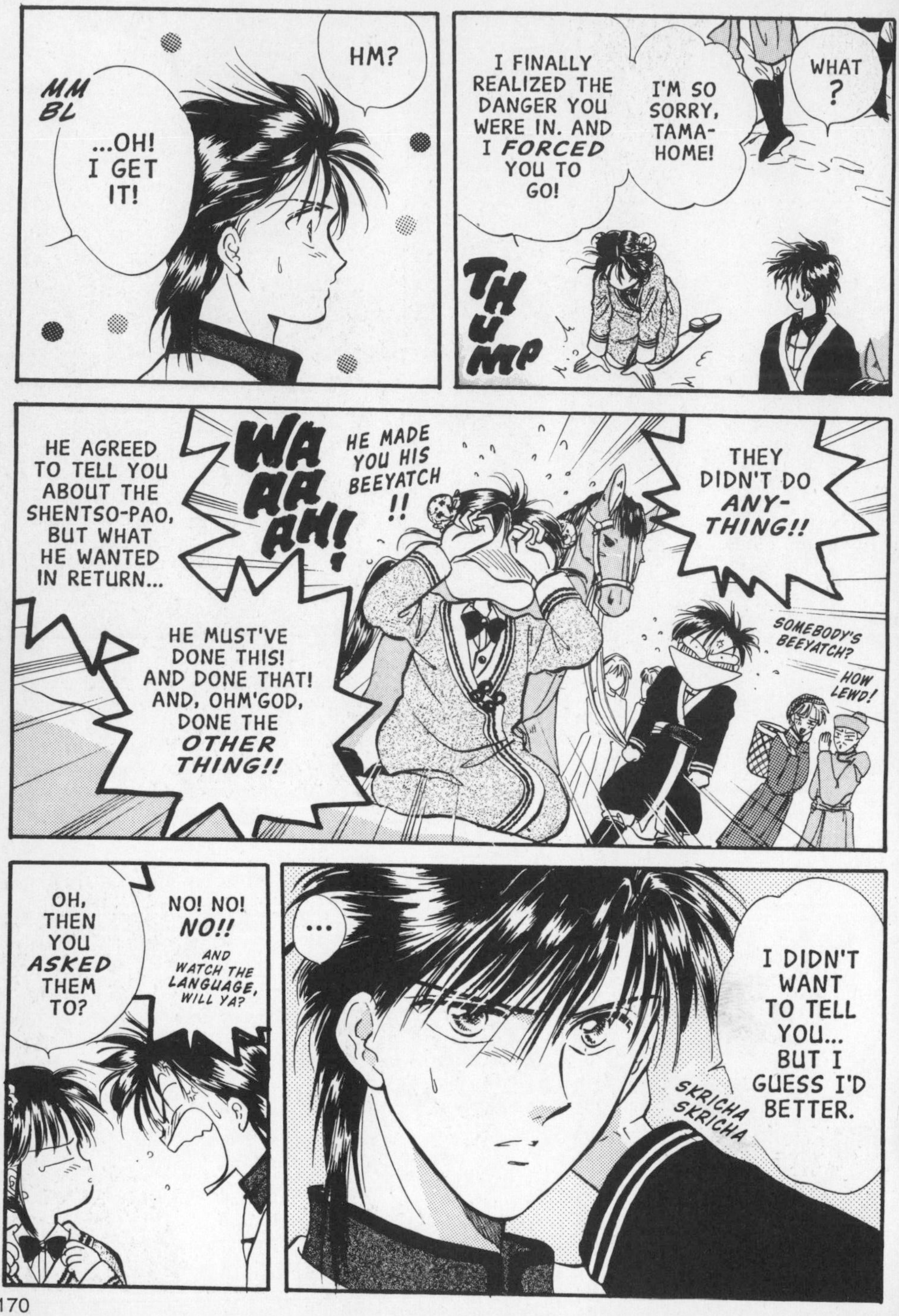
HM?
MM BL
...OH! I GET IT!
I FINALLY REALIZED THE DANGER YOU WERE IN. AND I FORCED YOU TO GO!
I'M SO SORRY, TAMA-HOME!
WHAT ?
THUMP
HE AGREED TO TELL YOU ABOUT THE SHENTSO-PAO, BUT WHAT HE WANTED IN RETURN...
WAAAAH!
HE MADE YOU HIS BEEYATCH !!
HE MUST'VE DONE THIS! AND DONE THAT! AND, OHM'GOD, DONE THE OTHER THING!!
THEY DIDN'T DO ANY-THING!!
SOMEBODY'S BEEYATCH?
HOW LEWD!
OH, THEN YOU ASKED THEM TO?
NO! NO! NO!!
AND WATCH THE LANGUAGE, WILL YA?
...
I DIDN'T WANT TO TELL YOU... BUT I GUESS I'D BETTER.
SKRICHA SKRICHA

I SAW YUI.

....!!

I DID MY BEST TO CONVINCE HER... BUT I DOUBT IT GOT THROUGH.

SUBOSHI SHOWED UP, SO THERE WASN'T ANY TIME TO TALK.

...REALLY? IS SHE DOING OKAY?

DID YOU... TALK ABOUT ANYTHING ELSE?

...

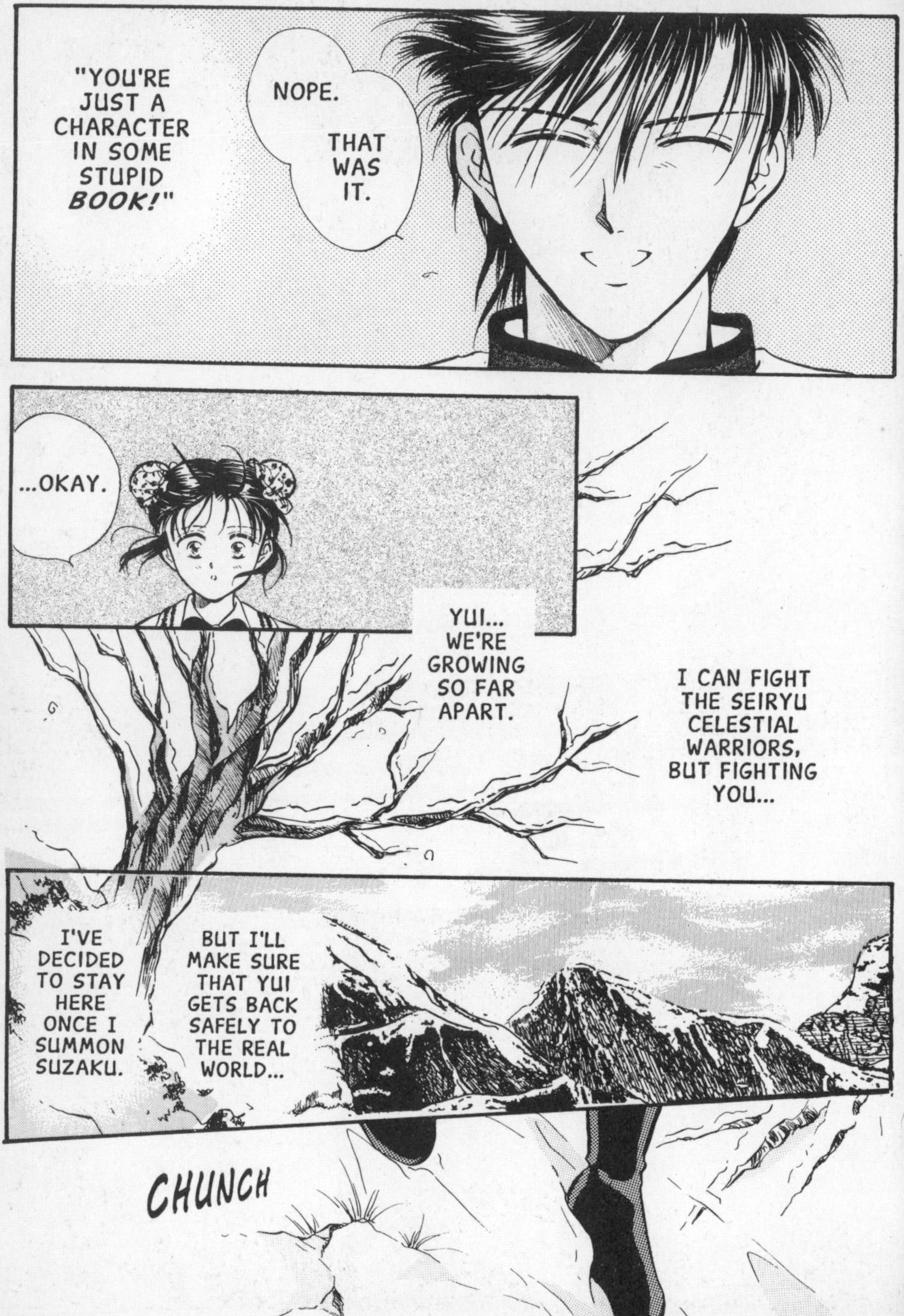
"YOU'RE JUST A CHARACTER IN SOME STUPID BOOK!"
NOPE.
THAT WAS IT.
...OKAY.
YUI... WE'RE GROWING SO FAR APART.
I CAN FIGHT THE SEIRYU CELESTIAL WARRIORS, BUT FIGHTING YOU...
I'VE DECIDED TO STAY HERE ONCE I SUMMON SUZAKU.
BUT I'LL MAKE SURE THAT YUI GETS BACK SAFELY TO THE REAL WORLD...
CHUNCH

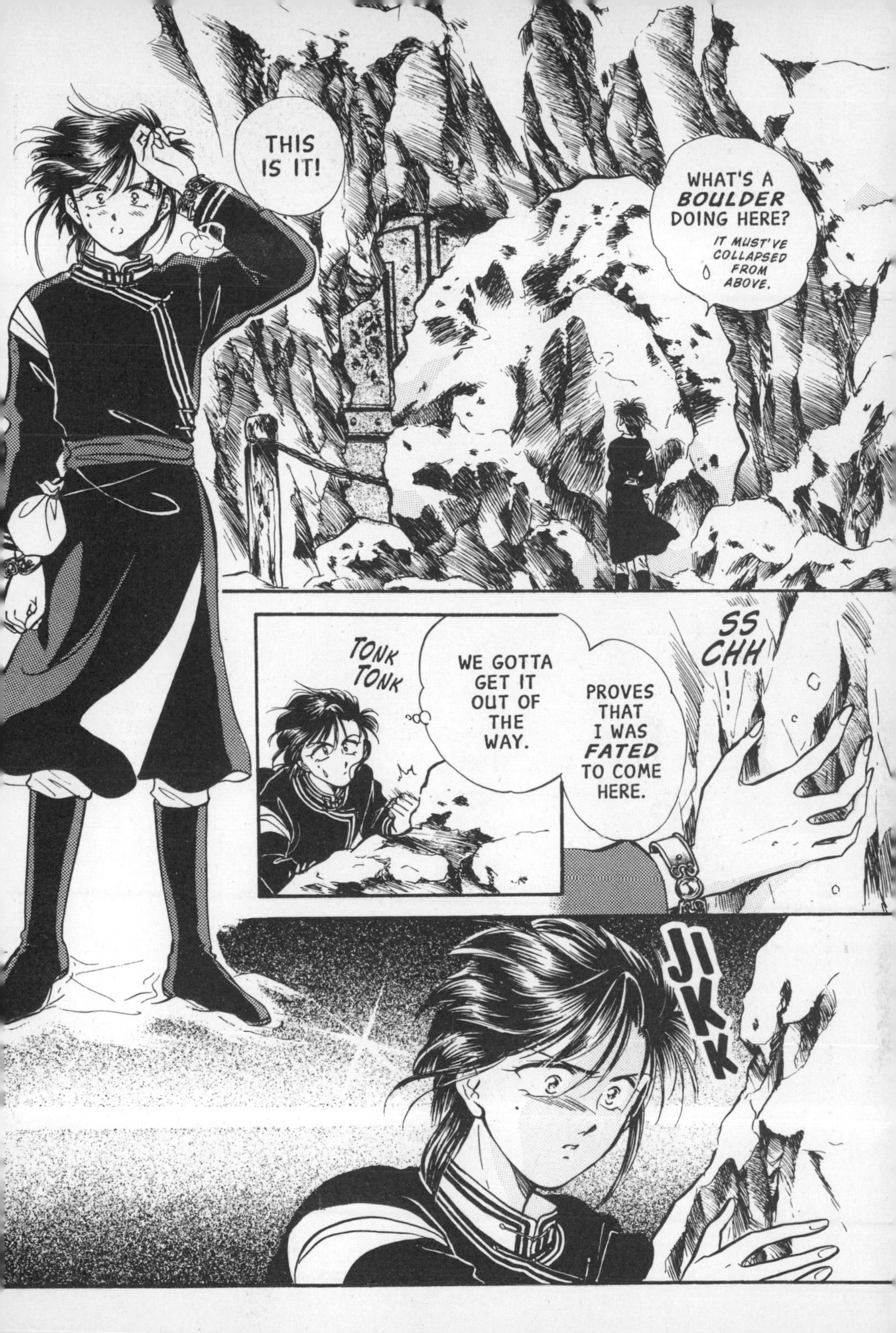
THIS IS IT!
WHAT'S A BOULDER DOING HERE?
IT MUST'VE COLLAPSED FROM ABOVE.
TONK TONK
WE GOTTA GET IT OUT OF THE WAY.
PROVES THAT I WAS FATED TO COME HERE.
SS CHH
JIKK

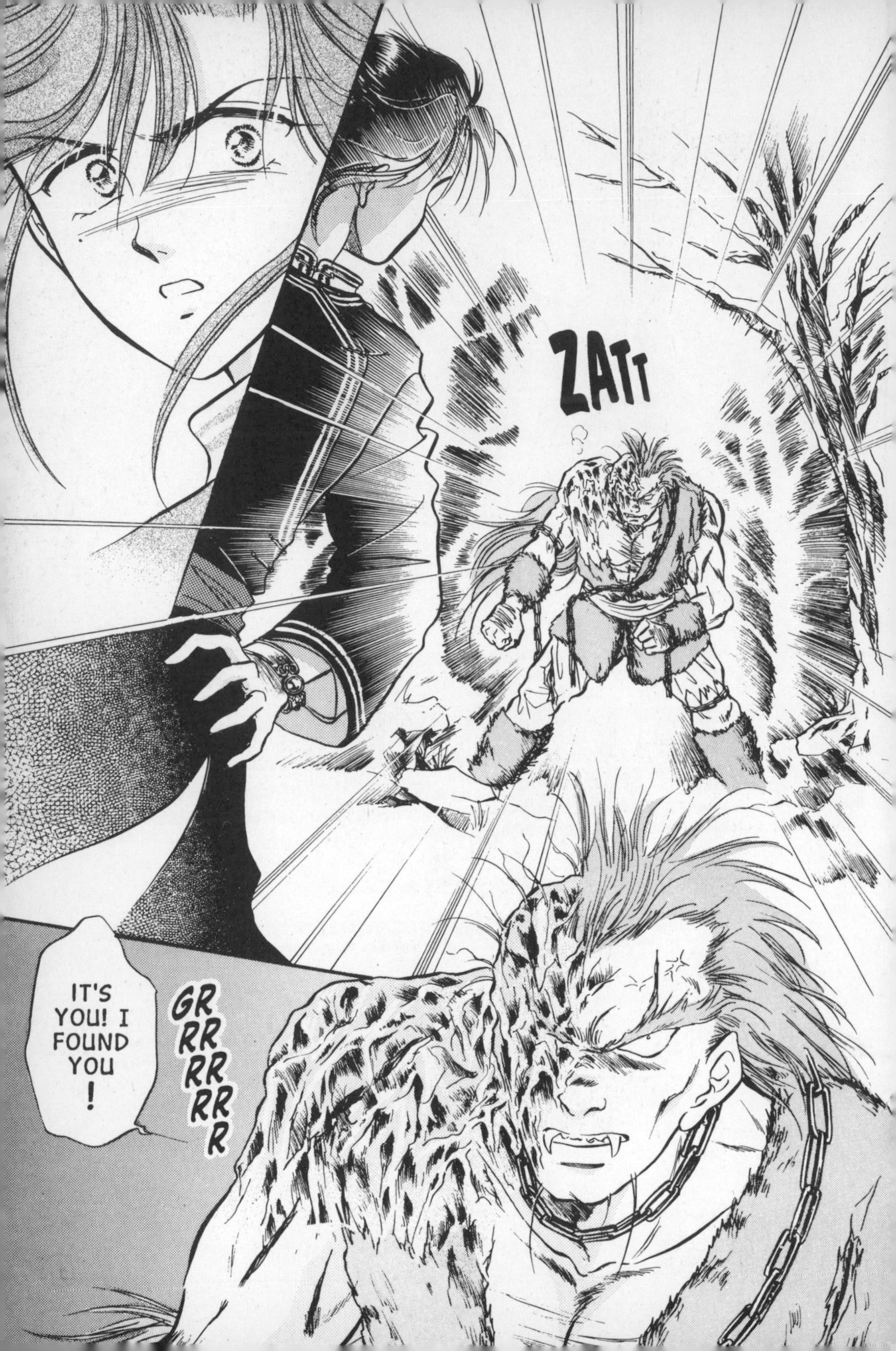
ZATT
IT'S YOU! I FOUND YOU!
GRRRRRRRR

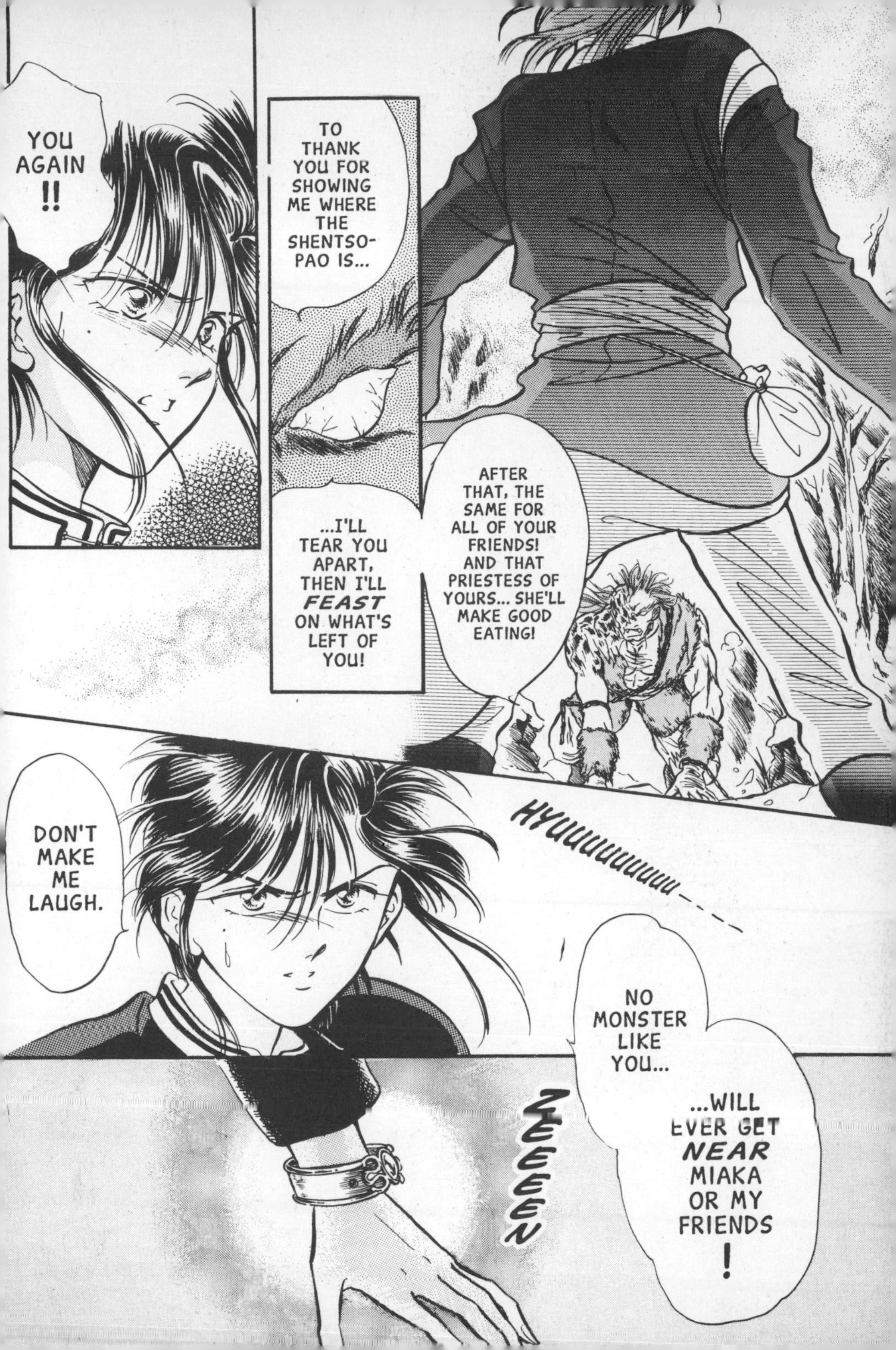
YOU AGAIN !!
TO THANK YOU FOR SHOWING ME WHERE THE SHENTSO-PAO IS...
...I'LL TEAR YOU APART, THEN I'LL *FEAST* ON WHAT'S LEFT OF YOU!
AFTER THAT, THE SAME FOR ALL OF YOUR FRIENDS! AND THAT PRIESTESS OF YOURS... SHE'LL MAKE GOOD EATING!
DON'T MAKE ME LAUGH.
HYUUUUUUUUUU
NO MONSTER LIKE YOU...
ZEEEEEN
...WILL EVER GET *NEAR* MIAKA OR MY FRIENDS !

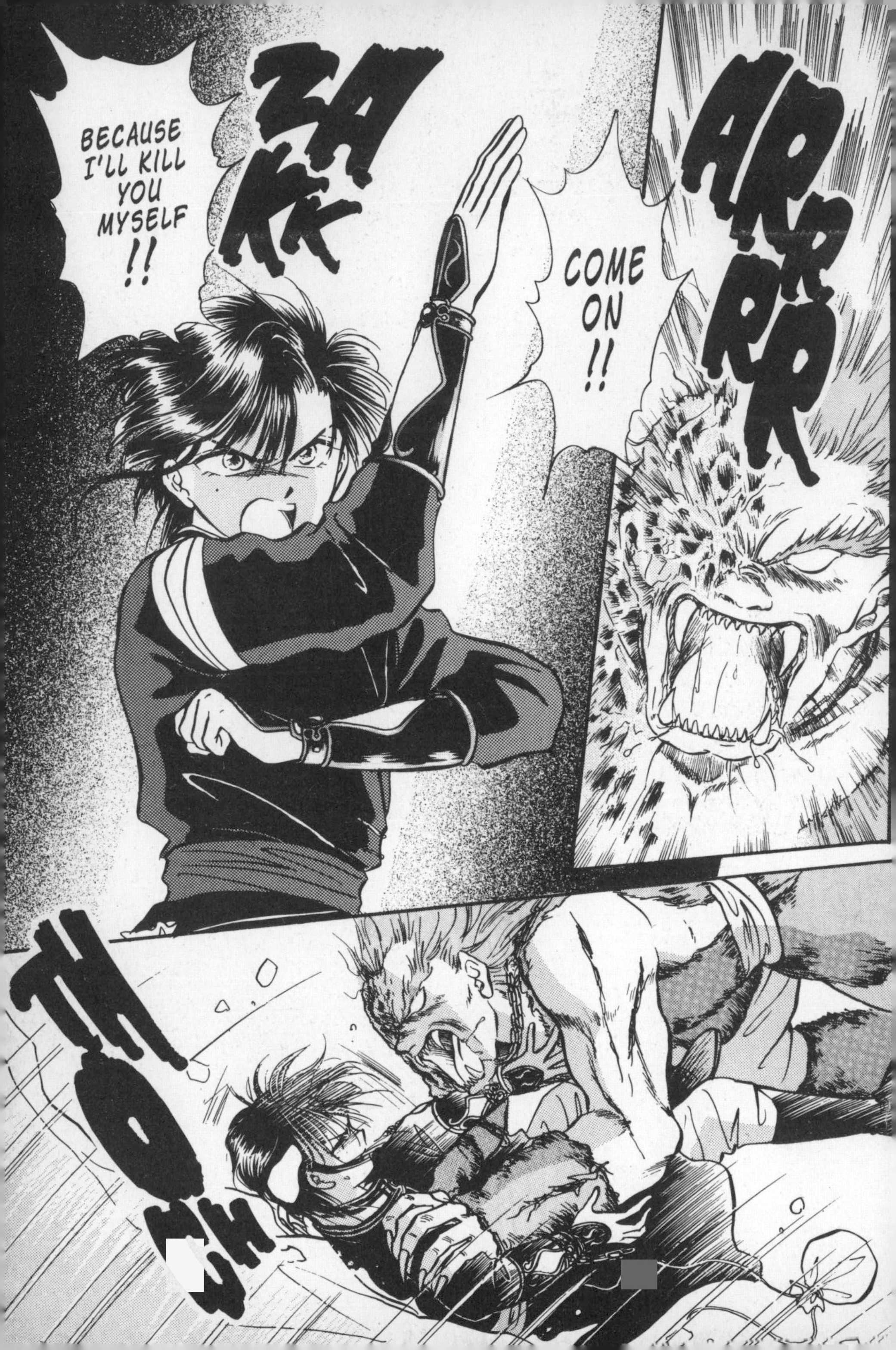
BECAUSE I'LL KILL YOU MYSELF !!
ZAKK
COME ON !!

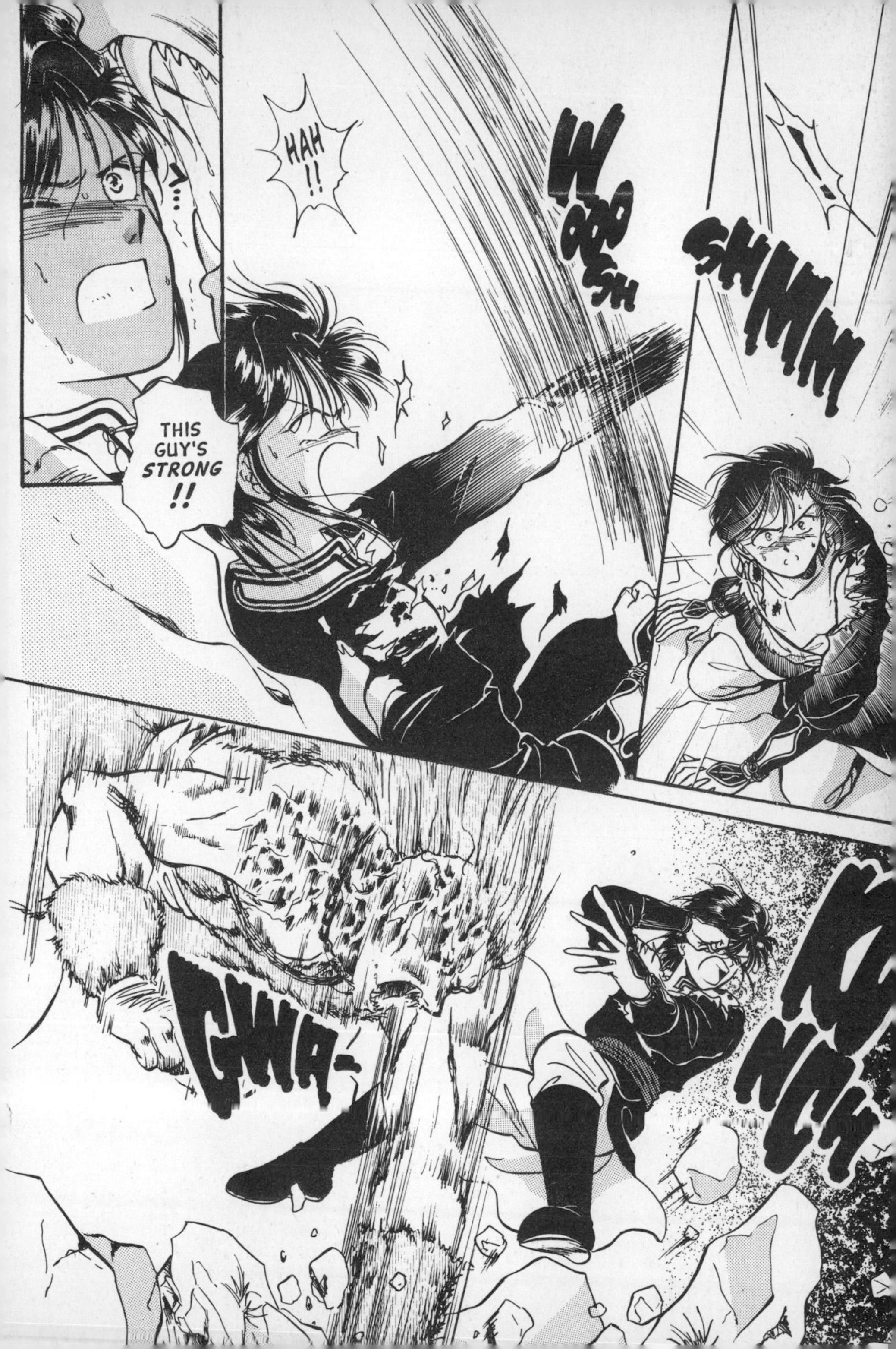

HAH !!
THIS GUY'S STRONG !!
SHMMM
GWA-

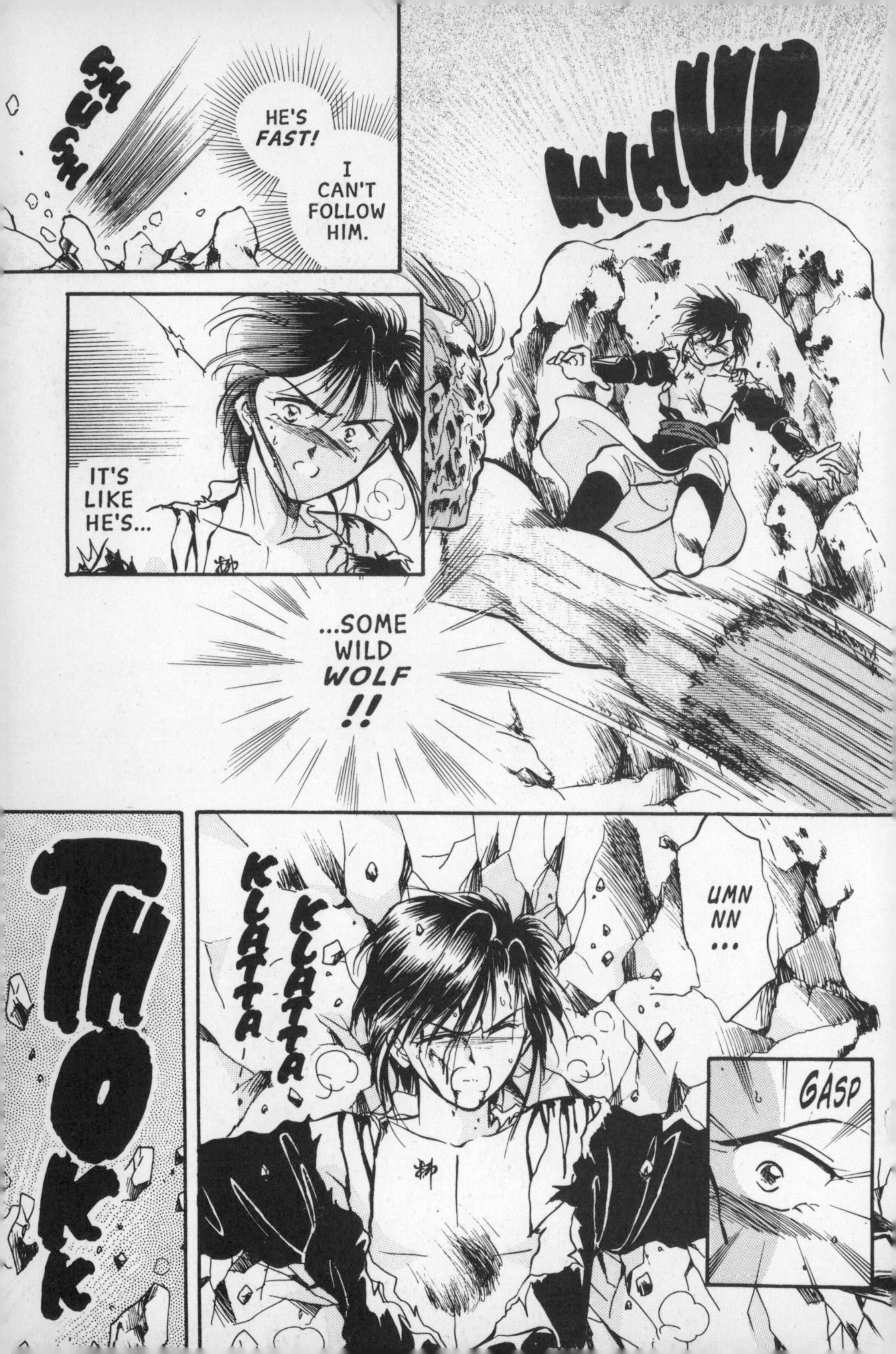
SHUSH
HE'S FAST!
I CAN'T FOLLOW HIM.
WHUD
IT'S LIKE HE'S...
...SOME WILD WOLF !!
THOKK
KLATTA KLATTA
UMNNN...
GASP

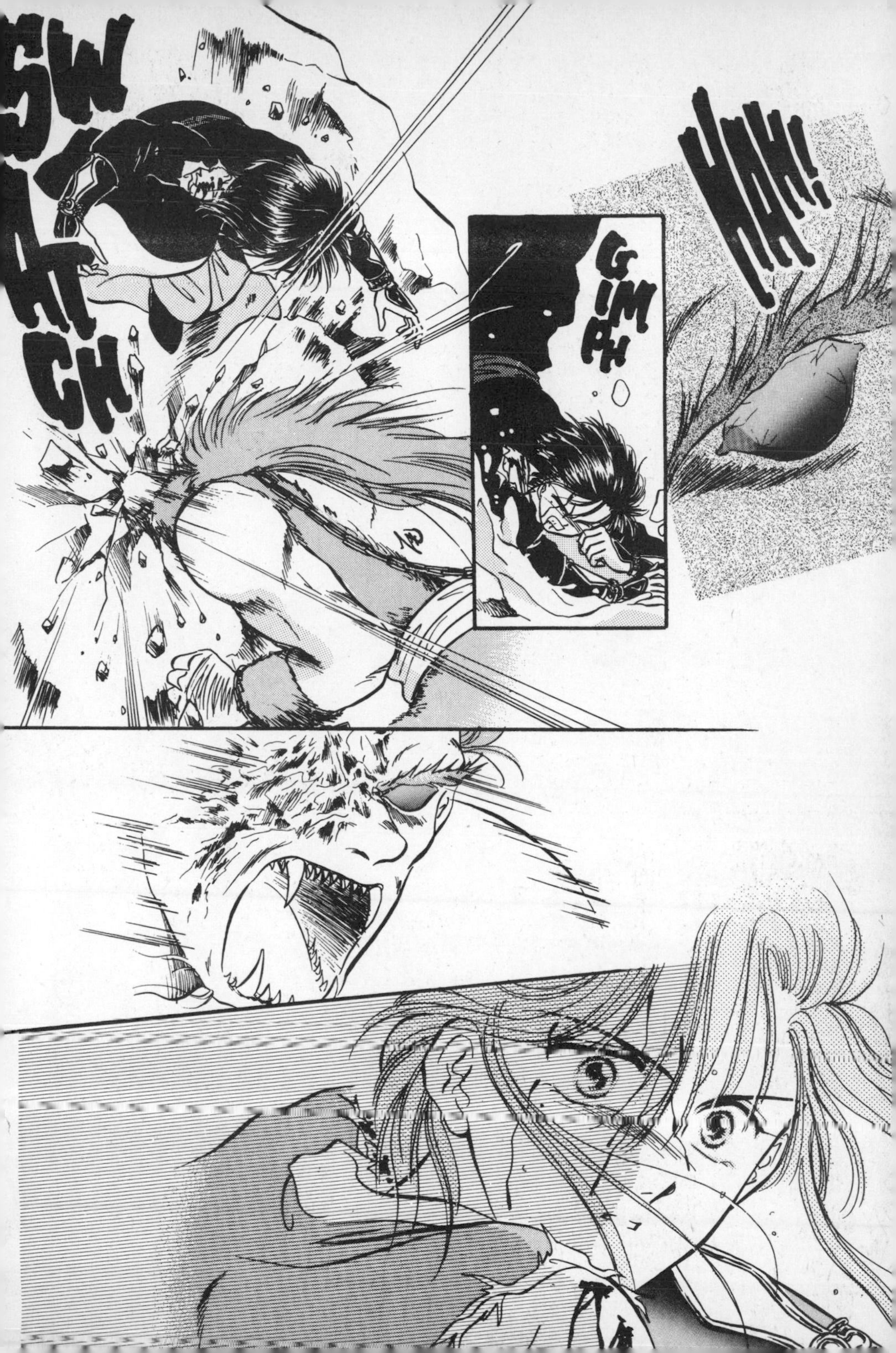
SWATCH
GIMPH
HAH!!

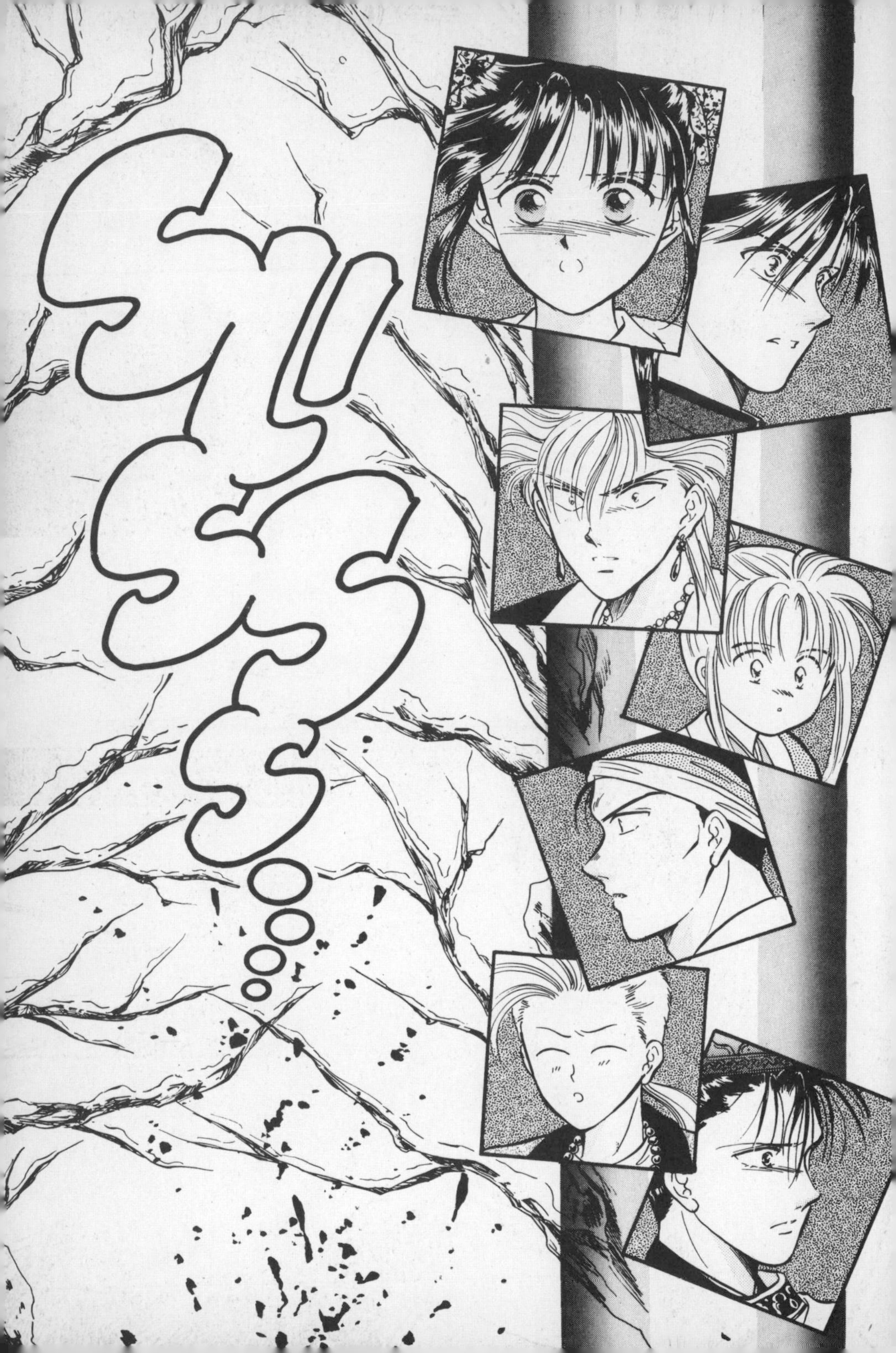

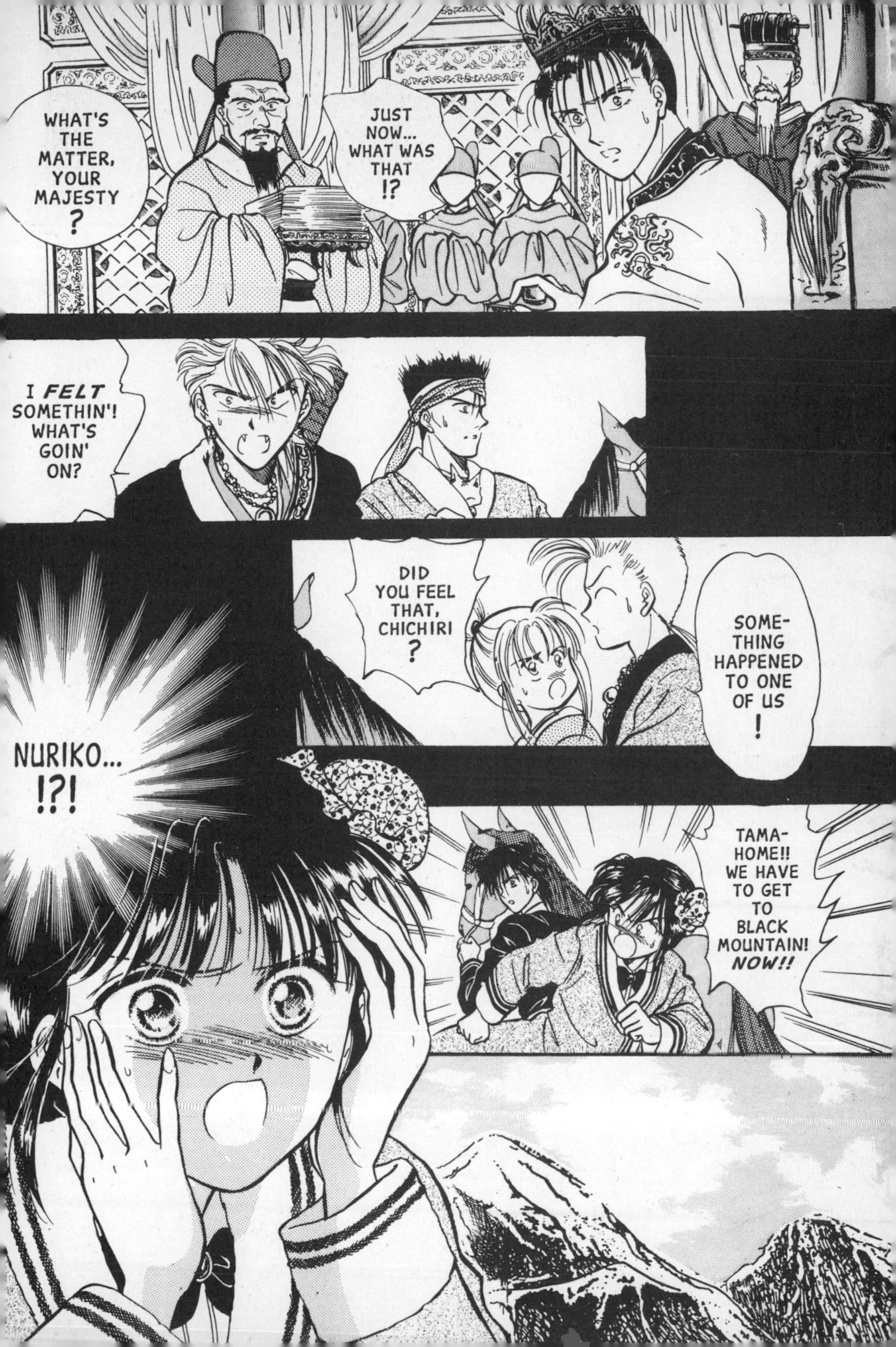
WHAT'S THE MATTER, YOUR MAJESTY?
JUST NOW... WHAT WAS THAT!?
I *FELT* SOMETHIN'! WHAT'S GOIN' ON?
NURIKO... !?!
DID YOU FEEL THAT, CHICHIRI?
SOME-THING HAPPENED TO ONE OF US!
TAMA-HOME!! WE HAVE TO GET TO BLACK MOUNTAIN! *NOW!!*

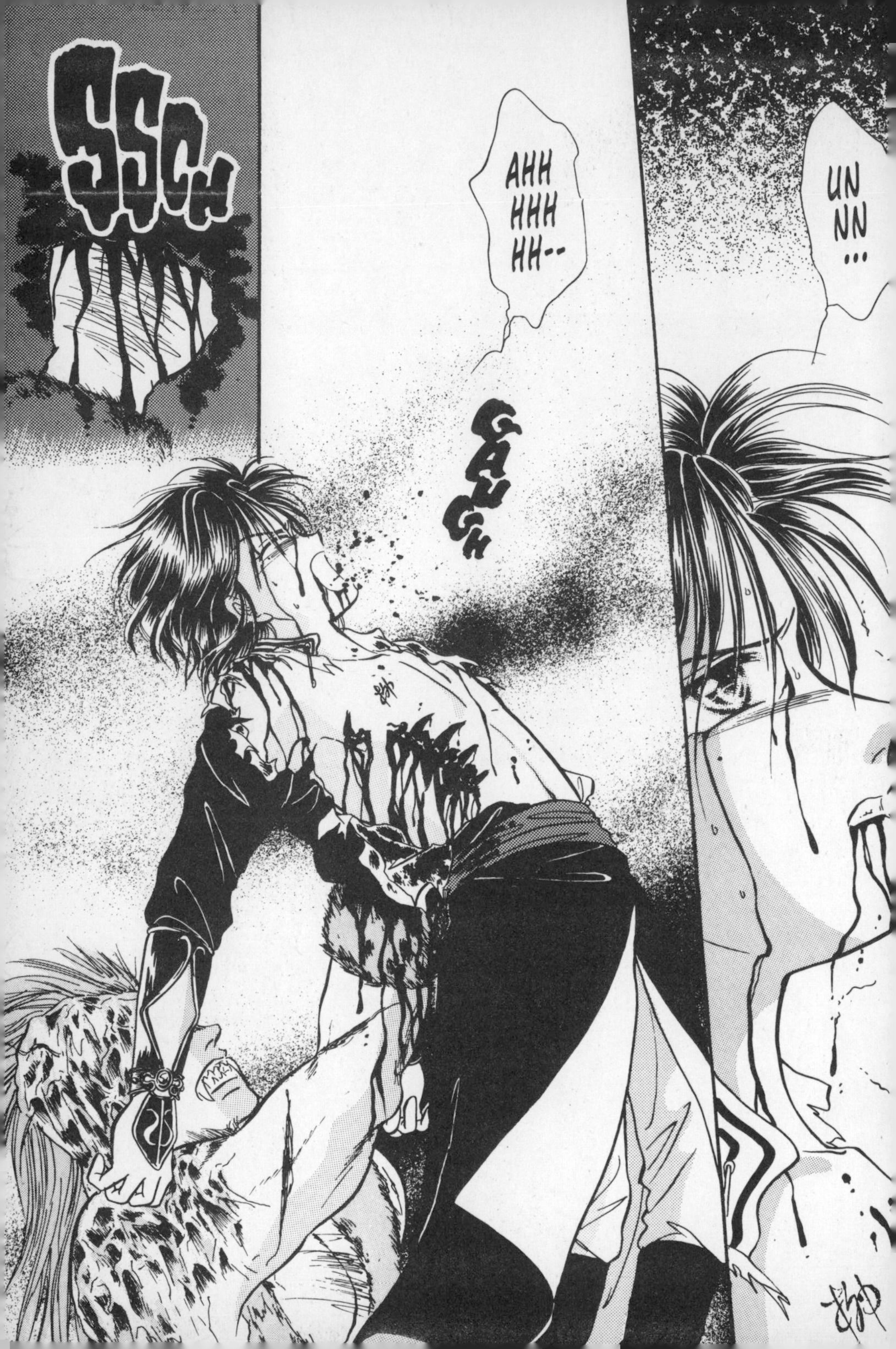
SSCH
AHH HHH HH--
GAUGH
UN NN ...

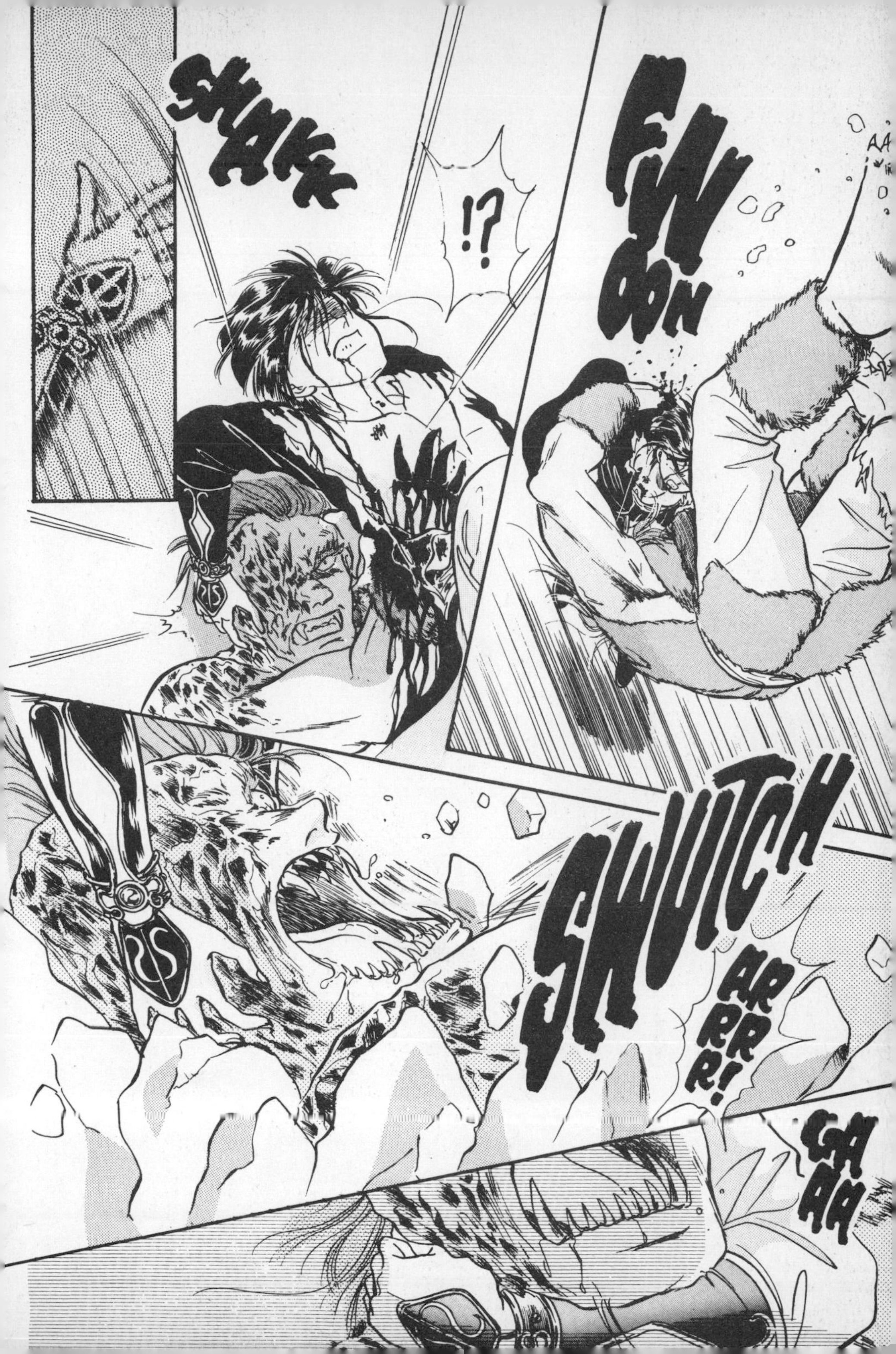

SHAKK
!?
FWOON
AA
SHWITCH
ARRRR!
GAAA

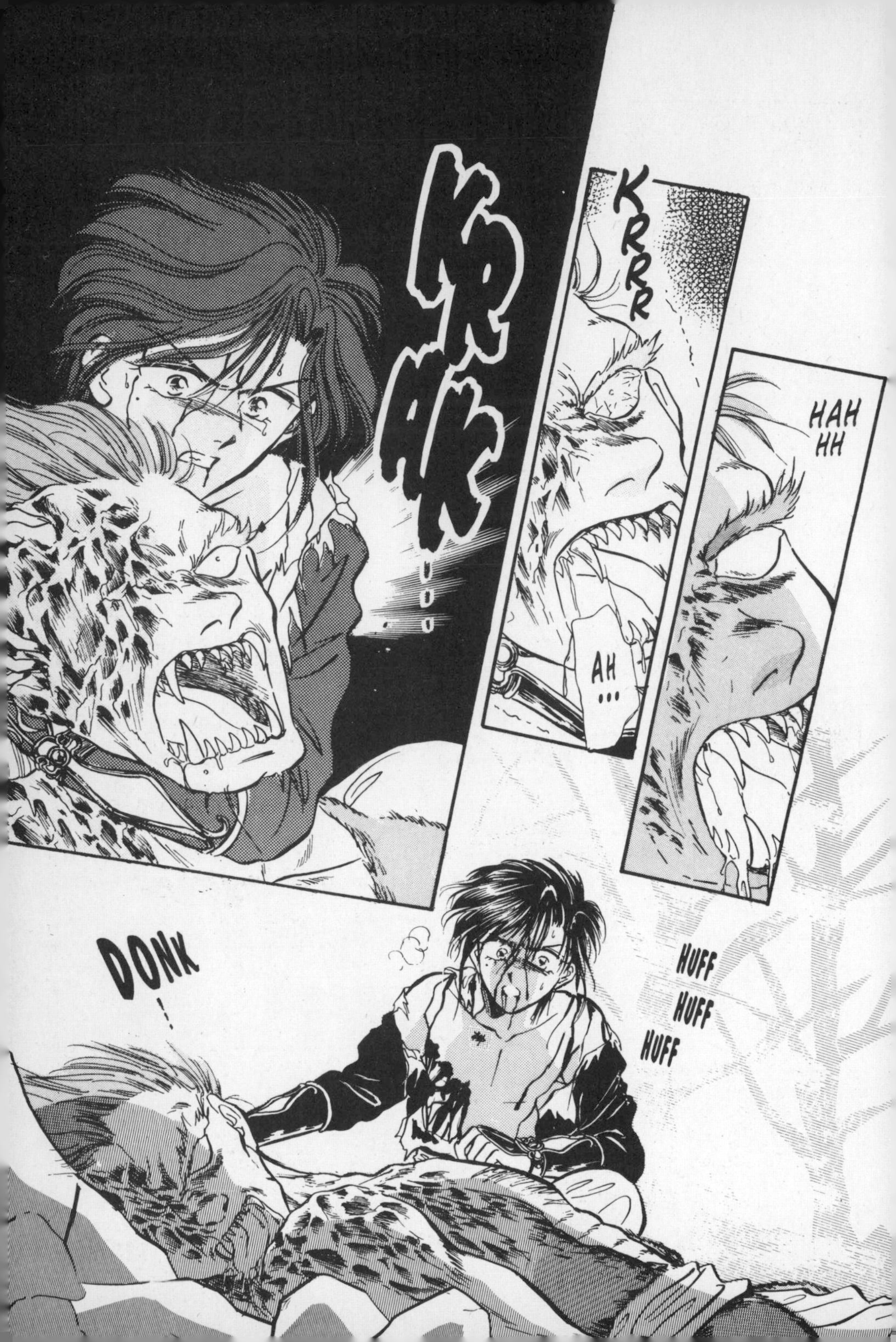
KRAK
KRRR
AH ...
HAH HH
DONK
HUFF HUFF HUFF

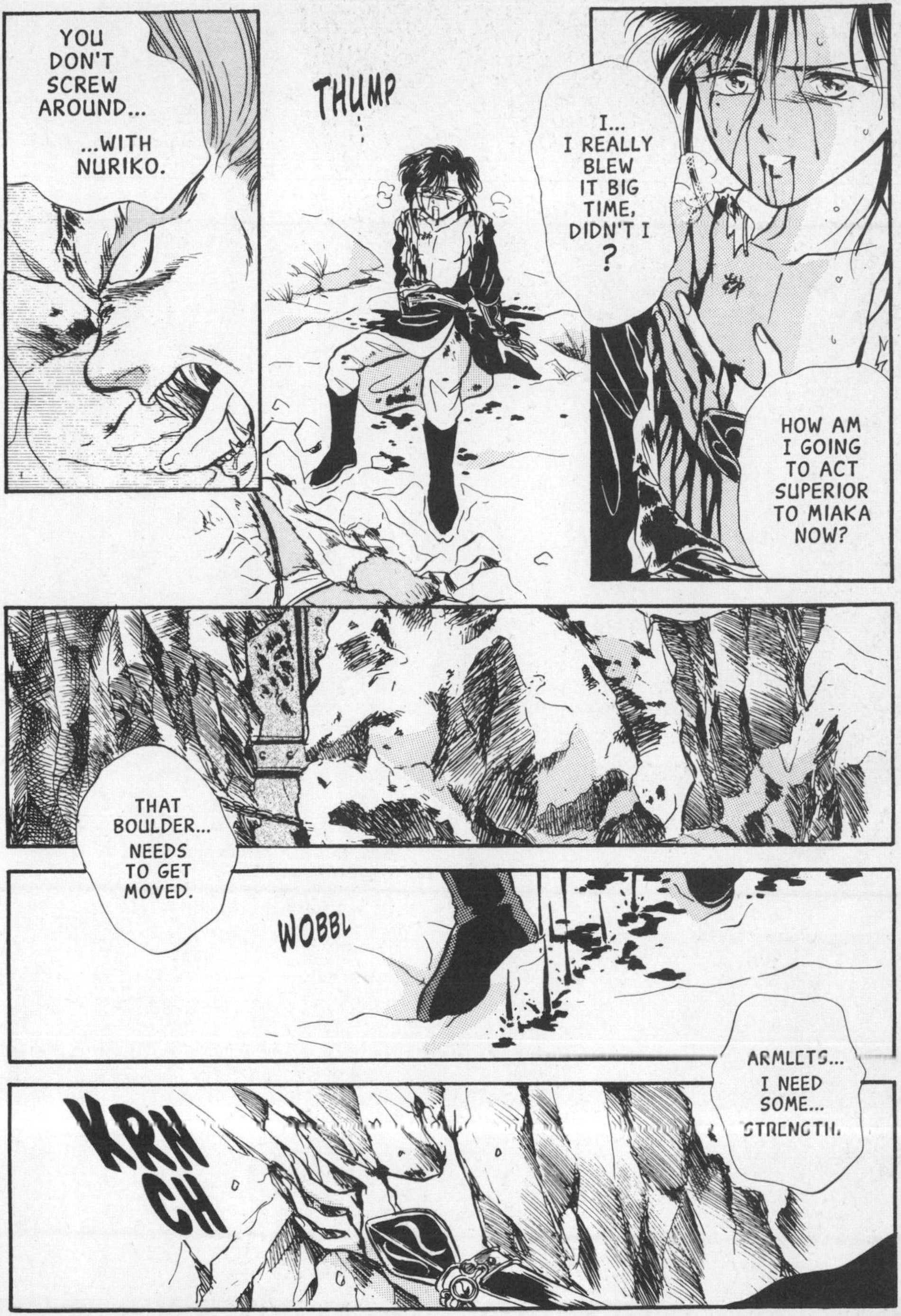
YOU DON'T SCREW AROUND... ...WITH NURIKO.
THUMP
I... I REALLY BLEW IT BIG TIME, DIDN'T I?
HOW AM I GOING TO ACT SUPERIOR TO MIAKA NOW?
THAT BOULDER... NEEDS TO GET MOVED.
WOBBL
ARMLETS... I NEED SOME... STRENGTH.
KRNCH

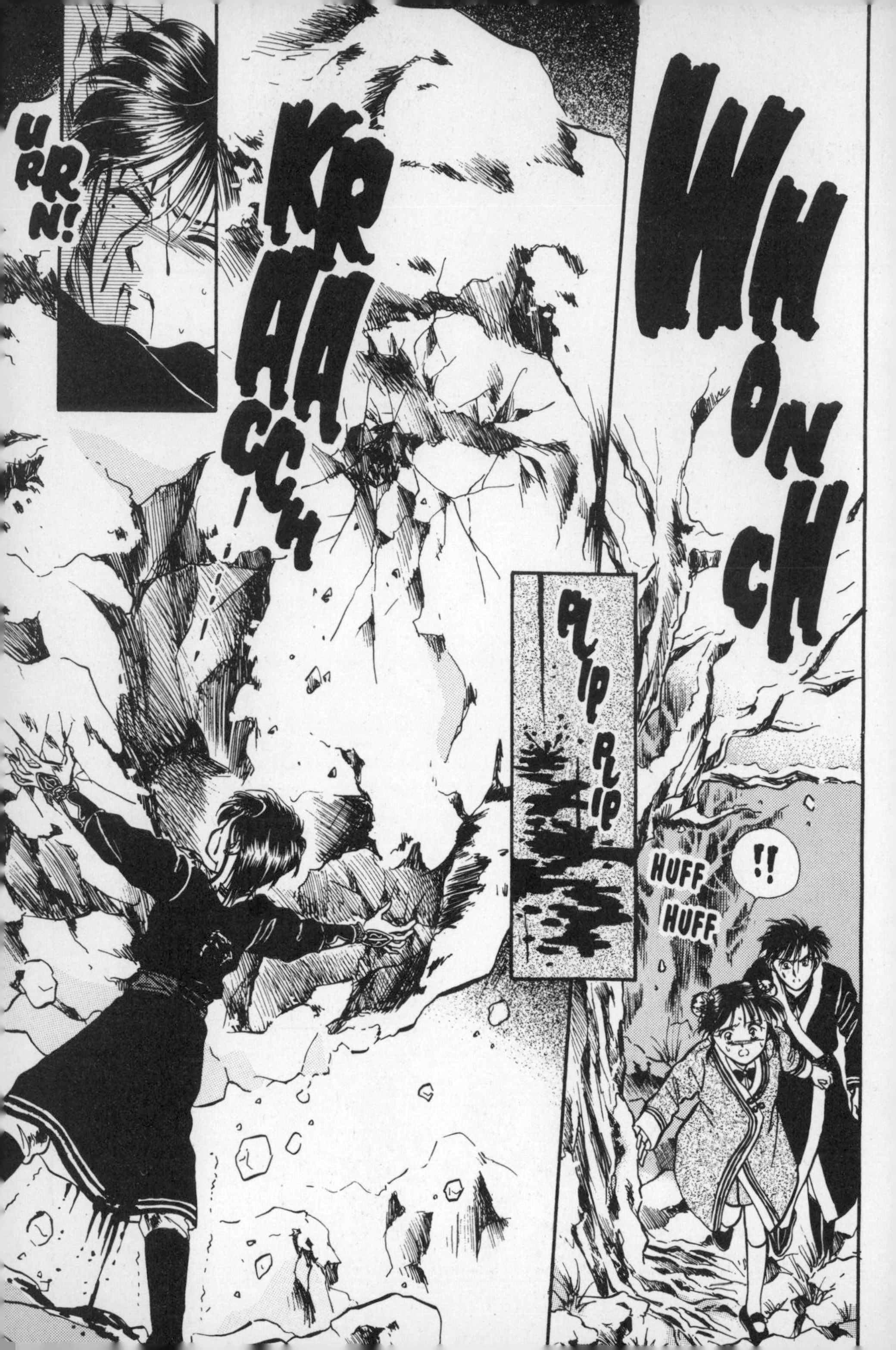
URRN!
KRAACCH
WHONCH
PLIP PLIP
HUFF HUFF
!!

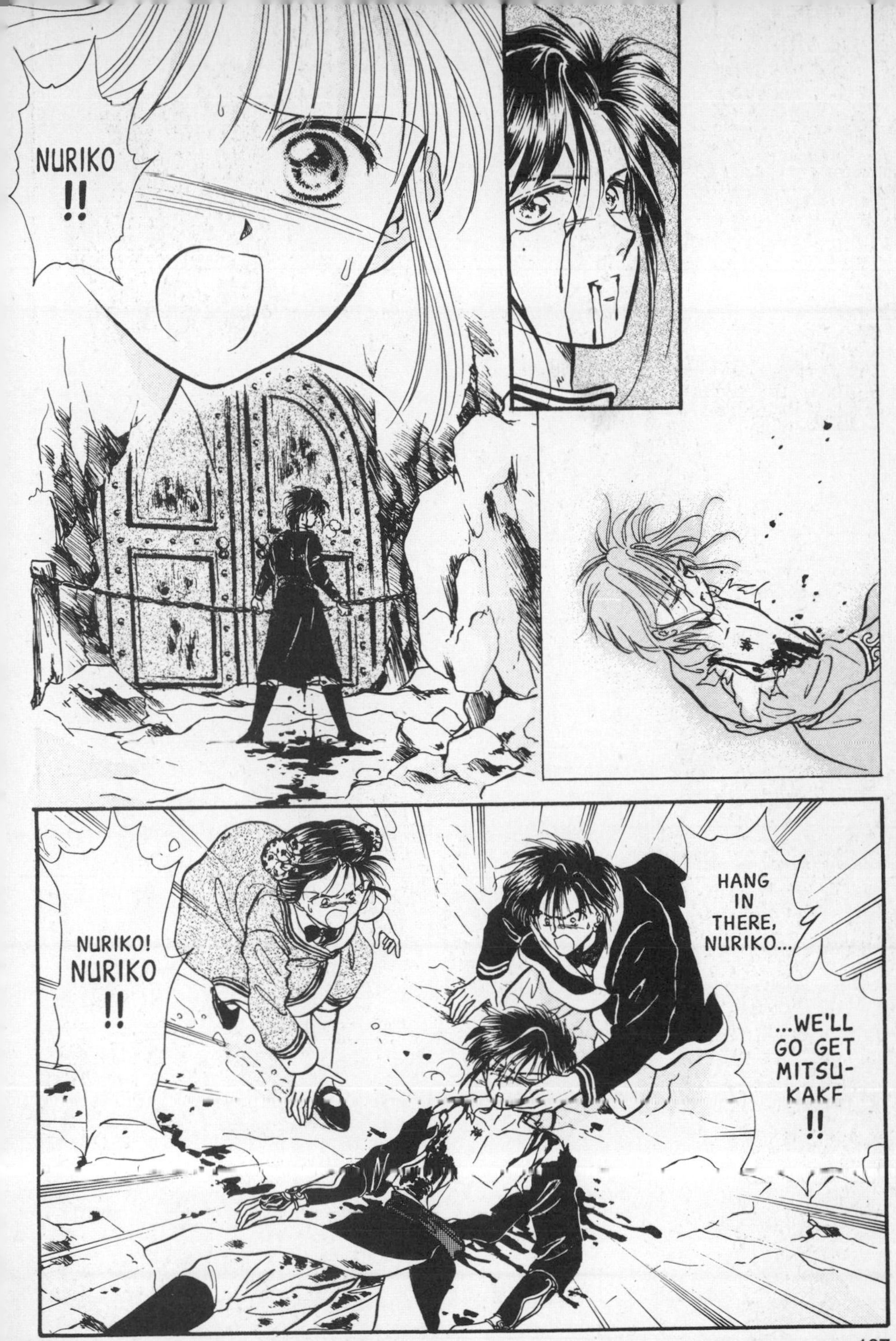
NURIKO !!
NURIKO! NURIKO !!
HANG IN THERE, NURIKO...
...WE'LL GO GET MITSU-KAKE !!

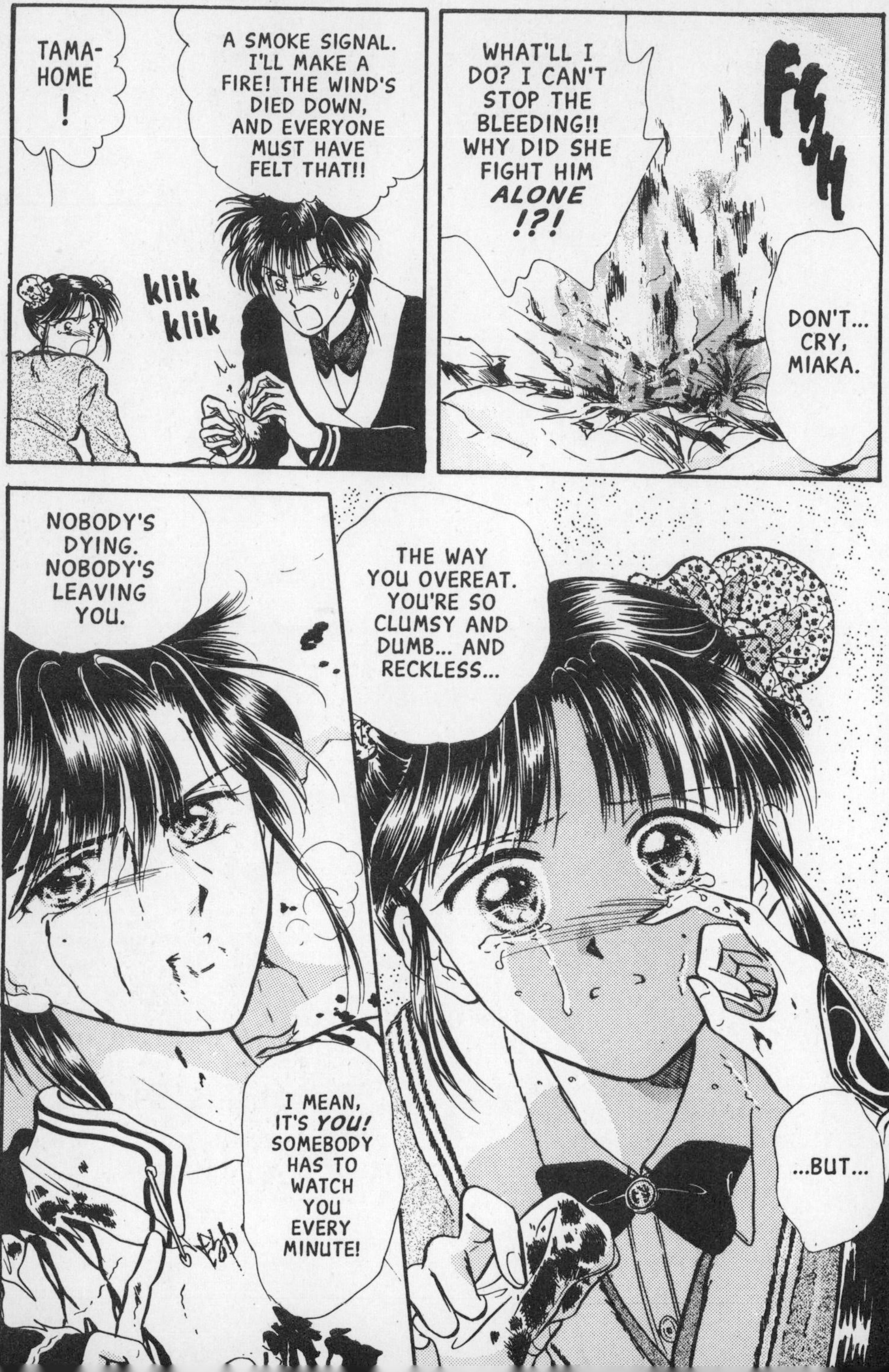
TAMA-HOME!
A SMOKE SIGNAL. I'LL MAKE A FIRE! THE WIND'S DIED DOWN, AND EVERYONE MUST HAVE FELT THAT!!
klik klik
WHAT'LL I DO? I CAN'T STOP THE BLEEDING!! WHY DID SHE FIGHT HIM *ALONE* !?!
DON'T... CRY, MIAKA.
NOBODY'S DYING. NOBODY'S LEAVING YOU.
THE WAY YOU OVEREAT. YOU'RE SO CLUMSY AND DUMB... AND RECKLESS...
I MEAN, IT'S *YOU!* SOMEBODY HAS TO WATCH YOU EVERY MINUTE!
...BUT...

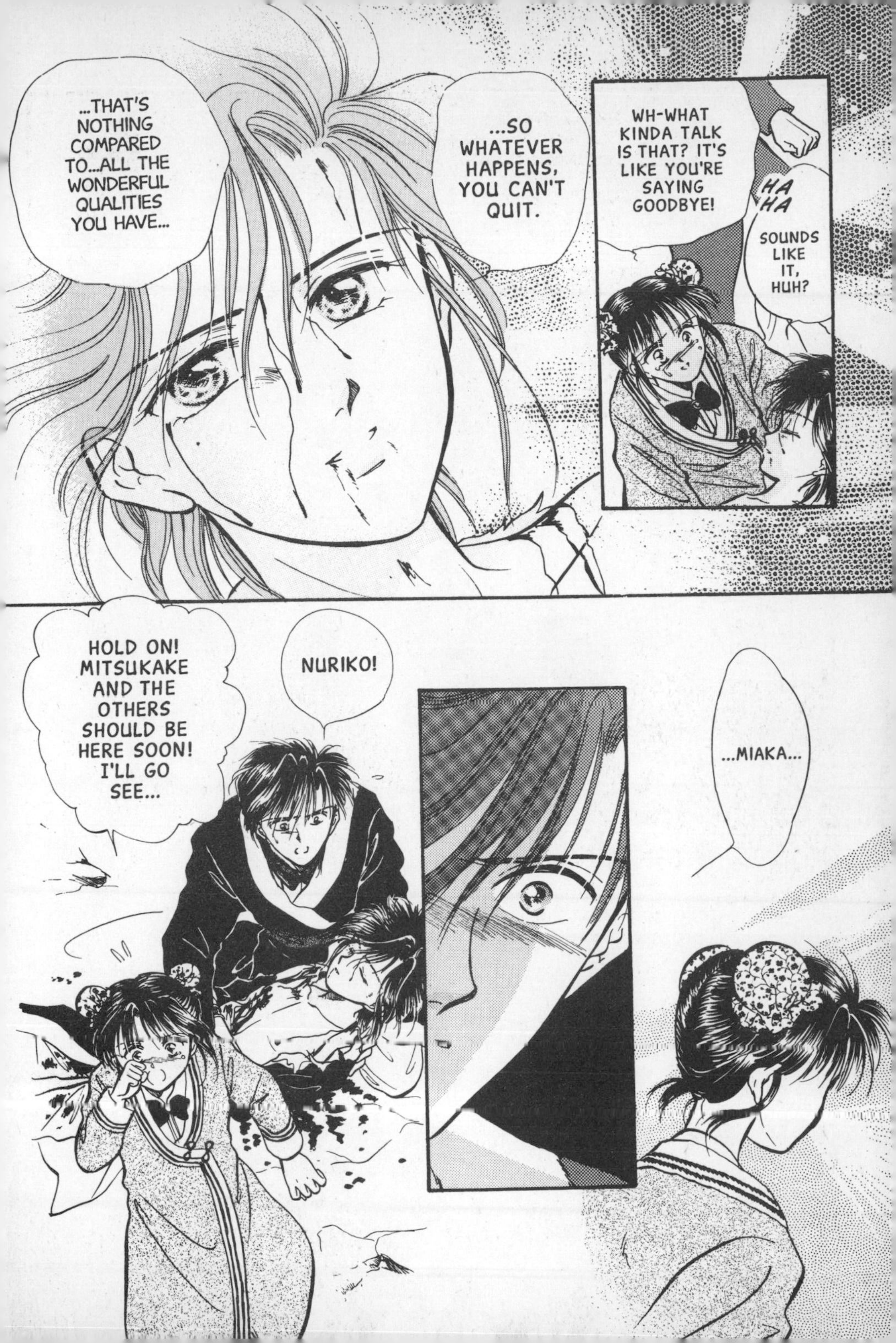
...THAT'S NOTHING COMPARED TO...ALL THE WONDERFUL QUALITIES YOU HAVE...
...SO WHATEVER HAPPENS, YOU CAN'T QUIT.
WH-WHAT KINDA TALK IS THAT? IT'S LIKE YOU'RE SAYING GOODBYE!
HA HA
SOUNDS LIKE IT, HUH?
HOLD ON! MITSUKAKE AND THE OTHERS SHOULD BE HERE SOON! I'LL GO SEE...
NURIKO!
...MIAKA...

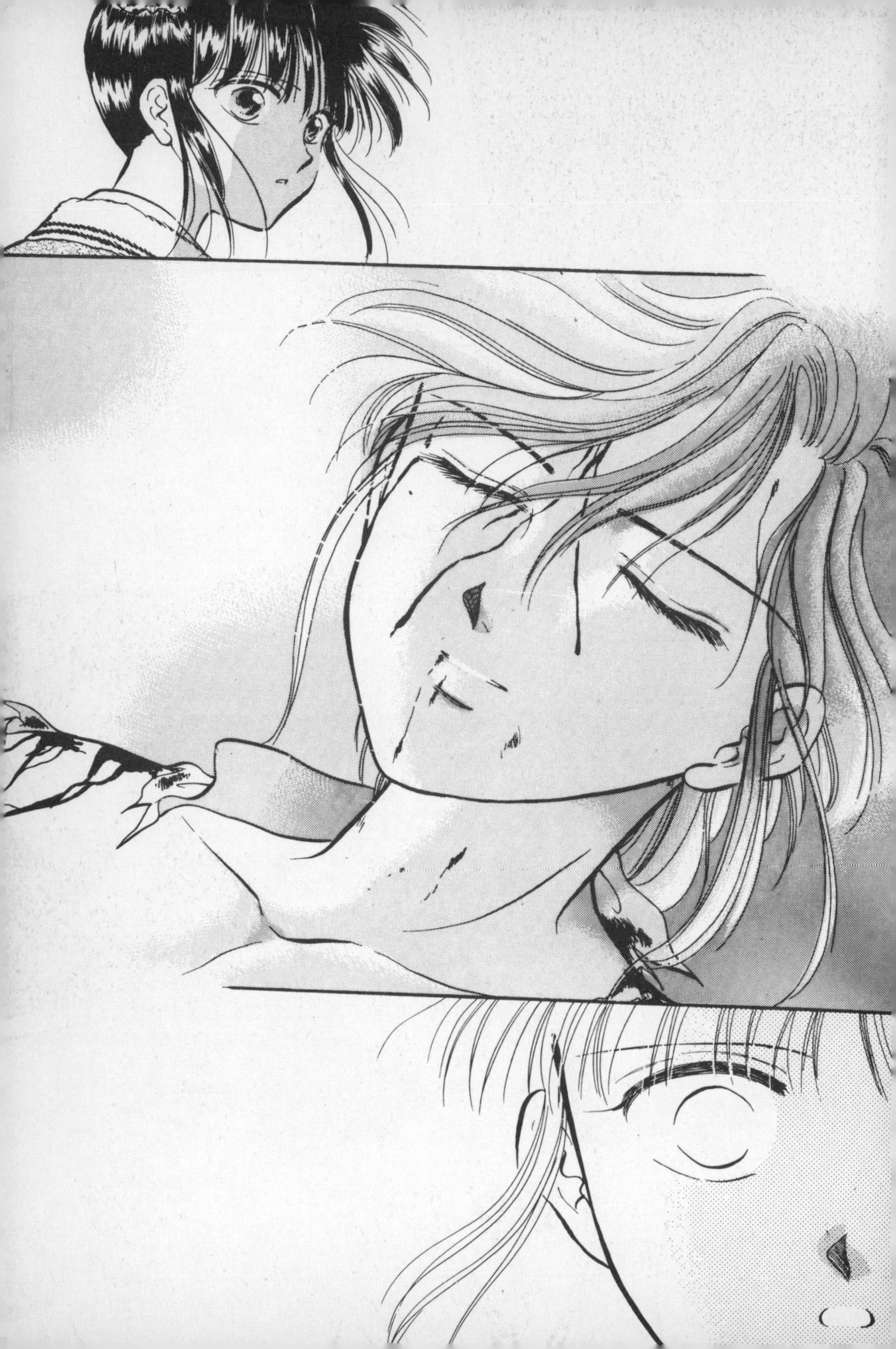

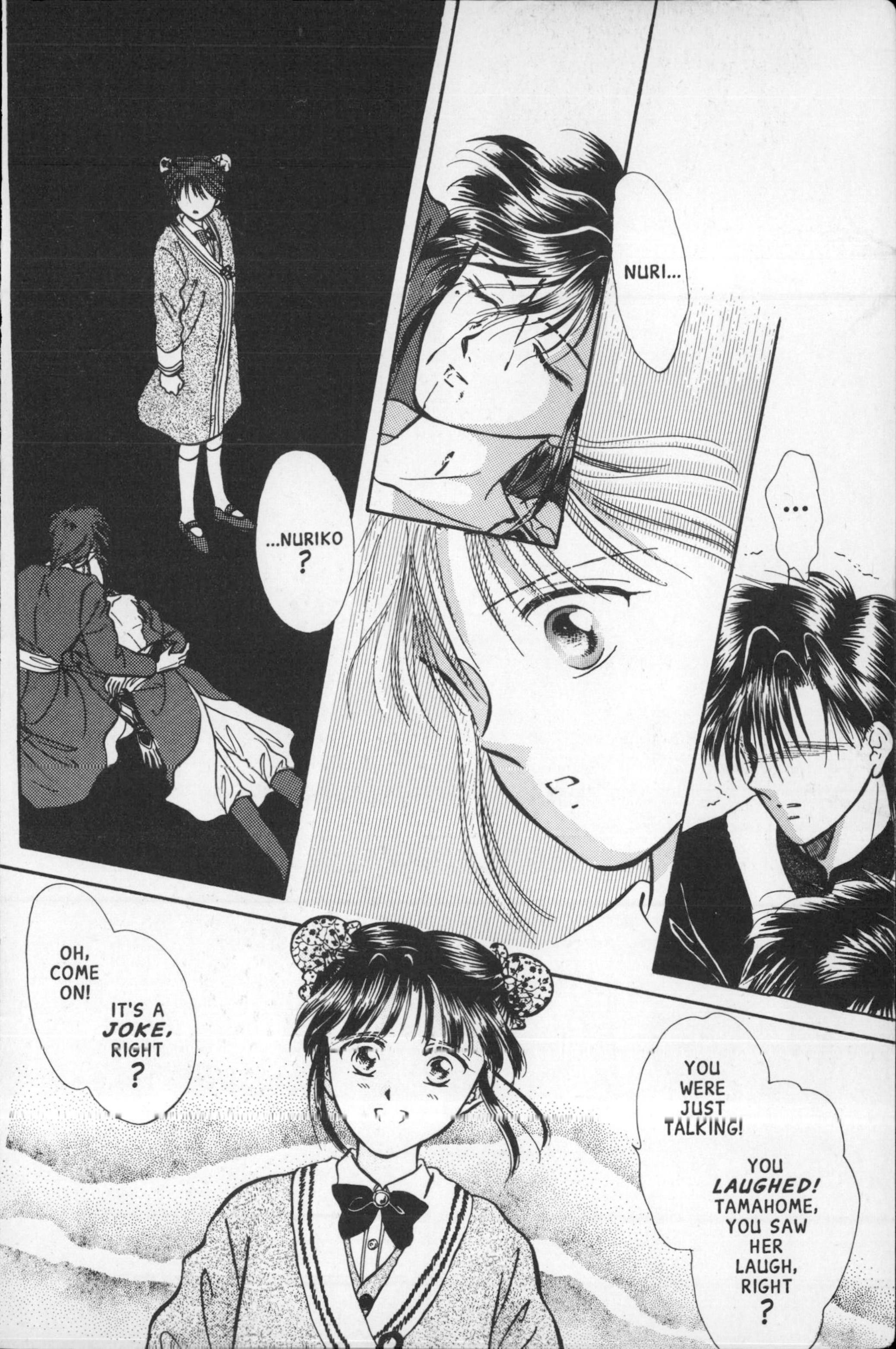
...NURIKO ?
NURI...
...
OH, COME ON!
IT'S A *JOKE,* RIGHT ?
YOU WERE JUST TALKING!
YOU *LAUGHED!* TAMAHOME, YOU SAW HER LAUGH, RIGHT ?

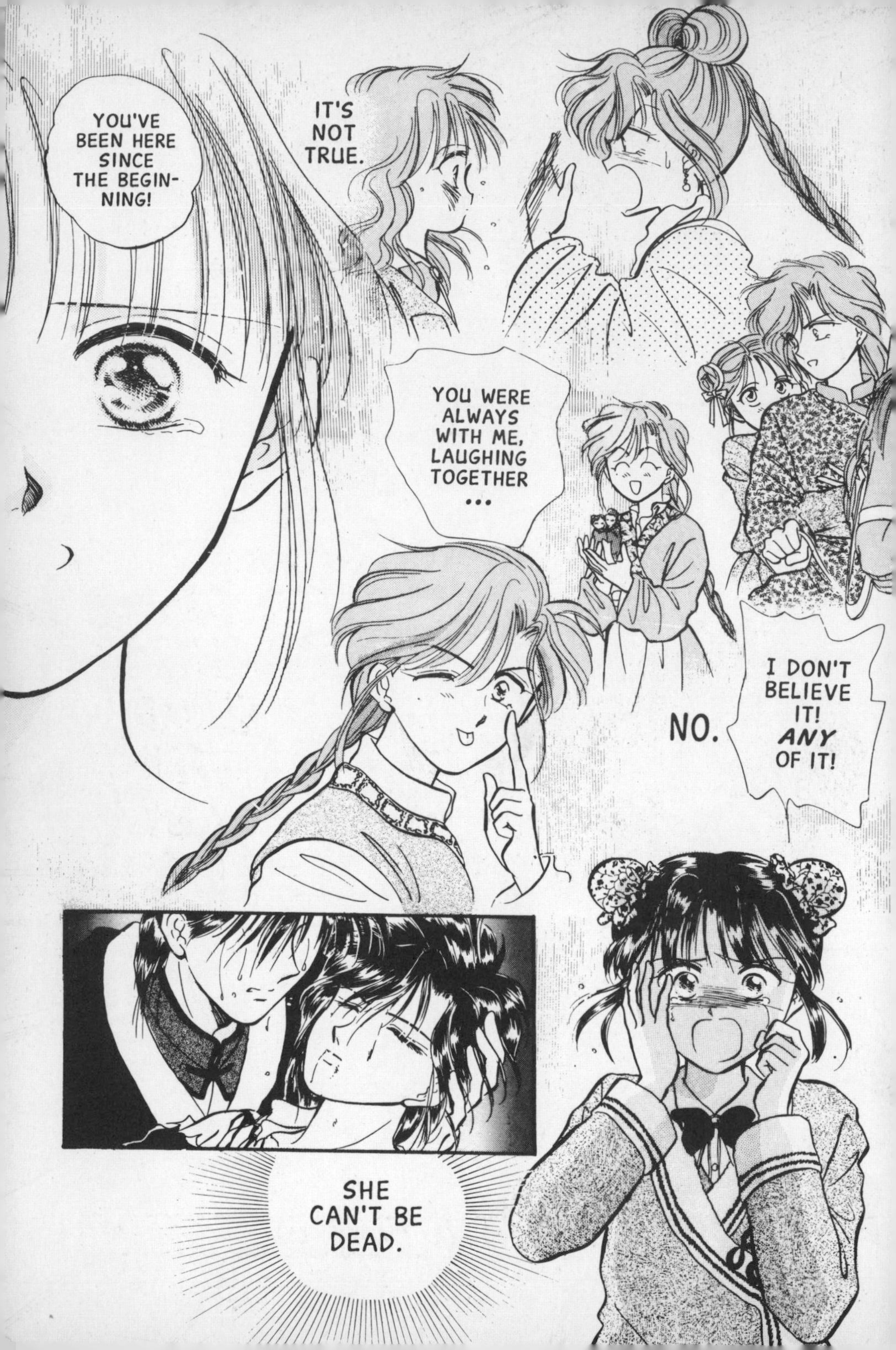
YOU'VE BEEN HERE SINCE THE BEGIN-NING!
IT'S NOT TRUE.
YOU WERE ALWAYS WITH ME, LAUGHING TOGETHER ...
NO.
I DON'T BELIEVE IT! *ANY* OF IT!
SHE CAN'T BE DEAD.

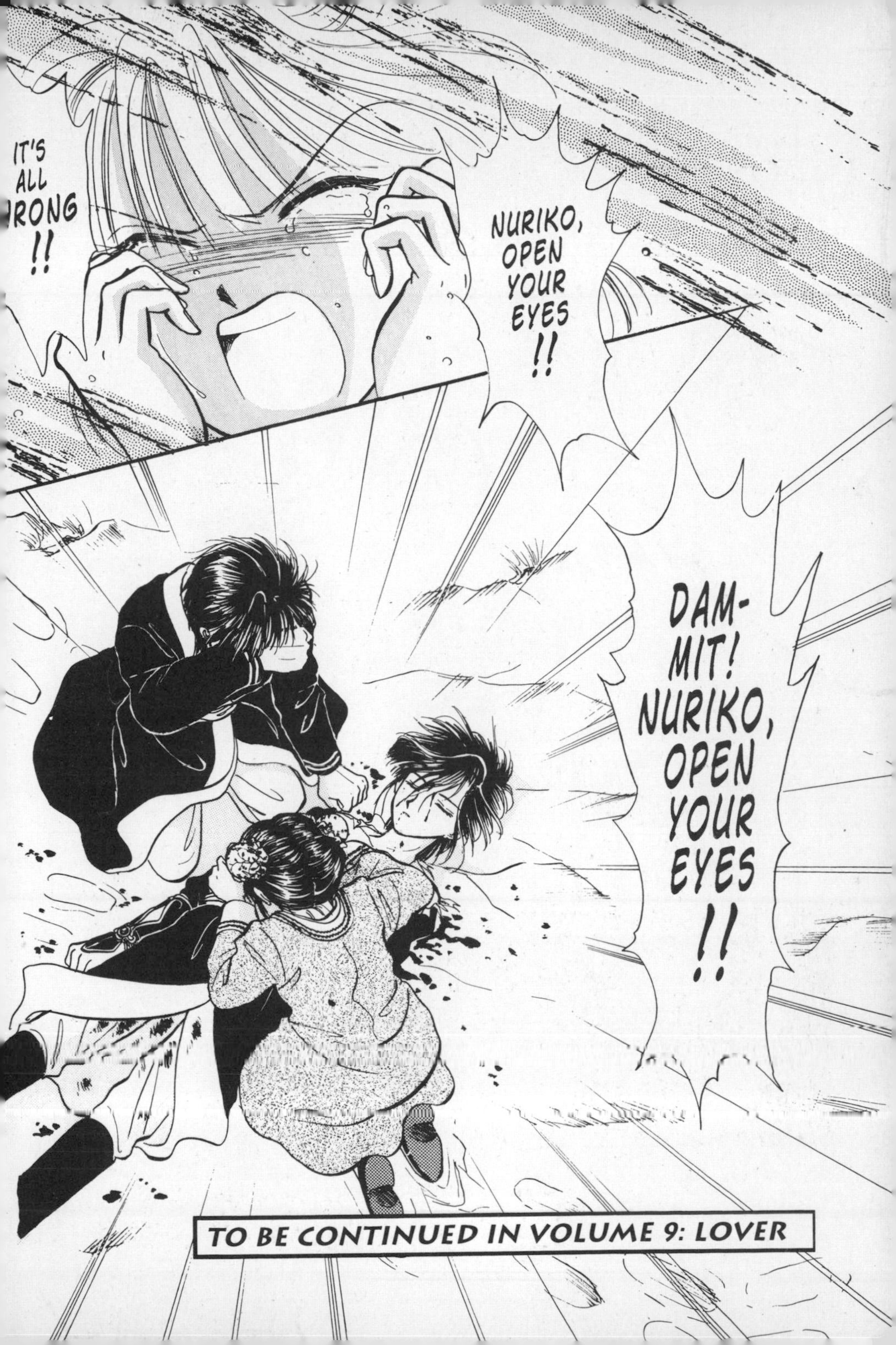
IT'S ALL RONG!!
NURIKO, OPEN YOUR EYES!!
DAM-MIT! NURIKO, OPEN YOUR EYES!!
TO BE CONTINUED IN VOLUME 9: LOVER

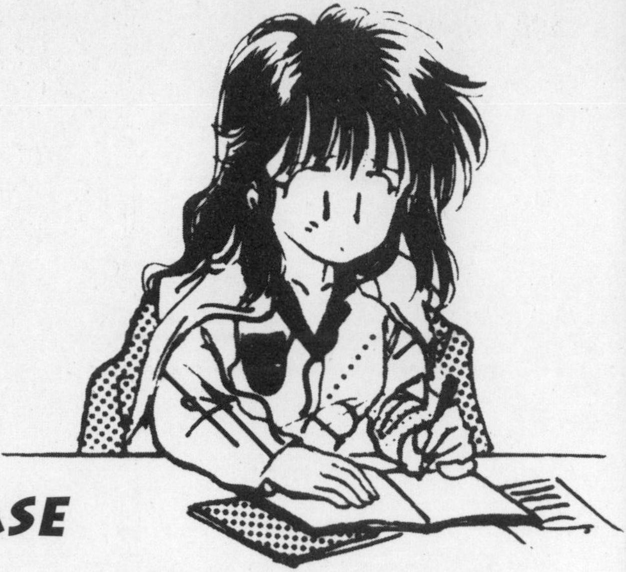

Yû Watase

Yû Watase was born on March 5 in a town near Osaka, and she was raised there before moving to Tokyo to follow the dream of creating manga. In the decade since her debut short story, *Pajama de Ojama* ("An Intrusion in Pajamas"), she has produced more than 50 compiled volumes of short stories and continuing series. Her latest series, *Alice 19th*, is currently running in the anthology magazine *Shôjo Comic*. Her long-running horror/romance story *Ceres: Celestial Legend* is now available in North America, published by VIZ. She loves science fiction, fantasy and comedy.